SECRET AGENT "X"

THE COMPLETE SERIES

VOLUME 7

CONTAINING THE NEXT FIVE STORIES:

THE DOOM DIRECTOR

HORROR'S HANDCLASP

CITY OF MADNESS

DEATH'S FROZEN FORMULA

THE MURDER BRAIN

WRITTEN BY
G.T. FLEMING-ROBERTS

ALTUS
PRESS

BOSTON
ALTUS PRESS
2015

TOM JOHNSON

IN THIS VOLUME, we again find some very interesting stories by G.T. Fleming-Roberts. "The Doom Director" and "Horror's Handclasp" (August and October 1936, respectively) were both headed Detective Mysteries, while the next three stories, "City of Madness," "Death's Frozen Formula," and "The Murder Brain," December 1936, February and April 1937, were headed G-Man Action Adventures.

Some may consider "The Doom Director," "Horror's Handclasp," and "The Murder Brain" as minor entries, but they do have their merits. Of note, we see "X" save Inspector Burks' life in "The Doom Director," and in return the inspector allows "X" to escape. And femme fatale Vina Trumaine appears in "Horror's Handclasp." While in "The Murder Brain," we have a woman with two identities. But, in my opinion, our main stories this time around are "City of Madness" and "Death's Frozen Formula," two of my favorites. "Death's Frozen Formula" was actually the first pulp of Secret Agent "X" that I ever owned, and it happened to be a good one.

Zerna is the femme fatale. This woman was exotically beautiful. She possessed a dark, secret beauty that warmed to gay colors and daring costumes. Her dark, soft skin had a faint yellowish coat that suggested mixed bloods. Her lips were warm and scarlet; her eyes cold and sea green. She was as evil a woman that Agent "X" had ever faced. She dispensed drugs and death while never displaying any emotion. She was a cold and heartless woman.

Yes, the novel is dark, and "X" is faced with a drug syndicate of pure evil.

But "City of Madness" may just be the best Secret Agent "X" story in the series. Here he is faced by his most evil adversary, Shaitan, and Betty Dale sees his true face for the first time. Betty was with the Agent from the very first, although a few novels featured her in no active part, merely giving the Agent information over the phone. However, she was usually right in the middle of his cases, and getting captured, being drugged, put in dungeons and tortured. At least once in every novel, Agent "X" was forced to penetrate a criminal stronghold to rescue the young reporter. She saw the Agent's true face for the first time in "City of Madness" (December 1936). She remained with the Agent for another year of the magazine, making her final appearance in the December 1937 issue, titled "Plague of the Golden Death." At that time she was dropped from the series (but the Agent still finds other fair damsels to rescue).

Betty had relatives in a town named Branford (no state given, but assumed to be New York), an aunt and cousin. The cousin, Paula Channing, is very wealthy in her own right, and popular in the community ("City of the Living Dead," June 1934).

Also important to the series was the love interest for the Agent's two aides, Jim Hobart and Harvey Bates; though the two ladies involved were only featured in one novel each, their parts were very important and deserve mention:

Leanne Manners ("The Murder Monster," December 1934) — Leanne was a red-haired young girl from a mid-western town. The fiancée of Jim Hobart, she was refined and educated (and also a graceful dancer). Agent "X" got her a job at the Diamond Club, where she quickly became the star of the nightclub show. However, she actually had another job there, which consisted of keeping tabs on the mobsters that frequented the club.

Leanne and Hobart were soon to be married, but she only appeared in the one novel and was never mentioned again. However, as Jim Hobart only remained with the Agent for two more years it might be assumed that they did get married and, due to the dangerous work in which he was involved, he was released from active service by the Agent.

Charlotta ("City of Madness," December 1936) — Darkly beautiful, her narrow velvety-lidded eyes were almost black and extraordinarily shrewd. High cheekbones accentuated a small, pointed chin. Her rouged lips suggested determination without in any way detracting from her beauty. She wore a short, flared black skirt and the postage stamp apron of a housemaid.

Though American born, nature had endowed her with brains as well as beauty, and she had served Russia in the early days of the war. Her mastery of foreign languages and her love for adventure had enticed her to seek fortune in strange lands at an early age. She later left Russia and transferred her abilities to the French Intelligence Service. Wherever adventure and intrigue could be found, there too was Charlotta.

Harvey Bates fell in love with her (and so did I) in the novel and she returned his love. But after this novel Bates was active in only four more cases and seldom placed in a position of danger. Thus, it might be assumed that Charlotta added the name of Bates to her own—and Agent "X" once again lost another very capable operative.

G.T. Fleming-Roberts was a master storyteller, and his plots always worked well. During the final years of the series, I believe his stories were edited for length, thus we missed out on some exceptionally good writing during this period. But even then, the characters he created carried the stories even with the word count cut. I think this current volume proves that George Thomas Fleming Roberts was, indeed, one of the top pulp authors of his day.

Happy reading!

Tom Johnson
Seymour, Texas

BOOK XXVII

THE DOOM DIRECTOR

Invisible doom came to change the living into strangled,
purple-faced gallows corpses. And Agent X's cunning
inventions and courage were failing before the wile
of a fear-mad killer, who could send his unseen death
to Sing Sing in time to cheat even the electric chair.

CHAPTER I

CORPSE CARGO

A **MINIATURE CONSTELLATION** of red, green and yellow stars moved against the black dome of sky—the night plane from Chicago, riding the blast of her three propellers, flying due east. The motors, three steely hearts, throbbed dutifully. Much depended on their pulse that night, much more than the human lives marooned upon that moving island in the sky.

Seemingly alone in the dark was this giant of the skies. Yet phantom wires linked it to the earth—wires, oddly enough, that tangled in a maze of conflicting purposes and emotions. At Ossining, thirty miles up the Hudson, Tony Lizio paced a cell in the prison death house. He might not have to die if the plane and all aboard reached New York safely. Fortunately, he did not realize that his salvation winged across the sky, else the suspense might have driven him to madness.

In a filthy East Side lodging house, another man thought of the night plane and was greedy for its arrival. Fifty thousand dollars' worth of jewels were aboard, and if every cog of criminal planning meshed, they would change hands in mid-air. Change hands without, he doubtless thought with a chuckle, benefit of monetary consideration.

Certain officials in police headquarters were edgy with excitement as they clocked the progress of that plane. Out of the dark and secretive night, a radio message had flashed from Chicago. A desperate criminal was aboard the airliner, masquerading as the radio operator. And when Inspector John Burks had received that message he had glanced significantly at the police commissioner, clenched his big fist, and said: "Well, that's just one place where Secret Agent X can't possibly get away from us." For in Burks' mind, one, and only one, man would have the sheer audacity to impersonate a member of the crew of the airliner.

A projectile of snarling
steel and screaming men,
the truck crashed.

The scales of justice swayed between heaven and earth that night. Yet within the plane itself the passengers showed no indication of their importance to the events that took place on the earth below.

"Yes, sir," declared Samuel Hempstead, folding his paper vigorously, "he ought to get it and get it proper. The chair's too good for him. But if that's all we've got I say I hope he gets it and gets it proper." He added insult to injury by slapping the picture that loomed largely from the front page of the paper. The picture was that of Tony Lizio, wide-eyed and frightened by the photographer's flashlight. That same Lizio who at the moment paced his cell in Sing Sing's "dance hall" and alternately prayed and cursed.

The villainy of Tony Lizio, his chance of escaping the chair had been the chief topic of conversation among those inclined to talk. Hempstead was obviously rabid on the subject. All criminals, regardless of their crime, ought to be quickly removed from the earth, in his opinion. Lizio was a man found guilty by the courts of the kidnaping and murder of young John Jonalden IV, the likeable,

inoffensive heir to the Jonalden fortune.

"Personally, I disagree," said a young man in front of Hempstead. He had been personally disagreeing all evening. "We have no right to take a man's life on circumstantial evidence. I admit that it looks rather bad for this Lizio, the half-completed ransom notes in his possession and all. But—"

Hempstead was deaf to all but his own voice. He began again with a glowing but inaccurate description of Tony Lizio writhing in the chair and getting half the voltage he deserved. Back of Hempstead, a bullet-headed man squirmed, hid his diminutive nose behind a magazine, and kept an eye on Mr. Hempstead.

Across the aisle from the bullet-headed person, a young pleasant-looking man kept his eyes toward the window. There was nothing to see in the glass but blackness—blackness and the reflection of the bullet-headed man. The young man knew that regardless of what name the bullet-headed person had put on the passenger list, his real name was Turney. He also knew that Mr. Turney's reason for being on the plane was none other than Samuel Hempstead, or rather Mr. Hempstead's diamonds.

But Turney and the young man and the old woman had said not a word since the plane had taken off. The old woman occupied the last seat in the compartment. Her large, unlovely figure was completely shrouded in black. A heavy, black veil draped her face. She was entirely surrounded by flowers so that she looked like a mourner at a funeral. She carried a small, brass bird cage in which a canary hopped from perch to perch and now and then tweeted when the old lady whispered to it.

HEMPSTEAD enthusiastically damned Tony Lizio for the last time and had plunged headlong into the crime problem. "I believe it the duty of every person to take particular pains not to put temptation in the way of criminals," Hempstead told anyone who would listen. "There'd be much less crime if everyone was careful. Now you take me. I could travel by train or bus. But do I? Not me. What's the use of tempting the crooks with all the stuff I've got to carry."

"I take it," said the man inclined to debate with Hempstead, "that you believe the patrons of the airlines to be very superior persons."

"They're higher up in the world," Hempstead guffawed. "But seriously, that's not it. Any one of you might be crooked. The point is, well—" Hempstead reached into his pocket and brought out a flat black case. He tapped it significantly. "There's fifty grand in unset diamonds in this case. I bought 'em for our shop from a collector in Chicago."

The young man across the aisle watched Mr. Turney's reflection in the window. Mr. Turney had lowered his magazine a little. He had even bent forward to make sure he knew in which pocket Mr. Hempstead carried his jewels.

Hempstead droned on as tirelessly as the motors themselves: "Just suppose some of you are crooks. Suppose you hold me up for the jewels. Where would you run to after you got 'em? Where, I ask you? You can't jump out of the plane. You got the jewels, maybe, but you can't get away with them. Yes sir, I feel perfectly safe on a plane."

Mr. Turney couldn't repress a smile. And the young man across the aisle saw the reflection of it. His jaw squared suddenly and his eyes narrowed. His hand went into his coat pocket and bulged there. He slipped quickly across the aisle and dropped into the vacant chair beside the bullet-headed Mr. Turney. The bulge in his pocket jabbed into Turney's side. His lips smiled amiably while his eyes threatened. The drone of the motors and Hempstead's lecture effectively muffled the young man's voice.

"Hughes is my name, Turney," he announced to the bullet-headed man. He reached into his pocket with his left hand and produced a small gold badge that made Turney squirm. "What Hempstead says about a crook not being able to get off one of the planes is pretty true. When we land in New York, you've got your choice of leaving a free man or going up to police headquarters on the charge of carrying concealed weapons as a starter. But that's just a starter, Turney."

"Lolly" Turney, one-time gang czar, forgot about Mr. Hempstead's diamonds. He knew only that there was a gun jabbing his side and a G-man's steady eyes prodding his brain.

"I learned a whole lot about you in Chicago, Turney," went on Hughes. "I'm assigned to the Jonalden case."

Turney jumped. "Listen, mister—"

"*You* listen, Turney. Before this plane lands, you're going to tell me what you know about the Jonalden job. There's enough stuff on you to put you on Alcatraz for life. But I can forget a lot of that if you'll come across with the information I'm looking for. Who killed young Jonalden? It wasn't Tony Lizio. And you know who it was, because on the night of January sixth—"

Turney mopped his brow. "You win," he croaked.

"And the truth, Turney."

THE WOMAN in black got to her feet. Head and shoulders stooped, she shuffled along the aisle toward the nose of the plane. Hempstead watched her, nudged the man in front of him. "The old lady's bird must be getting sleepy. Bored stiff with the stuff she's been whispering to it."

The man in front of Hempstead looked around. The old woman's bird was in the bottom of the cage. The man looked disgustedly at Hempstead. "Sleepy? Say, birds don't sleep that way. That canary's dead."

Hempstead's shoulders wriggled uncomfortably. "Say, don't those flowers give you the creeps? Smells too much like a funeral around here to suit me."

He hung on by the man's wrist.

Ahead, in the radio compartment, the operator slumped forward on his tiny table, apparently asleep. The door of the compartment was opened by a hidden hand. A small, glistening object dropped to the floor and slid noiselessly across to the wall as the plane banked. The door of the radio compartment closed.

A few minutes later, the man at the controls of the plane motioned to his companion, the co-pilot. The co-pilot nodded. In front of the nose of the ship, the horizon glowed faintly. Only a few minutes of flying time remained. The co-pilot got up and went to the radio compartment. He merely glanced through the door, but he saw something that caused him to take a sharp gasp of breath.

The radio operator lolled across his table, sleeping. But it was the sleep without an awakening. The man's face was blue-black. The black, puffy thing between his teeth was his tongue. His wide-open eyes stared blankly, and protruded like the eyeballs of a corpse cut down from the gallows.

Horror did not hold the co-pilot long. He turned at once to the passenger compartment. And there he was shocked into immobility. The plane was a flying morgue of garroted corpses. Six passengers and the air stewardess drooped in their seats or sprawled in the aisle. All dead, all apparently strangled. And the air was heavy with the funereal smell of cut flowers.

The co-pilot came out of his daze. He picked his way among the bodies. The stewardess had made an effort to get her medical kit open and had died in the attempt. Hempstead lay crosswise of the aisle, his blue, bloated face mooning up hideously. The jeweler's coat was open and the lining ripped. The co-pilot knelt and slipped a gloved hand into the man's pockets. Empty.

Pockets of the other passengers were similarly gutted. Not a paper remained on the body of Hughes. Only his gun and gold Department of Justice badge had escaped the thieving murderer. Lying beneath Hughes, his bullet head doubled under him so that there could be no doubt that his neck was broken, lay "Lolly" Turney. G-man and criminal must have fought side by side for the breath of life.

But the woman in black—what had become of her? The co-pilot went to the seat that she had occupied. In its cage, her canary lay dead. On the floor was a little puddle of water that the co-pilot found chill to the touch. All about were flowers, wilting a little now. On the seat lay a small, square case like an actress's makeup box. The co-pilot opened it, disclosing a polished black panel. On the panel were mounted knobs and a single calibrated dial. The instrument was an extremely compact short-wave radio receiver. Its dial was set at twenty-five hundred kilocycles—the same wave as that of a police transmitter in Chicago.

But where was the woman in black? The co-pilot picked his way among blue-faced corpses to the small door opening into the baggage compartment in the tail of the fuselage. He opened the door with steady hands and peered into the darkness beyond. He squeezed through the opening and stood there a moment until his eyes became used to the gloom. He stooped over and moved slowly forward to stop a moment later and stare at a jagged opening cut in the aluminum plates that covered the fuselage. He dropped to his knees and crawled to the opening. His gloved hands gripped the ragged edges.

SUDDENLY, something within the compartment moved with the swift silence of a cat. It struck the crouching co-pilot from the rear. The force of that blow sent the co-pilot lurching head foremost through the opening. One gloved hand groped instinctively the rushing emptiness. The other gripped the edge of the opening. For a moment, only one hand and the toe of his shoe kept him from pitching into space.

In the baggage compartment, the shadowy form moved again. A fist clenched, struck out at the man precariously balanced between life and death. But the co-pilot was ready for such a move. Where another man might have clung to the plane in a panic until the attacker had beaten him into releasing his grip, the co-pilot gripped the edge of the opening with both hands and twisted around so that he faced the one who was determined he should die. As the murderer in the plane struck out, the co-pilot seized his assailant by the wrist. For a moment it seemed that the co-pilot would draw his would-be assassin through the opening. Then abruptly, the co-pilot released his grip on the attacker's wrist.

The shadowy form lurched backwards, crashed into some baggage beyond. The co-pilot scrambled back through the opening. He seemed uncertain as to the exact point of danger because of the darkness. Suddenly the murderer came at him with head lowered. He sidestepped, drew a pistol, but held his fire. For the murderer flung himself sideways through the opening in the fuselage.

The co-pilot wasted no time debating whether his assailant's action meant suicide or escape by means of a parachute. Only one thing he knew: it was the old woman in black who had killed all the passengers in the cabin as well as the radio operator.

The co-pilot moved back through the cabin, walking warily among the dead. He entered the tiny control room and tapped the pilot on the shoulder. "Let me take her," he shouted.

The pilot shook his head and pointed mutely at what the co-pilot had already seen, the lights of the airport. The plane was already circling the field.

The co-pilot's voice suddenly grew harsh as he said: "Think it over, brother!" And at the same time he pushed the muzzle of his gun under the pilot's nose. The pilot jerked startled eyes from his instruments. The gun in the co-pilot's hand spoke inaudibly above the roar of the motors. There was only a cloud of white vapor that spat from the muzzle of the pistol into the pilot's face. The pilot sagged forward on his controls. The plane dived dangerously, but in another moment righted itself as the skilled hands of Secret Agent X took over the controls.[1]

THE SECRET AGENT'S errand in Chicago had been exactly the same as that of G-man Hughes. Agent X, too, had been dissatisfied with the result of the Tony Lizio trials. It seemed impossible that so ignorant and unintelligent a man as Lizio could have been behind the kidnaping and murder of John Jonalden. And in his fight to save a man, whom he believed to be innocent, X had encountered evidence that indicated that Lolly Turney might have known more about the crime than he would have cared to tell. One of the Agent's informers had seen Turney leaving Lizio's shanty just before the police found evidence there, in the form of unfinished ransom letters, that led to Lizio's arrest.

Lizio denied any knowledge of the affair. He claimed that he was too ignorant of the English language to have composed the ransom letters. Still, this ignorance might have been feigned.

Confident of Turney's connection with the case, X was determined to follow Turney back from Chicago. Turney, X felt certain, would make an attempt to rob Hempstead, the jeweler. X had hoped to use the threat of punishment for attempted robbery to compel Turney to talk. But on arriving at the airport, X had discovered that all passenger room had been taken. At the last minute, X had run across the plane's radio operator, knocked him out, and impersonated him.[2]

Long after the plane had left, police had discovered the unconscious radio operator locked in a washroom in an airport hangar.

---

1 AUTHOR'S NOTE: *Friends of Secret Agent X are by now well acquainted with his favorite weapon, his gas pistol. Though believed by the police to be a dangerous murderer, Agent X doesn't even permit himself lethal weapons. His gas pistol, for example, shoots a charge of concentrated anesthetizing gas, producing almost instantaneous unconsciousness without harming the human system in any way.*

2 AUTHOR'S NOTE: *The Agent's unique skill in imitation and vocal impersonation is augmented by the finest makeup equipment obtainable. He is seldom without a compact kit which contains a plastic substance for changing his facial contours. In addition, he supplies himself with a number of toupees and special pigments for imitating the complexion of any man. His kit even contains a dye which enables him to change the color of his eyes.*

Their radio message to New York, to be on the lookout for an impersonator on board the night plane, had been intercepted by Agent X. He had acted at once, luring the co-pilot into the radio compartment, knocking him out, and switching identities with him.

But one other person had intercepted that message besides Agent X—the woman in black. And to the woman in black, as to every other criminal, the presence of Secret Agent X meant trouble. It was because the woman in black believed she was destroying her most dreaded enemy that the man in the radio compartment had been killed. For undoubtedly, she thought this man was Secret Agent X.

As Agent X handled the controls of the airliner, compelling it to circle the field time after time, a man at the airport slowly melted with anxiety, excitement and suppressed rage. That man was Inspector John Burks.[3]

Burks paced the ground, shook his fist at the circling plane, and perspired. His fingers gripped the arm of one of his subordinates. "He's up there, like a cat up a tree, and I got a damn good idea he knows that he can't come down without falling into our trap."

"How could that be, sir?" demanded the detective. "According to the message from Chicago, Agent X will be impersonating the radio operator. If that's the case, he wouldn't be in control of the plane."

"Huh, you don't know Agent X," Burks grumbled. "Changes his face like a woman changes her mind. You get this, and you, too, Henderson, nobody leaves that plane until I get a look at every man on board. I've been given free hand by the airport officials."

"The plane's coming in now, sir," one of the detectives pointed out.

Burks nodded. "Come on. And there's going to be no funny stuff when I get my hands on him. There'll be no talk until I get him where I want him—behind the bars." And he was off, running toward the plane that was taxiing in from the field.

The motors were cut, the plane stopped. Burks and his five picked men circled the ship. Burks took up his position in front of

---

3 AUTHOR'S NOTE: *Though Agent X and the police were working toward common ends, the Agent's crime fighting methods are unhampered by ordinary routine. His weapons are so strange, his methods so obscure, that he is greatly misunderstood. His most unrelenting foe is none other than Inspector John Burks of the homicide department. Burks has met X many times and knows more of the Agent's tricks than any other servant of the law.*

the door from which passengers usually alighted. His hand rested uneasily on the butt of his gun. There was something queer inside that plane. There was none of the usual bustle. Only foreboding silence.

Suddenly, the oval door slid open. A very white-faced young man leaned against it and looked dully down at Burks. The man wore a pilot's outfit. "They're dead," he told Burks flatly.

"Dead? Who's dead?" Burks put out his hand and seized the edge of the door. "Let down the steps, can't you. I'm coming on board."

Burks swung up through the door. "Where's your radio man?" he demanded.

"Dead," replied the pilot tonelessly.

Burks frowned. He nodded at one of his men. "Watch this pilot, Henderson. Something I don't like about—" Burks stopped. Just beyond where the pilot stood, Burks saw the figure of a man squatting in front of a small, mirror-topped case. The man's fingers were covered with some puttylike material and were pressed against his cheeks. Burks crouched, sprang, whipped out his gun. He took no chances this time. He had caught Agent X in the very act of changing his makeup, He raised his gun and hacked down with the barrel to the side of the crouching man's head.

THEN he could restrain himself no longer. Years of suspense and anticipation were behind that movement. No possible trick could avail Agent X now. He was absolutely helpless in Burks' hands.

"I've got him, boys!" shouted Burks. "Got Agent X!" And as the other members of the police force were scrambling aboard the plane, Burks whipped out handcuffs and fastened them to the wrists of the unconscious captive.

The face of the man he had captured was indistinct, for it was covered with the plastic volatile material that Agent X used for his marvelous transformations, and this material had not yet been modeled over into features. But it was only a matter of minutes until he would remove that plastic and reveal, for the first time, the true features of Secret Agent X.

Burks' men pressed around, filling the vestibule. One had dropped beside Burks and was in the act of peeling the makeup from their captive's face. Suddenly, the man stopped. His eyes met those of Inspector Burks. "Say, chief, what did you hit this man with?"

"My gun barrel," Burks told him. "Why? Is he a long way out?"

"Yeah. A hell of a long way. He's dead, and your sock on the head didn't do it, either. He must have been dead when you came in here."

Another detective, who had slipped into the passenger compartment reappeared. "Inspector," he said huskily.

Burks glared at him. "Well what?"

The detective gestured back toward the cabin. "They—they're all dead in there. Look like something off a scaffold. And somebody's cleaned everybody's pockets. That Hempstead fellow, the wealthy jeweler—well, he's in there. You suppose somebody killed off everybody in the plane just to get Hempstead's diamonds?"

"Who brought the ship to the ground then?" demanded Detective Henderson.

Burks turned to glare at Henderson. "Who brought the ship to the ground then," Burks repeated slowly. Henderson flinched beneath his superior's gaze. "What the devil did you do with that pilot, Henderson!" Burks roared.

"Why—why nothing. You said—" Henderson gestured mutely at the handcuffed corpse on the floor. All knew, then, that this was but another trick of the crafty Agent X. He had posed one of the dead passengers before the makeup kit that X always carries. But a moment had been required for him to slap some of the plastic material onto the face of the corpse. Then, at the moment when the police were positive they had Secret Agent X, the Agent had quietly slipped from the ship.

A few minutes before the police made this startling discovery, X had hurried across the flying field to be accosted near the hangar by a man of above average height His black eyes watered slightly and his long, thin nose twitched with a threatening sneeze. His black hair, gummy with brilliantine, had lost its patent-leather appearance and was all upstanding. He seized the Agent's shoulder, clutched tenaciously, and got rid of a sneeze that seemed to come from his boot soles.

The man whisked out a handkerchief and waved it frantically at the airliner. "You came on that ship?" he demanded of the Agent.

X nodded.

"Well, was there a Mr. Hughes on board?"

X nodded again.

The man relieved himself of another sneeze and started for the plane. X caught his coat tail. "Wait," he ordered. "Why do you want to see Hughes?"

The man stared in amazement at X. "Don't you know me?" he gasped. "I'm Dean Winton, defense attorney for Lizio. Maybe you don't know it, but Hughes is a federal operative. Department of Justice men are not convinced that Lizio pulled off the Jonalden kidnap-murder any more than I am. Hughes was following a lead that might bring in new evidence. Somehow, we've got to swing a reprieve for Lizio. But what business is it of yours, Mr. Flyer?"

X shook his head. "None at all. Only somebody beat you to Hughes. You better look somewhere else for the makings of a reprieve. And the person who beat you to Hughes shut him up—permanently."

But as Agent X left Dean Winton alternately gasping and sneezing, he vowed solemnly that Tony Lizio would never go to the chair. How he could possibly save the man, he did not know. But some brain beside the one inside Lizio's thick skull had designed the slaughter on board the airliner. And in spite of the fact that all on board had been robbed of loot that must have totaled over fifty thousand dollars, X felt that the true motive behind the wholesale murder was to remove Lolly Turney and Federal Agent Hughes.

Turney had known something about the Jonalden case. Hughes might have forced Turney to talk. Both had died, and Hughes had been robbed of every scrap of paper that might have contained a record of what Turney had told him.

And only a few hours separated Lizio from the chair....

CHAPTER II

THE WOMAN IN BLACK

A **MAN LOUNGED** against the wall of a disreputable East-side lodging house. The shadows effectively concealed his features but could not hide his rather remarkable body. Shoulders and head were square. His chest was broad and deep. This tremendous breadth seemed to deny the fact that he was over six feet tall.

His name was Harvey Bates and he was director of Secret Agent X's most important corps of secret operatives. For an hour or more he had leaned thus against the building where he had last seen the man X had assigned him to follow. That man was Pat "The Terrible" Turney, younger brother of Lolly Turney, and one of the few remaining members of the Turney gang. The power of the gang had dwindled since bootlegging days until now it was scarcely to be reckoned with at all.

Yet Bates knew that Agent X believed the Turneys to be in some way connected with the kidnaping and brutal murder of John Jonalden. The Jonalden case was not one that offered much of a foothold for the ordinary investigator. The ransom for the young millionaire had been raised by one of his terrified, irresponsible associates. Police had not been informed until the money had changed hands and Jonalden had been returned, a corpse.

Bates' reminiscences were cut suddenly short by the staccato click of high heels on the pavement. There was no sign of tenseness in Bates' big body, but he was nevertheless alert on the instant. At the end of the block, light from a street lamp found its way beneath the tilted brim of the girl's hat. Bates nodded in silent satisfaction.

The girl was not only petite and attractive, but what was more important, Bates recognized her as a girl who had entered the dwelling of "Terrible" Turney before. Her name, he had discovered, or at least the one she used as a night club entertainer, was Fay October.

16

The girl stopped in front of the dwelling, went up the front steps, and knocked at the door. There was no answer. She came down, passed so close to Bates that he could have tripped her, and disappeared beyond the door that Bates knew covered a closed stairway in the same building.

A few minutes later, Bates deserted his post. He staggered aimlessly along and half fell into the doorway through which Fay October had entered. He sang vaguely a few bars of a song in a lusty, drunken voice. Above him at the top of the steps, a man's voice cursed him. Then the man went into a room and slammed the door. Evidently, the occupants of the dismal place supposed Bates to be a genuine sot. Bates shouted back that if they didn't like his music he'd have to move along.

He moved, but noiselessly and straight up the steps into the dark hall above. At the first door he came to, he pressed his ear to the panel. Only the snap of cards sounded within. A man playing solitaire. Bates moved on down the hall and stopped. Ahead of him, Fay October came out of a room, left the door open and moved on down the hall to enter another room. Bates slipped into the room the girl had just left. Inside, was a table, some chairs and no bed. It looked a lot more like a meeting place than a lodging.

VOICES in the next room. Bates moved over to the wall and leaned against it. He listened intently to a voice that he recognized as that of "Terrible" Turney.

"Why did Lolly have to knock off a whole plane full of people just to get the Hempstead rocks, boss?"

A second man replied in a steady, low-pitched voice: "He didn't. Your brother didn't get the Hempstead diamonds. And he didn't do the killing. When I said that all the passengers in the plane were killed—"

"You mean Lolly? You mean somebody chiseled in on the Hempstead rocks? Lolly got rubbed out by a dirty chiseler?"

"Apparently," replied the other calmly.

There was a moment of silence, then Turney growled: "*You* got any idea who killed Lolly? Talk. Just name the guy. I'll get him."

"Only one man could have killed all the passengers on that plane and still escape the police," replied the unknown evenly. "Secret Agent X was on that plane. The police got word from Chicago."

Turney whistled. "I've heard of that guy. Well, he'll wish he'd kept his mug out of this when I get hold of him."

The other laughed softly. "Perhaps that won't be necessary. Perhaps I've already disposed of Agent X.... But who is that in the next room?"

"Just Lewey Strait," Turney replied. "Used to be a good guy. Gone soft now."

"Who's he talking to?"

"Hell, how should I know?"

"Sh-sh."

Bates listened eagerly, but the men in the next room were perfectly silent. Somewhere in the building, voices rumbled, but the words were indistinguishable.

Then an exclamation from Turney.

"Wait," cautioned the other. "You'll not get anywhere by breaking in there alone. We have to keep out of trouble."

"But suppose what he says worked? Suppose that bird next door did get Lizio out of the big house on a fake pardon or something? Who takes the rap for the Jonalden—"

"Shut up!" the other warned. "We'll keep out of this. But we'll send Fay October for the police. We'll let the police do our job for us."

A few minutes after Bates' entrance into the building, a second man had entered and proceeded at once to the room occupied by Lewey Strait. Strait was an ex-convict who had done his stretch for forgery. He was a stooped man with a crooked nose and a lower lip that snarled down from yellow teeth. His fingers had been made for pinching the pen and he had an uncanny knack for remembering signatures.

His visitor was tall, with lean, outstanding cheek bones and a rocky jaw. His eyes mirrored no emotion, but there seemed a tangible force in their gray depths. And no wonder. They were the eyes of Secret Agent X.

"Lewey," said Agent X quietly, "I've a job for you."

Lewey Strait looked distrustfully up at the man in the doorway. His stooped shoulders twitched nervously. He had never seen the man before but the man knew his name.

"A little forgery job that unfortunately I am not able to do for myself," Agent X continued.[4]

---

4 *AUTHOR'S NOTE: As has frequently been stated, Agent X is himself a skilled forger, an art he has found extremely helpful in a number of impersonations. However, in this*

LEWEY started to slam the door, shook his head. "You get out of here, mister. You got the wrong place."

"No I haven't, Lewey." X smiled at the transparency of Strait's acting. He stepped calmly into the room and closed the door. "Lewey Strait, I know your record perfectly. You did a long stretch when you forged the name of the man who is now our governor. I want you to pen that famous signature again—to a reprieve for Tony Lizio."

"A reprieve?" gasped Strait. "Say, you must be crazy. You get out of here. You're a dick, that's what you are. You're trying to get me in a jam. I've been on the level for many years, but you dicks don't give a man a chance to stay that way. If we go straight, you try to frame—"

"That will do, Lewey." Agent X was stern. "I am not a detective." He drew his dangerous-looking gas pistol. "Understand this—I can compel you to do whatever I want you to do. In my pocket, I have a paper that requires only the signature of the governor to stay the electrocution of Tony Lizio. I want you to supply that signature. No trickery, Lewey, or I'll kill you."

At that moment Agent X looked perfectly capable of carrying out his threat. His jaw was set and his eyes were unblinking. "On the other hand," he added, "I will see that you are richly rewarded if the forgery is perfect."

Lewey backed fearfully before the Agent's gun. "No—no," he muttered. "I'm through."

"One more job, Lewey," X insisted. He took a paper from his inner coat pocket and tossed it on the table. Beside it, he placed a pen. "Believe me, Lewey, if you really intend to go straight, I will see that you have your chance—after you have done this job for me."

"Who—who are you?" Lewey quavered. His screwed up little eyes were harnessed by the steady, gray gaze of his visitor.

"Sign the paper, Lewey," urged X gently. "You will be well rewarded. It is for the sake of justice."

Lewey Strait debated no longer. He sprang to the table and picked up the pen. Tongue between his teeth, brow scowling, he thought a moment. On the edge of a newspaper he practiced.

"I—I'm not sure that I can do it," he said huskily.

---

instance, he did not have a copy of the governor's signature in his possession.

"You have the art," X told him, "if you will have the courage. You are doing no wrong, Lewey. I would stake my word on it that Lizio is innocent of the murder of Jonalden."

Strait pinched his pen anew and set it to paper. Laboriously, he traced, while Agent X watched.

"Lift your mits, boys!" a hard voice demanded.

The pen in Lewey's hand sputtered across the paper. With a cry of fright, he swung around. He saw the man who was Agent X facing a burly policeman who had just entered the room. Behind the cop was another. In the gloomy hall beyond, X could see the slender form of Fay October.

Agent X was smiling that disarming smile of his. His hands were poised halfway to his pockets which contained numerous special defensive weapons that would have given him a few seconds of surprise in which to break for the open. Yet when he saw the pitiful, panic-stricken Lewey Strait, cringing before the police guns, the Agent's code would not permit him to act as he ordinarily would have done.

Lewey Strait had unwillingly undertaken what, in the eyes of the law, was a penitentiary offense. He could not hope to escape prison for the rest of his natural life. To escape with Lewey, at the moment, was impossible, X knew. Yet he could not leave the ex-con to face a penalty for a crime that was not of his own volition. It was a strange and precarious position that the Agent found himself in, a situation to which there seemed no solution. Slowly, he raised his hands above his head.

"What'd you say they were up to, miss?" asked one of the coppers of Fay October.

THE NIGHT CLUB dancer stared boldly through large, dark eyes first at Lewey and then at Agent X. Then she glanced at the table. "I heard them say something about fixing a reprieve for Tony Lizio. It sounded screwy to me, but I thought you boys might like to have a look."

"Screwy is right!" echoed one of the police. His companion, who had gone over to the little table and had been examining the piece of paper, said: "Well, I'll be damned!" He picked up the paper and waved it under Lewey Strait's nose. "Of all the cockeyed schemes I ever heard of— But I'm damned if I don't think it might have worked for a time."

And that was all that Agent X had hoped for—a little more time in which to get evidence that would liberate Lizio and see the real killer of Jonalden behind the bars. But that plan was frustrated now. He searched Fay October's dark, beautiful face. She was much too small to be the woman in black who had killed ruthlessly on board the airliner. Yet she seemed to have the same motive behind her— to stifle truth, to send Tony Lizio to the chair.

Lewey Strait was screaming about his innocence. He had not wanted to do this thing. He had been forced at the point of a gun to forge the governor's signature.

"Gun is it?" One of the cops strode up to X and frisked him methodically. Gas pistol, makeup kit, chemical kit, small bombs containing anesthetizing gas and tear gas, tiny tools, all passed over into the cop's pockets. The cop was amazed at the odd assortment. "Looks like we got a desperate man here. Cassidy," he told his companion. "We better just handcuff these two together. This guy's got enough stuff in his pockets to start a revolution."

In another moment, Agent X found himself handcuffed to the all but weeping forger. The two cops knew the value of the fake reprieve as evidence, but they did not realize that the special equipment removed from X's pockets would brand one of their prisoners as Inspector Burks' old enemy.

As the two police with their charges went into the hall, a tall, broad figure of a man flattened himself against the wall, watched closely, then ran for another stairway. Agent X did not see the man, nor did the police.

The Agent's right wrist was linked to Strait's wrist. His left arm was gripped by the cop who had searched him. X had paid particular attention to where the cop had placed all the special equipment he had taken from X's pockets. He knew that his left hand at the moment was only about eight inches away from a very surprising device that now rested in the policeman's pocket.

As soon as they had reached the sidewalk, X put his daring plan into effect. A totally unexpected twist of the left arm freed him from the cop's grip. His long fingers jabbed into the cop's pocket, and instantly selected the thing needed. Coming up, the point of his elbow crashed into the cop's jaw, and at the same instant his left foot went out for a trip that sent the cop sprawling.

THE SMALL, round object X had obtained was a chemical smoke bomb. Its self-lighting fuse ignited as soon as the bomb had struck the sidewalk. X shoved Strait violently against the second cop before the latter knew what had happened. The second cop lost his grip on the forger's arm, and X dragged his companion straight toward the police car parked at the curb.

A dense cloud of smoke separated them from the two policemen. But as they were on the point of gaining the police car, X saw that a third policeman was in the driver's seat. He saw, too, that the man had drawn a gun and that the muzzle was pointed directly at Lewey Strait. X sprang onto the running board, thrusting Strait behind him.

The bullet intended for the forger landed squarely in the center of the Agent's chest. The bullet-proof vest X always wore checked the slug from entering his flesh, but the impact of the shot would have laid another man out. A wince of pain streaked across X's face. His free hand went out in an effort to grapple with the man in the car. For a moment, the policeman's gun was centered on the Agent's unprotected head.

But at that moment, a tall, broad figure rose from the running board on the opposite side of the police car. For an instant, X glimpsed the face of Harvey Bates. He saw Bates seize the cop's gun arm and force it upward. At the same time, Bates' fist descended like a hammer to the top of the cop's head. The cop had hardly time to go limp before Bates had dragged him from beneath the wheel and into the street. Then Bates ran for an alley.

X pulled Strait into the car beside him. He kicked the gear-shift lever with his foot and gave gas for a quick start. Steering with one hand, he took the corner on screaming tires. For several blocks, he kept up the furious pace. Then he stopped.

"Lewey," he said to the frightened man beside him, "I'm sorry about what happened tonight. But you'll not regret it if you're really determined to go straight."

Lewey snarled: "You've finished me. They'll catch me. They always do. It'll be the fourth time for me; that means life."

X shook his head. He groped in his vest pocket with his left hand. The cop who had searched him had left him his personal effects and at the end of his watch chain was a ring of clever master keys. Among them was a key small enough to fit the lock of the handcuffs. Only a moment was required in which to unlock the bracelets.

"Lewey, I know of a plastic surgeon who will alter your features. They could stand a little improvement, you know. And—well, you'll have your chance." He scribbled something on a card he had taken from his pocket. He handed the card to Strait.

"Take this card to the address I have written down. You'll find temporary sanctuary there."

Strait took the card, looked at it curiously out of his small, squinting eyes. "I don't get you," he said quietly. "You're not a crook. You're not a dick. Who are you?"

X smiled whimsically as Strait got out of the police car. "Don't think about that too much, Lewey." Then he turned the car around and drove back within two blocks of the point where he had stolen it.

His makeup kit was gone. Nevertheless, his skilled fingers made hurried alterations in the plastic material that covered his real features. He removed the blond toupee he wore and revealed his own wavy, brown hair. No one would have recognized him as the man who had tricked the police a few minutes ago. He was determined to meet Bates for a brief check-up.

Two doors east of the lodging where X had found Strait, Bates waited and watched patiently. He failed entirely to recognize X when the latter tapped him on the shoulder. It was not until X spoke in the voice with which Bates was familiar that Bates knew that he was once again in the presence of his beloved employer.

"That was quick thinking," X commended. "But a dangerous move. I can't afford to have the police spot you. And by the way, how did you recognize me?"

"Didn't," Bates clipped. "Followed Fay October into that place. It's the old Turney crowd's hangout. Walls are pretty thin. I eavesdropped. Turney and another man must have heard you talking with the forger. From what I gathered of their conversation, some one was trying to fake a reprieve for Lizio. Only one man would have the nerve to try a thing like that. You, I mean."

X uttered a short laugh. "So you moved your listening post to a point just outside Strait's door. Where's Turney?"

BATES nodded silently towards the dismal house.

"And the other? You mentioned another."

"Gone," Bates told him. "I got a look at him. He's the boss, the man behind the Jonalden job."

"What did he—" X stopped. From the door of the tenement where he had met Strait, came Fay October. She turned north, moving at a leisurely, graceful pace. A big sedan rolled silently by X and Bates and slowed at the curb. A man put his head out of the car. It was Dean Winton.

"Hello, Fay," the attorney called cheerily. "This is a fine neighborhood for you to be in. Wouldn't you rather ride?"

The girl smiled, nodded and got into the car. As the sedan moved off, X glimpsed another woman who stepped from a doorway across the street. Her dress and carriage indicated that she, too, was entirely out of place in this neighborhood. She stepped quickly to a waiting cab, gave an order and drove off after the sedan. Agent X glanced at Bates.

The big, square-headed man said: "Mrs. Winton in the taxi."

X confirmed with a nod. No one could read the papers and not know of Dean Winton's beautiful wife. She had obtained a divorce from Winton only about a year ago.

"Now tell me quickly about this man who was with Turney," X urged. "What did he look like?"

"Couldn't say, sir. Wore a veil."

"A veil?" X echoed.

"Right, sir. He was a woman. Dressed like one. A woman in black."

X frowned. "Stick to your job, Bates," he ordered. "Watch the Turney crowd. The older Turney brother was in on the Jonalden job. And he was murdered, to shut him up, along with half a dozen others who happened to be on the same plane with him. Any information that he may have given Federal Agent Hughes, was stolen by the murderer, who is your woman in black. The woman in black must have got off the plane before it landed by means of a parachute. You proved that he or she, whichever it is, is hand in glove with the younger Turney. Grill Turney if you get a chance. Look sharp."

"But Lizio, sir. Not a chance of saving him now, is there?"

"There's only one way," X told him thoughtfully. "The lawless way. I've got to take it. Lizio will have to be removed from the death house." And that, he thought, as he moved off up the street, was almost an impossibility.

Directly across the street from where Bates stood, a short man who wore a black, furry felt hat stepped from the shadows and walked toward the street lamp. There he appeared to jot something down in a notebook. Then, like a boy who wants to run past a graveyard, the man in the black hat hurried up the street in the opposite direction to that taken by X.

CHAPTER III

DEATH-HOUSE BREAK

WHILE IN THE city, X was seldom very far from one of his many hideouts. After he had left Bates, he went to a lodging house only a few blocks away. There he had leased a room under one of his many aliases.

As soon as he had entered his room and locked the door, he went to a closet and took out what appeared to be a small suitcase. Actually, the case contained a five meter radio transceiver with a telescoping aerial mounted in the top.

A minute later, he was in contact with Jim Hobart, head of the famous Hobart Detective Agency.[5] His instructions were brief. Hobart was to take a group of picked men and go at once to Ossining where they were to be stationed outside the city limits and not far from the penitentiary. Hobart was to take orders only from a man who would say: *"Martin sent me."*

X returned the radio to the closet and immediately set about changing his makeup. All the plastic volatile material had to be removed from his face. Next the metal face plates that had been used to simulate high cheek bones were returned to the makeup box. Guided by a number of photographs taken from his files, he began rebuilding his face with quick, skillful movements of his fingers.

The impersonation he was about to attempt was a dangerous one. The man whose features were slowly forming on the face of Agent X was a famous novelist and close friend of Warden McCray of Sing Sing prison. The fact that Novelist Heldon was a shorter man than Agent X did not make matters easier. However, the

---

5 AUTHOR'S NOTE: *The Hobart Detective Agency is actually supported by funds supplied by X. Jim Hobart, who owes his mentor much, is always ready to act upon any order that X gives him. Hobart knows X only when the latter is masquerading as A.J. Martin, a well-known newspaperman.*

fact that Heldon and McCray were close friends would assure the Agent's admission to the warden's office.

This preparation occupied the early morning hours and it was nearly ten o'clock before he was inside the forbidding doomlike walls of the prison. When he had been admitted into the warden's office, he found that McCray had other visitors. McCray was in conversation with ex-Mrs. Winton and her father, Dr. Randolph Mills. Dora Winton was a tall, handsome blonde, every inch a sophisticate. Her father was tall and gray-haired. His shoulders were bowed beneath years of scientific research. He was noted for his work with chemical toxins.

Agent X slipped into an inconspicuous position near the door and listened carefully without seeming to.

"My daughter's request may seem odd to you," said Mills, in a reedy voice. "I myself know hardly how to account for it. She is not generally so—so charitably inclined."

Dora Winton's fine lips thinned. Her nostrils spread. She was obviously not thankful for her father's last remark. But she managed an appealing smile for Warden McCray.

"Lizio's case has interested me very much, naturally, because Lizio was one of my husband's clients. Surely if I can do something that will cheer the poor man up you would not deny me the opportunity."

Warden McCray looked gravely at the woman. "Frankly, I can't imagine what you could possibly do for the man." However, he reached for a visiting order slip. Agent X saw Dora Winton sigh. The warden handed the filled out slip to Dr. Mills with a smile.

When the two had left, McCray greeted X genially. But no sooner had their hand clasp been broken than a frown settled down on the warden's forehead.

"Do such cranks worry you?" asked X as he dropped into the proffered chair beside the warden's desk.

McCray looked at him shrewdly. "Such cranks don't. As a rule, none of them do. There is never a man executed within these walls but what we get threat letters." McCray ran his hands through his sparse thatch. "This time, I have a premonition that some of those threats may be in earnest." The warden opened the drawer of his desk and fumbled within it. He shot a nervous smile at X. "You've changed a little since I last saw you, Heldon."

Instantly on guard, X watched the warden's every movement. To all appearances, he was perfectly at ease. "A little fleshier, perhaps?" he suggested.

THE WARDEN shook his head. "No, taller than you were yesterday when you came to tell me you were slipping off to Europe." McCray's hand came from the drawer, fingers closed over the butt of a revolver. But his gun wrist met the Agent's fingers. X was on his feet as soon as he realized that his act had failed. At the same time that he twisted the gun from the warden's grip, he dealt a paralyzing blow to McCray's biceps that prevented the warden from pressing the electric call-bell on his desk.

McCray broke free, backed. X swung around the desk and came to grips with the warden. McCray was no mean opponent, for he had come up from a hard-boiled prison guard to his present responsible position. But for every blow he handed out, Agent X had an effective guard. At the very moment when X's face seemed to be open territory, X put over a short, chopping blow to McCray's jaw. McCray sagged, and X caught him before he could fall to the floor.

That one blow from the Agent's powerful arm would be enough to keep McCray out for some time. In that time, X had to accomplish miracles. First of all, he had to make over his face so that he might impersonate the warden. Crouching before his makeup kit, with McCray propped up in a chair as a model, the Agent's fingers flew, fashioning new features and adding color to the plastic material by means of his special pigments. He combed out a gray toupee after the fashion of McCray's hair. The dark suit he wore was very similar to McCray's and there was no necessity for a change.

He then concealed the warden in a closet and hurried from the office. He had hit upon one plan of liberating Lizio. But it was a scheme that involved considerable violence. He wanted some plan that would be surprising and subtle. First of all, he had to see Tony Lizio. It was very possible that if Lizio remained cool in spite of his proximity to the chair, X might manage some switch of identities that would enable Lizio to walk from the prison to freedom with none being the wiser until much later.

X passed numerous officials. Evidently, his disguise was perfect, for all greeted him as the warden. He gained the prison yard and walked to the death house. Lizio had been established in one of the six last-minute cells that extended in an obtuse angle from the corridor leading to the chair.

Lizio was a tall, big-boned man with no evidence of a neck and small, pointed ears set far forward on his head. A grin brightened his dull face as he saw Agent X. "Hello, warden," he greeted.

"How are you, Tony? What's going on here?" For X had noticed that the door of the condemned man's cell was open, and that two guards were standing in front of it. Another guard was in the cell helping Lizio with a large, ice-packed, ice cream bucket. Lizio was peeling paper from a brick of ice cream.

Lizio grinned. "You know what you says. You says da last time, I get anything I wanta to eat." He pointed at the brick of cream. "Ice cream from Luigi's. Gotta my name in whipsa cream."

The Agent's eyes were soft with pity. Condemned men made odd requests. Probably one of Lizio's childish ambitions had been realized—to have ice cream made to order. The condemned man cut off a slice and offered it to the Agent. X took it to humor the man, ate without relish, talked cheerfully, and all the while studied Lizio.

He was more convinced than ever that the man was innocent of the crime. But how to get him out? X knew that reporters were already waiting to get into the execution chamber. The clock crawled on. Given a few moments alone with Lizio, X could have made alterations in his features so that no one would have recognized him. But Lizio lacked the guile necessary to an impersonator, and his voice and manner of speaking would have given him away at once.

X LEFT Lizio to his ice cream and went out again into the yard. He was familiar with the layout of the penitentiary, knew the gate through which supply trucks were permitted to pass. If he could get Lizio to impersonate one of the truck drivers—but no, that was outside the reaches of even the Agent's fertile imagination. He looked at his watch. Only about ten minutes left in Lizio's allotted span of life. Well, the execution could not take place without the presence of the warden. That would delay matters for a little while.

X went back through the main building, stopped at the guards' arsenal. After a few minutes there, he started back to the warden's office.

At the end of the corridor, he came to an abrupt halt. Stretched on the clean, mopped floor was a man. He was unmistakably dead. His glassy eyes bulged, his blue and swollen tongue protruded from between his teeth, his face was that ghastly blue-black, of a hanged man. A few feet beyond was another guard. Again the hand of the blue death had reached out and killed. Beyond was another. The corridor was like the hall of death, silent and corpse-filled. All about was a funereal odor like freshly cut flowers.

Agent X sprang into the warden's office, he seized the phone, called the death house. But there was no answer to persistent ring-ing. He crossed the office toward the door, stopped, stared at the typewriter on the warden's desk. Curling around the platen of the writing machine was a piece of paper. On the paper was typed:

Keep out of this, Agent X.

X turned to the closet in which he had concealed the warden. The closet was empty. The warden must have known X's identity. Had he written the note? Was McCray actually involved in this super-crime?

The door of the office swung open. One of the prisoners, a trusty, rushed breathlessly in. "Lizio has escaped!" he gasped out. "The death house is a morgue. Prisoners, and guards all dead."

X went into the hall, nearly bumped into Attorney Dean Winton. Winton seized his coat lapels. "Warden, you've got to delay the execution. I'm expecting new evidence any moment. Lizio is innocent."

X said through clenched teeth: "I wish to heaven he was inno-cent. But if he never committed murder before, he has now."

Winton gasped. "Is that why the prison is in such a turmoil? Is that why Inspector Burks is outside? When did it happen?"

"Burks?" What was Burks doing at Sing Sing? He was a long way outside his province of law enforcement. Then suddenly it flashed upon X's mind that news of the attempted faking of a reprieve had reached the ears of Burks. Burks had recognized the Agent's dar-ing methods and had supposed that X would not stop there in his effort to free Lizio.

Though Burks would have no official capacity in the prison, still he was a splendid organizer and leader of men. He would bolster the morale that would otherwise be badly damaged by the absence of Warden McCray.

Down the corridor a way, he heard Burks' roaring: "Lizio es-caped, you say? With McCray as hostage? Expected something like that. It's the job of Mr. X. Watch every gate. Nobody goes out, not even me, without a double check-up. That's the only way. Agent X is apt to turn up looking like anybody."

X turned his head. His eyes encountered Winton's. The lawyer could not have helped but hear that which Burks had said. Win-ton's jaw dropped. Then with an oath, he sprang at X. At the same time, he shouted: "Burks! Burks! Here's your Agent X!"

X ducked as Winton leaped. His lowered shoulder caught the

lawyer waist high. His hand clasped Winton back of the knees. He straightened suddenly, released his grip, threw Winton head first to the floor. He wheeled around in a crouched position. The trusty who had followed from the warden's office got a blow to the point of the chin that sent him reeling across the corridor to heap against the wall.

Then X was off at a run down the corridor. The crack of shots and the scream of lead followed him, but he escaped unscathed.

But his escape was only to another part of the prison. With Burks the watch dog, he would find it harder to get out of prison than he had found it to get in. Yet, get out he must.

Somewhere, the Agent's deductions had slipped up. Was robbery the real motive behind the plane disaster? Could it be that Lizio, the apparent innocent, was actually commanding the forces of a powerful criminal organization?

But at the present moment, he was forced to concern himself with getting out of Sing Sing. There was only one method: he must organize and direct a large-scale prison break. And this must be effected without loss of life, and, if possible, without a single prisoner escaping the clutches of the law.

CHAPTER IV

PHANTOM FLOWERS

AT ALMOST THE same moment that X, in the prison, admitted to himself that he was completely baffled, Harvey Bates saw the opportunity he had been looking for. Pat Turney, re-christened "The Terrible" because of his bestial countenance and habitual scowl, left the East Side lodging house where he had been quartered during the night. And Turney, to all appearance, was depending entirely upon his grimacing face to protect him from any rival racketeers who might be seeking his scalp. Turney was alone.

Pat Turney proceeded on foot, and Harvey Bates leisurely followed, smoke puffing placidly from his square pipe that nearly matched the square contours of his head and torso. Bates' ambition at the moment was to get Turney alone, hand out much more fist work than Turney would take, and force Turney to tell him who his mysterious companion of the night before had been—the sinister man who masqueraded as the woman in black.

A few blocks north, Turney entered an apartment above a dance hall known as the Hoola Club. The club was known to be Turney property.

Bates followed without hesitation up the carpeted stairway and came to a stop outside the only visible door. He listened a moment. He could hear absolutely no sound. The door was open a crack. Bates deliberately tamped out the fire in his pipe and returned it to his pocket. Both hands free, he pushed open the door.

Turney sat in a chair. In each of his hands were automatics. On his thick lips was a smile that was more terrible than his scowl.

"Come in, colossal," he invited throatily. "You get it, don't you— or you will when these roscoes start talking."

Bates nodded. "Trap."

Turney looked Bates up and down. "Smart, too, and what a big

She drew back,
screamed: "Police—"

boy! I was watchin' you last night when you separated that flat-
foot from his car. A nice piece of musclin'. Who was the guy who
lammed with Lewey Strait?"

Bates said nothing.

"Secret Agent X," supplied Turney. "You don't have to tell me.
He was the guy who tried to fake a reprieve to save Lizio from the
hot squat. Nobody else would think up a stunt like that. You bein'
his pal, you get the idea why you're here. I gotta square things with
Mr. X. I'd just as leave start on you. Mr. X was the guy who rubbed
out my brother on the damned plane."

"That," Bates told him, "is crazy." He took a step toward Turney.

Turney shook his head. "Don't try it. I couldn't miss you with my eyes closed. What's more, I got only to raise my voice and bring in the rest of the boys. I kind of want to save you till your pal gets here. Then when Mr. X comes, you're goin' to watch each other take a long time dyin'."

"When X comes," Bates told him, "he's going to squeeze the truth out of you about the Jonalden case. He knows that you were in on it."

Turney laughed. He glanced at a clock on the table. "That's one case that's closed. Just about now, some doc's listenin' to Lizio's ticker and hearin' nothin'. He'll turn away from the hot seat and say—"

Turney choked on his words. His ugly face went white. He stood up, staggered back a little.

Over his shoulder, Bates saw a tall, big-boned man with a dull, dark face and no apparent neck. The man who had just pushed into the room was Tony Lizio. And as he advanced slowly, like a corpse from the grave, Turney backed, seemed to forget his guns.

"Fix me in da frame, eh?" Lizio growled. "You wanta me to fry, eh? I show you da t'ing or two."

Then Bates saw his chance. Lizio blocked the door through which Bates had entered, but there was a second door near Turney's table. Bates sprang for it, seized the knob and opened the door.

At that moment, the lights went out. But Bates plunged ahead. Arms came out of the darkness. He lashed out with his fists in blows that thudded into human flesh. But a tide of humanity swept over him, bore him to the floor. Stunned, he was half-dragged and half-carried into another room. A single impression was foremost in his mind. He was conscious of a faint odor that was sweetish, like freshly cut flowers.

In another moment, he was in a lighted room. He was completely surrounded by desperate-looking, armed men. Turney had not been lying when he had said that his boys were within the sound of his voice, and Bates cursed himself for having plunged headlong into their midst. He was considerably worse off than he had been before....

BACK in Sing Sing prison, Secret Agent X ducked through a doorway of one of the prison offices. There, trusties, who had clerical ability, were at work. Evidently, news of the escape of Lizio had not yet reached this office. X picked out a gray-headed individual about his own height and build. He beckoned to the man. The trusty rose from his desk and followed X into a washroom.

"You know there's been a prison break?" X demanded in a voice that was the exact counterpart of that of Warden McCray.

"Prison break, sir?" asked the man excitedly. "Who was it?"

X didn't answer the question. All he had wanted was to hear the man's voice. His gas pistol came from his pocket and spat its charge of gas straight into the man's face. The convict dropped in his tracks.

X locked the door of the washroom. His makeup kit was in his hands in a moment. His fingers flew in the alteration of the volatile substance that covered his face. Three minutes later, his features were identical to those of the unconscious man on the floor.

He changed clothes with the convict and immediately slipped from the washroom. Out in the hall, a party of guards, trusties and reporters were hurrying along. Reporters who would have covered the electrocution of Lizio had a totally different, and more thrilling, story to report. Among the search party, X picked out a short man who wore a black, furry felt hat. Immediately, he recalled the figure he had seen near the Turney gang's hideout on the night before. A glimpse of the man's face, and X recognized him as Tip Morgan, a reporter on the *Herald*. He had seen the man frequently with Betty Dale.[6]

The Agent's objective was the prison arsenal. Inasmuch as the searching party was moving in that direction, he joined them unnoticed. He was only a few feet behind Tip Morgan. So it was that when Morgan unwittingly dropped his notebook on the floor, it was Agent X who picked it up. He had only an instant to glance into it, but several pages, he noticed, were filled with jottings in which the names of Fay October and Dora Winton occurred frequently. X thrust the notebook into his pocket and slipped unnoticed through the door of the arsenal.

His reception was considerably different than when he had entered the same place disguised as the warden. Three guards were in charge of the room.

---

6   *AUTHOR'S NOTE: Betty Dale, the Secret Agent's best friend, has shared many an adventure with X. Though she has never seen his face, she holds him in high esteem. Betty Dale, a newspaper reporter, has frequently been a source of valuable information to X in many of his investigations.*

"What is it, Ridgeway?" the guard nearest the door demanded of X.

FOR ANSWER, X sent a light blow to the guard's jaw. Immediately, the other two guards threw themselves upon X. He ducked under the hail of blows from their clubs, reached into his pocket and brought out a small crystal sphere which he dropped and crushed on the floor. At the same time, X held his breath. The effect of the concentrated anesthetizing gas, that the glass sphere contained, was almost instantaneous. As soon as the three guards were stretched on the floor, X went to one of the gun cases and took out six automatics. These, he was careful to unload before concealing them on his person.

There had been an emergency lockup order and all the convicts had been returned to their cells with the exception of a number of trusties who were aiding in the search for Agent X. The first cell block X came to had but one guard on the lower tier.

"Message from the head keeper, sir," X announced as the guard took notice of him.

"Let's have it." The guard was standing beneath the second tier of cells which extended out over the first and in such a position that the guard on the second tier could not see him.

"Here is a list of men who are to be taken from their cells to aid in the search." X brought out a perfectly blank piece of paper from his pocket and handed it to the guard. At the same instant that the guard reached for the paper, the Agent's left fist landed with terrific force at a point just above the man's heart. It was a particularly sensitive nerve center and the blow had a paralyzing effect. The guard dropped with scarcely so much as a groan.

Though the guard was unconscious on the floor, the excited prisoners in the cells witnessed something little short of a miracle. The voice of the unconscious guard was speaking—speaking from the lips of Ridgeway, their fellow convict! As he moved along the cells, X, in perfect imitation of the guard's voice, read from a mythical list of prisoners those who were to be liberated from their cells—this for the benefit of the guards on the tiers above.

X cautioned the prisoners to remain perfectly quiet. He stopped outside the barred door of the cell occupied by a particularly desperate-looking man. He took out one of the unloaded automatics and started to pass it through the bars. The convict reached for it eagerly.

Agent X had judged the man correctly. With a gun to give him confidence, this convict would fight to the last ditch. Just what he would do when he found the gun unloaded, X was not certain. X took out his master keys and quickly unlocked the cell. The convict came out, looked furtively about.

He clasped X's arm. "At a pal. Where to now?" he asked, whispering out the corner of his mouth.

"We're going to make a break for it," X told him. "We gotta have more men. I've got the guns. You pick the boys with guts. Whole prison organization is disrupted. Now's the chance of a lifetime."

The Agent's strange ally moved down the line of cells, pointing out men who were eager to take a chance on escape. Ten men were thus picked and six of them were armed with harmless automatics. Each looked to X as the man who would lead them to freedom.

But as the men moved through the door of the cell block, the guard on the second tier spotted them. The guard hesitated a moment, as X knew he would do because he could not have helped but hear X and the guard on the lower tier talking over the fake order to release certain of the prisoners to help in the search. But when he glimpsed an automatic in one of the prisoner's hands, he sounded the alarm and grabbed for his gun.

But by that time, X had moved his little army of desperados through the cell block door. But the alarm was out. The jangling gongs threw the men into a panic. Frightened eyes looked to Agent X. One of the men raised his gun and would have shot anyone or anything had not X knocked down his arm.

"Fool!" X whispered harshly. "Use your gun to threaten. Shooting will only bring more trouble. Follow me." He led off down the corridor, took a sharp turn to the right. Two guards, hurrying to the call of the alarm bell, ran into the army of prison breakers. The Agent's gas pistol accounted for one. A convict jumped the other man's gun, sent the guard's shot straying ceilingward. A blow with a clubbed gun laid the guard out.

They moved forward now at a steady trot, guns drawn, eyes alert. Suddenly, an office door opened. A woman came into the hall, sent a frightened glance at the column of men with guns in their hands. The woman was Dora Winton, and her appearance gave the Agent an opportunity that he dared not neglect. As Mrs. Winton opened her mouth to scream, X sprang forward. He drove his gas pistol forward threateningly.

"Shut up!" he snarled. "One peep out of you and you're dead!"

X MOTIONED to one of the men. The convict understood. He came up beside the woman and thrust his gun into her side. The body of convicts moved slowly forward like a single ferocious animal in cunning retreat. Had they known that the guns with which they threatened were as harmless as toy popguns, that desperate courage would have been shattered.

Guards melted before the menacing body of men. It was not that they feared the snarling convicts. To all appearance any effort on their part to interfere with the escape would have meant the death of Mrs. Winton. There was only one thing that Agent X feared. And no sooner had they gained the prison yard than they met that one thing—tear gas.

Only the Agent's super-human sense saved them then. Some inexplicable warning told him to turn his head and look back over the heads of his convict army. Four guards had quietly stepped from the door they had just left. Each carried tear gas bombs. One had his right hand raised, ready to hurl the bomb into their midst.

"Stop!" And all the dominant personality of Secret Agent X became apparent in that one word. "Make the slightest effort to stop us, and this woman dies. You may blind us with gas, but you cannot prevent my finger from tightening on the trigger of this gun."

The man with the gas bomb lowered his arm. The guards stared helplessly at one another.

"Get to the two supply trucks," X whispered. "One man, the woman and I in the driver's seat of the first truck. We'll force them to open the gates."

The men moved cautiously, backing toward the trucks, nervous as wild beasts before a trainer's lash. And the guards watched helplessly. X stood beside Mrs. Winton while one of the convicts sprang in beneath the wheel of the truck. X nodded at Dora Winton. "Get in," he ordered.

The woman, white but courageously firm, lifted her head haughtily. "I positively refuse."

X brought up his gun slowly toward the woman's head. She stared into the muzzle fascinated. Yet she did not move.

"Let her have it!" shouted one of the convicts from the truck.

"Drive like hell for the gate!" shouted another.

X felt his throne of power crumbling beneath him. He could not harm Mrs. Winton. He would not had he been able. Beside him, the motor of the truck was roaring into action. X knew the fickle souls of the criminals who made up his army. They would not hesitate to make a break for the gates and leave X, their liberator, at the mercy of the guards.

There was no time for debate. X seized Dora Winton in his arms, lifted her, almost threw her into the cab of the truck. It was a move that required both hands, the move the guards had been watching for. X could not have used his gun on the woman then. A gas bomb performed an arc against the leaden sky. It burst only a few feet from the second truck. The first truck was already in motion.

Agent X was the only man of the escaping party who was not in one of the trucks. A white, vaporous tongue of tear gas reached out for him. The acrid fumes choked, blinded him. Yet, through a blur of tears, he saw the first truck rolling toward the gate.

GUARDS drew their guns, loosed screaming lead, all aiming at a single target—the lonely, staggering man who was Secret Agent X. A slug landed squarely between his shoulders. Protected by his bullet-proof vest though he was, the impact sent him lurching toward the ground. He snatched at the handle of the truck door, clung to it, felt himself jerked along the ground.

Suddenly, a gray-clad arm reached down from the truck, seized X by the arm and dragged him to safety. Half blind though he was, X saw the face of the man who had saved him. Just a convict, perhaps a murderer, but he was not inhuman enough to permit the man who had risked much to release them, to be shot down. Agent X was not one to forget such an act.

It was the second truck that had received the full effects of the tear gas. Yet in a desperate effort, the driver had got the machine going. Motor roaring, it lurched blindly ahead of the truck in which Agent X and Dora Winton rode. It charged at the gate like a maddened monster of steel. The driver, blind, choking, fed every possible ounce of gas into the struggling motor. Guards at the gate scrambled away in terror before the rushing monster.

The car swayed. Guided by the gas-blinded convict, it struck the steel gate-post, a ton and a half projectile of snarling steel and screaming men. Steel fence twisted. Glass shattered. The entire truck seemed to telescope. Its nose suddenly acquired pleats like the bellows of an accordion. Men were thrown out as the truck came to a sickening stop, front wheels halfway through the fence.

But the disaster had given Agent X and his party an unlooked for advantage. Not only were the guards at the gate thrown into disorganization, but the lock of the gate had strained and broken. Before the accurately guided charge of the Agent's truck, the gates swung open.

"Turn left!" X shouted. "Drive, man, drive!"

The man behind the wheel needed no urging. He let the eight-cylinder engine beneath the hood take the bit in its teeth. The truck lurched sickeningly along the state road. Behind them, sirens of the pursuing prison cars screamed their warning.

"Side road to the right!" shouted X.

Tire squealed. The truck careened into an unpaved road. Ahead, X sighted a large shed that was attached to an old dolomite quarry. "Ditch the car!" he ordered. "Everybody out. Make for that shed. I've prepared for this."

And he had prepared for just such a move. If all else failed, he had planned just such a prison break in order to liberate Lizio.

The truck slowed. Men sprang from it into the tall weeds at the side of the road. The driver let the truck run into the ditch. Agent X, gripping Mrs. Winton by the arm, led and half dragged her across the field. X and the escaped prisoners stumbled through the door of the shed.

IT WAS gloomy in the building, but not so dark but what X made out the flame-red hair of Jim Hobart.

"Martin sent me," X cried. It was the signal he had previously arranged with Hobart. At once, Hobart's picked private detectives surrounded the group of convicts. There were oaths and shouts of "double-cross." Firing pins clicked upon empty chambers.

"Hands up, everybody!" shouted Hobart. And in the dim light of the building, X saw six convicts raise their hands. He slipped away into a small, dark room that had been used for storing tools. In the dark, his fingers worked swiftly and accurately, reforming his makeup material until his became the features of A.J. Martin, the newspaperman whose friendship Hobart valued so highly.

As soon as the transformation was complete, X joined the others. Hobart's eyes popped a little. "Mr. Martin!" he gasped.

"On your toes, Hobart," X said crisply in the voice associated with this most famous of all his aliases. "Hold these men for the prison officials." He glanced across the big room at the prison-pale faces of the convicts. One face stood out—that of the man who had dragged X into the truck.

X pointed the man out to Hobart. "That man gets full credit for having checked the prison break. You understand, Hobart? Make up a story that he got wind of the planned escape, got in touch with you, and led the men into this ambush. I don't know that man's offense. Whatever it is, there's good in him. Make him a hero and the very least he can expect is a shortened sentence. I owe him something."

"Just as you say," Hobart agreed readily.

"And Hobart, I'll take one of your cars. That's Mrs. Winton over there. I'd like to take her home."

Jim Hobart looked at Mrs. Winton. She was pale but firm-lipped. At the moment, she was very lovely. Hobart smiled, wondered perhaps, if Mr. Martin, confirmed bachelor, hadn't fallen at last.

But it was with a purpose quite different than romancing that X drove Dora Winton back to the city.

"This is my father's house," she informed him as X stopped the car in front of a magnificent mansion on West End Avenue. "I've lived here since my separation from Mr. Winton. It's really nicer looking on the outside than on the inside. Father's laboratory equipment is generally littered over most of the house."

"A chemist, isn't he?" X asked, as he escorted Dora Winton toward the door.

She nodded. "And a tireless worker. But I have my wing of the house where I can get away and be with my birds."

"Oh, you like birds?" X asked, opening the door for her.

She shrugged. "Not particularly. But Mr. Winton hates them."

X turned and stared into the woman's face. Beautiful perhaps, but there was a hard expression of cold hatred in her blue eyes. She smiled, invited him to enter. As they crossed a beautifully appointed hall, she added: "I like to think of the birds as keeping him away."

"Just why did you go to see Lizio in the prison today?" X asked suddenly.

The woman's eyes widened with surprise. "How did you know that? But I suppose in your capacity as a newspaperman you would get that information."

X nodded. The woman was scrupulously avoiding his question. She put her hand on the door that led into her apartment. "Forgive me, won't you, for not asking you in. This entire experience has been rather terrifying. I'm quite fagged out. But come sometime, won't you, Mr. Martin?"

He took her hand, bowed slightly. "It would indeed be a pleasure," he assured her. As she opened the door, he glimpsed the interior of Dora Winton's drawing room. A pleasant, sunny room, with flowers all about and birds in cages. Little chirping canaries.

Inasmuch as X was certain that the strangling death was of a chemical nature, he had good reason to suspect Dr. Mills. But at the moment, Lizio's escape worried him more than anything else. It was inexplicable. There seemed only one sure way of finding out why Lizio's escape had been planned and put into execution: that was to disguise himself as Lizio and walk the dingy corridors of the underworld—an unusually dangerous move inasmuch as the police would have orders to shoot him on sight.

CHAPTER V

HIDDEN DOOM

THAT NIGHT IN a cheaply furnished, two-room apartment not far from the Hoola Club, a man moved furtively through the dark. He went to a window and looked down upon the street. Light from the street partially illuminated the man's face. He was young, but his face was weazened and wrinkled. The big furry felt hat he wore on the back of his head seemed to weigh heavily upon him. The man was Tip Morgan, reporter of the *Herald*.

Morgan's indrawn breath whistled between his teeth. Down below, two men lounged against a lamp post. Morgan drew back from the window. He took a small flashlight from his pocket and used its feeble beam to guide him across the room. He went into the bedroom, straight to the bed. He lifted a pillow and removed a sheaf of paper.

This he carried back to the living room and laid on a small table that stood beneath a book shelf. Then he went out into the hall and picked up the telephone. He called a number that was evidently familiar to him.

"This Betty Dale?" he whispered into the transmitter. "Well listen, Betty. That story we've been working on—it's finished.... Yeah, but I don't know that I can get it to the office.... I'm being watched constantly. Can you come and get it? They won't be suspecting you.... You will? Good girl!" Morgan hung up, stood looking down at the phone.

Back in the living room, a flashlight beam picked out the table where the manuscript lay. A somber figure moved to the table. A hand reached out, picked up the paper and pressed a bit of wax to the last sheet. From the wax, a length of fine, silk thread was suspended. Attached to the thread was something like a small flask that glittered like quicksilver in the light of the flashlight. The hand lifted the glittering thing and put it on the book shelf....

Sometime later, in his hideout a few blocks away from Morgan's flat, Agent X was accomplishing another miraculous disguise. What was most amazing was that he worked without either model or photograph to aid him.[7] His head, at the moment, was monstrous and machinelike.

A cap of flexible metal was pressed over his head. The metal was curved so that it hid the natural hollow at the nape of his neck. When covered with plastic, it appeared that X had no neck at all. Heavy plates beneath his coat hunched his shoulders up nearly to his ears and added to the neckless effect he was trying to get.

He had spent much time on the toupee of close-clipped, black hair with which he covered the metal head plate. This toupee came far forward in front to simulate a low forehead. With plastic material he fashioned features that were expressionless and almost brutal. Then he tinted the plastic so that it resembled the skin of an olive-complexioned man.

When he had completed the subtle touches with a lining pencil, he surveyed his work in the mirror. With the exception of the position of his ears, Agent X looked very much the part of Tony Lizio— enough like Lizio, certainly, to attract bullets from any policeman who saw him.

DRESSED in a shoddy suit, the pockets of which he filled with his own special equipment, and with a hat pulled well down over his head, he ventured out into the ill-lighted street. He walked with a shuffle such as most convicts acquire. He had scarcely proceeded the length of a block before he heard the heavy tread of a policeman ahead of him, Agent X was frankly courting trouble, but not with the police. He slipped into a dark doorway to wait until the cop had passed.

When the policeman's tread had diminished, X breathed again and stepped out into the street. At the end of the block, he turned left and shuffled to the mouth of an alley. He was now within the boundaries of the territory of the Turney gang. He entered the alley unafraid, his head lowered, his eyes darting from one shadowy hole to another.

---

7 AUTHOR'S NOTE: Not the least of the Agent's assets is his photographic memory. It has been said that once he has successfully carried out an impersonation, he can repeat it at any time and under any conditions. His art extends even farther than that. Once he has studied a face carefully, he can, a short time later, duplicate that face, in plastic makeup material, from memory. Voices and mannerisms of people he has studied seldom slip his mind.

Steps sounded on a stairway. X paused, watching and listening. A husky voice burst into song. A squat figure clumped from the dimly-lighted stairway, lurched into an ash can and cursed. Light fell across the man's face. X recognized him as one of the Turney brothers' pals.

Agent X shuffled forward, pushed his hat back from his face. The man put one foot back on the stairs.

"Whatcha want?" he demanded hoarsely.

X uttered not a word but continued forward. Light from the stairway fell across his face—a hideous face, made up as it was, and somehow terrifying to the man at the foot of the stairs. He gasped:

"Lizio! Whatcha want, dammit!" He made an ineffectual stab at his shoulder holster. His brow had suddenly become beaded with sweat.

"Why you wanta to have me dead?" asked X in a whisper. His voice, intonation and accent were an exact imitation of Lizio's. "Why you put me in da frame?"

"I—I didn't," choked the man. "Not me, brother. When the others wanted to do it, I voted thumbs down. I don't frame guys. I—don't you touch me!"

The Agent's hands went out like the talons of a hawk. He seized the man by the shoulders, shook him until his teeth rattled. "Who did then? You tella me quick or I tear you in bitsa pieces!"

"I—I—it was— I can't tell. They'll kill me."

"And I tear you to bitsa pieces!"

The man struggled, but the Agent's grip only tightened. Somewhere above, X heard a window open.

"It—it was Agent X, that's who it was," the hood gasped out, as if it was the inspiration of the moment.

"Don't be da fool. I kill you."

"No—no," the frightened man pleaded. "It was—it was the Turneys. The Turneys and—"

Something moved behind the Agent. He flung the frightened hood from him, half turned. A blackjack descended upon his head with terrific force. The leather sack split and its leaden contents scattered like shrapnel. It was a blow that would easily have fractured his skull, but the metal head plate, that was a part of his disguise, broke the force of the blow.

DAZED though he was, half blinded by the brilliant lights of threatening unconsciousness that flashed before his mind, X turned and struck out at his shadowy opponent. His fist landed on the man's shoulder, rocked him backwards. As light from the stairway fell across the man's face, X recognized him as another of Turney's henchmen. The man snatched out a gun, fired straight at the Agent's chest.

At such close range the force of that shot as it thudded into his bullet-proof vest was stunning. Its effect, coupled with the blow he had received on the head, brought X to the ground. He fell flat, rolled sideways, lay perfectly still for a moment. Somewhere, a man was running, his shoes sounding hollowly on the pavement. If the police came, and the sound of the shot was bound to attract them, Agent X would be helpless to defend himself. X ground his teeth, clutched at consciousness that threatened to fade any moment.

Laboriously, he hauled himself to his feet, staggered to the wall of the building and leaned against it for support. Footsteps on the stairs again—the crisp click of high heels. Fay October stepped from the doorway. She turned, looked directly at the Agent, then moved off in an opposite direction.

X took a long, deep breath that was like a tonic to his fagged senses. Then with that same shuffle, he hurried after the night club woman. She jerked a frightened glance over her shoulder, started to run. X sprang after her, seized her arm. She writhed away, leaving something in his hand. At the same time, she screamed: "Police! Help! Police!" And she ran toward the mouth of the alley.

The sound of the shot had already alarmed the policeman on the beat. He came around the corner just as X was on the point of pursuing Fay October. The girl screamed again, pointed back toward X. The policeman ran into the alley, shouting at X to halt.

But X was running like a rabbit, turning, twisting, dodging, zigzagging from one side of the alley to the other. It would only have been luck if one of the cop's bullets had landed, and luck was not with the law that night. X vaulted over a fence, landed in a small court, ran up a narrow runway between buildings and gained the street. He ran to the corner, then proceeded at a more leisurely pace toward his hideout.

He was forced to detour twice to avoid meeting the police, but eventually, he gained his room. There, in the light of a lamp, he examined the thing that he had torn from Fay October in that brief struggle. It was a piece of paper and on it was written:

Agent X, if you want your big spy come and get him at the Hoola Club before 11:00.

The Agent's brow rippled with a frown. Fay October had deliberately given him that. The "big spy" could mean only Harvey Bates. But how had the woman known that he was Agent X? There was only one answer to that question: either some one knew exactly where the real Lizio was or Lizio himself had seen X fighting with the Turney hoods in the alley.

He had accomplished just one thing in his disguise as Lizio. Turney's crowd lived in deathly fear of Lizio. He looked again at the slip of paper before him. And quite suddenly, he made an astonishing discovery. The handwriting on that slip of paper was easily recognizable. It was identical with the peculiar scrawl in the notebook that Reporter Tip Morgan had dropped in the prison....

A few minutes later, a small roadster stopped in front of the old building where Tip Morgan had his apartment. The girl who got out of the car was small, exquisitely proportioned, and had brilliantly beautiful features. With hesitant, almost fearful steps, she approached the doorway. Her clear-blue eyes darted right and left. Betty Dale saw none of the watchers that Tip Morgan had feared. Still, the very silence of her fellow reporter's abode was sinister.

She entered the building and walked quietly up the steps. On the second floor, she found Morgan's door in the dim light of the hall lamp. The door was unlocked. She entered, guided by a small flashlight she had taken from her purse.

The beam of the light pointed out the small table beneath the shelf of books. On the table was a typed manuscript. Betty stepped to the table, jerked up the script. Something clinked. The silvery, flasklike object rolled to the edge of the book shelf, fell....

CHAPTER VI

THE YELLOW FEATHER

IN HIS HIDEOUT, X considered the trap prepared for him from every angle. There was the possibility that Bates had not fallen into the enemy's hands. But he dared not turn the matter aside with this optimistic conjecture. Then there was Tip Morgan to think about. Undoubtedly, Morgan had written the note that was intended to trap X. It was therefore possible that Morgan was responsible for the nefarious work of the terrifying, strangling death.

The best possible defense was a strong offense, he knew. Why not carry the war into the enemy's camp? Why not strike at Morgan instead of blindly walking into the pitfall arranged for him at the Hoola Club?

So it was that he set out immediately for Tip Morgan's apartment, two blocks away. The building was dark and silent. The door of Morgan's second-floor flat was open a little way. Inside, a pale beam of light was darting about. X pushed the door slowly open and stood there for a moment watching the moving light. It was a flashlight in the hands of a woman. It pointed to a small desk and a manuscript thereon. The woman crossed to the table quickly.

X took another step forward. The woman's hand went out to the manuscript. As she picked it up, X's keen eyes noticed something that the woman failed to see—a tiny black line of thread that passed from the manuscript up to the book shelf. Something on the shelf moved with a faint metallic *clink*. Something that gleamed like silver fell from the shelf.

Agent X leaped the eight feet that separated him from the desk. His long arm darted from behind the girl. His grasping fingers caught the falling, silvery thing, dropped it, caught it again when it was but an inch from the top of the table.

The girl uttered a small scream, turned. Her flashlight beam fell across X's face. "Lizio!" the girl cried.

"Betty!"

"Oh! *You*—" And for a moment of panting relief, Betty looked as though she was on the point of throwing herself into the Agent's arms. He sensed the impulse and slowly shook his head. "This little glass bulb is too easily broken. It's a great wonder I didn't smash it with my butter-finger antics." He broke the thread that connected the flask to the manuscript.

"What does it mean?" Betty demanded. "Oh, I knew when I came here I was walking into danger. But poor Tip—"

"Poor Tip," X told her grimly, "may find himself on a very hot spot for this night's work. This was a trap. Picking up the manuscript caused the flask to roll from the shelf."

"But the flask—what is it?"

X LOOKED at the silvery bulb closely. "It appears to be a small edition of a Dewar flask. Invented by a Scotchman for saving gases in a liquid state. Actually, it's a very superior form of thermos bottle. Just eggshell-like glass formed into a vacuum bottle and coated with mercury. Had the flask burst, the liquid it contains would have been immediately transformed into its true gaseous state because of the sudden rise in the temperature that the gas would undergo when it met the warm air in the room." X pointed with his flashlight at a vase of cut flowers resting on the shelf above. "They're something more than a floral offering for funerals yet to come. They act as masks."

Betty shook her head. "Much too deep."

"This gas—" indicating the flask in his hand—"is as deadly as cyanogen. Like cyanogen, it has a flowery odor which might warn the victim of its presence. So, whenever possible, the woman in black masks the odor with flowers."

"And who is the woman in black?" asked Betty.

"It begins to look very much as though she is your good friend, Tip Morgan."

Betty shook her head vigorously. "That's impossible. I know Tip. He couldn't do a thing like this. These horrible deaths are in some way related to the Jonalden affair. Why Tip and I have been engaged in hunting down a new angle of the affair!"

X uttered a short laugh. "Morgan wouldn't be the first man to investigate his own crime in order to throw off suspicion. But lay that aside. How did you happen to come here?"

"Tip asked me to. He was being watched, he said. He was afraid that if he left here with the manuscript, the manuscript would never reach the editor's desk. We did get information that would open an entirely new line of police investigation. Do you know that a woman was used as a decoy to get Jonalden away from his bodyguards?"

"That's believable," X agreed. "He was susceptible."

"That's what this story is about." Betty pointed to the manuscript. "It says here that Fay October, popular night club entertainer, was seen with Jonalden the night of his disappearance. Tip's been working for weeks to find the name of that woman."

"And the manuscript being bait for a trap that was intended to kill you, can't be believed at all. Unless—" X paused. "Unless the killer doesn't care at all what happens to Fay October. I hadn't thought of it in that way, but it's just possible that the killer is playing a lone hand." X glanced at his watch. It was ten minutes to eleven. He snapped his fingers.

"What's the matter?" asked Betty anxiously.

X put down the flask carefully, seized Betty's arm, and led her from the apartment. "I've got a job ahead of me. I'll have to put you in your car and send you home." They hurried down the steps and X helped Betty into her car. "Be careful, Betty," he warned. "Tonight's attempt may be only the first of many."

"You—what are you going to do? I know you are going into some terrible danger."

X knew that, too. He merely laughed, gave Betty's hand a quick squeeze, and told her to hurry. He stood for a moment on the curb, watching gloom swallow her car. The fingers of his right hand toyed with something soft and fuzzy—a downy, yellow feather. And he had found it on the floor near Tip Morgan's writing table.

As he hurried across the street, a somber figure stepped from the shadows of the building and followed.

IT WAS four minutes of eleven when X reached the Hoola Club. He had made no attempt to change his disguise. As Lizio, his entrance might create a surprise. If Lizio was really the brains behind these criminals, X might be able to run some sort of a bluff, telling them that he was Lizio and that Lizio was Agent X.

X detoured the gaudy front of the building where couples danced in the front room to the music of a small orchestra. He went around to the back, mounted an ash barrel so that he could reach one of the first-story windows. It required less than a minute for him to jimmy the simple latch. He raised the window, crawled over the sill. When he turned on his flashlight, he found himself in a deserted kitchen.

Three doors led from the kitchen, one into a gambling room that adjoined the dance hall, one into the backyard and a third into the basement. A glance through the keyhole told him that Bates was not in the gambling room. There remained the basement and the upper regions of the house to explore. He decided upon the basement first in as much as it was easily accessible.

He walked down the steps and into damp, clinging darkness. There was no need of walking softly. The band upstairs would have muffled a gunshot. The basement was the perfect place for murder, because of this effective sound shielding. At the foot of the steps, X saw a narrow thread of yellow light that marked the bottom of a door beyond. He went to the door, his gas pistol in his hand.

He tried the latch of the door. It worked easily—too easily. On the other side of that door, death awaited him. He raised the latch and suddenly kicked the door open.

Instantly, the light went out. A gun jabbed into X's side. A hoarse voice said: "Keep movin' straight ahead, Mr. X."

X obeyed. But he retained his gas pistol. If the darkness was a hindrance to him, it was also a disadvantage to the man behind him.

"Stop," ordered the husky voice. "Turn around."

Again X obeyed.

"Just want a glimpse of your face before I turn the heat on you, Mr. X. They say nobody's ever seen your face and lived."

A flashlight switched on. Reflected rays struck the face of the man with the gun. He was the same who had attacked X in the alley, but his was a face that suddenly went ghastly white. The light in his hand trembled. The gun trembled, too. "Lizio!" he cried. "Killed you once, and by heaven I'll do it again!"

But in his terror at meeting the man he believed he had killed, the man had taken no notice of the Agent's gas pistol. As soon as X's captor had cried out the name of Lizio, bedlam had broken loose in the next room. X heard feet pounding toward the door. He wasted no time. Even before his opponent's finger could tighten on the trigger of the gun he carried, X's gas pistol spurted its charge of gas in a straight line to the man's face.

As the man dropped, his fingers released his automatic. X

snatched it up just as the door behind him opened up and men poured into the room. X pivoted and raised up. The first attacker met some of the gas which had not entirely dissipated after X had loosed it from his pistol. The man, half groggy, fairly bumped into X's flying fist. At the same time, X sent a shot from the automatic he had recovered. The slug whined over the heads of the criminals and crashed out the light-globe in the next room.[8]

He was fighting in total darkness, then. The blows that landed upon him were powerful but panic-driven. Occasionally, a pistol roared and darkness was ripped by an orange-red sliver of flame. Had there been the slightest organization, weight of numbers would have borne X to the ground. As it was, the fight seemed to be a free-for-all and the battle cry was: "Kill Lizio!"

From somewhere, seeming far away, came the wail of a police siren.

"Cops!" somebody cried.

A PLUNGING body struck X, took him off balance, hurled him to the floor. To a man, the criminals made for the door, stumbling over X, falling over each other, in a mad stampede to leave the building. X picked himself up. He was apparently alone. He could little afford to meet the police in the guise he wore. He started for the door. As he did so, gray light from a window fell across his face.

Suddenly, out of the darkness, a man sprung like a black panther. X swung around. Powerful fingers locked on his throat. Sheer weight threw him back against the wall.

"Got you!" a voice chopped triumphantly.

"Bates!" X snapped.

Instantly the fingers released their grip. Harvey Bates uttered a dull groan. X got out his flashlight and turned it on the big man. Bates' square face was haggard. His eyes were dismal. "Sorry, sir, but you looked—"

"What happened to you?" X asked.

"Trap, sir. I've been a fool."

"Not necessarily," said X. "They would have trapped me, too, had it not been that they were frightened by my face. You were bait for the trap set for me. Some one in the gang knew that I was mas-

---

8 AUTHOR'S NOTE: Though he dislikes lethal weapons, there are few pistol marksmen who can compare with Agent X. It might be stated here that as soon as X discharges his gas pistol, he holds his breath to avoid any of the powerful vapor that might be blown back on him. Pulling a trigger and holding his breath are synchronous actions with him.

querading. That some one managed the trap but neglected to tell his henchmen that I might appear as Lizio. And for some reason, all the Turney crowd is scared of Lizio."

"Good reason," Bates said. "Lizio is out to kill some one who might have had something to do with framing him. I think that Lizio is the man behind the strangling deaths."

"Why?" demanded X.

"Because when I walked into Pat Turney's trap, Lizio followed me in. He accused Turney of framing him. He wanted to kill Turney."

"Then what?"

"Lights went out. I tried for a getaway and didn't make it. About all I knew was that somewhere somebody had opened some flowers—"

"Flowers?"

"That's what it smelled like."

"Where's Turney now?"

"Don't know. He wasn't in the bunch that was going to bump me off. He was in his apartment above the club, but if Lizio—"

"Where's Tip Morgan? Who was at the head of the men who were holding you? Morgan?"

"Don't know. I never heard of Morgan. After what happened up in Turney's place, I was sure that Lizio was the man we were after. When you came in and some one called out that you were Lizio, they all forgot about me. Then I thought you were Lizio."

X shook his head. "Things are fogging up pretty fast. I still don't understand—" X paused and for a moment was in deep thought. "Poison gas used on the plane. Later, the same gas was used by some one, probably Lizio, to get out of prison. The whole thing is beginning to look like another case of dragon's teeth."

"What's that, sir?" asked Bates.

"Oh, a certain Roman gentleman planted a crop of dragon's teeth. Armed men sprang up. He sicked one armed man on the other until they'd killed each other off. The Roman gentleman, actually the culprit, remained in the background and watched them fight until they were all killed. One thing is certain: this man kills because he fears something. But he is mighty careful to conceal the fact that he is the source of the trouble."

"Who's this Morgan?" asked Bates.

"A reporter. He apparently set a trap for Betty Dale. I say apparently, because I can't be certain. I found a canary feather near the trap. That might indicate that the woman in black set the trap. It might mean that Morgan is the woman in black. It might mean nothing at—"

A dull groan sounded from the next room.

"Been going on for a long time, sir," Bates told him. "It's in the furnace room. They've been torturing some one."

X HURRIED to the door of the furnace room and opened it. In the light of a single globe, a man lay on the floor, muscles of his arms and legs working in agony. His feet were bare and there were scars of burns on the soles. Nearby there was an open fountain pen. The man was Tip Morgan.

X walked over to Morgan. Now he understood why the note that had brought him to the Hoola Club had been written in Morgan's hand. The poor devil had been tortured into doing it.

"What's this?" Bates asked.

"What's what?" X was kneeling beside Morgan, attempting to revive him.

"Ice cube. But why here?"

X dropped his pocket medical kit, stood up and whirled around. Bates, hands in his pocket, was idly pushing an ice cube with the toe of his shoe. An ice cube—that was just what it was. But Agent X nearly knocked Bates over getting to it. He picked it up and sprang across the room. He picked up a piece of coal, threw it through the glass of the basement window, and sent the ice cube following the coal. He turned to Bates, sighed deeply.

"That thing dangerous?" asked Bates.

"I believe it contained the strangling death. That is a gas that is as dangerous as cyanogen, but with different properties. Evidently, the gas can be kept a liquid at temperatures as high as the freezing point of water. That's exceptionally high for a gas. In the liquid state the gas is harmless, evidently. I believe that it was carried on the plane as the liquid center for hollow ice cubes. I feel certain that somehow the gas was concealed in the ice cream delivered to Lizio's cell—evidently in small quantities so that Lizio could make several killings. The gas evidently is unstable and dissipates rapidly in the air."

"If it was in the ice cream, why not hunt up the man who made the ice cream?" Bates suggested.

X nodded. "Your first job on getting out of here." He returned to Morgan's side. With a hypodermic needle, he injected a powerful restorative. It was only a matter of moments before Morgan revived.

Morgan groaned, opened his eyes without seeming to see. "The woman in black," he moaned.

"What about the woman in black?" X asked.

Morgan tried to sit up. "Met me just outside my room. She—she's no lady. A mauler, stuck a gun in my ribs—" Morgan's roving eyes flicked across X's face. He grunted, looked puzzled, tried to grin. "Gave me a start at first. Thought you looked like Tony Lizio, or like Tony would look if he got punched in the face."

As a matter of fact, the Agent's makeup had been seriously damaged in the fight.

"What we want to know is how you got here," X told him.

"The woman in black stuck a gun in my ribs. She brought me over here and locked me in this room. He—the woman in black is a man—said I was going to write a letter. I told him he could go to hell. A girl came in—Fay October. And are the police going to open up on her when I get out of here! You know she was the one who lured Jo—" Morgan stopped. "Guess I'm delirious, shooting off my mouth. You fellows cops?"

X shook his head. "But its perfectly okeh. We know about the October girl and Jonalden. Who is the woman in black?"

MORGAN shrugged. "Turney, maybe. Maybe its Lizio. I don't know. Anyway, I wrote a letter to Secret Agent X—heard of him?—after they'd burned my feet nearly off. The woman in black told Fay to go out and find X. Said he was wandering around looking like Lizio—" Morgan's jaw dropped. He sat up very straight then and goggled at Agent X. "Say, mister you—you're—"

X stood up quickly. "Never mind who I am. The point is, you owe us your silence, at least. One thing more. Were any members of the Turney crowd in on the torturing?"

Morgan shook his head. "The girl held the gun. The woman in black did the dirty work. The woman in black slid out when I was about half shot. Fay October told the Turney bunch to sit around and watch for Agent X to turn up. The woman in black seems to be damned scared of showing her—or his—face around the Turney boys."

X drew Bates to one side. "I thought it was something like that. The Turney crowd is working with the woman in black though they don't know it. And, unless I'm miles wrong, the woman in black is going to destroy the Turney bunch. Why? Fear again. Bates, the woman in black is boss of the gang that kidnaped and killed Jonalden. And the woman in black is killing now because of fear of exposure. One person seems to be in the killer's confidence—Fay October. Understand?"

Bates nodded. "Want me to look up Fay October?"

"Right. But first get a doctor for Morgan. I'm going up to Pat Turney's apartment."

If X wondered what had become of the police who had been heralded by the siren outside the Hoola Club, he knew when he tiptoed up the back stairway to the apartment above. As he slipped into the kitchenette at the rear of the apartment, the first thing that he saw was the broad, blue-clad back of a uniformed policeman.

With the stealth of a cat, X slipped into a bare pantry. Through the half-open door, he could see across the dining room and into the living room. A man was stretched on the floor and a police medical examiner was bending over him. The man was Pat Turney, and he had died the strangling death.

Burks was there, red in the face, hands on hips, eyes glaring at Attorney Dean Winton. Winton pulled his thin nose and looked embarrassed.

"It's because we've got lawyers like you that we've got crime like this," Burks lectured. "Just what do you think of your angel-faced Tony Lizio now? This is another of his jobs. And that's the kind of a man you've got the nerve to defend in court!"

"I will have to admit," said Winton slowly, "that it does look rather bad for Lizio. Rather bad indeed."

"One thing I'll have to admit," said Burks, "that it does look as though Lizio was framed for the Jonalden job. Now, he's out to get square with the men who framed him." Burks turned to one of his men. "You look for fingerprints in the kitchen?"

"Getting at that now, chief." And followed by several of his assistants, the print man went out into the kitchen.

Anyone could have seen Agent X in the tiny pantry with the door partly open. But as soon as X had heard Burks direct his men to the kitchen, he had pulled the door of the pantry shut—and the hinges of the pantry door had squeaked alarmingly.

"What was that noise?" asked one of the men.

"There wasn't any noise. You always get the jitters when you work around a stiff. Get busy and powder up that window sill. What we want is prints. Burks will howl if we don't find Lizio's prints around here somewhere."

"Let him howl. I still think that pantry door was moving when we came in here."

"Well look, if it will do you any good."

Inside the pantry, Agent X had drawn out and recharged his gas pistol. He held it in his hand when the man swung open the door.

The print man turned white, uttered an oath that didn't get out of his mouth before the powerful gas wilted him to the floor. X hurdled the fallen man and fell upon another with both fists working like trip-hammers.

But the familiar voice of Inspector Burks rang out: "It's Lizio! Shoot to kill!"

A ring of threatening steel surrounded Agent X. Grim-jawed police squinted over revolvers. X slowly raised his hands. "No need to shoot. I surrender," he said quietly.

CHAPTER VII

VOICES IN THE DARK

"**JUST A MOMENT,** gentlemen." It was Dean Winton who spoke. He came forward, elbowed through the circle of police, and confronted Agent X. Winton's dark eyes were shrewd as they scrutinized X. "He does not look exactly like Tony Lizio," he said slowly. "Nor does he talk like Tony Lizio. As a matter of fact, he *isn't* Lizio."

"I was thinking that," Burks growled.

X knew there were good grounds for Burks' and Winton's suspicions. His makeup had been entirely ruined.

"Give him a frisk," Burks ordered.

Two men stepped forward. Agent X looked over their heads. Leaning against the door of the next room, looking very rueful, was Harvey Bates. X looked away quickly. His right foot began tapping. Apparently, he was all impatience with his searchers. Actually, he was tapping out a code message: "Bates, get lights out and get out of here."

The searchers brought out the Agent's gas pistol. It aroused no particular interest because in pattern it was identical to an automatic. Next, they took out his medical kit. X saw Bates reach out for the switch that operated the lights in the next room. In his right hand Bates held a gun he was aiming deliberately at the globe suspended from the kitchen ceiling. The searchers took a box of small, glass bombs containing anesthetizing vapor from Agent X. These were passed to Burks. Next, his makeup kit changed hands. And a slow smile twisted Burks' lips.

Lights in the next room went out. And simultaneously, Bates shot out the kitchen light. Total darkness. A door slammed. That would be Bates leaving, according to X's orders.

"Steady!" growled Burks. "He can't get away. We got him

57

hemmed in!"

"But you can't shoot him!" That was Winton's voice. "You might hit some one else. You can't take him. He may kill us all!" Winton's voice but it had come from the lips of Agent X.

From across the room came Winton's voice, but from Winton's own tips this time: "I didn't say anything. That sounded like me. It wasn't me!"

A flashlight beam stabbed through the dark, found Burks' face, grim and immobile.

"Steady," said Burks. "This man is Secret Agent X."

The flashlight jumped, crossed beams with another light. And Burks' voice came again—but from another part of the room: "Quick! Make for the front room. He's going out the front door." Burks' voice, but this time from the Agent's lips.[9]

"Stop, damn it!" roared Burks. "I didn't say a damned thing."

"What the hell you want us to do?" a voice demanded another of the Agent's thousand voices, speaking from another part of the room. His order, in Burks' voice, had had the desired effect. The ring of menacing guns was broken, and X was moving stealthily for the back door.

But if X was thinking fast, so was Burks. It was a battle of wits and Burks was a wily general. "Nobody move. Nobody speak," came Burks' tense voice. "Shoot the next man who moves or speaks. Watch the doors."

"That wasn't me! That was a trick! I didn't speak!" And that was X speaking again in Burks' voice. At the same time, he slid a little nearer the back door and felt instinctively the presence of a man in front of that door.

"Turn a light on the spot where that voice came from," ordered Burks.

A beam flashed across the room, caught X in the act of reaching for the door. But if the light marked X it also marked the detective who stood in front of the door. X's left fist came up in a short, fast punch to the detective's jaw. He flung the man aside, yanked open the door. He was in the clear, but for a moment a perfect target for Burks. Burks shot, aimed straight for the Agent's head, for he well knew that X's torso was completely protected by his bullet-proof vest. The bullet tore through the Agent's toupee and creased the

---

9   AUTHOR'S NOTE: *Coupled with his ability to impersonate voices, is X's unequaled skill as a ventriloquist, an art that has served him well on previous occasions.*

metal cap that was part of his makeup. Stunned, he pitched forward on the steps.

BUT HOURS of jiu-jitsu practice had taught X how to fall. He tumbled down the steps, head over heels, but with every muscle limp. By some miracle, he landed on his feet, and straightened up in time to meet two avid slugs that buried themselves simultaneously in his protecting vest. Pain-wracked, senses slipping, he ground his teeth and lurched across the backyard into the alley beyond.

Fagged muscles, leaden senses, demanded that he stop, drop where he was, give up. But his unconquerable will lashed his aching body into activity. He ran not seeming to know what he was doing. And suddenly he realized that the roar and crash of shots had ceased; that he was in a lonely and deserted street; that he was comparatively safe.

His first move was to make brief alterations in the makeup material that covered his face. When his fingers had completed that job, he returned to his hideout.

His investigation seemed to have reached a dead end. The two Turneys were dead, their henchmen were terrified ruffians—afraid of the police and afraid of Lizio. Was Lizio wreaking a horrible vengeance upon the Turney crowd because they had framed him for the Jonalden crime? It seemed impossible that Lizio could have directed the plane disaster from his cell in the death house. Yet Lizio had had outside associates who had helped him to escape.

In the solitude of his hideout, X shook his head wearily. He was back where he had started from. Lizio simply didn't have the brains to conceive such a thing. X discarded the revenge motive. Fear was the other possibility—some one, who had directed the Jonalden crime, feared treachery from some of his associates. And there was good reason for such fear. "Lolly" Turney must have squealed to Hughes on board the plane. What other reason was there for the killer to have stripped Hughes of all his records and papers?

But X was getting nowhere. Inactivity was irksome to him. He took his radio transceiver from the closet and contacted the headquarters of the intelligence force directed by Harvey Bates. Bates was not in his office, but one of his assistants was always ready to take calls and receive messages.

X asked if Bates had learned anything about the ice cream delivered to Lizio's cell. Bates' report had just come in. The ice cream had been specially made and packed by Luigi's Delicatessen. The driver of the truck, that delivered the cream, remembered distinctly seeing a man leave the truck when the truck had stopped to make a delivery. The driver had investigated, but nothing in the truck had been disturbed. No, the driver couldn't give much of a description of the man.

X signed off. The perfection of Lizio's prison escape indicated much pre-arrangement. Lizio couldn't have just happened upon the gas bombs and known what to do with them. And there was still that unexplained visit to Lizio from Dr. Mills and Dora Winton. X suddenly decided to visit the Mills house again, and this time in the disguise of Sergeant Keegan, detective on the force.[10] That, he hoped, would have some weight with the sophisticated Mrs. Winton.

In spite of the late hour, X left for the Mills house at once, arriving there shortly after midnight. The wing of the house occupied by Mrs. Winton was lighted up. X went around through the flower gardens at the side of the house, intending to knock on the French doors that opened off Dora Winton's drawing room.

Suddenly, a thin, frightened cry knifed the silence of the night. It was followed instantly by a cry for help. Dora Winton's voice, coming from the drawing room.

X SPRANG over the flower beds and leaped to the terrace. Through the French doors, he saw Mrs. Winton just picking up the telephone. X knocked furiously at the window. Mrs. Winton dropped the phone, stared for a moment in fright at the face of the man in the window. The features of Detective Keegan were pleasant and when worn by Agent X inspired confidence and trust. Dora Winton walked over and unlatched the French doors.

X flashed a neatly-counterfeited detective's badge. "Thought I heard some one cry for help. You, Mrs. Winton?"

"Why—" she seemed to hesitate.

"I'm Sergeant Keegan," X said with a smile. "Anything I can do for you?"

"Yes." Mrs. Winton held the door wide and X entered the room with its many flowers, and its caged canaries kept awake by the electric lights. "I was just going to call the police," Mrs. Winton explained. "Some one has been prowling around here. I'm all alone. Father received a call to go down to police headquarters early this

---

10 *AUTHOR'S NOTE: Keegan, Inspector Burks' right-hand man, has frequently been a model for X to impersonate. Knowing every line of Keegan's face and all Keegan's gestures and oddities, X can act the part easily at any time.*

evening and he hasn't returned yet. All the servants have been given the night off."

Mrs. Winton went to a chaise longue, sat down, and nervously picked at the embroidery of her negligée. "I am rather keyed up, I'm afraid." She gestured to a chair. "Please sit down. I had an experience yesterday at Sing Sing that was a little too much for my nerves. But about this prowler—I was on the point of retiring and I had just decided I needed a drink if I was going to sleep at all. I prepared a highball, was just raising it to my lips, when I heard a strange noise which seemed to come from my bedroom. I went to the door, looked into the room, and saw no one. When I returned here, I saw a dark figure going into the outer hall."

"A man?" asked X.

Mrs. Winton shuddered. "No. It was a large woman wearing mourning."

"A woman in black?"

Dora Winton nodded. "I could not see her features because of the black veil she wore. I screamed then, but the woman disappeared. I was afraid to follow."

X nodded. "And you were quite right not to. I'll make a careful search."

"Please do," Dora Winton urged.

"I'll only be gone a minute," X assured her. He left the drawing room and went stealthily into the hall. Mrs. Winton's scream had been genuine enough, but he wondered if perhaps she was not laughing at him.

From the hall, X worked himself into that part of the house generally occupied by Dr. Mills. That wing of the house was scarcely livable. There was hardly a chair in the doctor's living room and library that was not eaten by acid or occupied by some bit of scientific apparatus. Only two rooms were intended for the laboratory, but the equipment had overflowed its dominion.

On a laboratory table was a typed manuscript, to which marginal notes had been added. The script dealt entirely with the unusual properties of a gas of Dr. Mills' own compounding. Its possibilities in chemical warfare were immense, the notes explained. Thanatogen, he had named it. Its one freak property was its ability to be kept in a liquid state at a comparatively high temperature.

There was not the slightest doubt in X's mind that the strangling death had been born in this laboratory. For the description of thanatogen tallied exactly with what X knew of the killer's poison gas.

As for the woman in black, she or he seemed to have vanished. X returned to Dora Winton's drawing room to find her nervously pacing the floor, a tall, clinking glass in her hand. She put the glass down on a coffee table and came to X. No doubt of it—terror lurked in her eyes.

"You—you found nothing?" she asked eagerly.

X shook his head. "The house is com—"

Clink. It was just a faint sound like a sliver of glass breaking. Or like ice popping. But to Agent X, it was a warning of lurking doom. His eyes darted about the room. One of the canaries dropped from its perch and lay there dead. Another bird dropped. Mrs. Winton walking back toward her drink, suddenly staggered forward, choked.

UNSEEN fingers seemed to close on the Agent's windpipe. Across the room, Dora Winton's highball was bubbling furiously.

"Hold your breath!" shouted X, a command that could scarcely be obeyed because of the choking sensation in the atmosphere. He sprang across the room, seized the woman in his arms, bore her the length of the room and rushed through the French doors.

Half strangled though he was, he went to work furiously upon Mrs. Winton. He knew then that the woman in black had visited the Mills house. Perhaps, it might even be her permanent abode. One of those deadly, hollow ice cubes containing the powerful poisonous gas had been dropped into Dora Winton's drink.

The Agent's curative measures were simple. He knew that if she had inhaled one lungful of that gas in its concentrated form, his task was hopeless. Stretching her limp form on the ground, he bent over her, his powerful arms working tirelessly in artificial respiration.

Suddenly, he found that he was not working in darkness. Twin beams of light from a car fanned around the corner of the drive and came to a stop so that they spotted X and his patient. A man slammed the door of the car and came across the lawn with long, swinging strides. It was Dean Winton, sleek-haired, red-eyed, a handkerchief daubing at his nose.

"What the devil, Keegan!" he cried. "Who's that? Dora?" He was surprised, shocked even, but not particularly pained. X could understand that. His life with Dora Winton had been no bed of roses.

X nodded grimly. "Got to get her to a doctor—if there's anything left to doctor." His fingers, forcing lazy, poisoned lungs to breathe, felt a lifelike quiver in the woman's soft flesh. She choked spasmodically. Then came a sob. X straightened up a minute and then knelt beside her. He turned her over and gently raised her in his arms. The woman was alternately coughing and crying hysterically.

"Good Lord, if only we could get hold of her father. He's an M.D. as well as a chemist. He might help her."

X shook his head. He stood up with the woman in his arms. "Get to the car. We'll take her next door. I believe that's where Dr. Janes lives."

Winton started to say something, sneezed violently, and blew his nose. He led off toward his car. "What I was trying to say—" Another sneeze threatened. He couldn't get it out. "What I was trying to say is that Dr. Mills has disappeared. Inspector Burks sent for him early this evening. I just came from police headquarters. I've been trying to work with Burks on this Lizio affair. Feel responsible for Lizio's actions. What I suggested was that we get Dr. Mills' ideas on this strangling death. Poison gas is right along his line. But Dr. Mills has never showed up."

X lifted the woman into the car and got in beside her. Winton went around and slid in under the wheel. Dora Winton was mumbling like a delirious person. Hysterical laughter and sobs made her words incomprehensible.

"Thought you and Mrs. Winton were on the outs with each other," said X in the voice of Sergeant Keegan.

"You might call it that," replied Winton dryly. He started the car and let it roll from the drive. "But I did think she might know something about what had become of her father."

"That's all you know about it—he just disappeared?"

WINTON nodded. "Burks put a couple of men to work on it. I left before he had had any report." He steered the car a few hundred feet down the street and turned into the neighborhood property. As they passed through the gate. Dora Winton laughed again. "Fence," she choked out.

"Good Lord!" gasped Winton. "Is she going mad?"

"Diamonds," gasped Dora. "Oodles of diamonds. Hempstead...." Then she began to cry like a little child.

"It isn't madness," X explained as he lifted her from the car in front of Dr. Janes' door. "She's a woman whose nerves have been strained to the breaking point. Then the attempt on her life tonight was the last straw."

"You mean some one tried to kill her?"

X rang the doctor's bell. "The woman in black. And very nearly succeeded, too." And the two men stood in silence, listening to the woman's frightened sobs.

A sleepy servant ushered them in. Dr. Janes put in his appearance a few minutes later. X told him briefly what had happened.

"You deserve a medal for this, Sergeant," the doctor told him. "This is the first survivor of what the newspapers call the 'strangling death.' If I were the police, I would have looked in the Mills house the very first thing. A strange man, Mills. Very strange."

"Then Dora will recover?" asked Winton.

"Oh, undoubtedly. Needs rest mostly. My wife will put her to bed here. I'll give her a sedative just as soon as I have made certain that the dangerous results of the gas have passed. If the sergeant hadn't thought quickly—well, where is he?" Janes looked bewilderedly about the hall. Agent X had disappeared.

Birds—always birds. A bird on the plane that had turned into a flying morgue. A bird feather, that had evidently clung to the voluminous skirts of the woman in black, found at the scene of the death trap set for Betty Dale. Dead birds in Dora Winton's drawing room. And X hurried through the darkness, across lots to the Mills home, hunting birds.

By the time he had reached the Mills house, he felt it safe to enter Dora's drawing room. The gas, he had reason to believe, was an unstable compound. After a brief, deadly life, the poison gas seemed to unite with some element in the air, forming other harmless compounds. But before it dissipated, it killed. And it had killed every canary in the room.

X went from cage to cage, taking out the dead birds, removing yellow feathers from the still, little bodies. At last, he had a whole heap of downy yellow in the center of his handkerchief. He formed the handkerchief into a bag and slipped it into his pocket. By microscopic comparison, by careful analysis, he hoped to prove that the canary that had been carried by the woman in black had come from the Mills house.

His list of possible suspects was beginning to narrow down. The killer's moves, some of which he had thought maniacal, were beginning to indicate a terrible sanity. The killer knew what he was doing. And he was doing it well—killing as the coward kills because fear compels him to.

At the present moment, everything seemed to center about Dr. Mills. "A strange man," Dr. Janes had called him. Why had he suddenly disappeared when Burks had wanted to confer with him? Had the man a guilty conscience?

Winton had been very hazy about Dr. Mills' disappearance. Perhaps they would know more at police headquarters. There was one way for X to find out: he could go to police headquarters and ask. It was a bold stroke, but results might be extremely gratifying. X felt that he was on the point of a solution to the whole affair. He was willing to take any risk that would bring the matter to a head. A fear-killer, he knew, was the most dangerous kind. There was no telling where the next blow would fall.

CHAPTER VIII

DEATH AT HEADQUARTERS

BETTY DALE WAS returning from a news assignment that had kept her working late. She had parked her car in a garage near the apartment and was hurrying along the sidewalk when a large machine slid along the curb beside her.

"Betty," a voice said quietly.

Betty stopped, turned quickly, saw in the shadowy rear compartment of the big sedan, the head and shoulders of a man. It was a figure familiar to her, and her heart bounded with sudden terror. The man in the rear of the car was Tony Lizio. What she should have done at the moment was to call for the police. But why had she been called by name? Lizio did not know her. Then, of course, the figure in the back seat must be Agent X.

She stepped to the door of the car. The man in the rear seat made no move. If he were X, why hadn't he made one of his secret signs? [11] From the first moment she had sighted the car, she had been so fascinated by the figure in the back seat that she had not noticed that the driver of the car had slipped out as soon as the car had stopped. Now, she noticed that the driver's seat was empty. Betty took her foot from the running board, started to turn around. Something jabbed cruelly into her back. An arm reached around her and opened the rear door of the car.

"Get in," the soft voice ordered. Then, when she would have hesitated, a hand seized her roughly and thrust her into the car.

Betty fell back against the motionless figure in the back seat. A chill of terror passed over her entire body. She screamed then, or

---

11 *AUTHOR'S NOTE: Because Betty can never tell by appearance when she is face to face with Agent X, X has arranged several signals by which he can identify himself to Betty.*

tried to. A shadowy figure bent over her. A black silk veil brushed her cheek. Then something struck her a sharp, stunning blow on the head....

An hour later, as the first gray light of morning tinged the sky, a man entered a long, low, river-front shack that extended out over the water. He wore a visored chauffeur's cap that helped to support the black silken veil that covered his face. A woman met him in the front of the building. The woman was Fay October.

"Why did you come here?" the man demanded in a soft, chill voice.

Fay October's graceful shoulders shrugged insolently. "You used to be glad enough to see me." She took a cigarette from an enameled case. The match flame shivered when she tried to light a smoke. "Have you seen anything of Lizio?" she asked.

The man shook his head. "Have you?"

"No, thank heaven." The girl's dark eyes grew suddenly narrow as she studied the black veil that served the man for a face. "How did Lizio know that the Turneys had framed him?" she asked, trying to keep her voice even.

"Some one must have told him," replied the man. "The same some one who helped him to escape from prison."

"*You* couldn't have told him, could you?"

The man laughed harshly. "Don't get imaginative. I put him in prison. I had to, even if I didn't approve of his being framed."

The girl nodded. "You had to keep peace in the gang. And Lizio got his revenge on the Turneys for the frame-up. Or did he? I've been thinking about that. Lizio's vengeance made it rather convenient for you, didn't it? The Turneys weren't satisfied with their split of the Jonalden ransom money. They were beginning to threaten you. Then Lizio removed them—or did he?"

"Lizio and some one else."

"You think anyone would have killed Lolly Turney just to help Lizio with his revenge? That wholesale murder on the plane was a risky job."

"You're forgetting the Hempstead diamonds," said the man.

The girl shook her head. "No, I'm not. And I'm not forgetting the fact that there was a G-man on that plane. And he might have known something that would have made Lolly talk—talk about you."

"Look here, Fay," said the man harshly, "what are you getting at?

Weren't you satisfied with what you got out of the Jonalden job? I took most of the risk. I killed Jonalden. Why should you expect more than a grand for what you did?"

The girl came closer to the veiled man. Her expression softened. Her arms twined in his. "It's not the money," she said quietly. "I would have done my part for you and you alone. But I'm afraid, just as the two Turneys were afraid. And the Turneys died, horribly. They were afraid. A person who is afraid sometimes squeals. And the Turneys were murdered.

"Morgan, that reporter, found out how I lured Jonalden into the net you had prepared for him."

"And Morgan is dead," the man declared.

THE GIRL shook her head. "I'm not sure. It's never appeared in the papers. He might have been rescued. What about the girl reporter? Oh, I'm not going to take any chances. If my part in the kidnaping gets out, I'll talk. And I'll talk about you and the murder and the other crimes. Enough to send you to the chair a dozen times. I'll talk, because they'd let me off on a shorter stretch if they could get you for the chair. Don't you see, you've got to protect me. Protect me from the police—and from Lizio."

"I am doing just that," said the man softly. "The reporter, Betty Dale, is here now."

The girl started back. "Here? Now? Dead?"

"No, she is alive."

"Alive? You've got to kill her. Oh, you can't take chances like that. You can't take chances with me, for your own sake. You've got to kill her."

"Never mind. She shan't escape. No need to kill her just yet. There's something more important just now. There's a man across the street. He's hiding. Two detectives have been following him. If they find him, I'll have to act. No, the girl will have to live for a while."

"Oh." Fay October drew away from him, watched him coldly. Her eyes were perfectly dry, yet there was a quivering about her red, well-formed lips that suggested that she was on the verge of tears. "She's very beautiful, this Betty Dale, isn't she?"

The man sighed as though exasperated. "Really, I hadn't noticed."

The girl put her hand on the door knob. "But you will," she said in a scarcely audible whisper. "You always do." And she left the room, closing the door softly behind her.

The veiled man seemed not to notice her exit. He was standing beside a metal smoke pipe that reached up through the roof from the top of a small, iron stove. He had removed a metal plate from the rounded surface of the pipe, revealing an opening where a piece of mirror glass slanted across the interior of the pipe. He took the pipe in both hands, turned it, moved it up and down, until the front of a little tavern across the street appeared in the mirror of the disguised periscope. A car pulled up in front of the building. Two men got out. A sound like the click of a steel trap from behind the killer's veil. There was no mistaking the two men. They were plain-clothes police.

IN THE GUISE of Detective Sergeant Keegan, X entered the headquarters building without difficulty that morning. He proceeded at once to the office of Inspector Burks, opened the door quietly, and saw that the inspector's broad back was toward the door. Burks was using the phone. X entered to discover that Burks had another visitor—Sergeant Keegan himself.

But at the moment, Keegan was staring up at the sky, visible through one long window in the office. X slipped soundlessly into a coat closet and pulled the door partway shut behind him. As soon as Keegan was gone he intended to get the information he desired from Inspector Burks either by force or by bluff.

By the time Burks had hung up, Lawyer Winton came into the office. Winton was all smiles and his hair was polished to a jetty gleam.

Burks turned round, drummed on his desk and said: "I wish they'd quit bothering me with Lizio. That was some one else who has seen Lizio riding around with a blonde woman. It's the style, seeing Lizio, these days. And they all think they have to give me their information personally.... What are you grinning about, Mr. Winton?"

"It's Sergeant Keegan, inspector," declared Winton. "He is a damned capable man. Did he tell you what he did last night?"

"What, in particular?" asked Burks.

"Why, he saved the life of the woman who was once my wife. But what I'm here about is Dr. Mills. Any trace of him yet?"

Burks shook his head. "No trace. And it looks funny.... But what about Keegan playing hero?"

"Yeah," said Keegan from his position at the window. "I'm interested to know that myself."

Winton told a puzzled sergeant and a puzzled inspector what had happened to Mrs. Winton at Dr. Mills' house.

"Well, it's not the first time," said Keegan when Winton had concluded.

"What do you mean?" asked Winton.

"Keegan means," Burks interpreted, "that the man you found stooping over your wife was none other than Agent X. In all probability he was trying to kill her instead of save her."

Winton said that he would be damned. He glanced at his watch. "Let me know if you hear anything from Dr. Mills. I've got an appointment." He hurried from the office.

"Look here, sir," Keegan addressed his superior, "if Lizio is out to get square with somebody, why take it out on Mrs. Winton? That dame isn't mixed up in any kidnap gang."

"Nobody said Lizio was trying to get square." Burks picked up his phone. "Get me Dr. Janes' residence," he ordered. To Keegan: "And there have been fancy dames mixed up with crime before. And the more I think of it the more firmly I'm convinced that Dr. Mills has had plenty to do with this."

Keegan nodded. "Why did he run out when you asked him to come down here?"

Burks got in touch with Dr. Janes. He talked for a few minutes and then put down the phone. He pointed a thick finger at Keegan. "Send some men over there right away. Mrs. Winton is still unconscious. Dr. Janes is keeping her under the influence of dope until she can rest up. Nerves shot and generally out of her head. She may have something to say when she comes to. Anyway, if there's been one attempt made on her life, there may be another."

"Okeh." Keegan started for the door. "Say, what about this X guy impersonating me? We ought to do something about that."

Burks groaned. "Just let me get my hands on that guy. First thing we know, the people will wake up and find Agent X in the White House disguised as the President.... But you get out."

KEEGAN left reluctantly. From the closet door, X watched Burks closely. Just as soon as Burks' back was turned, he intended to come out of the closet, cross the office to the door, slam the door and pretend to be Keegan returned on some pretext.

But X was given no opportunity to carry out his plan. A few minutes after Keegan had left, two men burst into the office. Burks paused in the act of lighting his morning cigar. "Well," he rapped, "let's have it. And if you two have come back with empty hands and a vacuum in your heads, you'll be pounding a beat inside of twelve hours."

The two detectives both started to talk at once. The result was an incomprehensible scramble of excited words.

"Shut up!" Burks stamped across the floor, lighted his cigar, and apparently calmed himself down. "I tell you, if somebody doesn't find that Tony Lizio I'm going to take myself off to a padded cell. I get called up about every ten minutes by some one who's seen Lizio. Dancing at the Central Park Casino, driving a WPA truck, or playing the races at Belmont—it doesn't make any difference to a panicky public. I'll bet I've got half the force out chasing Lizios that always turn out to be men that look something like Lizio." Burks stopped, mopped his brow and nodded at the two detectives. "Go on. Had to blow up. I guess I'm going nuts. Let's hear your story, but one man at a time."

"Well, we've got him," said one of the detectives with some pride.

"Not Lizio," said the other dick. "Doc Mills."

Burks sighed. "Thank heaven there's some men on the force you can send out for one man and not have them bring in somebody else.... Where'd you put Mills?"

"Well, we didn't bring him in exactly," one of the detectives admitted a little lamely. "It'll take a whole squad to do that. Dr. Mills is the second cousin to a maniac. He's surrounded by a regular arsenal and he says the first man to step into his room gets the gong. The man's crazy with fear."

"Didn't you tell him you were from headquarters?" demanded Burks.

"Sure, but Mills says he don't come to headquarters or jail, or any place else. He says he wouldn't feel safe from the killer."

"Then he knows something," Burks decided emphatically.

"He does that. But imagine him bein' scared of gettin' bumped off in police headquarters. That's what I call a laugh. You can send a squad out to get him. The point is, though, that he not only knows the stuff that's doing the killing, but he's got a darn good reason to suspect the man behind it. What was it that Mills said was being used to gas the people?"

"Thanatogen," replied the other dick. "The point is, Mills traced the Hempstead diamonds, or rather he happened upon them accidently."

Neither Burks nor his two men were in a position to watch the office door, but Agent X was. While he had been listening intently to all that went on, his dangerous position kept him on the alert. So it was that X saw the door of the office open, saw a hand that opened it, and saw the two fragile globes of glass that had the power to turn his blood to ice. Instantly, X knew that he had been called upon to make the greatest sacrifice of his career to save a man who had good reason to hate him and had made a vow to send him to the electric chair. For the figure that appeared for a brief moment in the door was that of the treacherous, cowardly killer, the woman in black.

Across the room, the hand of the killer simply released the fragile flasks that X knew contained the deadly thanatogen. They burst. The door slammed. And instantly the office of Inspector Burks was converted into a lethal chamber.

Realizing fully what he was doing, X sprang from the closet. "Hold your breath!" he shouted. "Get to the window!" And at the same time, he threw himself upon Inspector Burks' back. Both of his hands came up, slapped across Burks' nose and mouth to clamp out that sweet-smelling, deadly vapor that had instantly spread throughout the room.

The two detectives wheeled around, saw that some one was apparently attacking their superior. Both snatched for their guns; neither drew them. Instead, they were simultaneously seized with a paroxysm of coughing. But that was not long lasting. Marble-eyed, tongue lolling, they staggered grotesquely. They were like men who had dropped through the gallows trap, who had broken the hangman's rope, kicking, strangling, clawing at strictured throats— men who had been hanged without gallows or rope.

And all the while, Inspector Burks fought furiously to break that hold X had upon him. It would have meant death to Burks had X released him. Burks was one of the few men who might have hoped to match the Agent's strength. He bucked and squirmed, but teeth gritting, breath locked, X struggled to save the very man who would exert every effort to send him to the chair.

With an almost super-human effort, X shoved Burks ahead of him into the next room. There was an air shaft there and inch by inch X forced Burks toward it. Then he kicked Burks legs out from under him and the two collapsed in front of the grating of the air shaft.

"Get a good breath," X ordered. "The gas dissipates in a short while."

But as soon as he was released, Burks sprang to his feet. He stood there, half suffocated by the grip that had saved him. He spluttered, glared, got red in the face. From his position, he could see into the office he had been forced to leave. The real Sergeant Keegan was just opening the door. Burks drew his revolver, leveled it at Agent X. "Well, Mr. X," was all he said.

CHAPTER IX

BURKS PAYS OFF

NO ONE ON the police force knew that the herald of the strangling death wore widow's weeds, so the killer had had little trouble entering police headquarters. While some may wonder at the fact that the woman in black no sooner reached the inspector's office but what "she" turned around and went back, no one understood the purpose of that brief visit until the two detectives in Burks' office were found to be gas-strangled corpses.

The killer went down headquarters steps, voluminous skirts dragging, jumped into a waiting car with a celerity that might have aroused suspicion, and drove away.

Yet no one took any notice of this dark disciple of sudden death except Harvey Bates. Bates had been charged by Agent X to carefully check Fay October's movements. But until that morning he had been unable to find the girl. It was only by chance that he had stumbled upon her shortly after she had left the river-front shack. Immediately, Bates sensed that the girl was ill at ease. She wandered aimlessly for a time before she seemed to make up her mind to act. Then she had taken a cab and Bates had followed.

The girl's destination was evidently police headquarters. The cab stopped in front of the building and Bates, who was following in his own car, saw that she hesitated to alight. But about that time the black-dressed killer left the building. Bates immediately forgot all about Fay October. He felt positive that under the circumstances, Agent X would want him to turn his attention on this masquerading killer. He had no idea what had been the result of the killer's visit to headquarters, but he was certain that no good had come of it.

Heart pounding with excitement, Bates got his car rolling again and tenaciously followed the zig-zag trail set by the murderer. The killer seemed to be in no great hurry, and for that very reason Bates suspected some sort of a trick. Nor was it long before he discovered just what that trick was.

The killer drove deliberately into a traffic jam. Bates nosed his car in a few cars behind his quarry, only to discover that he was caught in a lane of traffic that couldn't move. The line of cars to Bates' right was in motion, being routed to the right at the next corner. Bates saw the raven-black figure of the killer get quickly from his own car and climb into a taxi that was just getting into motion. Bates knew, then, that he would have to sit quietly and watch the murderer get away.

A glance in the rear-vision mirror told Bates that he was effectively bottled up from behind with not more than a foot to spare. Bates suddenly thought he saw a way out. He threw the car into reverse, let the clutch bang in and sent the car back to crash against the bumper of the car behind him. The car behind him rolled back about five feet before it tangled with the next car. There was much horn tooting, explosions of profanity and angry glares. But Bates twisted his front wheels and sent the car plunging forward and to the right.

Ahead, all traffic had been stopped, but the taxi with the killer inside had just squeezed around the corner. There were three cars between Bates and the intersection. A traffic policeman was coming out from the curb with his summons book in his hand. There remained no clear lane except the sidewalk. Just as the traffic officer began his tirade, Bates stepped on the gas, bucked the curb and rolled onto the sidewalk. Pedestrians uttered shouts of terror and scattered before this apparent maniac and the juggernaut he drove.

At the corner, Bates jounced from the curb, scraped fenders with a car going east and at the same time sighted the murderer's taxi. Nothing could have stopped Bates then. The taxi was moving rapidly, but Bates steadily crept up on it. As the traffic thinned out, Bates slowed down. The taxi turned south on Jackson Street, went two blocks farther toward the river and stopped.

Bates stopped a respectful distance behind. The killer got out, paid the fare, and moved off up the street with a dismal fluttering of black skirts. Four blocks more and then the river front. Bates was following too closely, he knew, but he feared that the killer would enter some building, shed his disguise, and come out again. So complete was the killer's disguise, that Bates feared that he would never be able to identify the man beneath it.

"Steady, man! He's opening the valves—"

The killer entered the office of a small warehouse. From his position, Bates had no way of knowing that the warehouse and its office had long been deserted. Bates went to the long, low, frame building that jutted out over the water and adjoined the warehouse. The door yielded after a moment of knob-twisting, and Bates went inside. The small front room was fitted up like an office. There was a telephone on the desk and the place was unoccupied. Bates picked up the phone, called a number that was listed in no phone book—his own secret office. One of his own assistants would be on duty to take his message and relay it to X as soon as possible.

But even before the man in Bates' office could answer, something cold and hard was pressed into Bates' back. "Put that phone down," ordered a chill voice.

Bates' heart sank. Slowly, he replaced the receiver and set the phone down on the desk.

"You didn't know that the building next door was connected with this one," the chill voice jeered. "You didn't know, my great fly, that you had walked into a spider's web. You didn't know that I knew you were following me. Do you know that you are going to die and that Agent X will die with you?"

Bates set his teeth. He might be going to die, but not without a fight. His heart was pounding as though in a frantic effort to get in as many beats as possible before the last. Bates clenched his fists, pivoted. His eyes widened, his jaw dropped. "You!" he gasped.

Then suddenly, the floor deserted him, fell away as a secret trap swung downward. Bates fell into blackness that became oblivion as his head struck the wood floor beneath.

BACK in police headquarters, X saw no possible way out of the predicament his generosity had placed him in. Burks, armed and squared off in front of him, had the whip hand of the situation. There was but one door leading from this inner office and no window that he could possibly use for an exit. Keegan was only the first to come into the outer office. There would be others, and the slightest alarm would bring many more.

But there was something wrong with Burks. His broad face was the picture of bewilderment and rage, but the gun in his hand was shaking—something that X had never seen a gun in the hands of Burks do.

Suddenly, Burks shouted over his shoulder: "Get out, Keegan. And close the door after you. Get out and stay out until you're called. Guard that door and let no one leave or enter."

"But, inspector—" Keegan started to object.

"Did you hear me?" Burks roared. And Keegan meekly did as he was told.

Burks gestured toward the outer office with a slight movement of his head. X stepped into the outer office, his hands raised above his head. Burks nudged X, on the point of his gun, to a small door at the rear of the room. The inspector's face was red, but there were odd white circles around his eyes. His teeth were clenched, the muscles of his jaw quivering.

"They're guarding the door, Agent X," Burks said in a crackling whisper. "The other door. Unless you're very unlucky, there's no one outside this door. I'll give you two minutes start before I take after you." Burks was actually panting. His lips moved, laboriously getting the words out. "You—you get the hell out of here before I change my mind and put a bullet in that damned clever brain of yours. I'm a fool—a colossal fool. But I'm not an ungrateful fool."

Agent X said not a word. He realized fully what the payment of the debt was costing Burks. Burks, who had grown up among policemen, who had struggled year after year to develop every faculty that would aid him in becoming the successful, respected official that he was, was deliberately failing to do his duty. And duty, as Burks saw it, must have been far dearer than life. X simply bowed his head, opened the door and left the office by the back way.

Burks crossed the office woodenly, and sank into a chair before his desk. He stared dully at the dead men on the floor. Then he ground his teeth and looked at his watch. Two minutes he had given Agent X. Had he been too generous? The man always seemed to move like the wind. Outside the office, sounded the excited muttering of voices. Burks paced the floor impatiently. Never before had he known the eternity of two marked minutes.

As soon as the second hand of his watch approached the meridian for a second time, Burks grabbed his hat and sprang to the door. Keegan was there with several other detectives. They all seemed to heave a sigh on seeing Burks. Burks looked Keegan squarely in the eye. "You'll take care of Saunders and Kelly"—indicating the two victims of the killer's gas bombs. "Poor devils. It was that fiend and his poison gas again."

Keegan nodded. "I'd swear I saw somebody else in there with you—somebody that looked enough like me to be my twin brother."

"Have your eyes examined," Burks growled, and started off across the hall.

When he had gained the front of the building, Burks looked right and left. There were plenty of people around. Any face might be one of the thousands of faces that Agent X owned or freely borrowed. Burks turned to a cop who was standing in the door. "Did you see Keegan go out about a minute ago?"

The man replied in the affirmative. "Went down the street that way," he pointed. "A girl passed him, sir. He seemed to take notice of her. He turned and followed her, grabbed her arm. They talked together a moment, then he hailed a cab and told the driver to drive to the Linden Café, or something like that."

Burks frowned. "Linden Café? Never heard of it." But he started

out on his strange quest, hunting the game he, himself, had liberated two minutes ago.

CHAPTER X

WATER TRAP

AS X, DISGUISED as Keegan, had hurried from police head-quarters, he had noticed Fay October walking along the side-walk approaching the building. X had turned, caught the night club lady by the arm.

Fay's deep, dark eyes had passed slowly up the tall figure to meet the bright, compelling eyes of Agent X. "I must see Inspector Burks," she said tonelessly.

"Yeah?" said X, in imitation of Keegan's voice. "Well, you're coming with me. I've got to talk with you."

"No," she persisted. "I will talk only to Inspector Burks. This is very important. You see, I know the murderer of John Jonalden. I want to talk, but I'll only talk to Burks."

X had been forced to think quickly. He knew that Burks would be as good as his word and follow as soon as the allotted two minutes was up.

"Burks isn't in the building now," X told her. "But I'll take you to him." Then he had hailed a cab and ordered the driver to take them to the Lynn Café—the place incorrectly referred to as the Linden Café by Inspector Burks' informer.

The Lynn Café was a quiet place with an excellent reputation. X had chosen it for two reasons: first, the air of refinement about the place would not provide Fay October with any reason to suspect trickery; second, it was conveniently located near one of the Agent's hideouts.

X engaged a tiny, private dining room, told the girl to wait and he would send Inspector Burks to her. Then he hurried to his hideout, changed both clothes and makeup. Since he had been frequently called upon to impersonate Burks, it took him but a short time to alter his appearance. He was back with Fay October before fifteen minutes had passed.

The lunch he had ordered for the girl was untouched, but the ashtray on the table was filled with cigarette butts. She heaved a sigh of relief when the man she supposed was Burks put in his appearance.

"You wanted to see me, young lady?" X demanded. He sat down opposite the girl.

Fay October nodded. "But we're not going to stay here. If you'll come with me, I'll show you the man who directed the kidnaping of John Jonalden and later murdered him. He is the man who has been the brains of plenty of other crimes, too, I have been told." She got up, ready to leave, but X gently forced her back into her chair.

"I go on no wild goose chases. Or if I do, I like to know more about the goose I'm chasing. How do I know you're on the level?"

"You don't," Fay admitted calmly. "Play square with me and I'll do the same with you. I'm taking a big risk."

X nodded. "Say, I know when to keep my mouth shut. You don't think I got to be an inspector without meeting a stool pigeon now and then? But maybe you don't have any information. How do I know you're not leading me into a trap? There's a lot of men who would like to see me dead. Suppose you tell me just who kidnaped Jonalden."

"All right," she agreed. "The Turney brothers were in it. They acted as guards for Jonalden. They weren't nuts about the job from the very first. But the big boss was careful to see that Jonalden never saw anybody but the Turneys and one or two of the old Turney gang. The Turneys did the actual kidnaping just as the big boss told them to do."

"What about the woman who lured Jonalden into their hands?" asked X.

"I don't know anything about her," Fay October answered hastily.

The Agent's eyes twinkled. "We'll leave her out of it. The Turneys did the kidnaping. The Turneys guarded Jonalden until the ransom was paid. Now, who collected that ransom? Who killed Jonalden?"

"The big boss," she replied. "He killed Jonalden because he got scared. The Turneys didn't want to get mixed up in murder, so the big boss did it himself. He got the ransom money, gave us each—I mean gave the two Turneys each a grand. He kept the rest. After the murder, the Turneys got scared. They framed Lizio for the job."

"The boss, as you call him, wasn't in on the framing?"

She shook her head. "That's why he's alive today—I guess."

X nodded. "You guess. What do you think?"

Fay October didn't answer.

After a moment of scrutinizing the girl, X nodded. "I believe you're thinking just what I've thought for some time. Now, just one thing more: who is the big boss?"

"I don't know," she said. "Oh, it sounds crazy, but I don't know who he is. I've never seen his face. It's always veiled. The Turneys knew his name. They had worked with him before."

"And you don't know him?"

"I have never seen his face," she repeated. "But I can, and will, take you to him."

"In just a minute. One more question: who is the other woman?"

FAY OCTOBER looked surprised. Then she smiled wryly. "I suppose it's very elementary, my dear Holmes, but why do you ask that?"

"Because," replied X gently, "you love this man. Oh, perhaps you haven't seen his face. You love the glamour and mystery about him. You've been proud to be—shall we be blunt about this?—to be the moll of a big shot. And now the big shot has looked at another woman. That's the only motive behind this desire to give me information. Now, who is the other woman?"

"It's not entirely that, Mr. Wise Guy. Oh, I'm a first class dope, but I feel sorry for the girl. I'm no softy, but this girl's a nice kid. Works on one of the newspapers. Just can't think of her name right now—Betty something."

For a moment, Agent X sat like a man of stone, so shocked was he by this announcement

"You've heard of this Secret Agent X?" Fay October went on. "Well, this X has been making it warm for the big boss. The boss kills anybody he even suspects of trying to track him down. He's out after X, and he saw X and this reporter girl together. He thinks the reporter is X's girl friend. He's got hold of her. He won't hurt her until after he's used her as a decoy to get hold of Agent X. After he's removed this X, Lord knows what becomes of the girl. Might be better for her if he killed her."

Agent X scarcely heard what Fay October was telling him. He knew the girl was trying to put herself in the best light. He knew that she was insanely jealous, knew that no desire to help Betty

Dale had led her to make this statement. It would not have surprised him in the least if this was all a trap to snare him—a trap deceptive because Fay October's statement was so blunt. Yet, she had really told him nothing that he had not known or guessed, except what she had told about Betty.

Perhaps she had discovered X's real identity. She had been lurking around police headquarters. Perhaps she had seen two Keegans enter the building. But as long as there was even a suspicion that Betty was in the power of that ruthless murderer, X would suffer the tortures of the damned. He realized that his brain was fogged with hideous visions that speculated on all the terrors that might befall Betty before he could reach her.

He stood up suddenly. "Let's go." And together they hurried from the café.

"This hideout of his," Fay October explained as they rolled along in X's car, "is a regular fort. He and the Turneys fixed it up. It's filled with traps and crazy passages. A squad of police wouldn't have a chance of getting at him, but one man might be able to."

X was driving according to the girl's direction. He noticed that a taxi had been following them ever since they had left the café. But as compared with the peril of Betty Dale, all other dangers seemed of secondary importance.

"Stop here," Fay directed when they had reached the river front. "It will be safer if I go the rest of the way on foot. You can follow. It will not seem as though I deliberately brought you here."

X agreed. He would have agreed to anything that he thought would bring him closer to Betty Dale. Impatiently, he drummed with his fingers on the steering wheel while he watched Fay October hurrying down the street. When she had gone about half a block, X got out and followed. He saw her enter the door of the long, low building that extended out over the river. As he approached, his keen glance took in every detail of the building.

It appeared to be a simple, flimsy structure, yet Fay October had told him that it was a fortress. Then he noticed something peculiar about the stove pipe that passed through the roof of the front part of the structure. The stove pipe was moving, slowly turning. The pipe evidently served the purpose of a periscope, enabling the hidden killer to see without being seen.

X knew that there was no possible chance for a surprise entrance. At the moment, he wasn't thinking about catching the criminal. His one hope was that he would not be too late to make an effort to save Betty Dale.

All windows in the front of the building were securely shuttered. The door looked flimsy enough until he touched it Then he knew that it was solidly fitted and very thick. The door was unlocked. He knew that he was thrusting his head into a trap, yet he twisted the knob and eagerly entered.

The door closed immediately after him. The darkness was stunning. For a moment, X stood perfectly still, his gas pistol in his hand. Then light came gradually, glowed dimly from an electric bulb set in the ceiling. X's quick-drawn breath whistled between his teeth. A man sat at a little desk. In front of him was what appeared to be a radio microphone. And the face of the man at the desk was that of Tony Lizio.

Lizio's eyes were half closed. He made not the slightest move. X took a step forward, his gun leveled at Lizio's head. "Lizio," he whispered. Then his eyes narrowed shrewdly. He took another step. Then it happened.

X SENSED the quivering of the floor. But on the instant when he would have sprung back, the floor opened like jaws of a mighty beast. He was precipitated into a pit of inky blackness. There was a rush of chill, damp air. His feet struck a slime-covered floor and instantly deserted him. His body twisted sideways as it fell. His head struck the wall. Something in the back of his neck snapped. A bombshell seemed to burst within his brain. Then there was nothing—nothing but an infinity of darkness.

So dark was the pit into which he had fallen that X was scarcely able to discern the division between consciousness and unconsciousness. The blow on the head had knocked him out, but it was that twist of the neck as he fell that had increased the period of unconsciousness. Perhaps the first thing he heard clearly was the distant rush of water. Then he discovered that he was sitting bolt upright in water that covered his thighs. He groped out with his hands, splashed the water on the floor, encountered something that was dead, gelid flesh beneath the water. His fingers found a face covered with water. He explored the features of the corpse and shuddered involuntarily.

He stood up with difficulty, remembered his flashlight, and turned it on. The place was narrow, seemed endless in length. It was about fifteen feet to the floor above. Rays of his light struck the features of the corpse beneath the water. Ripples distorted the features beyond recognition, but the Agent's sensitive fingers had seen what his eyes could not.

Ten feet away, sitting with his back against the wall, was another man. Blood from a cut in the forehead flowed down one cheek and dried there. The man was Harvey Bates.

With fear for Bates in his heart, X waded over to the man. A hasty examination assured him that Bates was only unconscious. X took out his medical kit, stuck his flashlight in a chink in the wooden wall, and hastily prepared a hypodermic injection of a powerful restorative, and let Bates have the full dose. Then X turned out his flashlight to conserve the battery, and waited, his hand placed gently on Bates' eyelids.

In a few minutes Bates groaned. His eyelids fluttered. X snapped on the light. Bates stared dully at it for a moment. Then he saw X and grunted: "Hello."

"As soon as you can make it, get on your feet, Bates," X told him in the voice that Bates could identify him with.

Bates' eyes started. "You—you're—but I thought you were Inspector Burks. Where are we? Where's the man with the veil on his face?"

"Not so loud," X cautioned. "Just get on your feet as soon as possible. The water's rising. That devil would have drowned us like rats. And we've got work to do—plenty of it."

"Try it now, sir, if you'll give me a hand."

X HELPED Bates to his feet. The big man staggered around, clung to X for support. His muscles were stiff. The pain in his head caused his features to contort in a grimace.

"How are we going to get out?" he demanded, looking about the room.

"Shsh," X whispered. Above their heads, footsteps sounded loudly. Then a voice said: "I killa dem all. All die for whats da do to Tony."

Chill fingers played along X's spine.

"That's Lizio's voice," Bates whispered.

"That's Lizio's ghost then," X replied. "Lizio is dead. He's been dead for a long time. His body has been posed in a car and that car driven all over town so that people would be convinced he is alive, so that he would get the blame for these strangling deaths. His body was posed up stairs behind that desk. The microphone on the desk was there for effect, so that those people the real murderer intends to dispose of, would think that Lizio was speaking to them through a loudspeaker system. Everyone brought into this building must have seen Lizio's body sitting behind that desk."

"How do you know that, sir?" asked Bates.

"Because this place we're in seems to be a sort of cesspool for corpses. The killer probably thinks we're dead. Lizio's body is down here under the water. It must have been pushed through the trap after I landed down here."

"Then the killer got Lizio out of prison to—to—"

"To act as the fall guy for all the murders contemplated. The killer was scared to death of his own gang. The two Turneys and Fay October helped with the kidnaping of Jonalden. But it was the big boss that killed Jonalden. Then, because the Turneys were grumbling about their split in the ransom money, the boss was afraid they'd make trouble.

"Lolly Turney was killed when Federal Agent Hughes tried to force information out of him. All the records Hughes had about what Lolly Turney told him were taken by the killer—the woman in black. Stealing the Hempstead diamonds and any other thievery that went on in the plane was simply incidental.

"Then, when Pat Turney became mutinous, the killer sent Tony Lizio out to get Pat. That was to give the other members of the Turney gang the idea that Lizio was out to get them for framing Lizio for the Jonalden job. But Lizio was just dumb enough to be dangerous to the killer. I believe that when Lizio went after Pat Turney with a knife, the real killer dropped one of his gas bombs in the room and killed them both. Then he removed the body of Lizio, for Lizio was to continue to be the fall guy even after he was dead.

"The killer began to get panicky. He tried to kill everyone who was investigating the case—Tip Morgan, Betty Dale, you and me. He murdered two detectives in police headquarters just as they were about to give Inspector Burks some valuable information. He's a fear-killer, the most dangerous kind. But he was clever enough to make everyone believe that the escaped Lizio was responsible."

"Then he was—"

"Wait," X cautioned. "There's another voice."

"The man with the veil," Bates whispered.

In the room above their heads, they could hear the soft, chill voice of the man with the veil—the man who had been the woman in black: "I shall call the roll of those condemned to die here tonight. Dr. Randolph Mills, Warden McCray, Fay October, Dean Winton and Secret Agent X—all condemned, by Lizio, to die."

"Keeping up the show to the end," Bates whispered.

Another voice sounded in the room above. It was unmistakably that of Inspector Burks: "Get it out of your head that I'm Agent X," Burks roared.

"I would expect you to deny it," went on the killer calmly, "but, when I meet two Inspectors Burks, I know that one is Agent X. If I've picked the wrong one, it doesn't matter. The other is dead by now. In a minute or two I shall turn on the gas that will promptly rid me of all of you."

"Come out and face me man to man!" shouted Burks. "I can't fight a voice."

AGENT X had listened carefully. There was some consolation in the fact that Betty Dale was evidently not among those in the lethal chamber above. It was just possible that she had never fallen into the killer's trap. But what of the others? They were going to die, and X was as helpless as though he wore a straight-jacket.

"Stand here, Bates," he whispered. "There has to be a way to get up there. We've got to stop this slaughter some way."

X waded along the gloomy corridor, his flashlight ray becoming feeble. The water was deepening all the time. The floor beneath him slanted steeply downward. Every now and then his feet found an opening through which the water entered. How much below the level of the river this section of the building was, he did not know. The water was up to his waist now. He slipped certain small articles from his pocket into his hat, together with a wadded up handkerchief. With the hat on his head he could hope to keep these materials dry for a time anyway.

The water was coming in with the force of Niagara near the end of the building. No possible outlet that way. He was on the way back to join Bates, when he saw a small door on the left side of the corridor. Just as he was about to investigate this door, he heard a strangely bubbling sound above his head. He turned the flashlight toward the ceiling. Two glass globes fully two feet in diameter were hanging from a steel frame halfway up the wall. Leading from the top of the globes were copper tubes that passed through the floor above. The bubbling sound was caused by the activity of a frosty-blue liquid in the globes. X knew that it was the deadly thanatogen in its liquid form.

"Bates!" he called huskily. "Come here."

He heard Bates floundering through the water that had now risen nearly to the Agent's armpits. While waiting for Bates, he studied the deadly-looking contraption above his head. He understood that as the liquid warmed to room temperature, it would gradually pass back into the gaseous state, expanding at the same time. This expansion would force it up through the copper tubes into the execution chamber above.

The Agent pointed out the globes to Bates when the big man came panting up to him. The long period of unconsciousness in this damp hole had taken a lot of Bates' herculean strength.

"What is it?" he gasped.

"That's the gas," X explained. "If you've got the strength to get me on your shoulders, I may be able to bend those copper tubes so the stuff won't get through when the killer turns the valves. Of course, there's a chance I may break the tubes. We won't have a chance when those big globes burst. They'll have to. As that liquid becomes a gas and expands to many times its present volume, with the copper tubes closed, there'll be no other way for it to get out except by smashing through those globes. You know what that means?"

Bates nodded. "But we could save the others."

X nodded. "And, of course," he added as cheerfully as he could, "we may find a way out of here before the gas gets us. Are you game?"

"Certainly."

"Good man! Stand ready to give me a leg up."

CHAPTER XI

DEATH BY INCHES

BATES WAS ALREADY leaning against the wall, his broad back bowed. X handed Bates the flashlight. Then he planted a foot on Bates' thigh and climbed to his back. He held to the wall, put a foot on each of Bates' shoulders. "Straighten up. But take it easy."

Bates grunted, strained, straightened slowly. X groped gingerly around the glass globes and got hold of the steel supports. "Another inch, Bates."

Bates strained up a little more. X let go of the supports and grabbed one of the copper tubes with both hands. If he lost his balance, if Bates slipped, the whole hellish contraption would come crashing down on them. The muscles of the Agent's arms swelled until it seemed they must burst through the skin. But slowly he twisted that tube, kinked it, squeezed it until it was completely closed.

"Got one!" he called triumphantly. "How are you doing down there?"

Bates did not answer. X could feel the man's exhausted body trembling. X reached around the second globe and got hold of the tube.

At that moment, the chill voice of the killer sounded hollowly in the room above: "I am going to open the valves. In another moment, you will smell flowers—the distinctive odor of thanatogen. Flowers you will never see. Flowers for your own funeral."

X felt a vibration in the tube he was gripping. The valves were opening. He clenched his teeth, exerted all his strength upon the tube. It yielded slowly. Sweat beaded X's brow. Beneath his feet, Bates swayed slightly.

"Steady, man! He's opening the valves. In another second, I'll have this one closed."

"I—I'm going under," Bates gasped.

"No! Bates, you can't!" X brought all his strength to bear on the copper pipe. It weakened suddenly. For a moment, he thought that he had broken it. He gave it a twist, a quick kink, just before Bates keeled over in the water.

It was only by an acrobatic twist in mid-air that X avoided bringing the infernal machine down upon him as he fell. X struck the water feet first and by some miracle kept his head up. A beam of light from the flash came shooting up through the water. X was about to dive for Bates when the big man's head bobbed to the surface. He coughed, sputtered, regained his feet.

"Sorry, sir. Foot slipped." He waded over to X's side. The water was up to the top of his shoulders now. "Thought for a moment I couldn't hold out at all."

"You didn't find a way out of here while you were exploring the bottom, did you?" X asked lightly.

Bates shook his head. He pointed the flashlight up at the glass bulbs. "Did that do the trick?"

X watched the fuming liquid in the bulbs. The liquid was slowly disappearing as it gradually became the invisible gas. X nodded slowly. "It worked. The gas is expanding right now."

Above their heads, some one was praying and cursing alternately.

Bates grinned feebly. "Won't they be surprised when the gas don't get them?"

X nodded. He was watching the glass globes above them.

"If those globes burst," Bates said, "well, there's something I'd like to say before they do. It's been great, just knowing you and helping a little. I've got a big kick—"

A shrill scream cut through Bates' sentence. And it came from somewhere near at hand. Agent X turned the color of paper. What had he done? Saved those in the room above, perhaps, by making a lethal chamber of their own quarters. But that scream of terror could have come but from one person—Betty Dale. She was somewhere in that under-water hole, sharing the death by inches that X and Bates had designed for themselves.

"Betty!" X called hoarsely. "Where are you?"

"Something struck this door over here, sir," Bates told him. "I was just going to suggest we try to get through that way. Look, some one's trying to open it."

"Betty!" X shouted. "Don't open that door. Stay where you are!" For X had good reason to believe that the deadly gas would dissipate before it could penetrate that door.

But he had warned the girl too late. The door swung open a little. Current caught it and swung it wide. For a brief moment, X saw Betty knee deep in water that had seeped into the next room. Then she disappeared in a veritable avalanche of water that poured through the door.

THERE was one thing in their favor: the next room had an electric light close to the ceiling. X swam through the door, saw Betty's golden head rise above the water. In another moment, he was beside her. The water was not yet up to X's and Bates' chins, but Betty was forced to swim to keep her head above water.

X clasped the girl in his arms. She was sobbing with relief. "Oh, I'm so glad you're safe," she choked out. "When I heard that fiend say he was going to turn on the gas in the room above, when I heard him say that you were there, I nearly went mad. I tried not to—"

"There, there," X comforted. "Everything is all right." There was no use telling her of the fearful proximity of death.

Bates pointed to the ceiling. "Door up there. Suppose we could get through?"

"It's locked," Betty told them. "I tried it hours ago. I've lost all track of time. I haven't seen a soul since the veiled devil put me down here."

"How did you get up to the door?" asked X.

"With the bed spring," she explained. "The bed is under water now. But it's no use trying it. The door's locked."

X squinted up at the narrow trap door. There was something in it that looked a lot like a keyhole. He took off his hat and handed it carefully to Betty. "Can you manage to keep that above water? Bates and I will dig up the spring."

"It's right under the trap door," Betty informed them.

X allowed himself to sink beneath the surface. He opened his eyes. Enough light came down through the water so that he could make out the outline of the iron bedstead. Bates was standing within a foot of it, groping for it beneath the water.

X got over to the other side of the bed. Together, he and Bates tilted the spring up so that one end rested on the bedstead and the other against the wall. Then X groped in his pockets beneath the water and got out his master keys. He turned to Betty, took back his hat, and placed it firmly on his head.

"If you hear anything like a lot of glass smashing, hold your breath," he ordered. Hardly were the words out of his mouth before a dull explosion sounded from the corridor outside. There was a tinkling of glass on steel.

"That's it!" X snapped. "Hold your breath. Steady the bed spring, Bates." X dug a toe into one of the coiled springs, climbed quickly, reached the ceiling. How long could Betty and Bates hold their breath? That was what worried him. A minute, perhaps? Two minutes at the most.

THE AGENT steadied his trembling fingers and examined the lock. The first key he tried failed to take hold. He discarded it for another, shot a worried glance down at the two anxious faces above the black water. The air was already heavy with that sweetish, cloying odor of the unseen flowers of silence. X inserted the second key in the lock and twisted it. The lock clicked. He dropped the keys into his pocket and pushed up on the door. The door banged down on the floor above. X looked into the room. It was empty.

X went down the spring. He motioned to Bates and pointed to the opening above. Bates nodded. The spring sagged under his great weight, but he moved with a swiftness born of desperation. Once through the trap, he dropped on his belly and extended both arms down through the opening.

Agent X turned to Betty. He could see the oxygen-starved blood throbbing in the arteries at her temples. He reached under the water, seized her about the waist and lifted her to the spring. She climbed slowly, but in another moment, Bates had seized her and dragged her through the opening. X joined them at once and slammed the door.

He put his fingers to his face and began to work with the plastic material while Betty and Bates watched in amazement. Quick, skillful alterations here and there and he appeared like quite a different person than Inspector Burks.

"Any weapons, Bates?" X snapped.

Bates shook his head. "Lost my gun in the water."

"Maybe we won't need any. Something tells me this killer works alone." X went to the door of the room and opened it cautiously. Beyond was only darkness and the sound of some one groaning. Bates pressed the flashlight into X's hand. X took it, snapped it on. The feeble ray brought out the figures of men and one woman standing with faces to the wall. Evidently, they were fastened to the wall in some manner.

"Where in hell is your gas?" Burks roared. "If you're going to kill us, get it over with. Just remember my boys are going to fill you with lead for this work."

X found a light switch near the door. He turned it on and looked about the room. Fastened to the opposite wall by means of handcuffs, were Inspector Burks, Dr. Mills, Warden McCray, Fay October, and Dean Winton. There was no one else in the room, but a loudspeaker hanging from the ceiling indicated the source of the killer's voice.

X motioned to Bates and Betty to enter. Then X took off his hat, carefully removed the wadded handkerchief. "There isn't going to be any gas," he said calmly. "And there's going to be no more murder." He opened the handkerchief, took hold of one corner, and shook it out. Hundreds of downy canary feathers floated out into the room.

Then X approached Inspector Burks.

"Who are you?" Burks snapped over his shoulder.

"Oh, I'm a G-man," X replied vaguely. He examined Burks' bonds and discovered that they were simply handcuffs to which a link to fix them to the wall had been added.

"Did you run across Tony Lizio?" asked Burks. "He's the man behind all this."

"Couldn't be," X contradicted. "He's dead, and been that way for some time. If you heard his voice, it came from a dictaphone record made before he was killed. The gas bombs with which Lizio managed his escape from Sing Sing were supplied to him by his worst enemy."

"When you two get done conferring, I'd appreciate it if you'd let me loose," said Warden McCray harshly. "I've been in this place ever since Lizio escaped."

X found a key that fitted Burks' shackles and turned the inspector loose. "Yes, I know about that, McCray." He went over to the warden.

"Lizio forced me to leave the prison with him," McCray explained. "I was a shield to prevent anyone from shooting him. But there was some one in my office before Lizio got there—some one who waited for Lizio and told him what to do. That some one wrote something on the typewriter. Might get his fingerprints from the keys."

"That won't be necessary. The man who wrote that note also visited Lizio before his escape and gave him instructions on where he would find the gas bombs and how to use them. We'll get him, don't worry about that."

"What's the matter with this building?" demanded Dean Winton at the end of the line. "It feels like it's swaying."

X unlocked the warden's shackles. "Didn't you get a look at the face of the man who helped Lizio escape, McCray?"

McCray shook his head. "He wore a veil."

"What gets me," Burks was growling, "I go on a wild goose chase all over town because some dim-wit got the Lynn Café mixed up with a nonexistent Linden Café. I finally track down Agent X, come here, and get in this jam. Then the killer slides out from under me."

Down the line of prisoners, Dean Winton struggled with an explosive sneeze.

"Wasn't Agent X your killer?" asked X mockingly as he moved to Dr. Mills.

"He was not!" snapped Burks. "Or if he was, there's no sense to him doing what he did. Why, he saved—well, never mind that. Let's get out of here. Feels like this place is coming apart."

"Can't get out this door," Bates said from one end of the room. "Door's locked and all of steel."

"We'll get out in due time," X said deliberately. He inserted his key in Dr. Mills' shackles. He looked shrewdly into the aged doctor's face. "Was it the Hempstead diamonds that worried you? I gathered as much from what your daughter said in her delirium."

Then X crossed quickly to the door. He looked at the lock, then held up his keys in order to pick the one most likely to fit. Bates and Betty Dale were near him.

SUDDENLY, came the crack of an automatic. Betty screamed as she saw the fingers of X's right hand stiffen out. The keys rattled to the floor. At the same moment, the entire building lurched to one side. There was a brilliant flash of blue flame, then instantaneous darkness. All lost their footing. There were screams from the women, oaths from the men. It was as though a giant unseen hand had the building in its clutches. X rolled down the steeply slanting floor, collided with Betty Dale. She uttered a sharp, pained cry.

"Hurt, Betty?" he whispered anxiously.

"No. But you are. You're hurt. That bullet—"

"Just grazed my arm. Made me drop the keys. We've got to find them some way. The killer is in this room."

Near at hand, Harvey Bates said: "Water rushing in somewhere. I can hear it. Feels like the whole place is settling."

"Who fired that shot?" roared Bates.

"I saw him do it!" shrilled Fay October. "It was—"

The sound of a clenched fist striking flesh. The sound of some one falling. Then, the soft voice of the killer: "This structure rests on rather flimsy piles. As long as there was the buoyancy of the water beneath the building, those piles were enough. But I flooded the lower floor to get rid of certain persons, and the weight of the water-logged lower structure seems to have been too much for the piles. Electrical connections also seem to have broken. The building will sink in the river.

"No one will be able to get out except myself. It is not exactly as I had planned your deaths—you who are my betrayers, my enemies, and you who have clumsily stumbled upon my trail. But you will all die, and none will know the truth. Don't move, anyone. I'm a very good shot."

"What does it mean?" Warden McCray asked in a husky whisper. "Is the killer in this room?"

Dean Winton sneezed violently.

"Most decidedly," said X in reply to the Warden's question.

Betty Dale clutched the Agent's arm. "The building is sinking. Water is spurting through the wall."

"Some of you may not realize it," the killer whispered, "but it's perfectly dark outside. Unless you have a light, nobody will find you until they drag the river. Very soon, I mean that you shall have a light."

Some one tugged X's sleeve. It was Bates. He whispered: "I've found the keys."

"Find the big key that feels like a Yale," X directed quietly. "Going around the ring from the left, the third key may open the door. The smallest key opens the shackles so that you can free the others. But don't make a move until I have attracted the killer's attention."

"What are you going to do?" whispered Betty.

"Wait." X stood up, took a step forward, sloshing through water that was running in between floor and wall.

"I said no moving," whispered the killer hoarsely.

"How did you expect to live in this room after you turned on the gas?" asked X. He took another step toward the whispering voice.

"A hole in the wall big enough for my mouth and nose," replied the man. "From my position against the wall, I could control the gas valves and also the cocks that let in the water. There was a microphone by means of which my voice seemed to come from the loudspeaker in the ceiling. At times, I may have seemed a whole gang of men, but I have played a lone hand, pitting my enemies against Lizio and even Agent X, while I alone destroyed my enemies. Though apparently I was shackled here, my hands were free at all times. My plan would have worked perfectly if—"

"If it had not been for a color," X interrupted. "That color is yellow. It was the yellow in you that made you kill off your own companions in the Jonalden crime. It was the yellow in you that made you attempt to kill the investigators that followed you, sometimes before they had any real evidence against you. Your powerful gas weapon gave you a synthetic courage, but even now, you are afraid to face me, man to man."

THE CRACK of a shot answered the Agent's challenge. The slug sang by his ear and imbedded itself in the wall.

"And the yellow feathers gave you away." X advanced another step. Across the rapidly sinking room, Bates was moving. But X held the killer's attention by moving continually forward and speaking in a calm, even voice.

"Did you hear that, Burks?" X went on. "Yellow feathers gave the killer away. Disguised as a woman, he boarded the Chicago plane in order to rub out Lolly Turney, whom he feared. He carried a canary bird with him, because canaries are particularly sensitive to poisonous gases in the air. The killer wanted to know just the moment that his poisonous gas began to escape. When the canary died, he knew it was time to clear out of the passenger compartment.

"But if canaries are sensitive to gas, the killer is also sensitive to canaries. I proved that a few minutes ago. I—"

Something flaming and white-hot streaked across the room, illuminating startled faces for a moment. It was a small, magnesium flare. No sooner did the flare strike the wall, than the wood burst into flame—a red, smoke-billowing flame. For the entire room seemed to have been soaked in oil.

"Now," screamed the killer, "they'll come for you. They'll take you out of here, blackened corpses!"

The wall of flame mounted, hissed across the floor to meet the water, climbed to the roof. On the other side of the flames, X saw the slinking killer, moving over the sloping floor toward the back of the building. X sent one glance over his shoulder. The steel door was open. Bates was herding the others through the opening. X hesitated only a moment. Then he pulled his sodden coat over his head and sprang through the wall of flame.

Beside the Agent, was another charging figure. The voice of Inspector Burks, already grown hoarse from the smoke, shouted: "Let's go, G-man!"

Through the flame, the boards sagged beneath their feet. The water had deepened. The entire building rocked with every step they took. Directly ahead of them was something that was as white as a tombstone in the lurid light. X could see that the floor ended sharply and water filled the rear of the building. The white thing was a boat, rocking at its mooring.

"He's getting in a speed boat!" shouted Burks. "I'd give half my life for a gun."

A MOTOR sprang into life, but X could see no one in the boat. As he sprang forward, his foot went completely through one of the rotten boards. He fell forward on his face. Pain shot through his leg. For a moment, he feared that it was broken. He gritted his teeth, regained his feet, just as Burks shot ahead of him and seized the rail of the boat.

A tall shadow reared itself above Burks. Burks tried to grapple with the shadowy figure, but something came down on his head. Burks sank to the edge of the floor, stunned, but did not relinquish his grip on the rail of the boat.

The speed boat got into motion. X saw Burks' body drag along the slopping floor and strike the water. All the strength in the Agent's lithe body went out in a leap that landed him on the rear deck of the boat. His left arm shot out. His fist struck the killer somewhere on the shoulder with the force of a projectile. The killer was knocked flat and the wheel of the boat spun in his fingers. But the throttle was wide open, and the boat, completely out of control, was tearing madly toward the rear wall of the shack.

As soon as he had landed in the boat, X dropped, seized Burks by the arms just as Burks' fingers peeled from the rail. With a backward lunge, X dragged Burks aboard. And at that moment, the prow of the boat struck the rear wall. There was a deafening crash. Planks splintered into hundreds of lethal lances. Timbers thundered down from the roof. A falling board struck X across the back of the neck, a stunning blow that flattened him.

He ground his teeth as though he clung to consciousness only with his jaws. Somewhere, among the red and yellow lights that flashed across his brain, he saw the dark and dangerous silhouette of an automatic. The muzzle of that gun was within inches of his temple. He felt for the moment as though he could not make another move. The blow seemed to have paralyzed him mentally and physically. Then he saw the gun again—more clearly, this time, because it was even closer.

He *had* to move. The fiend would murder both him and Burks if he didn't move. But a slow, laborious effort would only serve to warn the killer that he had not been completely knocked out. Everything depended on the element of surprise.

A confident, whispering chuckle from the killer. It seemed, almost, as though X could hear the *ping* of the trigger-spring as the killer's finger tightened. And then, X moved.

The law of self preservation, instinct, long practice, and perfect physical condition were instantly translated into smooth-flowing action that was swift as light and utterly surprising. His left hand came up to catch the killer's wrist in the fork between thumb and first finger. The gun went off in mid-air. The force of the Agent's blow brought the killer's arm down against the gunwale of the boat. Beneath gripping fingers, X felt the murderer's wrist bones crunch as they met the wood.

Desperately, the killer threw himself upon X. He clawed at the Agent's throat. But though he was under the man, X's right fist came up like a piston to crash to the point of the killer's chin. And the man went suddenly limp.

Somewhere, a hoarse-voiced whistle sounded. Out of the corner of his eye, X saw the hull of a river boat that was bearing down upon them out of the night. "Burks!" he shouted. "Look out. We'll be rammed!"

But Burks was already acquainted with the danger. He reached out a big hand, seized a wheel spoke, pulled down with all his strength. The speed boat veered instantly, shot by the river boat only inches from her hull. Then as Burks reached out and cut the throttle, they rocked gently in the wake.

"Nice work," grunted Burks. "Mighty nice work." He crawled to join X beside the killer. "Got a flashlight in my pocket if the water hasn't ruined it. We'll get a look at him."

X WENT back to the wheel, turned the boat back toward the shore, and advanced the throttle. A fireboat had pulled in toward the burning building. Its heavy jets of water arched up against the ruddy sky. Against the glare of searchlights, he saw firemen wrapping blankets around two women rescued from the building—one woman who would go to jail, and the other who was Betty Dale. Near Fay October, X could see Harvey Bates' square-shouldered form as he looked anxiously out toward the speed boat.

"Ho-lee smoke!" gasped Burks. "This—this guy isn't Dr. Mills."

"I didn't expect him to be," X said. "Mills was hiding from the killer because Mills and his daughter had evidence that put them in a dangerous position. Surely the killer's attempt on Dora Winton proved that. Dr. Mills and Dora somehow traced the Hempstead diamonds, which the killer picked up on the plane. You see Dora was following Winton, trying to get something on him so she could shake him down for more alimony. I think that's why they visited Sing Sing, trying get some information out of Lizio about Winton."

Burks looked down at the white face of Dean Winton, an ugly, hateful moon in the light of the inspector's flashlight. "You mean they actually ran across the Hempstead diamonds and didn't come to the police with the information?"

"That's it. Dr. Mills needed more money for research. They may not have connected Winton directly with the killings, but when they used the matter of the fenced diamonds to throw a scare into Winton, they might just as well have signed their own death warrants."

Burks nodded. "I'm clear on that now. And I see how Winton wanted to get Lizio out of the big house so that Lizio would be blamed for all the crimes. Come to think of it, who had a better chance to instruct Lizio on how to get out? Winton was Lizio's lawyer, and saw him nearly every day. And of course Winton got the formula of the gas from Dr. Mills. But what was that you said about feathers?"

X laughed. "Oh, that's a joke—but not to Winton. He's sensitive to bird feathers. A lot of people who have hay fever or asthma are. Bird feathers brought on acute attacks of hay fever whenever Winton got near to them. Naturally, he would avoid feathers. But he had to have a canary with him when he went on the plane with the idea of gassing all aboard in order to eliminate Lolly Turney and Agent Hughes. The canary, being sensitive to poisonous gas warned him when the gas began to escape. When I met Winton a little after the affair on the plane, he had an acute attack of hay fever. This attack was not repeated until the night he tried to kill his wife.

"Apparently, Winton had not entered Dr. Mills' house on that night, but nevertheless he was sneezing when I met him. Mrs. Winton had a lot of canary birds. She told me that she liked them around because they kept her ex-husband away. At the time, I did not know exactly why they kept him away. I really collected those feathers with the idea of comparing them with feathers found at another place where I was sure 'the woman in black' had been. You see, I was suspicious of Mills, too, at that time."

"I see," said Burks. "Tonight, it occurred to you that if you could prove Winton sensitive to feathers, you would really have something on him. Well, he started to sneeze almost as soon as you loosed the feathers."

X nodded. He was steering the boat up to one of the nearby piers. Burks sighed. "Well, I guess I have to give the Feds the credit for this case. Nice work."

"Keep the credit," X suggested.

"Nope. I believe in giving credit where due. I see Betty Dale out on the pier waiting for us. The kid ought to be in bed, but she'll never go until she gets her story. What's your name? We want to get it right in the papers."

X tossed a rope onto the pier. A man seized it, made it fast. X turned to Burks, smiled strangely. "All right. Here's my card. And be sure the name's spelled right." He handed Burks a piece of cardboard that was considerably sodden by the water. The Agent sprang to the pier.

Burks got to the pier more slowly. He was staring at the card in his hand beneath the light of his flashlight. It seemed blank on both sides, at first, but slowly, as though by magic, a black letter "X" appeared on the surface.

Burks vehemently told the world that he would be damned. He looked out across the pier. But there was no sign of Agent X. He was lost in the crowd. Perhaps, by now, he wore another one of his thousand faces and spoke with another one of his thousand voices.

BOOK XXVIII

HORROR'S HANDCLASP

The gods of evil sent forth a sardonic, murdering genius
of crime, whose unholy face struck terror to the hearts
of all who beheld it. And such was the powerful wile of
this fiend called the Fury, that even Secret Agent X had
at last met a checkmate opponent—a tantalizing sadist
who made famous men and gorgeous women his pawns
to play Satan's grotesque game of hopscotch upon a
gigantic chess board that dealt either death or madness.

CHAPTER I

KILLER'S CARESS

THERE WAS NOTHING about the house to suggest that it was inhabited, even by spirits. Beyond an iron gate that sagged back against the stone wall was a garden of neglect. A close observer, however, would have noticed that weeds that grew between the flags of the walk had been trampled lately.

The house itself had boarded windows. Its porch posts had a drunken lean. The architectural glory of its slate-shingled hip roof was overshadowed by the tall apartment houses that flanked it. Here was a lair for rats and spiders, a wide-eaved shelter for pigeons and sparrows. Surely nothing more.

Yet the old Marrow house was attracting the attention of two top-hatted gentlemen in the doorway of the apartment across the street.

"A clever, precautionary move of Madame Susu, you understand," said one of the men. A wave of his walking stick indicated the old house. "Not long ago the American Society of Magicians made the discovery that suicide, murder, financial ruin were often traceable to these so-called spirit mediums. The activity of the society, has pretty well weeded out the spirit fakers from New York."

"Surely, Moss," said the other, a lean-waisted, young man with an eager, intelligent face and inquiring gray eyes, "you a scientist, have no faith in this Oriental mystic and her abracadabra."

There was an amused gleam in the dark eyes of Alan Moss, one of the city's most promising young scientists. He shrugged. Energetic brows arched above round, rimless glasses. "No faith perhaps, Dale Emboyd, but novelties such as Madame Susu help prevent boredom. Tonight you will probably see stranger things than you have dreamed of in your philosophy."

A taxi stopped in front of the apartment. A gentleman whose

temples were gray, whose shoulders had a scholarly stoop, got out and assisted a woman to alight. Alan Moss and Dale Emboyd looked at the woman and forgot instantly that her escort was the world renowned Dr. Cornelius Arden. The woman was dazzlingly beautiful.

"Dangerously beautiful," Alan Moss expressed it in a whisper to his younger companion.

Dale Emboyd nodded. The woman was slightly above average height. Her black hair had the same silken sheen as the simple, black gown she wore. A short cape of dark fur was the perfect setting for her cameo-like features. Eyes of brilliant green had a ruthless glint in them that told Dale Emboyd why Moss had said: "Dangerously beautiful."

Moss took his companion's arm. They stepped to the sidewalk.

*Agent X's strength was fast ebbing
as he fought a losing battle to
stay that hand from the switch.*

Dr. Cornelius Arden pivoted, his lips parted in what was an almost terrified gasp. When his worried glance alighted on Moss's face, he smiled thinly. Then he looked quickly at Emboyd and frowned.

"Good evening, Dr. Arden," Alan Moss greeted. "Is it possible that your destination is the same as ours?" His glance indicated the apparently deserted Marrow house.

Dr. Arden admitted it with a timid jerk of his head. He awkwardly managed an introduction between Moss and the woman, a Mrs. Trumaine. Moss presented Dale Emboyd to the doctor and his dazzling companion. Emboyd bowed gracefully over the woman's hand. His keen gray eyes meeting her ruthless green ones was like the crossing of swords. Though he had not met her before, Dale Emboyd knew something about Vina Trumaine. He had made it his business to know. Vina Trumaine was a widow, over from Europe. By what right she held a position of social prominence, Dale Emboyd had been unable to discover. The right perhaps of a beautiful woman whose poise was perfection.

"I have begged Dr. Arden to bring me here," Vina Trumaine told them in a musical voice. "He, of course, does not believe in anything he cannot produce in a test tube."

She left Alan Moss and Dale Emboyd to divide the glory of her slow, alluring smile between them. Taking the doctor's arm, she proceeded toward the old house. Moss and Emboyd followed a little behind.

"By George!" Moss exclaimed in a whisper, "she is magnificent! And old Arden doesn't seem to be appreciating her."

It wasn't lack of appreciation for beauty that was affecting Dr. Arden, Dale Emboyd was certain. A more powerful emotion than that aroused by the presence of Vina Trumaine possessed him. Dr. Arden was afraid. Of what? Surely not of the conjuring of the mysterious Madame Susu.

AT THE GATE of the Marrow house, the quartet paused a moment, looked up and down the street. Undoubtedly, half the charm of Madame Susu's spiritualistic séances was due to the pledge of secrecy imposed upon all who attended them. They crossed the dismal garden, went around to a side door, and were eventually admitted by a plump Japanese with a face like a yellow moon, whose smile vanished as soon as Dale Emboyd appeared. Behind a short, yellow hand, he whispered to Alan Moss.

Again the amused twinkle behind the young scientist's glasses. "I assure you that Mr. Emboyd is a man of utmost discretion," he told the Japanese. "He is a fellow club member and I have known him for a long time."

Three days, Dale Emboyd thought to himself, scarcely constituted a long time. Yet Alan Moss's exaggeration seemed to assure the Japanese. Alan Moss scrawled his left-handed signature on the visitors' register. A moment later Emboyd put his name on the register. His name—rather one of his many aliases. For the man who signed as Dale Emboyd was nameless. His fine, almost delicate features were but a mask for a face that none had seen and lived—a mask cleverly modeled from a plastic volatile material of his own compounding and artfully tinted with flesh-colored pigments. For he was the man known the world over as Secret Agent X.

It was remarkable, thought the Agent, how sheer charlatanism could exert power over even the most brilliant minds. In the reception hall of the old house, where shaded lamps burned dimly behind boarded windows, he met Wilbur Kopsak, one of the most enterprising business promoters in the city. Tall, with a jaw that jutted furiously, with eyes that glowered beneath short black brows, Kopsak was a compelling, powerful figure. At the present time, X knew, he was engaged in organizing a cosmetic manufacturing concern.

Then there was Donald J. Lowery, a mild-eyed, kindly man of perhaps forty years of age—a very nervous man, judging by the way his trembling match-flame threatened his wisp of yellow mustache as he lighted a cigarette. Beside Lowery, stood a tiny, Titian-haired woman with soulful eyes and a warm, husky voice. Her pretty face was less famous than her voice, for she was Dot Dejong, torrid blues singer of Mr. Lowery's far-reaching radio network.

But it was a man of small importance in the business and social world who attracted most of the Agent's attention. That man was Paul Vost—thin-faced, pale-eyed, bronze-skinned Paul Vost. It was largely because of Vost that X was there. Vost, a debonair man-about-town whose reputation would not undergo too thorough an investigation, had visited Madame Susu's secret establishment for five consecutive nights. And just what amusement a man of Vost's caliber found in communicating with "departed spirits" X could not imagine.

In one disguise or another, X had been following Vost for a week. He had discovered that dangling from Vost's watch chain was an odd ornament of gold representing the head of a hideous woman. He had discovered that Vost was secretly meeting the sunny-haired, unsophisticated niece of Police Commissioner Foster. Yet it was not the attention of Paul Vost to unspoiled Doris Foster that had claimed X's interest.

FROM out of the underworld had come the whispered rumor that Europe had given America a criminal genius. A being whose identity was as secret as the Agent's own, whose cleverness, ruthless daring, and unprecedented cruelty had resulted in the loss of colossal sums of money in European capitals. That criminal genius was known simply as the Fury.

Through dark, crooked channels this information had come to the ears of Agent X. Immediately, he was on guard, watching for the Fury's first move. He did not know whether the hidden opponent he was about to face was a man or a woman. He knew only that as long as he lived he would exert every effort to block the schemes of this enterprising criminal. X was not suspicious of Vost

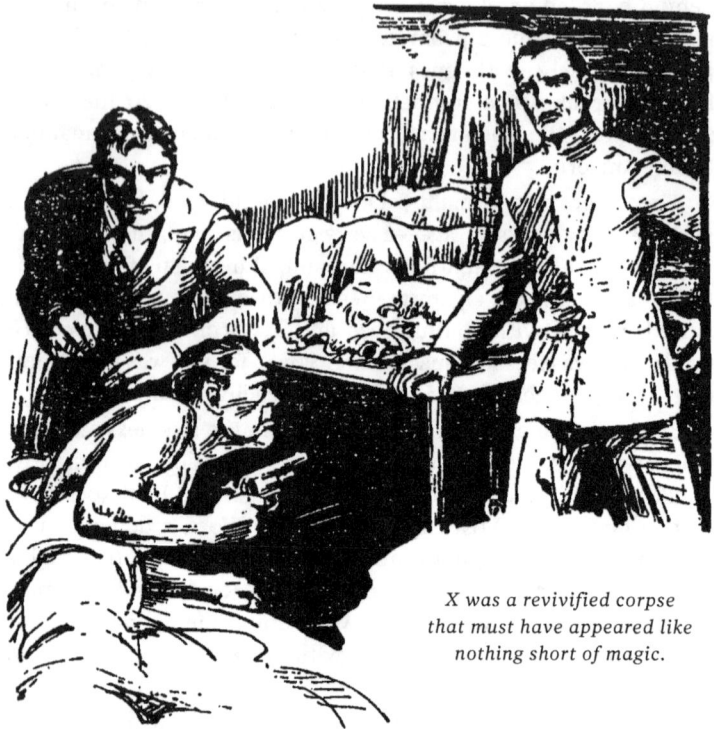

X was a revivified corpse that must have appeared like nothing short of magic.

simply because of the latter's unsavory reputation, but because the hideous gold head on Vost's watch chain was patterned after an artist's conception of the Fury of ancient Grecian myths.

No sooner had the Agent signed his name to the register, paid his twenty dollar fee which was exacted by the famous Madame Susu, than a silvery-toned gong sounded. A hush fell upon those in the hall. X glanced at the faces about him. The great Lowery twitched his thin mustache. His companion, the tiny Dot Dejong, made a grimace with her small mouth while a shudder rippled visibly across her bare shoulders.

Paul Vost's thin face was a study in sneering sophistry. Wilbur Kopsak's scowl might have been intended to frighten the spirits away. Dr. Arden looked dazed. Alan Moss's eyes sparkled with amusement. Doris Foster turned pale, smiled faintly when Vost squeezed her arm. Vina Trumaine alone was unchanged, neither thrilled nor frightened by the promise of finding herself in the presence of Madame Susu.

At the end of the hall, sliding doors were parted by hands unseen. Guests of Madame Susu entered the séance chamber. There was an eerie, foreboding atmosphere about the room that could not quite be described. Heavy oak timbers and panels formed walls and ceiling and absorbed most of the light from guttering candles in copper sconces. On silver tripods, brasiers of cloying incense smoldered. A curtain of exquisite Japanese embroidery work cut off the north end of the room. There were no windows, no visible doors save the ones through which they had just passed.

Agent X hung back, while others took places around a huge refectory table. He watched Paul Vost pull out a chair for Doris Foster at one end of the table, then sit down beside her. X took a position directly across from Donald Lowery, deliberately turned his back on Vost, and was apparently anxious only for the drawing of the Japanese curtain. Actually, his right hand palmed a small mirror by means of which he could watch Vost intently.

"If at any time any of you feel the slightest desire to move to another chair, it is because an unwelcome spirit is beside you." It was the moonfaced Japanese servant who spoke. "Do not hesitate to take another chair at any time during the séance."

Those about the table squirmed uncomfortably. There were hushed whispers. Dot Dejong forced a laugh, whispered to Lowery:

"I'm getting scared!"

Lowery patted the blues singer's hand kindly.

Wilbur Kopsak grumbled something beneath his breath.

The sliding doors closed softly behind the retiring Japanese. A lock click. Slowly, the embroidered curtain furled back. A chill wind seeming to originate in the gloomy end of the room revealed by the curtain, snatched out the candle flames along the wall. Then pale flickering light was born in a glass globe that centered the table. Its ever-changing colored beams passed from one strange face to another. But beyond the table all was darkness.

At the end of the room from which the chill draft had come, a concealed, yellow-lensed spotlight projected its rays upon a simple gilt stool and upon the glamorous figure that had suddenly appeared on it. Here was Madame Susu in a clinging gown of metallic sequins. She sat stiffly erect, her hands folded upon her breast, and her head bent low. A golden headpiece, like those worn by geisha girls of old Japan, concealed her dark hair.

Her cheeks were a satiny yellow, her eyes narrow and dark. Yet, except for her yellow skin and the exaggerated slant of her eyebrows, there was nothing about her that suggested the Oriental.

Here, no doubt, was a woman clever enough to fool men like Lowery and Alan Moss—a woman skilled in showmanship.

Madame Susu raised her head, staring with a faraway look in her eyes. "You have come," she began in a clear, sweet voice, "to exert an effort to commune with the dear departed. In a very few moments my mind shall wander back into the past. I shall evoke the shades, beg them to look with favor upon us. You may see fearful things. You may hear alarming things. Do not hesitate to ask any questions of any presence that may appear."

Madame Susu's head lowered again. For a moment, she seemed to be asleep. Then the muscles of her arms twitched as though she was in great pain.

"I feel the presence of a troubled spirit within this room," came the madame's whispering voice.

Agent X heard the men and women about him catch quick breaths. But without seeming to, X was watching Paul Vost closely. One of Vost's lean arms was draped across the back of Doris Foster's chair. With his other hand, he groped behind him, his fingers stretching to reach one of the incense brasiers.

"Come in, come in," moaned Madame Susu. "Come in, troubled one."

Vost's fingers touched the incense brasier. There was a faint click as his fingernails met the metal. Then cautiously he drew out a tiny square envelope from the metal bowl. His hands joined in his lap. There was the sound of paper tearing. A troubled frown clouded his brow. His right hand came up and thrust a crumpled ball of paper into his coat pocket.

X glanced at the strained, anxious faces about the table. Even Vina Trumaine's calm had deserted her. Her black-gloved fingers clasped and un-clasped. X pushed back his chair quietly and got to his feet.

NEAR where Madame Susu sat, the floor gave up an ethereal cloud of white vapor that swirled upward toward the ceiling. All watched it closely as it seemed to mature into something almost human in form. X moved quietly toward the foot of the table where Paul Vost sat. Within the room was a weird clamor of small voices.

Lowery groaned.

"Amazing!" whispered Alan Moss.

Agent X was directly behind Paul Vost's chair.

Suddenly, above the clamor of voices, one voice stood out distinctly: "Beware," it wailed. "Beware the Fury. The shadow of his hand lies upon you all. There are none here who shall not know his wrath."

A short, breathless curse from Paul Vost. He leaned forward, stared intently at the glittering figure of Madame Susu, and the ghostly thing of mist that stood beside her. Then the ghost-thing was gone. In its stead was blackness—a blackness that a second later gave up an arm. The arm seemed scarcely human. It was yellow, hairless and emaciated. Great, swollen veins stood out upon it and the hand was a talonlike thing. The arm moved inevitably forward, an arm without an apparent body. It extended above the heads of the terrified men and women around the table. It moved on and on, stopping above each head, as if counting those present.

But another hand beside that of the spirit presence was at work—the slender, graceful hand of Agent X. His fingers glided into Vost's pocket and scissored over the crumpled bit of paper.

At the moment that X withdrew the paper from Vost's pocket, Dot Dejong screamed. The yellow, unclean hand was above her head. Her wide, frightened eyes stared at it, fascinated as though by a hideous serpent. Slowly, the yellow arm was lowered. The thin, ugly fingers closed upon the firm, white flesh of the little songstress's shoulder.

It was hardly more than a caress, but it brought a scream of agony from Dot Dejong. Her scream was echoed by a sharp cry of terror from Madame Susu. All were on their feet now—all but Dot Dejong. With an agonized sob, the girl threw herself across the table. Her body writhed, muscles twitched, then suddenly were still and stony.

"Look!" shrieked Vina Trumaine. "The hand!"

But the yellow, emaciated hand had been swallowed in the darkness from whence it had come.

Doors of the séance chamber were thrown open. Brilliant light from the outer hall flooded the room. Three of Madame Susu's Japanese servants stood in the door. Each held a blue-steel automatic.

"No one move," came the order from the moon-faced Japanese. "Our register has revealed the name of Secret Agent X, he who is wanted by the police."

The eyes of the Japanese fell upon the figure of Dot Dejong, and seemed to point out to the others what they had failed to see before. On Dot Dejong's left shoulder was an ugly wound. It was like a brand except that it was in the form of a hand—a perfect impression of the emaciated hand that had come clutching out of the darkness.

Agent X was both horrified and amazed. Here, under his very eyes murder had been executed in its most horrible form. For there was no denying that Dot Dejong was dead. And on top of that, some one had found the Agent's name signed in the register. How was it possible? X had been most careful to sign the fictitious name of Dale Emboyd. Had some one, then, penetrated his disguise? His fingers went to his face, exploring the features he had so carefully modeled. His makeup was intact.

Everyone in the room was excited and horrified. The announcement that Agent X was in the house had provoked genuine fear, for the Agent's methods of crime investigation frequently led him outside the boundary of the law. And many, including the police, suspected him of criminal motives.... A beautiful woman had been murdered. Doubtless, in the minds of all present, the name of Secret Agent X was linked with the tragedy.

DONALD LOWERY slumped in his chair beside the body of Dot Dejong. There was grief on his kindly face, but his lips muttered mechanically: "I am ruined. I am ruined."

X thrust his hands into his pockets, feeling the store of weapons of defense that constant danger obliged him to carry.[12] His fingers encountered the crumpled ball of paper he had taken from Paul Vost. Cautiously, while all eyes were on the armed servants in the doorway, X unrolled the paper and looked at it. A small snapshot was pasted to the paper—the head and shoulders of a man. Beneath was written:

> "Meet this man at the corner of 59th and Amsterdam, and bring to the Fury's office."

Instantly, X recognized the man in the photo. It was Mark Brady, who stood high on the list of the nation's public enemies. There was no longer any doubt in the Agent's mind that Paul Vost was in the service of the Fury. He had come here tonight for the pur-

---

12   AUTHOR'S NOTE: Agent X has a hatred for lethal weapons, yet he is amply provided with equipment for any emergency. His gas pistol, containing a harmless, anesthetizing vapor is always with him. Bombs containing the same vapor are also part of his equipment, as well as tear gas and powerful narcotics. He also carries a compact makeup kit with which he performs his miracles of disguise: a small handy tool kit, master keys, and pocket amplifying device are also included. Such equipment coupled with supple muscles and an alert mind make him the criminals' most formidable foe.

pose of getting instructions from some one higher up in a powerful criminal organization. But what of Madame Susu? X glanced around the room to find that the medium had vanished.

At that moment, one of the Japanese servants gave place to a large, powerfully built man with a ruddy face. The Agent's pulse jumped. That man was Inspector John Burks of the homicide office, relentless hunter of Secret Agent X. Behind Burks were others associated with the police department. They filled the only visible exit from the room, and X knew that Burks would waste no time examining all present, searching for evidence of makeup on their faces. How could Madame Susu be associated with the Fury and still call in the police?

Suddenly, X hit upon a clever plan that combined not only a chance to escape but also a chance to get within striking distance of the Fury. If he could manage an impersonation of Public Enemy Mark Brady, a man evidently essential to the Fury's plans, he would probably be protected from the police by the criminals themselves. But such an impersonation required several minutes alone.

Only the disappearance of Madame Susu gave him hope. Somewhere in the room, was a secret door, one that had facilitated the appearance of the madame's "spirits." Could he find it before the keen eyes of Inspector Burks penetrated his disguise?

Burks strode into the room, stopped within a few feet of the body of Dot Dejong. For a moment he stared, speechless with horror at the scarlet brand against the white flesh. Then he extended his large, capable hand and pressed a finger to the girl's wrist. He turned quickly, squinting at the Japanese.

"This is murder," he said through clenched teeth, "and the most damnable thing I've ever seen. I thought you said Secret Agent X was here? Why didn't you say something about murder? And what kind of a place is this, anyway?"

The Japanese bowed low. "This is the meeting chamber of those who devote time and mental effort to communication with the spirits of the departed. Madame Susu rents this house. These are her guests. When I called you, I had no idea that there had been murder. Only I knew that Secret Agent X was among those present, for I have seen his name upon the register."

BURKS grunted. "It all sounds phony. But by the Lord Harry, the killer that would kill like that—" The Inspector's eyes roved challengingly about the chamber. "Anyone left this room?"

"No," declared Wilbur Kopsak.

"Madame Susu has disappeared," ventured Vina Trumaine.

"She has, has she?" Burks shot a glance at Vina Trumaine. "Well, more of that later. The first thing to do is to find Agent X. I don't say he'd pull off a brutal killing like this, but if he's here he'll know something about this." And there Burks was mistaken. The Agent was quite as baffled as the inspector.

"Maybe," Alan Moss suggested, "Madame Susu is your Mr. X."

Burks snorted. "He's nothing, if not a man. That guy simply isn't a female impersonator."

Burks stepped over to Donald Lowery. "Mr. Lowery, I believe. I've seen your picture in the radio magazines. You've no objections to some rather rigorous examination of your face?"

"No," replied the radio magnate flatly. "But you're wasting your time."

While Burks was devoting his attention to Lowery, looking closely at his face, pinching his skin gently in an effort to prove that it was flesh and blood instead of makeup, Agent X was busily at work. He occupied the end of the room near the chair where Madame Susu had sat. His keen eyes had detected fine, hairlike wires leading from the bottom of the gilt stool to the floor. Closer investigation revealed a number of electrical buttons bulging the carpet near the foot of the stool.

The Agent watched his opportunity. As Burks moved on to examine Kopsak, X thrust out his foot and stepped upon the first bulge in the carpet. Almost at once, thin, tinkling music filled the air and sent Burks' suspicious glance darting about the room.

"What's that?" demanded the inspector. "Who did that?"

No one answered. Doris Foster crept closer to Paul Vost and looked frightened.

"The spirits!" whispered Dr. Arden.

Burks wheeled on the doctor. "Yeah?"

Agent X stepped on the button concealed by the carpet and checked the "spirit music." No use experimenting in this trial-and-error fashion. His next attempt might produce something that definitely would attract attention to himself. He stepped over to the oak-paneled wall behind the medium's stool. A little to the right, he remembered, the "ghost" that had prophesied the coming of the Fury had appeared. The Agent's sensitive fingers hurried along the smooth-grained wood and suddenly encountered something that pricked like a pin.

"You!" Burks' harsh voice. "What are you up to?"

X turned to see the inspector's eyes hard upon him. The Agent shook his head. "Not a thing," he replied timidly. "Just looking around."

Burks grunted, continued with his examination of Wilbur Kopsak. Fortunately, Kopsak's humor was not the most amiable. He was giving the inspector considerable trouble and attracting the attention of all within the room. X's fingers strayed back to the tiny pin point that jutted from the wall. He was certain that it was a marker of some sort so that a hidden button could be found in the dark. His fingers pressed the wall surface adjacent to the pin, encountered what appeared to be a knot in the wood. Instantly, a narrow section of the panel swung outwards. Without a moment's hesitation, X slipped through the opening.

CHAPTER II

HOUSE OF THE DEAD

A BOARD BENEATH the Agent's feet snapped. Instantly, the sliding panel behind him closed. He found himself in total darkness. He slipped his fountain pen flashlight from his pocket and sent its needle of light searching the room. It was small and unfurnished. A wire framework covered with luminous painted cloth and manipulated by wires appeared to be one of the madame's "spirits." Beyond it was a door.

X crossed to the door, opened it and looked out into a narrow hall. He closed the door. The secret room, where he now was, offered the best possible place for a change of makeup.

In the next few minutes, the Agent's fingers flew. His pocket makeup kit spread in front of him with its folding mirror to guide him, he removed a portion of the plastic substance that constituted the base of his disguise as Dale Emboyd.

The impersonation he was about to attempt was an exceedingly difficult one. While the features of Mark Brady were not difficult to imitate, the Agent had only the tiny snapshot to use as a model. X had seen the real Brady only once in his life and that several years before he had become notorious as a public enemy.

With plastic material, he built up Brady's thick, heavy features over his own, added special pigments to simulate the public enemy's complexion as closely as he could remember it. Having never heard Brady's voice his art as a ventriloquist and imitator would be of little use to him. He only hoped that those he would be called upon to fool knew Brady no better than he did.

As he was putting the finishing touches to his makeup, some sixth sense told him of unseen eyes watching. He turned quickly and strode to the door. He pulled the door open with one hand and at the same time drew his gas pistol.

The hall without was empty but there lingered in the air a faint, exotic perfume. X hurried back to his makeup kit, gave himself a critical once-over in the mirror, snapped the kit shut, and returned it to his pocket. It was not without a moment's thought that he stepped into the hall. Police had orders to shoot Mark Brady on sight, and there were police only a few feet away in the séance room. But there were others—servants of the Fury. Agent X was willing to trust his life to the Fury in an effort to hunt down the criminal.

X tiptoed along the hall, one hand in his pocket on his gas gun, ready for instant use. Even if he should fall in with the Fury's men, as he hoped to do, there was the danger that some of them had looked through the keyhole and seen him changing his disguise.

At the end of the hall, he turned to the left. Some one moved directly in front of him. The Agent whipped out his flashlight and turned it on. At the same time, a flashlight beam from the man in front of him struck X in the eyes. For a moment he was blinded. Then he saw that the man he faced was short and thick-set. He noticed, too, that a golden ornament, like a head of a hideous woman flashed on the watch chain across the man's chest.

"Brady!" came a husky exclamation from the stocky man. "What are you doin' here?"

"Turn out that light!" X said harshly in what he hoped was Brady's voice. "Turn it out before I plug you."

THE SHORT man turned out his flashlight. "What are you doin' here?" he repeated.

"A guy by the name of Vost said there was a job for me here," X replied. "But why all the cops? If this is a trap, I'll break that Vost guy's neck."

"No—no," said the short man hastily. "I got no love for meetin' cops myself. You come with me. I'll show you a way out."

"Okeh," X grunted. "But I'm right behind you. First time I even so much as smell a cop, I'll let you have it."

The short man uttered a hushed, unpleasant laugh, turned, and opened a door. Beyond were steps leading downward. "In the basement," he explained, "there's a passage leading out to the barn. The guy who built this place didn't like to get his feet wet. And it's a damn' nice way to fox the cops."

In the basement, they crossed the furnace room and entered what might have once been a wine cellar. A small door at the end opened on a passage. The entire building, X saw, was admirably constructed for Madame Susu's purposes, with this passage that could be used for a quick getaway in case of a police raid.

The passage ended in a garage. There, two men and a large sedan waited. The short man gestured toward X. "Look what I bagged. Will the chief be tickled, huh?"

"Brady!" gasped one of the men and instantly drew an automatic.

"What's the idea?" demanded X, eyeing the trio suspiciously.

"The idea is," said the man with the gun, "that we want no slip-ups. We want to be friends, but there's an order out to deliver you to the chief's office. We take no chances of gettin' in bad with the chief. You get in that car and act nice, and we'll treat you right."

X shrugged, opened the door of the sedan. Foot on the running board, he paused. In one corner of the back seat was a human fig-ure—or was it human? A loose, black garment covered it from head to foot and hung like a sack from its bony frame.

The short man behind X chuckled. "Get in. *That* can't hurt you. Not now, anyway."

X got into the car. The short man shoved in behind him. The black-shrouded figure remained stiff and motionless. Its cold clam-miness penetrated the Agent's clothing and sent a chill coursing along his spine. The thing in black was a corpse, apparently. The corpse of a man seemingly wasted away by a long siege of fever. X tried to steal a glance beneath the voluminous black hood that covered the head of the thing, but the shadows of the shroud were too deep.

The short man beside X pulled heavy shutters across the win-dows of the car. A blind prevented X from seeing the two men who entered the compartment in front of him.

X uttered a short, strained laugh. "This reminds me of the time Mike Gagan's boys took me for a one-way ride. Only something went wrong. I drove Mike's car back alone."

"Sure," said the short man. "You're great stuff. That's why the chief wants to take you in. But you won't be the head man. Get that into your head. When *he* says you lay off the booze, you'd better lay off the booze."

X grunted. "Who is this big shot?"

"Ask somebody who knows, and you'll get the same answer you get from me—who don't know."

THE CAR bounced out of the garage and took a direction unknown. They drove on in silence for nearly an hour before the car came once again to a stop. The door opened and X found himself in another garage the doors of which had been closed behind the car so that it was impossible for him to know his location. The short man took his arm, marched him up three steps and through a door. X found himself in a room, the walls and ceiling of which were painted white. In the center of the room was a canvas-topped table on which were rubber gloves, instruments and syringes. A glass-fronted cabinet near the table was filled with bottles of hair-cleaning fluid and skin bleach. Agent X knew that he was in an undertaker's establishment.

The short man nudged X with his gun. "Go on into the next room. You aren't ready for this room yet."

The room adjoining the embalming room was a small office. There at a desk a man leaned back in a swivel chair while the heels of his shoes scratched the desk top. A black derby was cocked over his face.

"Mitch," called the short man, "come to, can'tcha. Here's the guy we've been looking for."

The man pushed back his derby, revealing small, black eyes and a hooked nose. Surely this was not the Fury. This man was Mitch Beckridge, a small-time crook and tough from the lower East Side. Beckridge, the Agent knew, had a reputation for brains but was rather short on courage.

Beckridge looked X up and down carefully. Then he held out his hand. "Never expected to shake the hand of a number one public enemy," he said nasally. "How yah goin'?"

X thrust out the heavy jaw that was so essential to the part he was playing. "Get this: I gotta know what this is all about. What's the idea of dragging me into a dead joint like this? I got a right to know, see? I'm goin' to know if I have to hammer down the ears of every man in this dump."

"You're tough," Beckridge said coldly. "But *you* get this: you're about the size of a pimple on an ant compared with the guy we're workin' for. Now here's our proposition. You kick in with us and it's your chance to get in on the ground floor of the biggest racket anybody's brains ever worked out. It's a safe racket, 'cause we don't do the work ourselves. The big chief thinks up the stunts. All we got to do is direct the lads who do the dirty work, and keep our traps shut."

"Who's this big brain?" demanded X. He helped himself from a package of cigarettes on the desk.

Beckridge squinted his tiny eyes. "You ever hear of the Fury?"

X nodded. "Who hasn't? What's the racket he's in?"

"That," chimed the short man, "is his business. We don't ask questions."

"One thing," declared Beckridge, "you're supposed to direct a hoist job at the Bastion estate. You know Rex Bastion? He's lousy with money."

X KNEW Rex Bastion, had met him frequently at his club.[13] He knew that Bastion's wealth was largely a myth, knew that his club dues were in arrears. Rex Bastion was an inventor and impractical dreamer. Surely Bastion was too small game for the famous Fury. What was the criminal up to? It worried X to be groping in the dark.

What had the archfiend expected to gain by the killing of defenseless Dot Dejong? What did he expect to gain by robbing a man who was all but a pauper? He could not even hazard a guess. Some crime of tremendous scope was forming in the brain of the Fury. So large a crime, in fact, that he concealed his plans even from his henchmen.

"What do I have to hoist?" X asked aloud of Beckridge.

The man in the derby shrugged. "I got no idea. The point is, tomorrow night you've got to pull off the job. Money maybe. Maybe jewels."

"How much in it for me?" asked X. Beckridge looked at the short man. The short man said: "You don't get it. We work for the Fury because he's goin' after something big. This stuff is just small fry, but it's the foundation for a big take. He'll treat us fair enough when the big take comes!"

X shook his head. "Not me. I sign no blank checks. You guys—"

The door of the office burst open. The two men who had driven X over from Madame Susu's place brought in the madame herself.

The spirit medium had changed to a simple suit of dark blue. She was none the less a striking, regal figure. Her dark, narrow eyes smoldered with suppressed anger and she stood stiffly erect as though she loathed the touch of her two male escorts.

The medium raised her right arm, pointed directly at the Agent.

---

13   AUTHOR'S NOTE: X has frequent contact with the clubmen of the city through one of his most famous aliases—that of Elisha Pond, wealthy philanthropist.

Her soft, musical voice whispered from vivid red lips: "That man will destroy you all. Madame Susu has said it. None shall escape him, for he is Secret Agent X."

Whether it was sheer guess, mystic prophecy, or because she had watched X through the keyhole when he was in the act of changing his makeup, X did not know. He knew only that he would have to act and act quickly. He lunged straight at the two men in the doorway. His right fist cracked to the jaw of one. His gas pistol came out and spurted its anesthetizing charge straight into the face of the other. A thrust of his elbow sent the man lurching to one side to heap beside the door.

X sprang through the opening, slammed the door. Bullets from Beckridge's gun jagged splinters from the door inches from the Agent's hand. X sprang across the embalming room, opened the door that led into the garage, and slammed it without going out. Escape would have been an easy matter for him, but he had his teeth deep in the crime and he was loath to let go.

Instead of leaving the mortuary, he pushed through a door in the side of the embalming room and closed it quietly behind him just as Beckridge and the short man crashed into the embalming room.

The Agent found himself in a small room where heavy drapes of purple velvet hung over long windows. The room was indirectly lighted and here two plain coffins lay in the middle of the floor. X was on the point of investigating further when he heard soft footfalls outside the door of the small room. Instantly, he ducked behind one of the purple curtains and held his breath lest the waving of the drapes betray his hiding place.

Two men entered the room. X was unable to see them, but he could hear their voices clearly.

"These coffins," explained one of the men, "have to be taken to the Fury before morning. Is the hearse ready?"

THE OTHER replied that the hearse would require gas and oil before the trip.

"Okeh," the other said. "We'll get to that right away. We'll all have to clear out of here tonight. Something tells me this joint is goin' to be hot."

The two men left the room and X slipped from his hiding place. The two coffins were to be taken to the Fury. Very well, X was determined to go with them. He crossed to one of the coffins and threw back the lid. Involuntarily, a gasp of horror escaped him. The corpse within was that of a man, briefly clad. Every rib was clearly defined beneath the yellow, parchment skin. The arms were like slivers of bone covered with tissues. The face was as gaunt as the victim of an East Indian famine. And this thing, this wasted corpse was to go to the Fury.

It required courage to lift that feather-weight, chill, stiff body from the coffin and hide it behind the curtains. It required even more courage to take its place. X thought grimly of another time when he had entered a coffin and had learned the terror of premature burial.[14] This time he would take every precaution against suffocation. As he lay down on the soft death couch and pulled down the lid, he wedged a pencil between the lid and the side to allow air to be admitted.

In spite of the grisly bed on which he rested, in spite of the stuffy blackness, X forced himself to relax. It was only a matter of minutes now before he would learn what was behind the inexplicable moves of the Fury. There were many questions that a few minutes in the Fury's presence might answer: why had the name, Secret Agent X been written on the register at Madame Susu's? Why had the hideous hand of death reached out to leave its mark on Dot Dejong? Why were such wealthy and powerful men as Dr. Arden and Donald Lowery trembling in the grip of terror? Why—

The Agent felt that his mind was wandering. Relaxation was easy. It was difficult to concentrate on anything. Once, he caught himself dozing off and it was only with an effort that he roused himself. What was the matter with him? The night's activity was hardly enough to exhaust his powerful body. Yet he was sleepy now, utterly worn out, like that yellow corpse—

Again, X found himself jerking out of a doze. Doze? It seemed more than that. Breathing was an effort. His hands crept up to his throat slowly and laboriously. His fingers pressed against an artery in his neck. His pulse was scarcely perceptible. Or was he too tired to detect any pulse at all?

A panicky thought burned across his mind. Terror wrung sweat from his body. When pulse stopped, when breathing stopped, you were dying. He had to get out of that coffin. Throw back the lid. That was it—the cushions of the lid were soaked with something

---

14   AUTHOR'S NOTE: This incident in the eventful life of Agent X occurred when he was fighting valiantly to prevent the destruction of New York at the hands of a criminal known as Emperor Zero and was related in the novel titled: "The Brand of the Metal Maiden."

that was affecting his breathing. He would die if he didn't get out of that poisonous darkness.

He exerted every effort to sit up. But he could not move. All feeling seemed to stop at his thighs. His legs, as far as he knew, did not exist. A smile curved slowly across the lips of Agent X. It was all very pleasant just to lie there in spite of the encroaching cold that passed over his body. Thoughts flickered across his mind in rapid succession. He thought pleasantly of Betty Dale, the sweet girl reporter who had shared so many of his adventures. This was one she would not share. This was death. Too bad so many men died in pain. He felt no pain. Only a desire to sleep eternally and not dream....

CHAPTER III

BATES CARRIES ON

A **MAN WHOSE** six feet two inches of height was hidden by the squareness of his immense body paced tirelessly up and down in front of the arched gate of the morgue. His square-shaped head hung low as though he were in deep thought. He wore no hat and the chill rain of the afternoon had draggled his shaggy hair down over his forehead. Now and again he would impatiently yank at the sleeve of his trench coat and glance at his wrist watch.

Across the street a car pulled up. A young man with a scraggy jaw and bleak eyes got out. The atrocious bottle-green hat he wore had lost its snap long before it had faced this afternoon's drenching. As he crossed the street it was easy to see that Detective Timothy Scallot, of the Homicide Bureau, was extremely nervous. No more so, however, than the big, square man he joined a moment later. Timothy Scallot attempted to convey nonchalance as he grinned at the big man and said:

"Nice afternoon, Mr. Bates." [15]

"Right!" Bates clipped.

"This is going to be ticklish," Scallot confided in a whisper. "I've told the assistant medical examiner that you're a professor from Northwestern University's criminological school. Think you can act absent-minded?"

Bates could see nothing to be jocular about. For over twelve hours now, he had heard nothing from Secret Agent X, his beloved chief. It was seldom that the Agent didn't call upon Bates when

---

15   AUTHOR'S NOTE: *Harvey Bates is the key man of Secret Agent X's group of operatives. Regular readers of these chronicles may recognize Timothy Scallot who is one of Bates's best men. Scallot has a dangerous post in the Agent's organization. Since he is on the police force, his connection with Agent X must be kept secret. His chief duty is to keep Bates well-informed as to what goes on behind the doors at police headquarters.*

he was working on an important case. When the announcement of Dot Dejong's murder had come to the ears of Bates, and still no word from X, he had commenced to worry. For he knew that X had attended the séance at Madame Susu's.

At last, in desperation he had decided to strike out alone, attempt to fathom the mystery of the Fury, but above all try to locate Agent X. His first move had been to get Timothy Scallot to arrange for Bates to attend the autopsy on the body of Dot Dejong.

"We've accomplished absolutely nothing on this Dejong kill," Scallot confided as he opened the front door of the morgue. "Burks has held up the autopsy as long as possible. He's trotted in all the suspects for a look at the body when he's grilled them. He seems to think that Lowery, the radio man, knows something. But Lowery won't talk."

"Madame Susu?" clipped Bates.

"The cops followed her to an undertaker's establishment, lost her there. The woman's a real magician when it comes to the disappearing act. By the way, I don't think I should have told the assistant medical examiner that you were a professor. There'll be a real scientist here. A fellow by the name of Alan Moss. You may not be able to bluff him."

Bates grunted. He was anxious to see Alan Moss. It was Moss, he knew, who accompanied Agent X to the séance.

They passed through a corridor lined with refrigerating compartments and entered the post-mortem room at the end. Men in white were bending over a table where the body of Dot Dejong rested.

Scallot beckoned to the assistant medical examiner who was watching the proceedings. The doctor came over and shook hands with Bates whom Scallot introduced as Professor Westfield.

The medical examiner turned to Alan Moss. The young scientist was sitting on a high white stool holding his round-lensed glasses in his right hand and polishing them with a wad of cotton in his left.

"Have you come to any conclusion regarding the murder method in this case, Mr. Moss?" asked the medical examiner.

MOSS raised his energetic eyebrows. "Oh, it's quite obvious that some corrosive was used. An acid perhaps that not only has the power to destroy flesh, but also unites with the oxygen carried by the blood stream. This, I think, will be proved conclusively when

the heart is examined. An acid, I should say, that is not only a corrosive but also a deadly poison when used intravenously. Do you
agree, Professor Westfield?"

"Not well enough acquainted with particulars," Bates skillfully
evaded. He coughed, looked around the room. Near-by was another table supporting a sheeted form. The medical examiner followed Bates's gaze.

"Another puzzling case," said the doctor, pointing at the sheeted
form. He stepped over and turned back the sheet to disclose the
body of a man with heavy features.

"Mark Brady!" Bates exclaimed involuntarily.

"Exactly," said Moss. "Some one has saved the G-men some bullets."

"Brady," explained the medical examiner, "hasn't a mark on his
body. There are no outward traces of poison. I am anxious to learn
just how he met death."

"He was too tough to die naturally," put in Scallot. "We found
his body all laid out in a coffin at the mortuary to which we traced
Madame Susu."

Moss, the medical examiner, and Scallot returned to the operat-
ing table, but Bates hung back. He had no taste for the gruesome
details of a post mortem examination. He wanted only to know the
exact cause of death. Now and then, the medical examiner would
ask Bates's opinion on the condition of this or that organ, but always Bates managed an evasive answer.

Bates was troubled with an unaccountable feeling that he was
being watched closely. Nerves perhaps, for masquerading as a scientist was indeed nerve-racking for him. But it seemed as though
two eyes like points of fire were burning into the back of his brain.
At times Bates, ordinarily hard to ruffle, felt that he must shout, so
persistent was the effort of those unseen eyes.

At last, he could stand it no longer. He swung around, his glance
jumping about the room, searching for the origin of that troublesome stare.

And when he found it, he could not shout. He was rooted to the
floor, his body cold all over and his scalp crawling. For the fixed,
compelling gaze was coming from the eyes of the corpse of Mark
Brady. Dead eyes staring with the gleam of life. And dead lips—
dead lips moving?

Bates blinked. It was all unbelievable. This was the morgue.
When a man was brought here he was utterly dead. Yet the corpse

of Mark Brady stared at him and whispered, though no sound passed the dead lips.

With legs that felt like fence posts, Bates crossed the tile floor to the table where lay Mark Brady. There wasn't the slightest doubt now. The lips *were* moving. Bates turned around toward the men gathered about the body of Dot Dejong. His lips parted to call out—

"*Bates!*" a strained, whispered voice.

Bates's heart leaped into his throat. His head spun. This was madness. Some one behind him had called his name. And there was no one behind—only the corpse of Public Enemy Mark Brady.

BATES turned slowly. It seemed as though he had to drag his head around. Once again, his terrified eyes met those of the corpse. He saw the dead lips twist slightly in a feeble smile.

"X," came the whisper from the lips. "I am X."

"You—you're—" Then Bates recalled that the slightest alarm might warn the others within the room that here was a corpse that was not dead, a Mark Brady that was not Mark Brady. He sent an anxious glance over his shoulder. Alan Moss and the medical examiner were enthusiastically debating some question pertaining to the corpse of Dot Dejong.

"I can't explain—now," came the whispering voice again. This time it was more like the voice by which Bates knew Agent X. "I—I can't move. Muscles tight—cold. Carry on if I can't—make it."

"Good heavens!" whispered Bates, "they'll perform an autopsy—any minute!"

Agent X smiled weakly. "No. I'm not dead.... Catalepsy."

"What you want me to do?" came Bates's agonized, hushed voice.

"Don't—know. It's passing—I think."

A hand dropped on Bates's shoulder. The big man jumped. His fists clenched. Had worst come to worst he would have fought, killed even to prevent anyone from touching that half-dead body on the table.

"Old Brady seems to have a fascination for you, eh, *Professor?*" It was Timothy Scallot, Scallot with a wink in his eye. Not even to Scallot did Bates dare to reveal what he had witnessed. For Scallot was not aware that his real employer was the mysterious Secret Agent X.

"Yes, sir, Brady still looks tough," Scallot commented. "Look at that chin. I'll bet the docs have to blast."

Bates took Scallot's arm, steered him back toward the table where the medicos were at work on the body of the murdered women. Scallot's coat pocket swung heavily against Bates's hand. The detective invariably carried his gun in his coat pocket.

"Look at Moss," said Bates. "What's he doing?"

Scallot craned his neck, and at the same moment Bates managed to get his big hand into Scallot's pocket and extract the detective's gun. Now if it came to a fight, the only member of the police force present would be unarmed. Then, too, Bates hoped to slip X the gun if the Agent obtained the use of his legs in time to try a get-away.

Agent X, where he lay upon the morgue table, felt his pulse quickening and warmth slowly penetrating his muscles. Beneath the sheet that partially covered him he found himself able to move his fingers. The strange trance into which he had fallen was passing. But would the full effect of the strange drug leave in time? A surreptitious glance across the room, and he saw the stitcher coming into the room to sew up the murdered woman. Only a few minutes more before the medical men would prepare to perform a second autopsy.

Two of the white-coated assistants approached the table where X lay. The medical examiner and Alan Moss crossed the floor, still arguing. At the door Timothy Scallot chewed a match. Behind Moss and the doctor, stood Harvey Bates, his face grave, his eyes haggard.

Now was the moment to move—if he could. The Agent felt the muscles of his legs tighten. Behind locked lips, his teeth were clenched. He felt the surge of vibrant power through his body. Sheer will goaded him into action. He sat up stiffly, the sheet clinging to him like a shroud.

The two assistants in white dropped their jaws. Their eyes seemed on the point of popping from their sockets. Across the room, Alan Moss uttered a shout. Timothy Scallot reached for his gun—the gun that wasn't there. And behind them all, Bates thought coolly, acted fast. Scallot's gun was in his hand, then flying through the air straight toward X. The Agent saw it coming, reached for it with an effort and snatched it out of the air.

It must have appeared nothing short of black magic. X had every advantage of surprise. Over the heads of the stunned doctors, X saw Bates raise his own gun and fire one wild shot in the direction of Agent X. It was a clever move to avoid suspicion.

"Drop that gun!" X ground out between jaws that still seemed stiff.

BATES dropped his gun. Agent X stood up, holding the sheet about him with one hand and covering all within the room with his gun.

"You!" X jerked at one of the medicos. "You take off that white tunic, your trousers and shoes. Move, man, or I'll make you into a corpse—that won't live again."

The terrified man moved to obey. Across the room, X saw Alan Moss trying to get through the door. He sent a warning shot in the young scientist's direction. Moss turned, his eyebrows high with surprise.

X sat down on the table and thrust out bare feet. To the partially undressed medico he said: "Put your shoes on my feet."

"I'll lose my job for this," said the terrified man.

"You'll lose your life in another moment. Move, man!"

The medico assisted X to put on the smock and trousers, then suddenly gave X a quick shove. The Agent's knees struck the top of the table. He fell backwards over the table to strike the floor on the other side. In a moment, Alan Moss and the medical examiner threw themselves upon him.

A quick upward hack with the barrel of the police revolver in his hand knocked out the medical man. An elbow thrust in the face turned Moss aside. Then on his feet, X sprang toward the door, yanked it open and fled along the corridor lined with refrigerating units, to escape through the front door.

That afternoon many people were startled to see a man in a surgeon's smock running along the sidewalk like a madman, a gun clenched in his hand. At last X ducked into a deserted alley, found his way to a fire escape and up to the third floor. He opened an un-latched window and stepped into a plainly furnished room.[16]

Ten minutes later, he left the lodging house feeling like a new man and certainly looking the part. A change of clothes, makeup, and toupee had made him a man that no one would have looked at twice.

He hurried back the way he had come just in time to meet Harvey Bates and Timothy Scallot leaving the morgue. Scallot was excitedly talking of the miracle they had witnessed in the morgue.

---

16 AUTHOR'S NOTE: Agent X, no matter where he may be within the boundaries of the city, is never very far away from one of his many hideouts which he rents or purchases under his assumed names. In these hideouts he keeps a complete wardrobe, elaborate makeup material, weapons and radio equipment for communicating with his operatives.

Bates, his usual laconic self, was answering in single, clipped syllables only when an answer was necessary.

X strode up to Bates and tapped him on the arm. "Mr. Bates, I believe?"

Bates looked wonderly at Agent X and nodded his head.

"I'd like a few words with you if you'll just step into the drug store here. A purely personal matter, you understand."

BATES complied with the Agent's request. They stepped to the door of the drug store, and when X spoke again it was with the voice that Bates was sure to recognize.

Bates's face beamed with pleasure. "Afraid you wouldn't make it, sir. But why were you there? Accomplish something?"

X shook his head. "Not a thing." He related briefly what had happened to him after he had disguised himself as Mark Brady. "I believe that some chemical in the top of the coffin lid was responsible for the trance into which I fell. It was genuine catalepsy, you may be sure, or I would not have been brought to the morgue. Undoubtedly the criminals found me in the coffin and decided that it would be good riddance of Agent X if they left me for the police."

Bates scratched his shaggy black hair. "Heard or read something like that. Man discovered some sort of anesthetic. Considered impractical. The stuff induced artificial catalepsy. Think it was in the paper about two weeks ago. Cardigan or Varden or some name like that was the discoverer of the stuff."

X frowned. "Dr. Cornelius Arden?" he suggested.

Bates snapped his fingers. "That was it. Arden."

"That's a new angle," said X thoughtfully. "Stick close to the central office. I'll contact you later. Up to now, the Fury has made all the moves. Now it's our turn." And he left Bates standing in the door of the drug store.

In spite of the fact that his mind had been a complete blank while under the influence of the potent drug that had produced catalepsy. X could still recall that the Fury planned a robbery scheduled for that night at the home of Rex Bastion. Unless the Fury had changed plans, Agent X was determined to meet him at Bastion's that night.

X returned to his hideout and there called the office of the *Herald*. A few minutes later, he was talking with Betty Dale, the capable newspaper woman who was the Agent's closest friend.[17]

---

17   AUTHOR'S NOTE: *The daughter of a member of the police force who was killed in*

"Can you give me a little information. Betty?" X asked, using the voice that was associated with his portrayal of the character of A.J. Martin, one of his disguises with which Betty was familiar.

Betty caught her breath. The sudden appearances of the Agent never failed to surprise her. "You know," she replied, "that I will do anything to help you."

"What can you tell me about a man by the name of Rex Bastion? You know the old Bastion place overlooking the Hudson?"

"Oh, you mean the death-ray man!" the girl exclaimed. "I'm afraid I don't know much about him. I've met him, but he's a man you can't get next to. He's always so busy bragging about his own achievements that you can't see the inner man, if you know what I mean."

"Death ray? What's that about a death ray?"

"Hadn't you heard?" Betty came back. "He's invented a ray, the exact nature of which he refuses to make public. But he hints it will be marketed soon as a defensive weapon. The man's a joke to every one in the newspaper office. He craves publicity. For all I know, the death ray may be only a gag. We did treat him to a column a few nights ago. He intends to demonstrate the ray tonight, I believe. I'm going to see if I can cover the demonstration for the paper."

X frowned thoughtfully at the transmitter for a minute. Perhaps this time Bastion deserved all the credit publicity could give him. Perhaps he had discovered a death ray that was practical. Some one was bound to some day. Why not Bastion? The man was really quite capable along the lines of electrical research.

"I wouldn't try to cover that story if I were you, Betty," X told her. "I can't tell you more than that it might be dangerous."

The girl's merry laughter came back through the receiver. "Personally," she said, "I don't believe anything that Rex Bastion invented would be deadly enough to poach an egg.... When will I see you?"

"I don't know," X said quietly, "perhaps tonight. Good-bye now, and remember what I said about danger at the Bastion place."

X hung up. Bastion, a man who had wasted his millions, claimed to have invented a death ray. Fair prey for the Fury.

---

action, Betty Dale has grown up in the very center of police work. As a reporter, she frequently has information to give X. Though she has never seen X's real features, she loves him for his courage, resourcefulness and human qualities. Betty's beauty and charming personality have always been a source of inspiration to Agent X.

THE BASTION RAY

IN THE TOWER room of a grim, stone mansion that centered on an island far out in Long Island Sound, a strange figure sat at a desk littered with scientific instruments. His face was as white as bones bleached by the desert sun—a mask of molded celluloid. Centering the forehead of the white mask, like a third eye, was a small golden device representing the hideous head of a Grecian Fury.

Standing on either side of tall oak doors that opened into the dome-topped chamber, were two human skeletons—men so thin that their bones seemed on the point of piercing their dry, yellow skin. They stood like statues, yet somehow they lived and breathed. Deep-eyed, dull-faced walking corpses who guarded the portals of the Fury's sanctum.

An impending storm had brought an early dusk. The tall, arched windows of the strange chamber, where sat Agent X's enemy, were now and again brightened by a flicker of lightning dancing across the horizon.

There was something dispassionate about the eyes of the Fury slotted by the openings in the mask. He seemed a chess automaton, a master-mover planning some clever gambit while he worked.

At last he racked a test tube, picked up a hand-set radio transmitter and looked at the watch on his wrist. On a panel in front of him a small pilot light glowed red.

"The Fury speaking," came a lifeless voice from beyond the mask. "What have you to report?"

The Fury listened a moment. "So Agent X escaped from the morgue, did he?" the man in the mask mused. "Then we can safely count on his presence tonight at Bastion's place." He drummed on the desk top with his fingertips a moment. Then: "At all costs we must obtain the Bastion Ray. We cannot go on without it. The death of the Dejong woman has produced no results as yet. If our plan is to succeed, we must obtain the ray.

"Be careful of Mark Brady—the real Mark Brady. We have won him over to our cause, but I believe that this afternoon, under influence of liquor, he let certain information drop. That information is probably now in the hands of the police. As soon as Brady has accomplished our purposes, he must be removed. We have nothing to fear from the police this time, but it may not always be so."

He listened a moment, drumming quietly on the desk top. "No, there will be no police interference, I assure you. As to any others who may attempt to prevent us from obtaining the Bastion Ray, we shall depend upon the death-touch to handle them. For all who interfere, the caress of death. But for Agent X—" the Fury paused. The strange, emotionless eyes wandered to the gaunt, living corpses standing at the door. He nodded his head slowly. "Do not kill Agent X. Leave him for me. There is no greater satisfaction than humbling a powerful opponent.

"Tomorrow I can promise you, we will have the situation well in hand. Huge reservoirs of wealth are ours for the tapping. Until then, every effort must be concentrated on obtaining the Bastion Ray. In two hours we move."

THE FURY replaced the hand-set, got out of his chair and strode to the window. In the distance thunder rolled ominously. Lightning fell upon his sombre figure and made a gleaming thing of his white mask. The Fury clenched his fists. It was as though he felt the power of the storm in his hands and hurled back the lightning in grim challenge to Secret Agent X.

Just beyond the gates of the Bastion place on Riverside Drive, a car was parked. Behind the wheel was a man with commonplace features and a sandy complexion. He was known to the newspaper world as A.J. Martin, a representative of the Associated Press. Actually Martin was but one of the many aliases of Secret Agent X.

The man beside him was unmistakably Harvey Bates, though the big man wore a neat black mask over his features.

"You have everything, Bates?" X asked. "Net? Glass cutter? You're well armed?"

"Right," Bates clipped, readily.

"And you say that the Fury's raiding party will be in charge of Mark Brady?"

"Such was the information given me by Scallot. Word got to the police from a stool pigeon. Believe Brady was drunk, talked."

"Then the police will be here. More trouble. On the stroke of nine, I'll knock out the lights in the laboratory. You'll be waiting on the skylight as planned. Drop your net on the end of a rope and pull it up when you feel a sharp tug."

"Don't see how you can get a big machine in a net like that," Bates said.

"It's not a machine. Just a metal vacuum tube. Of course there are a lot of accessories attached to the tube. But the main thing is to get the tube. After you have netted the tube, get across the estate and come out on West End Avenue. I have arranged for a fast car to be waiting for you."

"But the Fury?"

"I will try to cope with the Fury in my own way."

"And the police?"

X shook his head. He reached over to the dashboard and turned on the short-wave radio, with which he and Bates kept careful track of the movements of the police on their way to the Bastion house.

"Attention special squads on Riverside Drive," droned the voice of the police announcer. "Proceed no farther. Proceed no farther. Return at once. Orders given at eight-fifteen are cancelled. Return at once."

X looked at Bates, frowned.

"The group ordered to Bastion's?" puzzled Bates.

X nodded. "The police are withdrawing their protection. What can that mean? The Fury doesn't act like a person who might easily be persuaded to give up his plans. Perhaps he has tricked the police."

"Or already stolen the ray," Bates suggested.

X shook his head. "Hardly. We will go right ahead as planned." Saying this, he sprang from the car and hurried through the rusty, iron gate and across the ill-kept lawn. Beyond neglected sunken gardens, the huge Bastion house stood and still bore the Bastion name in spite of the fact that it was mortgaged from wine cellar to chimney pots.

A wooden-faced butler, whose long service with the Bastion family had become a tradition, admitted Agent X and examined his card. He bowed stiffly, said that Mr. Bastion was expecting Mr. Martin. X was taken into the drawing room where a number of guests had gathered, awaiting Bastion's demonstration of his invention.

In spite of the Agent's warning, Betty Dale was there, cool, clear-eyed and lovely in a simple gown that revealed soft, girlish shoulders. She sent a quick glance at Agent X and smiled. A.J. Martin was one of the aliases of Agent X with which she was familiar. She turned at once to Wilbur Kopsak with whom she had been speaking when X had entered.

"Just what is your opinion of the Bastion Ray, Mr. Kopsak?" she asked.

KOPSAK glowered at her, but her smile was contagious. In another moment he was talking and laughing freely. "Don't know a thing about it, my dear Miss Dale. Not a thing. I simply know that Bastion needs money to carry on his experiments. Undoubtedly that is why I have been invited."

Across the room, stooped, scholarly Dr. Arden was listening absently to a lecture from Alan Moss. His eyes were worried, red-rimmed from lack of sleep.

Moss was saying: "This man Bastion is mad. If he has accomplished what he claims, how on earth does he expect to shield his ray tube? He claims that it will fuse metal instantly. How then can he direct it?"

Vina Trumaine, all in black—gown, bag and gloves, was observing several oil paintings that hung from the walls. In her dangerous green eyes was neither admiration nor contempt. She turned, however, as X approached. He was certain that her quick glance photographed every detail of his face and dress.

Agent X bowed. "Since our host is too occupied to introduce us, suppose we dispense with formality and manage it ourselves. I am A.J. Martin."

Vina Trumaine smiled slowly. "Then we require no introduction. I am already familiar with your work for the Associated Press. I am Vina Trumaine."

X laughed quietly. "I'll ask for a raise. Some one really reads my articles." Then: "You are a friend of Rex Bastion, no doubt?"

"The merest acquaintance. Dr. Arden was kind enough to bring me."

Rex Bastion bustled into the room at the moment. He was a small, thick-set man with almost dwarfish hands and feet. His nose was large and bulbous, his mouth froglike, his eyes probing. He stood in the door, raised his strange hands, much as a master of ceremonies in a night club might do before introducing the star of the evening.

"My friends, my friends," he began in a blatant voice, "we can now begin. Bastion is here." He minced into the middle of the room perfectly conscious that he was the center of attraction and glorying in it. "I had to quell a minor uprising among the servants. Such a problem! It seems that some one saw fit to enter my safe without asking my permission. Questioning the servants, I found them highly indignant that I should even insinuate that they knew anything about it."

Bastion paused, coughed behind his palm. "Some plans were stolen."

"Not the plans of the ray, I hope?" Betty Dale asked.

Bastion chuckled. "Indeed no. I am too clever to leave anything decipherable about my invention lying about. Put that in your paper, my dear young lady. Bastion keeps his plans in—" he flicked his forehead—"his not altogether empty head." He laughed uproariously, pranced across the room, and looked the part of an idiot as he took Betty's arm and made off toward the laboratory.

"Our host has an eye for beauty, or is it a desire for the right kind of publicity," Vina Trumaine whispered to X.

"Under the circumstances, undoubtedly the latter," X flattered as he offered Vina Trumaine his arm.

BASTION'S laboratory had been built at the back of the house, a one-story structure the ceiling of which was centered by a skylight of glass now and again illuminated dully by a flash of lightning. The lightning, X thought, would increase the danger of the scheme that he had evolved. It would certainly silhouette Bates's big form against the skylight.

At one end of the laboratory was a grotto temporarily constructed. In this grotto was a box about three feet square and constructed of steel plates. At the opposite end was a contraption of generators, electrolytic condensers, rheostats and transformers connected by a maze of wires and having a porcelain socket in the center of it.

Bastion arranged his guests back of the maze of electrical devices, then crossed to a steel cabinet from which he took a curious cylindrical tube of some gleaming metal. This, he pointed out, was the heart of his powerful ray. Then he fitted the tube into the socket and crossed to a small bakelite switchboard.

Agent X was careful to stand close to an electrical outlet. In his pocket was an electrical device which, in spite of its simplicity, was extremely effective. It consisted of a forked piece of brass in an insulated handle. The fork, when thrust into a light-socket would produce a short circuit that would blow out every fuse in the electrical system.

"My friends," began Bastion with a gleeful rubbing of his dwarfish hands, "I have prepared a pamphlet which will explain the scientific principle behind my ray. The construction of the tube remains a secret, of course. For the benefit of the laity, I might explain shortly that my tube sends out a beam of charged electrical particles with such a tremendous rate of speed that terrific heat is generated."

"How do you point the beam?" asked Alan Moss.

"You will observe," Bastion went on, "that in the grotto at the opposite end of the room, there is a steel box that I intend to destroy."

"How do you direct the beam?" persisted Alan Moss.

Bastion yanked a switch on a panel in front of him. If he spoke at all, his words were lost in the hum of the generator as it started. He gestured toward the grotto at the end of the room.

X glanced upward. A flare of lightning illuminated the form of Harvey Bates sprawled out on the skylight. Bates was evidently courageously at work with his glass cutter.

Bastion pulled a switch, then stepped to his electrical contraption and advanced a rheostat slightly. The tube glowed with a faint purple light.

Then, suddenly, white-hot flame drenched the steel box in the grotto. There were hissing, sputtering sparks, a blinding flare. Metal dripped like water. Bastion cut his switches. The glow faded from the tube. At the end of the room nothing remained of the box save a shapeless mass of molten metal.

"Amazing!" cried Dr. Arden.

"Astounding!" Alan Moss echoed. "But I say, old man, how do you keep the beastly thing from snapping back at you, as it were?"

Standing behind all the others who crowded around the triumphant Bastion, Agent X pulled the forked tool from his pocket. Decidedly, the Bastion Ray was a deadly thing. He shuddered to think of what it might do in the hands of a person like the Fury. With a quick motion of his wrist, he jammed the forked instrument into the light-socket. There was a lightning flash of blue flame, then instantaneous darkness.

Now to yank the tube from its socket, toss it into Bates's net—

Agent X stopped. His thoughts suddenly left him. He was deaf to the startled cries of those within the room. On the wall directly in front of him, burning in cool flickering flames of green was the mark of the Secret Agent himself—a huge letter "X" drawn in luminous paint.

How had it come there? Had some one again penetrated his disguise? Was some one having a joke at his expense? Did the Fury plan to commit crimes in the Agent's name?

Some one shouted: "The mark of X! Secret Agent X is in the room!"

X PIVOTED, sprang in the direction of the deadly ray tube. His groping fingers encountered Bates's net. He gripped it, snatched out with his right hand for the ray tube—and encountered nothing. The tube was gone, completely disappeared. X sprang to the steel cabinet from which Bastion had taken the tube. A moment's delay had spoiled everything. The cabinet was open, but his exploring fingers found it empty.

At that moment the door of the laboratory burst open. A harsh oath sounded from the lips of Wilbur Kopsak. The Agent snatched out his flashlight and sent its piercing beam toward the door. For a moment, the dot of light paused on the heavy features of Public Enemy Mark Brady. Behind Brady, X saw the lean, hungry features of two beings who looked like walking corpses.

Bastion's old butler faithfully attempted to prevent the entrance of the invaders into the laboratory. One of the emaciated wretches lifted his right hand, brushed it lightly across the butler's face.

Instantly the old man's features were obliterated by an ugly acid brand. Pain sent him reeling into the room, screaming, clawing at blinded eyes. He spun around once like a top about to stop, struck the floor and lay still.

The touch of death. The long arm of the Fury was reaching for its prey. Screaming, cursing, the guests of Rex Bastion mobbed from the laboratory, through doors and windows, rushing pell-mell to get away from the cadaverous killers.

"The ray!" shouted Brady. "Get the ray, damn it!"

Somewhere out on the lawn, came the high-pitched scream of a woman in stark terror. Across the mind of Agent X flashed a hideous picture—the white, girlish shoulders of Betty Dale, branded by the hand of death. He turned toward an open window. One of the Fury's gaunt slaves stood there. X whirled up a chair, held it like a battering-ram, and rushed the man. The chair hit a body, blotted it from the window. Risking the death-touch, X sprang over the fallen man and gained the lawn.

The scream came again. Guided by it, X raced around a towering clump of lilac and came suddenly upon a woman. His protecting arms went out. Her small hands clutched his arm. He could feel her trembling body pressed close to his.

"Betty!" he whispered. "Are you all right? What happened?" He turned the light of his flashlight down into the girl's face. The beam awoke the dangerous, fascinating glitter of the green eyes of Vina Trumaine. Her red lips parted, quivered slightly. "So sorry to disappoint you," she whispered.

X RELEASED her, glanced down at her hands that slowly, almost reluctantly let go of his arm. It was the first time he had seen Vina Trumaine without her black gloves. Her fingernails were filed completely to the quick.

"What happened?" X asked her quickly. "Why did you scream?"

"Because," she said quietly, "I was afraid. Foolish of me, but I didn't know you were so near."

"But what frightened you?"

She touched her chest lightly with her fingertips. "Hush! Some one is coming."

X reached into his pocket and gripped the butt of his gas pistol. Baleful lightning revealed the shadowy form of a man coming around the lilacs. X turned his flashlight straight into the man's face. It was Alan Moss, his energetic eyebrows raised in mild surprise. In his left hand he gripped his yellow walking-stick.

"Martin!" Moss exclaimed as soon as he saw X. "And Mrs. Trumaine. Where are those hellish killers?"

"Mr. Martin is anxious about the little reporter," said Vina Trumaine.

"Oh, Miss Dale? She's all right. Locked up with Rex Bastion. I'm out to reconnoiter."

"You didn't hope to lay any of the killers low with that stick, did you?" X asked.

Moss smiled thinly. "Silly of me, but I always feel safer with the thing in my hand. Suppose we get back to the others. Dr. Arden is certainly worrying about Mrs. Trumaine."

They turned, started toward the house. X thrust out both arms, checked his companions. "Some one or something is in front of us," he whispered.

"A man," whispered Vina Trumaine. "No, three."

"A man and two of those mummy-devils," echoed Moss. "Good lord, Martin, have you a gun?"

X nodded, pulled out his gas pistol. The weird trio had stopped. A flashlight held by the man in the center turned its searching ray on X and his companions then flashed straight up to illuminate the glistening, bone-white mask of the Fury himself. Beside the man were two of his unclean, emaciated bodyguards.

The Fury spoke: "These grounds are completely surrounded by my men. We have the strength of numbers and the power none can thwart—the death-touch. This is my ultimatum: tell Bastion to hand over his ray within thirty minutes. Otherwise, I shall be obliged to kill everyone on this estate. Half an hour. No more."

The Fury and his corpselike escorts turned and moved back into the shadows.

"Great heavens, Martin! Why don't you shoot?"

X did not shoot for a very good reason. The Fury was beyond the range of his gas pistol. Furthermore, a charge of gas would have certainly blown back and knocked out both Moss and Vina Trumaine, for only those who held their breath were immune to its power.

X shook his head. "For the safety of all concerned, Bastion better hand over his ray." It was advice he hated to give, yet he could not stand by and watch Betty and the others slaughtered. Against the death-touch he was utterly powerless.

"But he can't do that, man!" Moss exploded.

"Why?" asked Vina Trumaine.

"He hasn't got the damned thing! Some one stole it from under his very nose."

It was a dangerous situation to which X could see but one solution. He must, at all costs, contact the police. Squads of armed police might mow down the Fury's cadaverous killers, break through their ranks, and come to the rescue. Never before had Agent X called upon the police for help. Now he must, though such a move might result in his own arrest.

CHAPTER V

BLACK GLOVES

AS SOON AS he had entered the house, X went to the nearest telephone extension only to find that the wires had been cut. Yet the main lines leading to the house were still intact. If he could connect one of the disabled instruments at the point where the lines entered through the roof, he might still be able to contact police headquarters.

After he had made certain that Betty Dale was safe inside Bastion's study, X went into the drawing room, knelt by the telephone box, and took a small, strong screwdriver from his pocket tool kit. He was on the point of removing the telephone when a soft voice asked: "Just what are you doing?"

He turned to see Vina Trumaine leaning against a table watching him. The woman dangled a cigarette in her red lips. Her green eyes gleamed unblinking through the blue smoke. "I am going to contact the police," X replied, continuing to work with his screwdriver. "Does that alarm you?"

Vina Trumaine shrugged gracefully. "No. Why should it?"

X stood up, glanced at the woman's hands. She had once again pulled on her black gloves. He approached her, gently took both her hands in his. "It's a shame to keep such lovely hands covered." He took hold of the fingertips of one glove and pulled. She tried to jerk away. His left arm went about her waist and held her tightly. She struggled a moment, eyes bright with fury, then melted toward him.

"Please," she whispered breathlessly. "Later, perhaps, if you wish to come and see me in my apartment—"

With a quick jerk, X stripped one black glove from one slender hand. The woman glanced down, bit her lips. Agent X smiled. "What have you done with the Bastion Ray?" he demanded coldly.

Her body stiffened. The green eyes registered amazement now, or perhaps it was fear. "I haven't the faintest idea what you are talking about. Will you give me back my glove?"

"You cannot deny that you opened Bastion's safe and made an attempt to steal the plans of his ray—nonexistent plans, it seems. I have never seen fingers filed as yours are except on the hands of professional safe crackers. Filing them close brings the more sensitive nerve endings close to the surface, enabling the expert safe operator to feel the resistance of the tumblers as he turns the combination dial."

Well-formed nostrils haughtily spread, she said: "This is quite the most absurd thing I have ever heard in my life. You do not seem to realize to whom you are speaking."

"No," replied X mockingly, "I haven't the slightest idea. But certainly you are not what you seem."

Somewhere outside the house came the crack of a shot. A body struck the hall door. X sprang into the hall, saw the front door buckle beneath the impact of a shoulder. X twisted the latch and Wilbur Kopsak almost fell into the room. He was waving a smoking revolver in his hand, breathing heavily, his thick lips dropping curses. He leaned forward, one hand clasping the Agent's shoulder, and kicked the door shut behind him.

"The man with the white face!" he gasped. "Two things like corpses. They're still out there waiting for us. Where in hell are the police?"

"You saw the Fury?"

Kopsak shrugged. "A man with a face as white as flour. A golden thing in the center of his forehead. He pointed me out to the two corpse things. I've been running from them as I never ran before. Fired a shot when I got close to the door. That seemed to scare them away. We can't get away from here. There are men spaced every twenty feet around the fence. Why haven't the police come?"

X NODDED reassuringly. "Please take Mrs. Trumaine into the study with the others. Stay there. I'll try to get the police out here."

Kopsak took Vina Trumaine and steered her toward the study.

Back in the drawing room, X lost no time in removing the telephone instrument. Then he tucked box and hand-set under his arm and hurried up the steps.

At the end of the upstairs hall, he found a stairway leading into the attic. Guided by his flashlight, he climbed their narrow length

The lean, corpselike servants
of the Fury moved stealthily
to surround him.

and found himself in a dark and cavernous chamber beneath the steeply slanting roof. He found the twisted phone wires in a moment where they led through a porcelain in the wall of a gable. He carefully scraped away insulation and cut one wire at a time. Then he attached the wires to the poles of the phone box, lifted the handset and heard the buzz of a live wire. He immediately called the office of the police commissioner.

"Good evening, Commissioner Foster," X said quietly when he heard Foster's familiar voice, "this is Secret Agent X speaking."

A gasp of amazement from the commissioner.

"I want action, Commissioner, immediately. You may know that

I am desperate or I would not have appealed to you. You owe me nothing, it is true, but your duty toward the people of this city is very great. I am speaking from the Bastion house, not for myself but for the people of New York. The entire household and six guests are trapped here, unable to leave alive because the Fury has the house completely surrounded by killers. You know what became of Dot Dejong. That was the Fury's work. All here are his prospective victims. Send a couple of squads of heavily-armed men over at once. Inform them to avoid hand to hand conflict with anyone here."

"I—I will see what I can do," Foster choked out and started to hang up.

"Foster!" shouted Agent X. "What do you mean, 'see what you can do?' There are lives in great danger, man!"

"The Fury," sounded Foster's strained voice, "is more powerful than the police. My hands are tied."

A faint click. X shouted, begging Foster not to hang up. He even offered to turn himself over to the police if Foster would send assistance. But the line was dead.

While X was talking to Foster, shadows in the dark attic moved. Gaunt hungry shadows, circling the Agent like wolves whose courage came from strength of numbers. The lean, corpselike servants of the Fury moved stealthily to surround him.

When he realized that Foster had hung up, X dashed the phone to the floor. Foster was not a man to shirk his duty. Something truly serious had happened to impair the courage of the police. But with the police force out of commission, there remained only Agent X and his force of operatives. To bring his own men to the Bastion place meant giving them orders to kill. Without the law to back them, it would make murderers of them all. There seemed no other way—

A LEAN, sinewy shape launched itself in a catlike spring that carried it out of the darkness to land on the Agent's broad back. X turned as he fell, wrenched his left arm free, sent a smashing blow into a yellow face that was all but a skull. But every shadowy corner of the big attic gave up gaunt, yellow men, slaves of the Fury, whose touch meant death.

X fought like a madman, wondering every minute why he did not feel the branding contact of acid from the lean hands that sought his throat. Then something crashed to the top of his skull. Consciousness flickered out. He lay perfectly still.

"Kill!" a thin voice screamed.

"No!" cried another. "It is against the master's will. This is the man called X. I heard him say so. Bring rope. Tie him. Gag him. Then go for the master."

The thin savages scrambled about the gloomy attic, obtaining trunk straps and rope. The Agent's jaws were forced apart and old rags thrust into his mouth and tied in place. Straps and ropes trussed him up helplessly. Had he been conscious he might have expanded muscles so as to obtain play in his bonds, but by the time the slaves of the Fury had finished, escape without aid would have been impossible.

The thin men walked silently on bare feet to the attic door. One of them said: "The master said we were to hide in the house, await his signal. When that signal comes, we kill. Now we must inform the master of what we have done to the man called X." And in single file they left the room.

Such was the Agent's perfect physical condition that he recovered from the blow quickly. As soon as his head had cleared and he recalled what had happened, he glanced about him. The windows of the attic were open. Casements banged, caught in the teeth of the wind that was driving the storm in from sea.

He found that he could flex his knees. He rolled toward one of the casements. There was a thin hope that he could break the glass window and use the cutting fragments of glass to liberate his hands. But this hope was shattered when he discovered that heavy leather straps had been used to bind his hands.

He crouched before the window, braced his shoulder against the sill and managed to get to his feet. Incessant lightning illuminated the scene before him; a tile roof slanting dizzily downward to the eaves of the first story, the shrubbery and dwarf trees on the lawn below and the recumbent figure of a man.

There was no mistaking the square shoulders and shaggy head of the man on the ground. It was Harvey Bates. Had the Fury struck while X was helpless in the attic? Were all within the house dead at the hands of the fiends? Or perhaps Wilbur Kopsak had shot Bates with his revolver, mistaking him for one of the Fury's men.

No, Bates moved, rolled on the ground, groaned softly.

Some twenty feet from Bates, a bush parted. A thin, mummylike face was visible between the leaf-covered twigs. Then a scrawny arm extended with fingers crooked like talons, with veins bloated like fat worms. The thing crawled from the bushes. There was no mistaking the lust to kill that burned deep in the cavernous eyes. Here was a murder-madman and in the touch of that extended right hand was the power to kill.

The Agent's heart thudded dismally. He was so utterly helpless. He must stand there, watch the murderous fiend lay his deadly hand on the flesh of the faithful Bates. It was mental torture more than he could bear. He tried to shout a warning, but the gag choked him. If there was only some way to warn Bates, he was certain that the big man would come out of his coma in time to defend himself. But there was no way. None unless—

X looked down the steep incline of the roof. There *was* a way. It meant risking his own life, but he was willing to pay that price if in return he saved Bates's life.

The one thing that he could do was to deliberately fall out of the window. He could not help but fall near where Bates lay and there was the chance that he could shock Bates to his senses. At any rate, he could not permit Bates to face death alone. And there was no mistaking the evil intentions of the yellow-skinned killer.

CHAPTER VI

THE DARK MASK

THERE WAS NO getting on the sill, preparing for the long slide down the slates and the drop through the air. There was only one way to get out of that window. He must throw his weight forward, allow the sill to trip him and plunge headlong down the roof. His short, awkward dive landed him on his face. The plastic material that composed his false features was smeared. The breath was hammered out of him. At sickening speed, he slid on his belly down the roof until a raised tile caught his foot and whipped him around. He rolled sideways, felt the bite of the eaves trough against his side, and pitched over the edge.

X landed on his back in a bush only a few feet from where Bates lay. The mummy-faced killer sprang backward, uttered a startled snarl. For a moment, he stood there, staring dumbly at the Agent's helpless form. Then a glimmer of intelligence crossed his face. He advanced cautiously, his right hand outstretched.

But the sound of X's body crashing into the bush had brought Bates to his senses. He rolled to his knees, lurched to his feet, saw the emaciated killer. He clawed for his gun, got it out, fired twice in rapid succession. Still hazy from the knockout he had received, he could not hope to hit his target. But the crash of the shots served him well. The thin killer took to his heels and ran back toward the rear of the house.

Bates staggered to the bush, seized the Agent's bound legs, and pulled him out. He could not have recognized the Agent's features as those of Martin because the makeup was ruined. But he did know that X covered his face with plastic material and consequently knew his chief.

In silence, Bates removed the gag from X's mouth. "Hurt, sir?" he asked anxiously.

"No," X gasped. "A little winded. That bush broke my fall. I didn't see any other way to warn you. What happened to you, anyway?"

As Bates took off the straps that bound X, he explained what had occurred: "When I pulled up the net and found that the ray tube was not in it, I got off the roof. Met a woman running from the house. Something shiny in her hand, looked like the tube. I tried to take it from her. Got my hands on it. She scratched at my face. Thought I had the tube when some one attacked me from behind.

"I heard the woman scream. Somebody cursed, said something like: 'Tomorrow Lowery gets it in the neck.' That's all I remember."

"A man or woman said that about Lowery?" X asked.

"Man."

"You said the woman scratched your face. No marks on your cheeks."

BATES scrubbed at his jaw with a big palm. "Funny, I didn't feel any pain either."

"Because she didn't have much in the way of fingernails," X told him. "Vina Trumaine was the woman you tried to take the ray from. Her fingernails are filed down to the quick. But if the Fury has the ray, then surely the danger has passed. Suppose we walk up toward the gate and see if there is a guard there."

"What became of the police, sir?" Bates asked. As they moved toward the gate, X repaired the makeup on his face. So familiar was he with the features of the mythical A.J. Martin that he could adopt them even in the dark.

"That's it. Something is wrong with Foster. And it will be my first move to learn just what the trouble is. The Fury must be immune from the police and there must be a very excellent reason."

They saw no one at the gate and passing through resulted in no attack. Obviously the Fury had the death ray. The danger of the moment was past. But a far graver danger loomed on the horizon—a danger that threatened the city, perhaps even the nation. The Bastion Ray appeared to be the most deadly weapon the brain of man had ever conceived. What it had done to steel it could more readily do to human flesh. And Donald Lowery was the first marked man.

"What now, sir?" asked Bates.

"Nothing for you to do but stay here and keep on the lookout. I believe that the devil who tried to attack you had strayed from the pack. If he puts in his appearance again, shoot, and shoot to kill. No hand to hand scuffling. I've seen the Fury's death-touch in operation twice. It is the product of mad genius, perhaps, but it works."

X left Bates on the lawn and hurried back to the Bastion house. They were all in the study—Bastion, Betty Dale, Moss, Kopsak, Arden and Vina Trumaine.

"The Fury has the ray," X said, looking straight at Vina Trumaine. "There is no reason why we should stay here unless you choose. I am heading downtown at once."

"Miss Dale," said Vina Trumaine, "I wonder if you could drop me off at my apartment on your way. Dr. Arden, I know, wants to stay a few moments longer and talk with Mr. Bastion."

"I'll be delighted," Betty said readily. Then perhaps she thought she ought to have consulted Agent X, for she looked at him strangely.

When Vina Trumaine had gone for her wrap, Betty approached X. The Agent led her into the hall. "Betty," he whispered, "don't trust Vina Trumaine for an instant. It was she who stole the ray from Bastion's laboratory tonight. Now the Fury has it, for he has withdrawn his guards. For all we know, Vina Trumaine may be one of the Fury's aides—and certainly she would make a capable one."

"She has done nothing but ask questions about you ever since you deserted us," Betty told him. "I really believe the woman is in love with you."

Agent X smiled. "Jealous?"

Betty's bright, blue eyes widened. "No. What right have I to be jealous?"

X pressed her hand gently. "Some day," he said quietly and nothing more. But the one word spoke volumes.

"I'll be most careful of the wicked Vina Trumaine," she said.

"Good night, then." And with a reassuring smile the Secret Agent left her.

ONE HOUR later, a man whose red hair was fading at the temples, whose nose was thin and hawk-beaked, whose eyes were squinted, entered police headquarters and demanded to see Commissioner Foster. "I have," he said nasally, "important evidence in the Dejong murder case which I will relate to no one but the commissioner."

In the commissioner's office Edward Neihart, for such was the name the hawk-beaked man had given, glanced across at a screen that hid a portion of the room. "It might be wise," he suggested, "to dismiss your secretary. The matter I am about to discuss with you should be heard by your ears alone."

The police commissioner whitened perceptibly and promptly dismissed his secretary. "Now, Mr. Neihart, if you will get to the point at once," Foster suggested. "My time is extremely valuable."

"Hardly that, judging from the manner in which you exercise your duty," said Neihart sternly. "You are busy retarding the normal police procedure."

Foster frowned. Neihart noticed that his white fingers trembled. "Sir, I am not here to listen to such insinuations—"

Neihart's fist thumped the table. "Yet you will listen."

The phone on Foster's desk jangled. The commissioner lifted it, listened, and hung up without a word. To Neihart he said: "You have information concerning the death of the Dejong girl? I know of no better time to hear that information. There has been another death-touch murder. Mark Brady has been picked up on West End near Seventy-eighth."

Neihart smiled one-sidedly. "That is no news for me."

Foster raised his eyebrows. "Just what is your profession? Are you a private detective? If so I do not remember signing your permit."

"My permit," Neihart declared, "does not need signing. I know of Brady's death because I ordered it so. When one of *your* men is caught drinking too much, you demote him or take his badge away. When Mark Brady failed me, I demoted him to a corpse. Had not you been putty in criminal hands, information Brady dropped while drunk might well have put the skids under a certain little plan that culminated in theft at the Bastion house."

Foster stood up. His eyes, red from lack of sleep, burned into Neihart's brain. "Who are you that you know so much?" he demanded.

"I am," the man told him, "one Edward Neihart, sometimes called the Fury."

Foster's lean figure trembled with ill-suppressed emotion. Suddenly, he flew into an uncontrollable rage, swung around the desk and threw himself at his visitor. "How much longer," he shouted, "do you intend to keep my niece a captive. Damn you, I'll strangle the truth out of you!"

Neihart warded off the commissioner's rage-driven attack with a capable forearm. When he saw an opening, he shot in a blow with the flat of his hand. Foster was caught in the chest and thrown back into his chair.

Neihart tapped his coat pocket significantly, and smiled down at the panting commissioner. "I have a gun, but I need not use it. If I do not return to my office within an hour, your niece—" Neihart smiled as his voice trailed off.

Then he dropped into a chair across from Foster and idly scribbled on the desk blotter. "I shall hold your niece just as long as is necessary to accomplish my ends. If you co-operate with me, she shall be returned safely. I want no interference with my work. Of course," he said, standing up, "I shall be permitted to leave this office without attracting any attention. If I should be followed, you can imagine the results. Or rather you can't imagine the results. For your niece would pay dearly and—shall I say?—on the installment plan."

With this final word of warning, Neihart left the office and the headquarters building.

FOSTER got up and paced the floor of his office. He was trembling like a man in the grip of the ague. Duty is a dear thing to a man who has worked his way up in the police force. But Foster loved his niece. His predicament was indeed a hopeless one.

As his pacing brought him back to the desk for the fifth time, his eyes dropped to the blotter where his unwelcome guest had scribbled. Foster's heart almost stopped beating. He bent low over the desk, and studied the penciled scrawl on the soft paper. It was more than idle scribbling; it was a message. He read it half aloud: "Things are not what they seem. Neither Neihart nor your horizon as black as they appear. Rest assured that I will exert every effort to return your niece to you, unharmed. And, incidentally, perhaps I'll send you the scalp of the Fury."

The note was signed by two pencil lines crossing to form the letter "X."

Commissioner Foster smiled for the first time in many dark and sleepless hours.

Had Agent X gone to the commissioner and asked outright the reason for his failure to permit police to go to the Bastion place he would have received no answer! He had known, as soon as he entered the office, that Foster was a badly frightened man. There was only one way for X to gain the information he wanted—by the indirect method.

And he had gained the information he had come after. Undoubtedly Doris Foster had been kidnaped by Paul Vost, probably directly following the séance at Madame Susu's. Her life was held as a check against police interference.

The next move that Agent X planned was against Dr. Arden. According to the information that Bates had given him, Dr. Arden had discovered a new anesthetic that induced artificial catalepsy. X was certain that something of the sort had been used in the coffin in which he had hidden himself. He was also inclined to believe that Arden's drug had something to do with the emaciated slaves of the Fury.

BEFORE entering the house of the doctor, however, X made brief alterations in his disguise while he sat in the car. He required no mirror for changing his toupee and reshaping his nose. Then from a dashboard locker which contained special accessories, he took a neat counterfeit of a police detective badge. If Dr. Arden were at home, this badge might gain X admission. If he were not at home, so much the better. X had ways of his own with which to enter forbidden places.

Thus equipped, X got out and went up steps to the door of Dr. Arden's old-fashioned, narrow house. His knock was unanswered. X was on the point of inserting one of his master keys into the lock when the door was jerked open by a man. X hastily palmed the key. He peered into the gloomy hall and recognized the stooped, scholarly figure of Dr. Cornelius Arden. At first, it looked as though the doctor had been dragged out of bed and was dressed in his pajamas, but as X's eyes became used to the gloom he saw that the doctor wore a white, acid-stained laboratory suit.

"Sorry to disturb you at this time of night, Dr. Arden. I am from police headquarters. If you've no objection, I'd like to look over your house."

"I certainly have objections," replied the doctor warmly. "Do you realize that it is nearly midnight?"

"All right." X allowed his voice to become flinty. "You want to be nasty about it, I got a search warrant here to show you." X took out a pocket case, opened it and flaunted an official looking paper under the doctor's nose. That it was not a search warrant made little difference in the dim light of the hall.

Dr. Arden coldly invited X to enter. X looked around the hall. For a man of means, Dr. Arden's home was not very pretentious. X nodded wisely at the papered walls and brassy chandelier. "You got a laboratory here, haven't you?" he asked.

Dr. Arden nodded slowly. "I am at present running a series of experiments of a rather delicate nature. I simply cannot allow anyone to enter—"

"Good!" X interrupted. "Let's go there now."

Dr. Arden paced dejectedly to a door at the rear of the hall. He was about to open it when he turned, made one last attempt to stall. "You haven't the slightest idea what you are doing!" he declared.

X shrugged. "Maybe not. Let's go."

The doctor's trembling fingers manipulated the lock. X pushed into a large, high-ceilinged room where glass tubes connected a huge retort, gas generators and condensers. All of the apparatus was familiar to Agent X.[18] But in the part he was playing he chose to act ignorant of the glass instruments and their bubbling contents. "What you got here?" he demanded.

"I am simply generating a gas," explained the doctor.

"Trying to put the public utilities out of business? Or maybe you're making an anesthetic."

The doctor's eyes blinked rapidly. "No—no," he denied hurriedly—too hurriedly. "It's just a gas that I am generating here and putting into solution—"

"I get you," cut in X. "In solution, it's easier to saturate the linings of coffins with it. Dr. Cornelius Arden Fury!"

DR. ARDEN'S shoulders seemed to droop the more. His eyes were downcast. His knees were folding slowly. His next move was totally unexpected and the Secret Agent was literally taken off his feet. From what appeared to be a fainting fit, Dr. Arden launched himself into a long, low spring. His head struck X like a battering-ram just below the belt. His arms whipped around X's knees.

X's head struck the floor. It was a spine-jarring, stupefying blow. X recovered in a moment, but there was time enough for the doctor to seize a weapon—a long glass tube cut diagonally to a point. The tube stabbed downward. X made an attempt to seize the doctor's wrist, missed and yanked his head to one side to escape being stabbed in the eye. The length of tubing passed down the side of his head and splintered against the floor. Glass particles rained across X's face. Glass needles pierced Arden's hand. Arden sprang to his feet, blood dripping from his fingers.

As X pulled to his knees, the doctor's muscles seemed to ex-

---

18 AUTHOR'S NOTE: *The Secret Agent is a student of all sciences. He has made intensive study of chemistry, physics and biology, especially those phases of science which pertain to crime and criminal investigation.*

plode in another of those battering-ram leaps that drove his body full weight against Agent X. Arden knew nothing of legitimate, hand-to-hand scuffling. There was no telling what sort of tactics he would apply next. His head struck X in the jaw, but at the same time the Agent's fist arced in a short hammering blow that landed on Arden's chest. Arden rolled to one side, the breath driven out of him. X reeled to his feet, his head fuzzy with the hammering he had taken.

At the moment, the rear door of the laboratory opened. Through mental haze, X saw Paul Vost, armed with a sawed-off shotgun. With him were two gaunt, hungry-lipped slaves of the Fury.

"Reach!" Vost commanded. "Keep 'em high."

X put his hands above his head, eyed the shotgun warily. It wasn't a weapon that a man rushed without considerable thought. If the charge of lead pellets found the Agent's chest, all well and good, for he wore a perfect bullet-proof vest. But if the gun were raised a little higher, its blast of shot might easily tear his face completely off.

"You all right?" Vost addressed the doctor.

Arden got to his feet, breathing heavily. He nodded, pointed at Agent X.

"Sure," Vost said, "he's wise." He nodded at the two emaciated criminals beside him. "Get started."

A look of insane glee brightened the normally dull eyes of the thin men. Their right hands became clutching claws. The veins of their bony arms swelled. They advanced slowly, approaching at an angle, the prospective point of convergence of which seemed to be Agent X.

The death-touch. To elude it meant a blast from Vost's shotgun. Surely possible death from the gun was preferable to standing there. X was weighing his chances, nerving himself for a spring at Vost—a leap that might well land him into eternity. Then a crisp, high-pitched voice cried: "Drop that gun! You're covered!"

Vost swung halfway around. His shotgun struck the floor, roared, tore plaster from the wall. Vost raised his hands.

Standing in the door of the laboratory was a slim, boyish figure—a very young man in evening clothes and a silk hat. His features were completely covered by a mask of black silk. His small, white hands clenched two heavy-caliber Colt automatics. One of the guns cracked. It was an untrained shot that kicked the gun nearly out of the young man's hand. With a howl of terror, the two mummy men plunged through the rear door. But the others stood like statues.

Silk Mask nodded his top-hatted head slightly at Arden. "Get the Bastion Ray, Fury. You have exactly two minutes to hand it over to me if you don't want to get shot."

"Who—who are you?" stammered Dr. Arden.

"I am Secret Agent X," said the Silk Mask haughtily.

CHAPTER VII

DRUG OF LIVING DEATH

IF THIS DECLARATION surprised Vost and Arden, it completely bewildered Agent X. A perfect maze of tangled thoughts struck his mind all at once. Arden had the ray—or did he? Arden was the Fury—or was he? Was it Silk Mask who had written the name "Secret Agent X" on Madame Susu's register and painted the Agent's trade-mark on the wall of Bastion's laboratory? If the Fury were executing crimes in the name of Agent X, then Silk Mask ought to be the Fury. Then why stick up Vost and shoot at his own slaves?

X was between three fires and he knew not which burned the brightest.

It was Dr. Arden who broke the silence occasioned by Silk Mask's startling announcement. His was an air of shocked surprise. Whether genuine or faked, X could not tell. "You don't mean that you think that *I* stole the Bastion Ray?"

Silk Mask nodded, though the gesture lacked assurance. X noticed, too, that the heavy, black guns in his hands were trembling slightly. Eyes in the mask glanced apprehensively about the room with its weird collection of instruments and its vessels of bubbling chemicals. But he did not see what X saw—Paul Vost's thin fingers closing on a metal ring-stand clamp.

A moment later, X realized the purpose of that piece of metal in Vost's hand. Vost moved with lightning rapidity, a faint, sneering smile on his lips. The ring-stand clamp flew across the room and smashed the big glass generator to atoms. Gas under pressure, the terrible drug that produced the sleep that was like death instantly spread across the room.

Only the Agent's presence of mind saved him. Breath held, he sprang toward the door, straight against the two automatics held in the hands of the young man in the black silk mask. One of the guns blasted. The heavy slug imbedded itself in the Agent's bullet-proof vest. The pain from the impact halted him only for a moment.

"Fool!" he cried between clenched teeth. "Hold your breath!" Then he bucked like a football player, knocked the young man through the door and leaped over the sprawled form. He swung around, slammed the door of the laboratory.

X dropped to his knees and peered through the keyhole to see what effect the gas had had upon Arden. But evidently the doctor had anticipated Vost's action and held his breath long enough to get clear of the room. The laboratory was empty and the rear door standing open.

X turned to the young man he had saved, the young man whose intervention at the critical moment had gone a long way toward helping X out of his predicament. The young man was sitting on the floor, head bent, chest heaving with sobs. Tears trickled down the surface of the silk mask he wore.

A smile flicked across the Agent's lips. He hooked his hands under the young man's arms and helped him to his feet. "Come now, Secret Agent X, don't cry," he said in a gentle, mocking voice.

The young man who was beginning to show very feminine weakness, stamped a small foot and cried: "Don't you call me Agent X. Don't you dare!" And with an angry jerk of white fingers, the silk mask came off to reveal the dangerously beautiful face of Vina Trumaine.

AGENT X took the woman's arm. In spite of the danger of the last few minutes, he could not suppress a chuckle. And the more he laughed, the more furious Vina Trumaine became. She struggled to get away, she kicked at his shins, she even drew one of her automatics and made an angry effort to blow out X's brains. Failing that, she apparently tried to commit suicide.

X, serious at once, disarmed her. She blinked back tears, turned a pout into a smile, and once more had control of herself. "Forgive me, please," she said huskily. "It's really my first offense as a hysterical woman."

"There's nothing to forgive," X told her. He guided her from the house and out to his car. She watched him remove his police badge and put it in his pocket.

"Am I under arrest?" she asked, as the motor roared.

X nodded. "In a way. Answer my questions truthfully, if that's possible, and we may get along together. Why the masquerade?"

Vina Trumaine shrugged as though the answer was obvious. "What chance would a woman have against those men?"

X said: "I don't know, but you managed pretty well. But why try to impersonate Agent X, of all people?"

"I shouldn't have," she said thoughtfully. "He's really inimitable. But I thought his name would lend greater weight to my threat. I really couldn't kill anyone."

"You tried very hard to kill me," X reminded her.

"I know. But I wouldn't have. I felt so very helpless when you had hold of me. Trying to shoot you was just a threat like pretending to be Secret Agent X. I am a great admirer of Agent X. I've tried to imitate him in my work."

"Even by signing his name to registers and painting his trademark on laboratory walls? That was to help create the confusion in which you stole the Bastion Ray."

"I didn't steal it!" she denied fiercely. Then more mildly: "How did you know about the 'X' mark on the wall?"

X smiled. "After all, I am a detective. What did you expect to do with the ray if you had kept it—for you did steal it right from under Bastion's nose, just as the lights went out."

"I—I wanted to destroy it," she told him. "Such a weapon has no right to exist. I am a militant pacifist. I wanted to destroy the ray because it makes war too easy."

Agent X had to admit that Vina Trumaine spoke convincingly and developed her alibi swiftly. A story that was good, but necessarily sheer fiction. Militant pacifists of the female variety didn't file their fingernails to the quick as a professional safe cracker would. The woman was a spy, perhaps, working for some European power. X knew there were hundreds of spies in the United States, attracted by the ingenuity of American inventors in creating new instruments of war.

Or perhaps she was a free-lance adventuress, wanting the ray to sell for her own personal profit. Still he could not tell her this without admitting that he was A.J. Martin. From such information she would quickly deduce that he was Agent X. It was possible that she already guessed his identity.

He could not deny that during that brief drive to her apartment she had used all her feminine wiles on him. He found himself alarmingly conscious of her intoxicating perfume and the alluring glances she turned upon him—glances that would have made another man giddy. Perhaps her only purpose was to try and gain his confidence so that she might profit from information he might drop while drugged by her lovely presence. Or again, it might be that by some strange quirk of emotion she was genuinely infatuated with him.

At any rate, he saw her to the door of her apartment. After he had unlocked the door for her, he coolly said good night and left her. But he was conscious of her green-eyed, burning glance that followed him all the way to the elevator.

X was not immune to the charms of Vina Trumaine. He would have never denied admiration for her beauty. But the chances of her winning his affection were slim. Two things prevented that: the love he bore for Betty Dale and which she returned, and the fact that X held his duty toward mankind above everything else.

In a very short while, X had reason to believe that doom would come for kindly, mild-eyed Donald Lowery. Though X had no idea what criminal scheme revolved in the Fury's brain, X intended to be with Lowery when the Fury struck. If possible, he even hoped to shift Lowery's danger to his shoulders.

CHAPTER VIII

MILLION DOLLAR CRIME

DONALD J. LOWERY was at home on his Long Island estate the following afternoon. He was expecting his doctor. Unfortunately Lowery's nervous condition was not to be alleviated by a visit from his family physician. The worthy doctor was at the moment quietly sleeping on the couch in his own office. Much to the alarm of his own patients who entered to consult him, the doctor could not be awakened. Such was the effect of a single shot from the Secret Agent's gas pistol.

X's operatives had learned of the doctor being called by Lowery. This gave X an unlooked-for opportunity of getting into Lowery's confidence. Shortly after noon, X had accosted Dr. Hykeman in his office, prescribed rest, and provided for it by giving him a shot of anesthetizing gas.

With a living model to work from, X had no trouble in molding his own features so that they were identical to those of Hykeman. All the doctor's mannerisms that X's keen mind could record in a few minutes with Hykeman were perfectly imitated by X as he entered the presence of Donald Lowery, some time later.

"I haven't the slightest idea what the trouble is, doctor," Lowery complained. "You know I have generally enjoyed perfect health."

"Now, now, don't trouble yourself about what's ailing you," X said, in the voice of Dr. Hykeman. "Your business is radio. Mind it. Let me find out your trouble." And as he looked Lowery over, X had not the slightest trouble in diagnosing the case. Lowery was overwrought, tired and worried.

After a brief examination, X said: "You work too much, worry too much. Why, I do not know. Surely a man in your financial condition, with everything in the world at your fingertips, has no right to worry. Just what's troubling you?"

"I—I can't say," Lowery whispered. "I—I don't know."

X opened a satchel that contained some of his own drugs, and took out a white powder. This he dissolved in a glass of water. "Just a little sedative," he told Lowery. But it was something more than that. It was a powerful opiate that would stimulate Lowery's imagination and weaken his will power. After the drug had had time to take effect, X took hold of Lowery's hand and gazed steadily into his eyes.

"Now, Lowery, you will tell me what is troubling you."

"I—I can't. I dare not!"

"Come, come. I am your doctor. You know that what you tell me will go no farther. Money troubles?"

"Yes," Lowery said sharply. "With the radio broadcasting business amounting to something like seventy-five million a year, I am none the less in hard straits."

"Because of the Fury?" X suggested gently.

"How did you know?" demanded Lowery, instantly on his guard.

"Relax," X whispered. "I have heard of the Fury. It was he who murdered Dot Dejong. Why?"

"It is death to tell! I don't want to die!"

"You're not going to. What has the Fury asked of you? Don't you see there's only one way out? You can't carry this burden alone."

"I'm not alone," replied Lowery. "Every broadcaster in this city is threatened." He paused a moment, took a long breath. Then he blurted it all out:

"The Fury is taking the broadcasting business. At first he threatened our star performers. Remember when Dick Coleman, the orchestra leader, was shot down? Scandal murder, the papers called it, because it occurred in a woman's apartment. But I knew better. The Fury told me that if I did not pay money for 'protection,' Coleman would not be able to fulfill his contract. After Coleman's death, I paid—sometimes as much as a thousand dollars a week.

"Others were threatened. Michial Norwich was a tenor under contract to the American Network. He disappeared. I know where he is. I was shown his body before it was thrown into the river. There was a brand, like the imprint of a human hand, across his chest. He died as Dot Dejong did, when I again refused to pay the radio 'tax' that had suddenly been raised. Now the Fury wants even more—fifty per cent of all the profits taken in by all the broadcasters of the city. If we do not pay, he threatens to strangle radio broadcasting."

"Is that possible?" X asked.

"Certainly. Think: tonight Uthskin Cosmetics is sponsoring a great new radio show over our network. If that program is successful, there will be a long-series contract signed. The show will be successful, undoubtedly, and on a thirteen week contract our profits should approach two hundred thousand. But the Fury has demanded a flat fifty thousand dollars to 'protect' the program tonight—more than the show is costing the sponsor. I can't afford to pay the Fury's demands. Nor can I afford to let this opportunity of netting a long-term contract slip by. I have raised thirty thousand dollars and paid that much to the Fury. But I can raise no more. And the Fury is still unrelenting."

"Rest assured," X told him, "there is no way your programs could be jammed by an interfering station. The Federal Radio Commission is too eager to catch some one trying to do that. Directional receivers could easily trace the origin of the interference. Besides, the Fury could hardly hope to jam all the stations in your network at once. He may, however, make an attempt to kill off the entire cast of this new show."

"You may be right. He made a good start. Dot Dejong was to sing on the Uthskin program. Fortunately, I found some one to take her place. But what am I to do?"

X RETURNED to his satchel, removed a hypodermic syringe, and a small vial. He loaded the syringe and approached Lowery. "I am going to see that you get some much-needed rest." He rolled up Lowery's sleeve and made the injection. The narcotic he used was harmless and would not conflict with the action of the opiate he had used before. A moment later, Lowery was unconscious. He would not awake for some time to come unless he received medical aid.

He carried Lowery to the bedroom and once again set about changing his features. This time, he took a great deal of care. He was going to impersonate Donald Lowery. He was not only going to attempt to deceive Lowery's associates, but also he must deceive Death when Death came stalking Lowery.

When he had completed his disguise, he left the bedroom and closed the door behind him. He returned to the library where he and Lowery had been talking. As he entered the room, his disguise was put to its first test, for Wilbur Kopsak was waiting for him, or rather for Lowery.

Kopsak's prominent jaw was outthrust belligerently. His short,

A hideous, emaciated hand reached out from the heavy drapes and snatched at Madame Susu.

black brows were crowded by a tight frown. He helped himself to one of Lowery's cigars and bit off the end angrily.

"Look here, Lowery, I couldn't help it," he began, shaking the cigar at X. "Couldn't help overhearing what you were telling the doctor. Your servant told me to wait in the room just outside. You mean to say there's actually some one trying to stop my program? This devil who calls himself the Fury?"

Evidently it was Kopsak's cosmetic firm that was sponsoring the new radio show. X nodded his head in answer to Kopsak's question. "I am afraid that what you overheard is all too true. I've paid all I can to try to buy him off. Time only will tell whether he is capable of carrying out his threat."

"But, Lowery—he can't do that. I've sunk ten thousand hard dollars into that single show. I'm expecting it to pull, and pull hard for my new firm. Why, I want at least twenty thousand return in new business from that single show. It's *got* to go on!"

"It will go on," X reassured him. "Whether it will go out through our transmitters I don't know. The wisest thing for you to do is to see some special insurance underwriter and have the air time insured if it means so much to you."

Kopsak was silent for a moment. X watched his big hands nervously peeling wrapper leaves from his unlighted cigar. Then Kopsak looked up. "Is it really that serious?"

"I am afraid it is."

"Then I'll take out insurance. I'll see about it this afternoon. Leeds and Son will take it up, I'm sure. They've insured weather for me when I owned a ball club. If you don't mind—"

Lowery's servant entered. "A lady to see you, sir. She would not give her name."

"What did she look like?" X asked.

"A foreign sort, sir. Yellow of deeply tanned skin. Attractive, I should say, but not exactly—" the servant coughed discreetly.

X smiled. "Not exactly my type. Nevertheless, show her in."

"Begging your pardon, sir, but are you quite well? Has the doctor left?"

X nodded. "Quite well, thank you. Dr. Hykeman has left."

The servant turned, and in another moment ushered Madame Susu into the room. The medium wore the same simple suit that X had seen on her in the undertaker's establishment. A dark veil dropped from the brim of her hat to halfway down her nose, concealing, to some extent, her exotic eyes.

X's pulse quickened. Perhaps now, the Fury would strike. Perhaps the mystic was the emissary of sudden death.

"Madame Susu!" exclaimed Kopsak. "The murderess! You're wanted by the police, my fine woman!"

MADAME SUSU dropped on her knee, brushed back her veil with one hand. She seized X's hand imploringly. Her dark eyes glistened with tears.

"Protect me. Oh, please don't let them take me! You owe me that, at least, for the risks I have taken for you. The Fury will kill me. He will have me die slowly, because of what I am going to tell you. But I must tell. I can go on no longer, hating myself for helping him. He compelled me to—frightened me into obeying his orders."

"Be careful," Kopsak warned. "The woman's a fox."

X shook his head slightly. If he had ever read sincerity in human eyes he read it now. "Go on, please, madame," he said quietly.

"Then you believe me! You will protect me. The Fury compelled me to allow him to use my séance chamber for his secret communications. I tried to warn you all that night something terrible would befall. I tried to warn you with the spirits. The Fury was there that night, though I know not who he is. He was there to watch one of his slaves kill poor little Miss Dejong. And he is not through. Listen, please!"

Madame Susu grasped the Agent's hand the tighter. "Your radio stations," she whispered earnestly, "are in danger. I do not know how he will do it, but I have heard him say that tomorrow night he will strike. You must pay money to stop the Fury. Much money."

She stood up. "There!" she was triumphant. "I have warned you. I have risked my life."

Agent X reached for the phone on Lowery's table. "You shall have your protection. I am very grateful for what you have done." He called the number of the Hobart Private Detective Agency.[19]

When Hobart answered the phone, X spoke to him not in the voice of A.J. Martin to which Hobart was accustomed, but in the voice of Lowery. He asked that two men be sent out immediately to escort a woman to her apartment and watch over her day and night.

"And now, Madame Susu," X said assuringly, "if you will just step into the hall and wait until these detectives arrive, I am sure you will have nothing to fear." He took the medium by the arm and led her into the hall. There he stopped. Madame Susu screamed.

On the floor at their feet was a man, just barely recognizable as Lowery's servant. His mouth and chin were a livid scar, like the imprint of a human hand, burned deep into the flesh.

"What the devil?" It was Kopsak who, alarmed by the woman's scream, had rushed to the door.

THE AGENT'S pulse hammered. His nerves grew taut. He thrust

---

19 AUTHOR'S NOTE: The Hobart Detective Agency is actually under the sponsorship of Agent X. Jim Hobart, its chief, is one of X's friends. Hobart, however, knows X only as A.J. Martin, newspaperman.

his hand into his pocket and gripped his gas pistol. "Back in the library, Kopsak. The Fury or some of his men are in this house. That man died from the death-touch!"

Kopsak rushed back into the library. X was on the point of forcing Madame Susu to follow, when a hideous, emaciated hand reached out from the heavy drapes that flanked the living room door, and snatched at Madame Susu.

X's movements were adroit. His left hand came up, slammed across Madame Susu's mouth and nose, jerked her back and at the same time prevented her from breathing. For the Agent's gas pistol was out, spitting its mist of sleep straight into the curtain. The curtain wavered, parted. The starved-looking killer fell forward on his face. Only a quick back-step prevented his deadly right hand from touching Agent X.

Kopsak could evidently withstand the suspense no longer. He yanked open the door, stuck out his head and demanded: "What's happened?" Then his mouth opened, remained so, silently shouting. His right hand pointed along the hall.

X's glance followed that pointing finger. Fifteen feet from him stood a tall figure clothed in a dark rain coat in spite of the fact that the afternoon was warm and fair. His face was the white of bleached bone—a mask of celluloid, the forehead of which was centered by the Fury's golden seal. Agent X wished that he had had time to reload his gas pistol. Or better still, he wished for an automatic. For if ever a man needed killing, it was the Fury.

The Fury threw back the folds of his rain coat and tilted up the muzzle of a machine gun he had concealed beneath. "Just in case you try some heroics, Lowery," he warned. "You, Madame Susu, have escaped me this time. But there will come a day when you won't be so fortunate. Lowery, this is your last warning. Unless you pay me what I have demanded I shall blot out everything in radio between the hours of eight and nine tonight. The Uthskin program shall not be broadcast unless you pay. When I speak again, it shall be with the voice of silence. Do you understand?"

The Fury backed slowly down the hall, uttering a peculiar, throaty signal as he did so. From the door at the end of the hall, another of the gaunt slaves appeared. The Fury pointed mutely at the slave's fallen companion, still unconscious because of the Agent's timely shot.

The second slave advanced boldly, lifted his fellow upon his shoulders, and moved back to join the Fury. Without another word, the Fury left the house. In another moment, X heard the roar of the criminal's car as he drove away.

And there was nothing that X could have done under the circumstances. He dared not risk Madame Susu and Kopsak by trying to rush the Fury as he might have done, even in spite of the menace of the criminal's machine gun.

In the deathly game they were playing, the Fury had won every hand. But X was making slow gains. At least he knew the Fury was out to tap the flow of millions that entered the coffers of the radio-network moguls. He was fighting a losing fight, to be sure, but he no longer fought in darkness.

CHAPTER IX

RADIO HI-JACKERS

AS SOON AS Kopsak had left, and Hobart's men had come for Madame Susu, X went to the satchel he had carried as Dr. Hykeman, and took out a compact, five-meter radio transceiver. He fixed the telescoping tube aerial in the top of the metal cabinet and immediately called the radio station which operated out of Harvey Bates's headquarters.

When he heard the answering call of the man on duty, he said: "Contact Bates at Bastion estate. Have him report at G.H.Q. at once. He is to report at the studio of Continental Broadcasters at six o'clock, there to await orders of Donald J. Lowery."

A like message, sent in the name of A.J. Martin, went out to Jim Hobart at the detective agency. Altogether, there would be twenty reliable men in the radio studio, surely enough to protect it against the Fury's attack.

X went to Lowery's bedroom, changed into one of Lowery's suits, which fitted perfectly, and obtained the radio magnate's keys. Then he left the house and locked the door behind him.

At six o'clock, he met Bates at the doors of the broadcasting building. He took Bates up to the tenth floor office of Lowery and wrote passes for Bates's and Hobart's men that would admit them to any part of the building. His forgery of Lowery's signature was perfect.

Two hours dragged slowly by. Nothing alarming occurred within the studio. A little before eight, Kopsak insisted upon accompanying X to the small listening booth off Studio D where the Uthskin show was to get under way. The booth was separated from the studio stage by a glass partition. Sound emanated from the studio through a loudspeaker in the wall.

Lowery's program staff had spared nothing to give the show variety. A symphony orchestra shared honors with a Harlem band. There was a popular comedian and a news commentator. A romantic tenor and a blues singer—imposing names and the best of talent.

There came the warning signal for silence. The orchestra director raised his baton. Continental's velvet-voiced announcer stepped to the microphone. Ten seconds after eight, the opening fanfare sounded. The announcer plugged the product and introduced the artists.

"Guess I didn't need the insurance policy after all," Kospak whispered. "The show is on the air and nothing has happened." Kopsak looked at X and smiled pridefully. "And it's a good show. I'd like to give a party for the cast on the roof garden afterwards."

X said nothing. The Fury had never given the slightest indication that he was a person who obtained what he wanted by sheer bluff. Yet it certainly seemed that this time the Fury had uttered threats he could not back up.

A tap on the door of the booth and X saw Harvey Bates through the glass. He got up and opened the door. "Anything wrong?" X asked.

Bates shook his head. "Not a thing. Perfect order, sir."

Kopsak rubbed his hands gleefully. "I knew it all the time. The Fury is a mere braggart."

"He was not bluffing the night he killed Dot Dejong," X reminded him.

"Come now, Lowery," Kopsak urged, "don't be a kill-joy. Sit down, won't you? I'm enjoying this immensely."

X sat down, but relaxation was impossible. He looked at his watch. Fifteen minutes had gone by. But this was an hour show and much could happen before it was over.

Two minutes later, the program director entered the booth without knocking. "I'm going to stop the show," he told them flatly.

KOPSAK sprang to his feet. He opened his mouth, couldn't say anything for a moment. "What the devil do you mean—stop the show? Why I'd just like to see you do it. Over my dead body you'll stop the show!"

The program director shrugged. "Just as you like. The artists may be amusing themselves and you are evidently enjoying it. But it's rather expensive entertainment for a handful of people."

"Do you mean it's not going on the air?" X demanded.

"That I can't say," the man replied. "I only know that no radios are picking up this or any other programs. We've received more calls than we can answer in the past five minutes from people wondering what has happened to the Uthskin program. Their radios are completely dead. As near as I can figure out, radio has been blotted out of the ether. It just doesn't exist. Completely strangled!"

X sprang through the door of the booth in spite of the fact that Kopsak clung to his coat tails. He ran the length of the hall and took an elevator to Lowery's office. He picked up the phone and called the office of Commissioner Foster.

"Foster," X began sharply as soon as the commissioner's secretary had turned over the phone to the commissioner, "this is the man who wrote on your blotter the other day. Do you understand?"

"Yes, of course. Any news?" asked Foster excitedly, thinking, of course, that X had some information concerning Doris Foster.

"Radio reception has been wiped out. The work of the Fury. What is the condition of the police radio system?"

"Oh," Foster murmured his disappointment. Then: "Nothing doing on the police bands either. No radio communication anywhere. There has been one airplane crash already because the signals don't seem to get through. Because of the crippled police radio, crime seems to be on the rampage."

But while Foster talked, X noted a persistent tapping on the line, as though the commissioner was rapping the transmitter with a pencil. In another moment he understood. Foster was tapping out Morse code.

X ceased hearing Foster's words. He listened only to the tapped-out message and rapidly decoded it: "X please come to the office at once. Help."

Obviously Foster feared to speak openly over the phone because of the danger of tapped wires. Had the Fury heard his appeal, Doris Foster's life would not be worth a penny. It was a desperate, pitiful attempt to contact the only man Foster believed capable of helping him. Or was it a trap? Perhaps the Fury stood beside Foster and tapped out the message in order to lure X into some hidden snare.

X would have to take that chance. He had never heard a cry for help and failed to heed.

BETTY DALE was enjoying one of her rare evenings of relaxation, driving her small roadster up Pelham way. She had passed through the park, was driving along the east side of the country club when the radio in her car was suddenly silenced.

The girl reporter had not been paying much attention to the program, for her mind was on Agent X, wondering where he was, what horrible danger he now faced. But the sudden silence of the radio brought her out of her dreams. The dial of the instrument was still lighted. Perhaps a tube had burned out. She switched off the instrument, thought nothing more about it until, looking due east across the Sound she saw a faint, purplish light flickering up against the sky. It was as if Northern lights had suddenly decided to wear only lavender and dance on the wrong horizon.

As she gained the top of a small acclivity along the shore road she noticed that the weird light seemed to come from Ghost Island, a small bit of land above Middle Reef. She had visited the island several times. It wasn't a particularly inviting spot. Two old sailors were ending their days there that their ears might never be far from the music of the sea. There, too, was an old deserted mansion that some millionaire who was medieval minded had built many years ago. The place was a veritable castle, part of which was crumbling into ruins. But the central tower of the old place was still standing, a hoary guardian over the bones of some of New York's early blue bloods who slept in the tiny private burial lot.

Betty had not the faintest notion what that purple light might be, and that was reason enough for her to investigate it. There might be, she thought, a very interesting newspaper story back of it all. She decided to charter a launch and go out to Ghost Island....

ACROSS the commissioner's desk, Agent X, once again the red-headed Neihart, faced Foster. The commissioner seemed to have aged years in hours. His eyes were dull lamps of discouragement.

"I have called you as a last resort, Agent—er, Mr. Neihart. I dare not send my men upon the mission I hope you will undertake.

"You know the reason." Foster fumbled in the drawer of his desk and produced a sheet of paper. "This should have been burned as soon as I received it." He passed the paper to Agent X.

Upon the paper was lettered in pencil:

My headquarters is on Ghost Island. Needless to say, it is not without good reason that I tell you this. I suggest that patrol boats take up the work of protecting me from curiosity seekers who might be attracted by certain phenomena which will occur. Of course, police must keep clear of the island or you will never see your niece again.

I have a network of high-voltage lines about the place, insuring certain death to anyone who makes an effort to investigate my sanctuary.

With a wish for the continued health of your niece, I am your eternal tormentor.

The Fury.

Agent X returned the paper to Foster. The commissioner eyed him eagerly. "You will do something?"

"My best," replied X simply. And without another word he left the office and returned to his car.

X drove furiously back to the broadcast studio, entered by means of one of his own passes, and hurried to find Bates. He beckoned the big man into one of the offices.

"Bates, we must get to a plane at once. We're flying out over the Sound tonight."

"You, sir!" Bates was open-mouthed with surprise at hearing his chief's voice coming from the lips of Neihart.

"We have a line on the Fury," X explained. "His headquarters are on Ghost Island. He has the island protected, but I intend to make a parachute landing. You'll fly the plane back and stand by for radio orders."

"But the radios are silenced," Bates objected.

"Not if I can get my hands on the Fury. I'm not coming back tonight without Doris Foster and the Fury. Come, let's get started." Together they left the studio to drive to the Agent's own airport.

BETTY DALE had visited Ghost Island before, but never at night. As the little launch which she had hired pushed through waters that were deceivingly placid, she saw Ghost Island in an entirely different aspect. Its rocky shore was fringed by wisps of rising mist from whence the island got its name. It was terrifyingly silent and the lights of a yacht steaming up the Sound seemed like things remote from the world of ghosts she was about to enter.

"Seems to me, miss," said the boat owner from his position at the little wheel, "that you got very strange tastes, though it's none of my affair, to go rambling round that place in the dark. I, for one, don't like the looks of that light. It's a tear-purple, that light is, a mourning sort of light. You don't hire me to set foot on that island tonight."

"You'll have to set foot on it to beach the boat," Betty told him. "And if you're afraid to come with me, I'll go alone."

The man shook his head. "It ain't that I'm afraid. Just a little nervous. Stomach is upset. Been eatin' too many oysters."

Betty could have laughed at his cowardice had it not been that she did not feel particularly courageous herself. She found it hard to face the dark of the wood that stood back from the narrow strip of beach. For a moment she hesitated, turned her head and said: "You—you'll wait for me, won't you?"

"Sure," said the boatman. "But I think you're plumb crazy, and don't forget I warned you."

Betty laughed, a mere pygmy of a sound mocking a giant of silence. She picked her way among rocks, found a rough pathway leading directly into the woods. Sharp stones underfoot were not meant for high-heeled pumps. Brambles caught at her skirt, seemingly to implore her to go no farther. But Betty had been endowed with courage. She plunged on through the woods.

At last her flashlight shone upon the gleaming cross-wires of a newly erected fence that stretched some twelve feet above the ground. Beyond, the flickering, purple light danced among the tree tops before it beamed upward to paint the sky.

Betty turned to the left and followed the fence closely until she came to a gate. The gate was open. She stepped through, knowing that she was not far from the ancient mansion. She had gone but fifty feet through the woods enclosed by the fence when somewhere in the distance a gong sounded once. Betty stopped, listened breathlessly to the dying of the bell note. She persuaded her legs to take her a little farther. Looking up through the trees, she saw the tall tower of the house. It was capped with a dome of glass or metal, and from the dome the purple light eddied upwards.

Suddenly, a cone of brilliant, blinding light cleaved the darkness. It was like a sword thrust to Betty. She turned sharply to the right and broke into a run, only to come to a quick stop. Her lips parted. She screamed. Directly in front of her, the darting beam of the searchlight flashed upon a hideous, yellow face with eyes so deeply sunken they seemed like holes burned in the brain beyond them.

Betty turned again, ran back through tearing brambles. Close behind her, bare feet pad-padded along in tireless strides. Something sure of its prey was pursuing her, wearing her down. And always that piercing searchlight from the tower pointing its accusing finger upon the frightened girl.

Ahead of her was the fence. She saw the gate, now closed. But perhaps it was not locked. She prayed that it wasn't locked.

Something sprang from the brush beneath her feet, sending her heart up into her mouth. Only a rabbit, probably little less frightened than she was. It bounded straight ahead of her as though leading her on. She saw the cottontail gain the fence, turn quickly to run down beside it.

Then there was a brilliant, blue-white fire leaping from the fence. A sputtering noise. The stench of burned hair hanging heavy in the air. Betty stopped, stared in terror at what she saw. The rabbit was dead, burned, electrocuted. It had run near the fence—the fence then was charged. There was no way out. And behind her—

She dared not think of the mummy-faced thing that pursued her. Giving the fence a wide berth, she ran on. She was breathing heavily. Weights seemed tied to her feet. A wire jacket seemed around her breast, a cage of steel against which her heart fluttered like a frightened bird.

The white light followed. The yellow slaves followed. And the distance to doom shortened.

She fell over something, picked herself up, her fingers digging into the mossy surface of a gravestone. Her breath came now only in sobs. She ventured a look over her shoulder. The gaunt forms, like the dead unearthed, came striding closer.

Suddenly, a tall tombstone begot arms. Another emaciated, kill-crazy being appeared from behind the gravestone. There was no time to turn. She struck out with a small, balled fist at the noxious face. A hand caught her wrist. She screamed. Other long arms lashed about her—bony arms, that looked as fragile as glass, yet had the strength of the hawser of an ocean liner. Hot, foul breath met her cheeks. She was thrown to the earth.

Then rope replaced those hideous arms, lashed round and round her like the coils of a boa. Her body was strained back against the tombstone. The bonds grew tighter and tighter until she no longer had the breath to scream, nor the will to struggle.

Then one by one, the thin, nightmare people vanished. The brilliant light went out. She was alone with the Silent Ones—those rotting old bones that lay buried in the earth beneath her.

CHAPTER X

TERROR ISLAND

IN THE HIGH, domed chamber on Ghost Island, the Fury watched, through eye slots in his white mask, the mounting purple light from the Bastion Ray tube. The tube centered a complicated hookup of electrical apparatus. Instruments required constant watching. The Fury paced from one meter to another, made adjustments in voltage and resistance.

An auto-call horn blared above the whir of generators and the thunderous crackle of spark gaps. The Fury shrugged disgustedly and crossed to the door. On opening the door, one of the yellow-skinned, emaciated slaves put in his appearance. For a moment, the sunken eyes were filled with a sort of animal fright at the sight of the flickering light that bathed the tower room.

"Speak, man!" the Fury whipped out.

A swallowing movement in the scrawny throat of the slave. "Ah—the girl. The golden-haired girl. She came through the gate. We have her tied to the stone near the entrance."

"I don't know what you are talking about," the Fury snapped. "How does it happen that anyone came through the gate? I have given explicit orders that the gate shall be closed and the switch set so as to charge the fence with electricity."

"So it is now, master," replied the slave humbly. "It was not I who failed. But no damage is done. We have the girl. What now?"

"I hold each man responsible for every error," the Fury chided. "I make no mistakes. Only slaves make mistakes. Next time, all shall be punished. As to the girl, leave her alone. I shall attend to her personally as soon as I am through. And—well, is she attractive?"

The slave's thin face twisted into a leer. He nodded his head eagerly. The Fury chuckled softly and closed the door of the laboratory.

In the old cemetery, Betty struggled fruitlessly against the ropes that bound her. She was exhausted. Terror's powerful stimulant raced her heart until she thought every beat must be the last. Finally she forced herself to relax. There was no use anticipating danger. So far, she was unharmed. Perhaps the boatman would become alarmed because of her long absence and would go for help.

A rustling sound seemed to come from the grass-and-weed covered grave beneath her. She looked down, thought shudderingly of snakes, wondered if snakes came out at night. But she saw nothing. The breeze perhaps—but there was no breeze. Only that fearful, rustling sound.

A full moon shed pale light through the branches of the old trees. She searched the ground about her as far as she could turn her head. The rustling sound continued.

She looked over her left shoulder, near the edge of the grave mound. There dry weeds stirred. There something squirmed. Tiny yellow snakes! No, fingers! Gruesome, corpselike fingers. Then a wrist and arm—mere bones covered with parchment. The terrified girl shrank back against the tombstone. Her mouth was open, but her throat too dry to scream.

The fingers were groping up through the grave, searching for her flesh. Dry, bony fingertips touched her bare arm. Skeleton fingers closed with the grip of steel.

Betty's head seemed to whirl. The earth became a hideous kaleidoscope where all was moonlight-silver and grave-mound green. And a thousand clutching hands, instead of one, grappled with her. Then, though she probably did not know it, she screamed—the agonized cry of a woman half mad with terror....

AGENT X, in the plane piloted by Bates, flew northeast. Fort Schuyler's light was far behind. In silken waters, City Island glittered like a jewel. The ferryboat to Hart Island looked like a tiny glowworm crawling through the darkness. They crossed the Blauzes. Somewhere below was treacherous Middle Reef and up from the black water came the purple ray of light, like an evil beacon.

"Ghost Island," X sang out into the telephone transmitter. "That purple light. Cut the motor and glide in. No use telling the Fury I'm on my way. I'll take the jump at about seven hundred feet. As soon as I'm clear, head back to the airport. Get to headquarters and stick by the radio."

The roar of the motor cut and there was only the banshee wail of wind playing on taut struts. X loosened his safety belt, stood up, began climbing over the edge of the cockpit. Just before the plane sprang into the flickering beam of purple light, he jumped. He rocketed down, down, down, tumbling over and over, to pull up with a jerk a scant hundred and fifty feet from the ground. The dead air let him drift almost straight down.

The chute cleared tree tops and settled in a small clearing. X ripped out his knife and began slashing at the cords that tangled about him. When he was almost free, he thought he detected the sound of footsteps behind him. He jerked his head around, snatched out his gas gun and at the same time felt the jab of a gun barrel between his shoulders.

"A machine gun, man. Don't take any chances," the voice of Paul Vost sneered.

A beam from a flashlight seared into X's brain. He dropped his gas pistol into the tangle of weeds at his feet. When his eyes became used to the light, he saw Vost and another man. It was Vost who held the machine gun.

X raised his hands slowly, allowing his knife to drop into his sleeve. Vost's companion came in close, severed the last of the parachute cords, and dragged X free. Then, while the Agent was under the watchful steel eye of the gun, the man emptied the Agent's pockets and loaded their contents into his own.

"Must be a peddler," the man joked, "with all this junk in his pockets."

"It doesn't matter a lot what he is now." Vost sneered. "It's what he'll be when the Fury gets through with him that he's got to worry about. Think he's a cop? The Foster girl gets it in the neck if he is."

"He's got no badge on. What'll we do with him?"

"It doesn't matter a lot what you do with me," X said, his voice cold and mocking. "It's what I'm going to do to you in a minute that you've got to worry about."

Vost sneered. "Yeah? Go on and start an argument. This Tommy can talk you out of damn' near everything!"

Out of the darkness, jabbed the shrill scream of a woman. A woman in pain or terror. Doris Foster, perhaps. And X had sworn that he would bring her back safely to the commissioner. The Agent's right hand swept downward. Centrifugal force shot the knife down his sleeve and across his palm. He caught it by the thin blade and threw it by the same motion. In daylight, the trick could not have succeeded. But Vost caught only the glimmer of the keen blade as it coursed the short distance from X's hand to Vost's shoulder.

Vost cried a curse. The knife was imbedded to the hilt in his shoulder. The machine gun clumped to the ground. X stooped quickly. His fingers darted out and recovered his gas pistol. Vost's companion landed full weight upon the Agent's back. A back-swing blow with the gas gun knocked the man off and X sprang toward Vost's machine gun. He seized the Tommy, lifted it, called out to Vost to halt.

But Vost was on the run and X dared not shoot for fear of alarming the Fury's entire crew.

A glance over his shoulder told him that the other man was fleeing in the opposite direction. The scream of the woman came again short and shrill. X plunged into the wood, following the direction of the cry. Branches whipped the machine gun from his hand, but he didn't stop to retrieve it.

Beyond the clump of trees, X saw another clearing where gray tombstones slanted from weed-grown graves. He saw, too, the frightened girl and the yellow arm reaching from the grave.

Where another man might have stopped to ponder the strange, unreal scene before him, X acted at once. He *had* to act, for he saw veins on the emaciated arm swell suddenly. X dove straight toward the grave, his hands outstretched to seize the yellow arm.

THAT yellow arm meant death, X knew. In its swollen veins flowed the poison, the mere touch of which would kill. X was not oblivious to his own danger. He knew that he might better be fighting with a rattlesnake. His one purpose at the moment was to save the girl.

The yellow fingers released their grip on the girl's arm, writhed and twisted in an effort to catch hold of the Agent. The strength in that withered arm was surprising. It required all X's strength to keep those yellow fingers from coming in contact with his own flesh.

Suddenly, strength went out of the yellow arm. For a split second, X relaxed his grip in an effort to gain a better hold. And in that moment, the arm darted free, darted back into an opening apparently in the crust of the earth.

X jerked out his gas pistol, turned its muzzle into the hole, and pulled the trigger. From the opening, came a dull, sobbing sound. Then the night again belonged to the silence.

"Oh, thank heaven!" sobbed the girl.

"Betty!" X exclaimed, for it was not until she spoke that he recognized her. "What are you doing here?"

She could not answer. Short, dry sobs prevented the utterance of words. Near the girl, X found her flashlight. His own had been taken when he had been searched. Aided by the light, he quickly loosened Betty's bonds. He raised her to her feet and held her one tender moment.

"Try to control yourself," he said gently. "Did you come here in a boat?"

Betty nodded. "But—but I can't go back. There's no way out. A fence charged with electricity surrounds this place. The gate was open when I came to investigate the purple light, but they—those horrible creatures—closed it."

X had no desire to leave the island until his work was completed, but he hated to have to risk Betty's life by taking her with him. He crouched by the grass-fringed opening in the grave and gingerly reached into it like a man exploring a serpent's nest. His groping fingers met something cold, hard and smooth, a sort of handle. He pulled up on it. A square of sod at his feet neatly camouflaged a trapdoor set in the earth. He beamed the light down the opening.

Behind X, Betty clutched his shoulder, shuddered.

"He can't hurt you now," X whispered. "Knocked out by the gas. But he is obstructing our passage." X went down three steps of a narrow, steep flight, hooked his hands beneath the arms of one of the Fury's emaciated slaves and moved the man to one side. Then he went back and helped Betty enter the narrow chimney holes that reached down between old graves.

X PAUSED to examine the right arm of the slave he had knocked out. It was covered by a long rubber glove that exactly matched the yellow color of the man's natural skin. The glove contained "veins" that were evidently rubber tubes extending to the wrist and entering the palm. The palm of the glove was pierced with many holes through the outer section of the rubber. Through these the killer's deadly acid passed when a large rubber bulb beneath the armpit was pressed.

"You see," explained to Betty, "the glove is the weapon. Because of its construction it looks almost as though these skinny devils had supernatural power. They have merely to touch their prospective victims with the palm of the glove, press on the bulb and the palm is flooded with that deadly stuff. The acid burns through the flesh and acts directly on the blood, producing death in a very few seconds. These devils don't mind killing. There's something wrong with their minds—enslaved some way by their master."

They went on. At the end of the flight of steps, they found themselves in what appeared to be an underground mausoleum. There were niches in the stone walls and in some of these crannies were coffins. New coffins that contrasted strangely with the inches of dust on the floor, and the mossy walls.

X went to one of the coffins and looked in. Inside was another of the slaves, to all appearances dead.

"But he isn't dead," X whispered in answer to Betty's question. "It's a cataleptic trance, induced by that new anesthetic that Dr. Arden makes. I had a taste of it. I believe that these slaves are down-and-outers that the Fury has picked up somewhere. He has given them anesthetic in some subtle manner. Then when he brings them from the period of catalepsy, he no doubt tells them that he has brought them back from the dead. Something that anyone who has tried the drug would readily believe.

"In that way, no doubt, he has gained their eternal fealty. By inducing the cataleptic trance frequently, the Fury is no doubt able to carry his slaves around conveniently in coffins, to be awakened when he needs them. That accounts for the Fury having a mortuary as one of his offices."

"But what makes them so thin?" Betty asked. "And why are their minds affected?"

"Undoubtedly, the habitual use of the cataleptic agent has something to do with their physical and mental condition."

"Then Dr. Arden—" the girl ventured.

"I can't say for certain," X said. "The Fury undoubtedly is a man of science."

"What about Moss?" the girl suggested.

"Hardly possible, for Moss was with me when I met the Fury for the first time. But we must hurry on. Doris Foster is here in this hell hole somewhere. She has been held a prisoner, her life as a pawn for Foster's protection of the Fury's activities."

Beyond Death's dormitory, where the Fury's slaves rested, was a narrow passage. Earth walls were held back by new lumber which attested the fact that the tunnel had been newly constructed.

"We're moving in the direction of the old house," Betty whispered.

X nodded. "No doubt this joins with the house somewhere."

The passage ended in a wooden door poorly fitted into a wall of stone. X swung back the door and they entered the basement of the old mansion. There was not a sound in the building, not even the squeak of a rat. Queer, that silence, and not especially conducive to peace of mind.

They climbed rickety steps. The Agent's left hand was behind him, clasping Betty's hand. At the top of the steps, a door yielded to a mere touch. They found themselves in a tall, old kitchen, long ago fallen into disuse. The tile floor beneath them uttered no telltale creak. Still that foreboding silence as though only the dead dwelled within the ancient stone walls.

THE NEXT ROOM showed some sign of habitation. A green-shaded light burned above a desk that was not particularly dusty. On the desk, beneath the lamp, was a leather-covered ledger. X and Betty approached on tiptoe.

"An account book," Betty whispered. "Look, it's something about radio. There's something about the Whisk-Away soap program."

X nodded. The entry read:

> $3,000 a week for nine weeks covering protection of Whisk-Away program. Obtained from American Broadcast Network.
>
> $27,000 Net.

As his eyes skated down a column of similar figures, X could not suppress a gasp of astonishment, so great were the profits which the Fury had realized by his extortion scheme.

"You see," he explained, "the Fury would threaten a broadcaster, demanded money. If the money weren't forthcoming, the star of the program that hadn't paid for protection would be murdered. That was the first scheme, before the Fury learned how to silence radio entirely. But if you think those are sizable sums, look at what he gained from tonight's work." X pointed to another entry:

> $50,000 demanded to protect Uthskin Series.
>
> $30,000 received from Continental Broadcasters
>
> less—$10,000
>
> $20,000 net
>
> $15,000 to be added which will make a total of $35,000 profit.

"You mean the Fury profited that much from silencing all radios tonight?" Betty asked incredulously.

"Virtually," X said quietly. "The queer part is that last entry—the $15,000 to be added."

"Could that be what Lowery charged for airing the show?" Betty asked.

"Lowery?" X asked sharply, as though he had not heard the name before. Then slowly he shook his head. "Betty," he whispered, "I think we've got it. I think we know who the Fury is. Only, it's utterly impossible because no man can be two places at once.

"But then again, it's right in front of us in black and white. That account book tells exactly who the Fury is, just as though he had signed his full name to it."

X turned from the telltale ledger to the drawers of the desk. If he only had a weapon of some sort. Searching the drawers might reveal a revolver. He opened the top drawer and stared into the startling, bone-white features of the Fury's mask.

At that moment, Betty screamed a sharp "Look out!"

Where another man might have turned around automatically to see what the danger was before acting, X thought for the merest fraction of a second. In front of him was the best weapon fate had dealt him—the white mask. He snatched it from the desk drawer and slipped it over his face before turning around.

Through the door of the Fury's office came a group of six emaciated slaves. And behind them was the Fury himself.

X and Betty were trapped. Had it not been that the girl was with him, X might have made some desperate attempt to lay hands on the Fury whose face was an evil gleam of white mask, identical to the mask that X wore.

There was only one possible way out. It depended entirely on quick thinking and psychological bluffing—an art in which Agent X was an adept. He must turn the slaves against their own master.

CHAPTER XI

WHERE MEN GO MAD

THE FURY SEEMED stunned into inactivity by this sudden meeting with his counterpart. As to the slaves, their dull faces took on a look of helpless bewilderment.

X knew that everything depended upon acting during that moment of surprise. With a movement of his left arm, he hastily thrust Betty Dale behind him and strode straight toward the slaves and their evil master.

"Masquerader!" he cried, pointing an accusing finger at the Fury.

The Fury gave the slave nearest him a push. "Get him!" he whispered. "Get the other man in the mask!"

The slaves surged forward in a body, stopped and looked from X to the Fury.

"Be careful," X warned. "I am your master. Do I not look like your master? You shall be punished if you disobey. Turn around and take the other masked man prisoner. It is he who is responsible for all your misfortune. You might live like other men, be like other men, instead of sleeping in the filthy holes he has assigned you. Turn on him. Be men! He is your destroyer."

"Get that man!" shouted the Fury. "Damn your empty heads! Get him!"

One of the slaves turned, snarled at the Fury. Then the Fury made his greatest mistake—he drew a gun. And X immediately took advantage of that mistake. "See," he cried, "he would shoot you. I do not threaten to kill you as he does."

The snarling slave sprang straight at the Fury's throat. The Fury shot. The man dropped back, wilted slowly to the floor. But that one shot was enough to send the other five slaves into a rage. They fell upon their chief, bore him to the floor. X strode as close as he dared and shouted: "Don't hurt him! Take him alive!"

But the snarling fiends had tasted battle and were not to be stopped. One of them wore one of those deadly rubber gloves on his right hand and arm. Too late X sprang to save the fallen criminal. That yellow, rubber-covered arm snaked out. Thin fingers locked around the Fury's throat.

There was a scream of agony from the Fury as the poisonous acid bit into his flesh.

"Kill, kill, kill!" screamed the slaves. One of them seized the Fury's gun, leaped over his fallen leader, ran through the door and shouted to the others to follow.

"Betty, come on!" X called as he followed the slaves through the door. He was thinking of Doris Foster, locked up somewhere in the house. The mad slaves were running amuck. He dared not think of what might happen if they found the commissioner's niece unprotected.

THE SLAVES raced down the hall and flung open a door. Beyond, X could hear their wild battle cry. He raced into the room, saw the five slaves standing in front of a steel-barred door. They shook the bars and snarled like animals. They reached scrawny arms through the openings, tried to clutch something.

X kept Betty behind him and approached the grating. In the room just beyond, X could see a man and three women cowering against the wall, just beyond the reach of the madmen.

"Back!" shouted X to the slaves. "Get back to your rooms!"

One of the slaves turned his snarling, skull-faced head toward X. He shook a lean fist. "Kill! Kill the other White-face. He will bleed, too. He is not a god, either!"

The slaves turned, to a man. Betty screamed, ran forward and threw her arms about Agent X as though to protect him. The Agent shook her off. "Back," he whispered. "We must show no fear." To the slaves he shouted: "Come on then. Try to kill me. The first to touch me dies a thousand deaths. Come kill, why don't you?" As he spoke he advanced step by step toward the mad band.

And step by step they retreated, their eyes flickering frightened glances at X. By sheer force of will and the compelling power of his voice, he forced them to back into another room, the door of which was made of steel like that of the neighboring cell. As soon as the slaves were inside, X slammed the door and twisted the key in the lock.

He took the key out and hurried back to where Betty waited in

front of the first barred door. Within the cell was Dr. Arden. A girl
of perhaps eighteen years of age was in his arms. X noticed the
marked resemblance between Arden and the girl. Very probably
she was Virginia Arden, the doctor's daughter. Doris Foster was
also in the cell and was all but hysterical. But Vina Trumaine, the
fourth prisoner, was perfectly self-possessed, aloof from the others, and quietly smoking a cigarette.

"The fortunes of war lead one into strange places, Mrs. Trumaine," X said with a smile. He fitted the key, which he had taken
from the lock of the other door, into the lock and opened the grating.

Vina Trumaine shrugged lightly. "The fortunes of war sometimes result in one meeting strange people. I have a vague notion
that we have met before."

"And may meet again." To Betty, X said: "Take care of Doris Foster."

Betty nodded, went over and put a comforting arm about the
commissioner's niece. "You'll soon be with your uncle, my dear.
The Fury is dead. Everything is over."

X went to Dr. Arden. The doctor's scholarly eyes squinted up at
him. "A—a policeman?" he asked timidly.

X shook his head. "No. But there is no reason for you to fear the
police. Very little explanation is necessary. I know that you tried to
purchase your daughter's life by aiding the Fury. He compelled you
to help him just as he compelled Commissioner Foster to protect
him. It was you who produced the catalepsy drug for the Fury to
use on his slaves."

"That damnable stuff!" Arden shouted. "I have cursed the day
I discovered it. The Fury used it on his slaves. It made them like
corpses so that when he revived them he could pose as their god. I
heard him telling them that he had restored them from dead bodies
and that they owed him their lives. Habitual use of my anesthetic
affects the mind. Men may not visit the dark halls of death too often and hope to retain their sanity."

"Enough, doctor," X said kindly. "I am sure there is small blame
on your shoulders for what you were compelled to do." He turned
to Betty and the others. "We will all go together. We must find the
switch that will break the electrical circuit running through the
fence. Then I will contact the police and have a boat sent out."

X HAD no idea where such a switch could be located. It was simply a case of trial and error. He went back down the hall and turned in at the first open door on his left. This led into an expensively furnished apartment, decorated in the modern manner. The floor was made up of black tiles alternated with squares of stainless steel. Furniture was all of chrome and leather. The walls were walnut, inlaid with ornaments of bronze. Beyond, through a curtained doorway, X could see a bedroom similarly furnished.

"It doesn't look as though there would be a switchboard in here," X told the others as he started to turn back.

A dull clanking sound. Doris Foster screamed shrilly. Dr. Arden's daughter renewed her terrified sobs. X turned around to see that a heavy iron grill had dropped from the top of the door frame, completely cutting off their escape. Beyond the grill, X saw an impossibility—the Fury alive.

The emotionless white mask, the heartless gleam of the slotted eyes, the tall, powerful frame—all were there. Yet there was no acid burn on the man's throat. X realized that here was an impossibility which made all of his deductions possible. The appearance of this second Fury revealed the whole clever criminal scheme.

On the other side of the grill, the Fury stamped his left foot angrily. "So, you would have escaped, would you?" he cried. "You *have* escaped. You've walked straight into hell."

No one moved. The Fury chuckled. "You will try to get out, eventually. They all do. This is the room where men go mad—or die. This is my own conception of hell. You notice the large amount of metal work in the room? Some of that metal is safe. Other pieces in walls, floors and furniture are heavily charged with electricity. There are even charged spots in the floor. Do you see?"

"I see, Fury," Vina Trumaine said calmly. "It's a game. Guess where the safety spot is."

The Fury laughed. "A woman with a sense of humor. Yes, this is a maze of death. There is no electric chair that could kill more quickly than certain articles in this room. Some of the most harmless looking are the most deadly. And I will be glad to be rid of you all. You—" he shot a glance at Agent X who had removed the white celluloid mask before releasing the prisoners—"I don't know you, but I can imagine that you are some sort of investigator. Perhaps you are the notorious Agent X. I'll know you better as a madman or a corpse. And Dr. Arden, I am through with you."

"But surely my daughter has a right to her life," the doctor pleaded.

"No, she and the reporter are too wise. As for Miss Foster, her weeping has annoyed me. I will still be able to bluff her uncle into protecting me. He need not know what has happened to her. As for you, Vina Trumaine, you know why I brought you here."

Vina Trumaine nodded coldly. "Because my persistent efforts to get the Bastion Ray were troublesome."

"Exactly. Too bad you wasted your efforts on something worthless. You would have learned, had you tried to sell the ray to some foreign government, that as a death ray it was a failure. Bastion knew that. His demonstration was faked. The box he apparently destroyed was fired by thermite. Bastion hoped that he could interest some one in backing his future experiments if he could prove the ray of value.

"Some time ago, I learned that the only value of the Bastion Ray was its ability to wipe out radio reception. Its rays are not unlike the rays of the sun when the sun is affected by what are commonly called sun spots. It was Bastion himself who told me that. Yet he had not the slightest idea how to make money out of his knowledge. It took a genius to figure that out."

"What do you intend to do with us?" Arden asked.

"Do with you?" The Fury emphasized his words with a stamp of his left foot. "You will either be electrocuted or go mad trying to guess where to put your foot or lay your hand *without* being electrocuted. This room was to be used in another extortion scheme I have yet to work out. For the moment, I shall use it as a punishment for meddlers. Torture by hope, you might call it. You hope the next thing you touch will not be charged. But then you never know until it is too late."

THE MAN in the white mask was gone. The Fury was still the master chess player. His chess board was the floor on which they stood and they were the playing pieces. The manner in which the prisoners stood, scarcely daring to breathe, made the simile more exact: they might as well have been carved from wood.

At last, Vina Trumaine drew a long breath. Her slow smile was for Agent X alone. "What have you to offer, Agent X?" she asked finally. "You are Agent X. No one else could have penetrated this fortress." She opened a mesh bag and took out a package of cigarettes. She lit one and threw the match to the floor. "Cigarette?" she asked the Agent.

"Please." And as she started to toss him the package, X added: "The whole bag if you please." Vina Trumaine tossed the metal mesh bag and he caught it deftly.

"You—you mean you see a way out of this?" asked Dr. Arden.

"P-please get us out," Doris Foster whispered.

"Keep talking sane things," X urged. "And don't move. Miss Arden!"

The doctor's daughter raised tearful eyes. "Yes?" timidly.

"You are inclined to move your right foot too much. Watch that," X warned. "There is absolutely no danger if you don't move."

"But good heavens—" gasped Arden.

"Doctor!" X said sharply. "Get a grip on yourself. Your nerves are farther gone than those of the women and I assure you that your daughter and Miss Dale and Miss Foster have been through more trying times than you. I am going to try an experiment. If it works, we walk out of here in perfect safety."

X flattened Vina Trumaine's metal hand bag after he had removed the cigarettes. Then he stooped without moving his feet and sent the bag sliding across the smooth floor. Nothing happened.

"Well?" asked Dr. Arden impatiently.

"What's the experiment?" asked Betty Dale.

X mustered a cheerful smile. "That was the one that didn't work. Lots of experiments don't. I was trying to touch two charged spots on the floor at once with the metal bag. I hoped to produce a short circuit that would put the whole electrical system on the blink. Have to think of something else."

"We—we'll have to start guessing soon," Virginia Arden whispered. "The guessing game with Death."

"Stop that!" X snapped. "Miss Arden, where do you go to school?"

"Why, City College—"

"Talk about that," X urged. "What studies do you enjoy most? Doris Foster, that fine man who is your uncle is planning to show you the sights of the city as soon as you get back. How long do you expect to stay in New York?"

"I—I don't want to stay at all," the girl whimpered. "I want to go back to Kansas."

X laughed. "Oh, you've got to see a Harlem hot spot before you go back."

"Don't talk drivel!" Dr. Arden shrilled. "I can't stand this. I can't stand anything. I've got to move!"

"Doctor!" X cautioned.

"You fool!" shouted Arden. "Do you think I can stand here until I'm paralyzed? I—I—" And with a harsh, mad laugh, he lurched across the room. Only Betty's quick action prevented his daughter from following. Betty reached out, caught the girl by the arm, held on. Her teeth were grinding and there was a deadly, determined light in her blue eyes.

ARDEN staggered across the room, threw himself against the steel grating. For a moment, his writhing features were illuminated by sizzling, crackling blue flame. His body was a gyrating, squirming mass of muscles seeming to pull one against the other in a fruitless revolt against the charge of current coursing through his body.

The doctor's daughter uttered a pitiful, hurt cry, and sagged against Betty. Doris Foster's knees gave way and let her drop into a chair. She sat there, white-faced and tense, utterly unable to move even so much as an eyelid. Back from the grating where his death dance had carried him, the body of Dr. Arden lay on the floor.

"Betty," X whispered, "can you hold the girl a little longer? I think I see a way out."

Betty nodded grimly. "I'll do my best." It was easy to see that holding the Arden girl taxed all her strength.

"Don't move, anybody. Doris Foster, don't even so much as touch the arms of your chair. Understand?"

"I won't," the commissioner's niece replied. "I don't want to die like that."

Vina Trumaine lifted her lovely head proudly. She smiled slightly and extended one slim foot in front of the other.

"Vina!" cried the Agent. "Stand still!"

Vina Trumaine took another step. Her smile seemed painted on her deathly white face. Then she reached out her hands and took hold of the shoulders of Dr. Arden's daughter. "I'll help you, Betty," she said quietly.

Agent X said nothing. In his mind revolved a strange pattern of black and white tiles. He saw the crooked footsteps of a man running headlong into hell against that checker board pattern. Could he do it? Could he cross the floor exactly as Dr. Arden had done? Could he touch only the exact spots that Arden had touched? The grating was charged. All other things that Arden had touched were not charged.

But first he had to get to the exact spot where Arden had stood before he made his wild dash. That spot was about a foot from the chair where Doris Foster now sat—fully six feet from X. X bent his knees and suddenly sprang. His standing broad-jump was so perfectly timed and executed that he landed both feet on the spot where Arden had stood. For a moment, it seemed that he would lose his balance. He waved his arms like a wire walker executing a dangerous feat.

"Please don't try it," Betty wailed.

X LOOKED into her eyes, saw the tears that glittered there. He looked hastily back to the floor, lest emotion crowd that pattern of tiles that indicated Dr. Arden's path from his memory. He took another step.

In the room where men went mad there was utter silence. There was not a face but what was beaded with sweat as all eyes watched the Agent's thoughtful, sure-footed progress toward the charged grating.

"What in heaven's name do you expect to do?" Vina Trumaine gasped. "You can't unlock the door."

"Hush!" X whispered. He took a wide swing to the right—a step that took him off the straight course to the door. But it was a step that Dr. Arden had taken and he dared not risk the short cut. His brain was on fire. He had to drive back the impulse to make a dash for the door, regardless of the path Arden had taken. Some devil of encroaching insanity within his brain whispered: "Take a chance. You *may* win. Plunge right into it. It's so much quicker and less torturing."

But doggedly X continued his labored progress and eventually arrived unharmed within a foot of the steel grating. Then he stood upright and took a long breath. "Courage," he whispered. "In a minute this grating will be open. The Fury will open it for us."

He *hoped* the Fury would open it. His entire scheme was based upon the assumption that the Fury Number Two had not seen the body of his partner, the dead Fury. For there were two chiefs in the crime. There had to be, simply because no one man could be in two places at the same time. X knew as well as he knew his own name the identity of the white-masked man killed by the slaves. Yet there was another Fury still alive— the one that had trapped them in this room of madness and sudden death.

X knew the identity of this living Fury, too. Both of the villains were men of about the same build. Wearing the white masks, both must have looked very much alike. But there was a slight difference in their voices and mannerisms that a keen mind like that of Agent X was bound to notice.

X reached under his coat and produced the white mask he had found in the Fury's office. He slipped it over his face. Now, if Fury Number Two didn't know that his partner was dead, the scheme might work, for X could imitate any voice and he was about the same height as the two criminal leaders.

X cupped his hands over the mouth opening in the mask. "Help!" he called. "Help. Come let me out of here. What in hell is the matter with you?" The voice that came from the mask was the voice of the Fury—the dead Fury.

"Uncanny," whispered Vina Trumaine.

A moment later, they heard footsteps on the stairs. Then footsteps moved across a floor. The white face of the living Fury matured from the gloom of the hall. The man stopped, stared at X. Was there a gleam of suspicion in his eyes?

X shook his fist at the Fury. "What do you mean by locking me in this room and turning the current on?"

"How did you get in there?" the Fury asked coolly.

"Get in here? Why I was in here all the time. I was back in the bedroom dozing. Let me tell you, had I not known every danger spot in this apartment you might have killed me."

If the Fury had the least suspicion, X's last statement should have dispelled it. It was for that purpose that X had chanced following Dr. Arden's footsteps. Such a move must convince the Fury that X was familiar with all the danger spots in the room.

"Will you let me out?" X cried. "This place gives me the chills."

Without a word, the Fury stepped to the side of the door. He returned a moment later, took out keys, and unlocked the grating. "Come out," he said quietly. "Next time, be more careful where you take your naps."

X knew now how a man approaching the electric chair felt. The Fury had made no move to open the grating. Perhaps the lock was insulated from the other metal. Perhaps the current still moved through the metal door. The Fury might have fathomed X's scheme and was using this way to trap him.

But a moment's hesitation would have excited suspicion. X reached out boldly, seized one of the horizontal bars, and lifted the grating back into its slot.

"Thank heaven!" came an audible whisper from some one in the room. The Fury's head jerked sideways as X passed through the door. X turned, too. Relief was so clearly indicated on the faces of the four women in the torture room that the Agent's ruse must have been apparent.

THE FURY'S icy gaze turned on X. "Take off that mask," he said softly, emphasizing his words with an impatient tap of his left foot.

"Why should I?" X asked.

The Fury kicked out with his left foot, touched a catch at the side of the door. The steel grating once more dropped over the doorway. "Take off that mask," the Fury repeated. "I must see your features."

X lifted his hands to the white mask. "May I suggest that you take off your mask, too. I know very well who you are." X slipped off his mask and dropped it to the floor, revealing the hawk-beak nose and red hair that were parts of his disguise as Neihart.

"Tricked," said the Fury softly. "Tricked? Not yet, quite." He whipped a small automatic from his pocket and centered it on the Agent's chest. "Raise your hands," he commanded.

X put up his hands. The Fury was backing slowly away from him. In the chill eyes within the slots of the mask, there was no indication of what he planned to do. "My compliments. You have played the game well. Not quite, I am happy to state, well enough." And all the time he talked, he moved backward.

Then X fathomed the Fury's plan. At the right-hand side of the door, a small switch board was revealed by a sliding panel. One switch was open—undoubtedly the switch controlling the current in the torture room. All within the room had moved. The four women stood in a group near the steel grating. For all X knew, Betty might be standing at that moment on a deadly spot that would shoot a charge of electricity through her body as soon as the switch was pressed.

X took a step forward. The Fury cried: "Stand where you are." X took another step, but the Fury backed at the same time. "One more step, Agent X, and I will shoot," he warned.

Instead of one step, X took two strides and a leap. The Fury fired twice. The slugs from the automatic thudded into the Agent's bullet-proof vest. But at such close range, the double impact brought him to his knees. He was certain, at that moment of agony, that the Fury's eyes were smiling. The Fury's hand shot to the switch lever, but stopped an inch away. X's fingers were locked on the Fury's coat sleeve at the biceps. All the weight of his tortured body hung on that arm.

The Fury's gun barked again, the muzzle but inches from the Agent's chest. In the torture room, Betty screamed. Vina Trumaine cried: "Soulless beast!"

The Agent's teeth ground together. He clung doggedly to that sleeve in spite of pain that felt as though his lungs were being torn out of his chest.

"Iron guts, eh?" the Fury said between clenched teeth. And the muzzle of his gun bobbed up, centered on X's forehead.

It was move now or never. X goaded fagged muscles into action. His right hand came up, seized the Fury's gun wrist, and deflected the gun barrel. At the same time sheer will brought him to his feet. He lurched forward unexpectedly, his head bent low. His head struck the Fury in the midsection, toppled him off balance. The Fury made one more effort to reach the switch as he went over backwards. His fingernails must have broken off against the switch handle, but the copper throws never reached their contacts.

FLAT on his back on the ground, the Fury fought. His legs worked like pistons, kicking at X in an effort to prevent the Agent from gaining an advantage. X gouged up with his thumb, caught the Fury in a particularly sensitive nerve center behind the right knee. The Fury's right leg went limp. X threw himself forward, completely smothering the Fury's body beneath his own. He seized the killer's gun wrist, forced it back. Then he risked a single blow with his left fist that had all the strength of his fagging muscles behind it. The blow landed, directly on the chin of the Fury's celluloid mask.

A long, sobbing sigh passed the Fury's lips. He lay perfectly still. For at least thirty seconds, X lay across the unconscious form of his enemy, breathing heavily. Then he sat up, turned his head, smiled at Betty.

A quick search of the Fury's pockets revealed the key to the grating. In another moment, he had the four women out of the torture room. Then he went to the switch board. One of the switches was marked: "Fence circuit." X opened it. They were free to leave the island where terror reigned no more.

X went over to the unconscious Fury and removed the white celluloid mask. Beneath, the handsome features of Alan Moss were slightly marred by a blackening lump on his jaw where X's blow had landed.

"Moss!" exclaimed Betty as the Agent lifted the unconscious man in his arms. "But you said that you saw the Fury when you were with Moss in Bastion's yard."

X nodded. "The clever part of their deception. There were two men known as the Fury—two partners in crime. To divert suspicion from themselves, they each took their turns appearing before us as the Fury. Moss, of course, held up the scientific end of their standard of crime and terror. It was he who rigged up the Bastion ray after he had stolen it from Vina Trumaine who took it from Bastion's laboratory that night." X looked at the adventuress. She made no effort to deny the accusation.

"I guessed this second Fury was Moss when I saw that he was left-handed—or rather left-footed. As you know a left-handed person is always left-footed, too. It was Moss who developed the powerful acid weapon which the Fury's slaves used."

X carried Alan Moss into the torture room. He placed the killer in the chair that Doris Foster had occupied. Then he went out, closed the grating, and turned on the current. X could think of no better prison for Moss than the hell of his own designing.

"That should keep him out of mischief until the police arrive," he told the women. His next job was to contact the police. A few minutes in the Fury's tower room and he was talking with Bates, by means of the Fury's own radio. The Fury had turned off the radio silencing beam as soon as he had fulfilled his promise of silencing radio between the hours of eight and nine. Bates would get in touch with the police through Timothy Scallot.

While they awaited the coming of the police boat, Betty asked: "But the other Fury—the dead one. Who was he? You said you knew."

X smiled. "Did you guess. Remember the ledger we looked into? Remember the entry concerning the profits made from threatening the Uthskin Cosmetic program? An extortion fee of fifty thousand dollars had been asked. Lowery had been able to pay only thirty thousand. You would naturally suppose the two villains netted thirty thousand from the deal. But there was an added factor—a cost of ten thousand to be subtracted, which was difficult to interpret until you saw that there was another sum to be added to the total—an amount to be added in the future."

"I remember," Betty said. "Fifteen thousand was to be added to that."

X NODDED. "Fifteen thousand yet to be collected—not from Lowery, surely. Only one man could have collected that fifteen thousand from a program that had not gone on the air. That was the man who had insured the air time. Insured it, evidently, for fifteen thousand dollars to be paid to him if the program didn't go on the air. Kopsak counted his money before he collected it. Kopsak had the air time insured at my suggestion. He later told me he had taken out the policy."

"You mean," Vina Trumaine interrupted, "that Kopsak and Moss tried to extort money by threatening to silence the program that Kopsak was paying for?"

X smiled. "And there you will see is the reason for the ten thousand dollars cost entered on the deal. That was the amount Kopsak paid Lowery for the first program of a prospective series. The series, incidentally, would have been canceled right after the first program, even though Lowery had paid the full fifty thousand dollars asked for. I am certain that Kopsak's cosmetic concern was a mere blind. He didn't need the cosmetic plant. He and his partner were already tapping a large portion of radio broadcasting's seventy-five million a year business."

Out across the Sound came the scream of a siren on a police launch. Vina Trumaine drew a long breath. Her green eyes met those of Agent X.

X smiled slightly. "What will you do now?"

"I was about to ask what you would do with me."

X shook his head. "I don't arrest people. I've nothing against you. As a matter of fact, I think you saved my life that night in Arden's laboratory. You have played a dangerous game. I suppose you always will."

"A dangerous game," the woman whispered. "And this time I have been badly beaten. And in so many ways." She extended her hand to the Agent, stooped quickly, and kissed Betty's forehead. "But no one," she added as she went through the door, "can say I am a poor loser."

Doris Foster was seated on a couch, comforting the sobbing daughter of Dr. Arden. She looked up as X started to leave the house. "You're not going?" she asked quickly. X nodded. "But," Doris insisted, "you can't. Uncle must know how wonderful you've been."

X smiled, patted Doris Foster's head. "I am very much afraid Commissioner Foster knows too much about me already." He looked at Betty, and left the room. He would, no doubt, return to New York on the police boat, impersonating one of Inspector Burks's best men.

BOOK XXIX

CITY OF MADNESS

Secret Agent X knew that the destiny of millions of
honest people rested in his judgment of a beautiful
but crafty woman. And all the Agent's plans fell
to pieces when his most important confederate,
Harvey Bates, rebelled against orders. For
Bates insisted that Charlotte, the glamorous and
powerful spy of old, was incapable of any evil.

CHAPTER I

STAGGERING DEATH

THE BROWN DIRT road writhed and squirmed around hills, down hills and up hills. The man in the open roadster crowded his body against the wheel, leaned forward like a trained jockey urging his horse toward the finish line. The flaring headlights now and then shot out across some dark, abysmal ravine as the car swung around hairpin curves and missed eternity by the merest measurable fraction of an inch.

This was a short cut to Brownsboro. And John Morris of the United States Secret Service was tempting the Grim Reaper with every lurch of the hurtling car.

John Morris's gray temples were shaved close; his ears flat against his head. His thin nose flared surprisingly at the nostrils, giving him an appearance of alertness that his ever darting, hazel-colored eyes did not belie. He was sensitive to danger that threatened the country he so loyally served. He knew to a certainty that no country in the world held so many foreign spies as the United States. And no one knew better than he that such men were a dangerous menace.

People had called John Morris a crank and a crape hanger. "Spies? Well, what if there were a few spies in the United States? Aren't we at peace with the world?" Such was the usual reply, even from government officials, when John Morris uttered his warnings. Yet Morris knew that one by one the nation's newest and best defensive weapons were being stolen. Who knew but what some day they might be turned against the very men who had developed them.

It was not until Washington had received an urgent message from Lorin Garvey, formerly of the Chemical Warfare Corps of the United States Army, that officials began to take John Morris seriously. That message had been short, giving scant information but leaving no room for even the most ardent optimist to doubt that trouble's cauldron boiled and bubbled in the hills of Pennsylvania. John Morris had seen it and he had nodded his head as he read:

> My safety be damned, but as you love the safely of all America, send some one to help me guard my secret.
>
> (signed) Lorin Garvey.

Morris knew what the officials had said: "John Morris is the man to send. He's a little cracked on the subject, but he's a man of action and has had wide experience in the Secret Service."

Cracked, was he! John Morris's jaw shot out as he angrily yanked the car that seemed a part of him around a curve and let it plunge recklessly down a hill with the clutch out. The car thundered over the loose planks of a bridge and started on the upgrade. When it had gained the top of a little acclivity, Morris could see the ragged horizon tinged with a gleam of lights from Brownsboro.

Only a few more miles. He jammed the accelerator to the floorboards only to slow down a moment later and listen to a strange sound, entirely foreign to the sweet song of his perfectly tuned motor.

It was a knock of metal against metal, almost as noisy as a broken connecting-rod. But it came from the rear of the car. A flat tire, broken spring leaf or a riddled gear in the differential couldn't have possibly been the cause of the noise, for when Morris gave the motor the gun the wheels responded immediately and the car remained on an even keel.

Morris threw the car out of gear, set the hand brake and sprang to the road. He hurried around to the car's sleek rear deck and immediately knew the origin of the persistent knocking that continued even after the car stopped. The sound came from the closed rumble seat compartment.

Morris got up on the step plate. His right hand dropped into his coat pocket, clamped on his automatic. His left hand grasped the handle of the compartment opening. He gave the handle a sudden twist and jerked up on the panel. He stepped down quickly and drew his gun. A shadowy form emerged slowly from the rumble seat. A whimsical voice said:

"Hello, John."

"A stowaway, eh?" Morris barked. "Get out."

"With considerable pleasure. It was getting stuffy in there, John, not to mention cramped. And besides, it's time I took over the driving anyway."

A strange sensation stole upon John Morris. Not at all a pleasant sensation. This was something like a nightmare. It was more than hearing a voice come from the rumble seat of his own roadster. Had it been a strange voice, it would not have been half as alarming. But it was a voice thoroughly familiar to John Morris. It might have been an echo of his own voice. No, more than that. It *was* his own voice.

THE STOWAWAY threw long legs over the rear fender and slid down the polished surface of the car to the ground. With magnificent unconcern for John Morris's gun, he proceeded to dust off his clothes, stretch out wrinkles and straighten his tie. Then he reached into his pocket, produced a package of cigarettes, and began peeling off the cellophane.

"Don't do that," said Morris.

"Don't do what?" the echo came back mockingly. "You didn't expect me to smoke in that stuffy hole, did you? I've been on board ever since you stopped at that filling station. You're not an easy man to follow, John. No—no—" as Morris reached toward the door of the car—"don't bother about a flashlight. I'll show my face in just a moment. Will you have a cigarette?"

"No thank you," said Morris levelly.

"Very well." A cigarette lighter flicked into flame.

John Morris took a staggering, backward step, stopped, let his jaw hang. It was almost as if by some magic a mirror had been conjured up out of the darkness. Not only did the stowaway have a voice exactly like John Morris, but his features were identical. And the glint of this stranger's eyes showed that he was getting considerable delight from Morris's obvious discomposure.

The secret service man's eyes narrowed. Something of the fires of hate burned in their depths. He leaned forward, his gun tilting slightly toward the face of his twin. "I know you," he whispered. "Know you in spite of that diabolic craft of yours. I met you once during the Great War when you established an enviable reputation for yourself. And I have heard what became of that reputation and how you deliberately perverted it. Money, wasn't it? You couldn't use your skill to make a living honestly. The very nation you risked your life for, during the war, you betrayed by becoming one of her worst citizens.

"Clever? I'll say you're clever! The only mistake you've ever made is following me. You haven't a chance now. You know there's not a better shot in the country than John Morris. Anyway, a child couldn't miss at this distance."

"Going to kill me, John?" asked the other calmly. "It's bad enough to be terribly misjudged by as worthy a man as you without being murdered in these dark hills."

"I'll kill you if you make a false move. Get back in that rumble seat. I've a key to that compartment and the lock doesn't extend through to the other side. You'll have to blast your way out if you escape, Mr. Secret Agent X!"

THE MAN who was the living image of John Morris raised his eyebrows. "Glad you reminded me of the key, John. I'll make sure to use it."

"Get back in that rumble seat, damn you!"

The Man of a Thousand Faces, known the world over as Secret Agent X, shook his head. "Sorry to do this, John. I was in hopes that we could work together amicably in this. But if you will have it this way—"

A sharp, hissing sound came without warning from the cigarette lighter in Secret Agent X's hand. While the Agent had been talking with Morris, his fingers had managed to press a secret button in the side of the lighter, releasing a small charge of anesthetizing vapor contained in a cartridge in the lighter. This anesthetizing vapor, while harmless, was extremely powerful. As the thin veil of gray vapor curled up around Morris's face, the secret service operative gave a short, coughing sound and crumpled forward into the arms of Secret Agent X.[20]

---

20   AUTHOR'S NOTE: As has been frequently stated, much of X's experience as a hunt-

X sighed a little sadly as he lifted the unconscious man into the rumble seat compartment. He seemed destined always to go his way alone. Few understood his unorthodox methods of crime detection. Even the police of the nation's big cities whom he had secretly aided for years, ranked him high on the list of public enemies. Yet he could not change his methods now. Let the regular city, state and national lawmen handle the usual crimes in the manner provided for by the law.

But Agent X preferred the thousands of risks his impersonations brought him, the life of high adventure when the balance of life and death was turned one way or another by some clever deception or some swift stroke of action.

No sooner had X dropped the panel of the compartment than he was under the wheel, driving as Morris would have driven. He looked like Morris, he acted like Morris, and for a brief span of his dynamic life he would actually be Morris. No actor on the stage ever lived his parts more realistically than did Agent X.

Oddly enough, the same assignment that had sent John Morris to Brownsboro also accounted for X's movements. Like Morris's, the Agent's orders had come from Washington, from the office of that mysterious official who preferred to be known only as K9—the Secret Agent's only official sponsor.

It was because of spies that might be surrounding Lorin Garvey that X had been summoned. But beneath the surface of the promised adventure, Agent X scented something that was far bigger and far more insidious than an ordinary spy plot to obtain secret formulas from the brilliant scientist, Lorin Garvey.

Harvey Bates, key man of X's own organization, had gone ahead to make preparation for his chief's arrival. And Bates's habitually terse reports had indicated that something more deadly than a poisonous serpent was being nurtured in the Pennsylvania hills.

Suddenly Agent X pressed firmly on the brake pedal. The roar of the motor dropped to a scarcely audible murmur. Head slightly on one side, the Agent listened intently to a sound that seemed to come from the thick woods that hedged the road. It was a high-

---

er of men and an unraveler of mysteries, has come from his service as a young Intelligence officer in the World War. There his uncanny ability for disguise and impersonation was a source of constant wonder to all his comrades. Neither Morris, nor X's other companions ever got a glimpse of the Secret Agent's real face. None knew his real name. It is little wonder, then, with all this mystery surrounding X, that Morris was ready to believe the rumors that unjustly claimed Secret Agent X to be an unscrupulous criminal.

pitched wail, with something of the animal quality about it and something that was like the cry of a human being in mortal agony. Such a shriek as the legendary werewolf of old might have made when it sought to satisfy its midnight hungering, came from the wood along the road. The hair on the back of the Agent's neck prickled in apprehension.

A moment later he was forced to tramp the brake pedal to the floor and swerve the car to the side of the road to keep from running down a man who plunged from the woods and threw himself directly in front of the car. Or was it a man? It was more like an eerie, staggering shadow of a man. It would take a few reeling steps, stop, dash blindly around in circles, and all the time it screamed and wailed like a lost soul in hell's torment.

X SPRANG from the car. The gaunt shadow ran headlong toward the car, struck the fender and sprang back, snarling, to bump squarely into Agent X. His fingers crooked like claws in an effort to rake human flesh to ribbons. He lowered his head and charged insanely, arms swinging like windmills.

X sidestepped, caught one of the flying arms and twisted it up behind the creature's back. He seized the other arm and held it firmly. The man struggled furiously and kicked blindly, all the time uttering unholy shrieks.

But X's grip was not easily broken and the staggering man seemed to have used up most of his energy in his pointless battle. Soon, he was hanging as limp as a sack in X's arms. The Agent dragged him out in front of the car where the yellow stream from the headlights found his captive a thing so horrible to look upon that revulsion almost swept pity aside.

The gibbering creature had four or five days' growth of beard on his face and the stubble was stiff with blood from many a scratch that thorns and twigs had given him in his dash through the wood. But the creature was a living corpse. So it seemed to Agent X when he looked into the man's eyes. The eyeballs protruded, looked dry and hard and were encrusted with dirt and grime and numerous bodies of small insects.

Then pity triumphed over horror. The blood raced in X's veins as he saw what some fiend out of hell had done to this fellow human. The man was blind simply because his eyelids had been completely removed by some satanic surgeon's scalpel. And his lips were snarling because fine copper wire had been used to sew the upper lip into a perpetual sneer. Mad? Of course he was mad. Nothing made of human flesh could have withstood such cruelty and remained sane.

X started to carry the gasping maniac toward the car. The man was uttering something between his malformed lips. He was wailing one word piteously in a high, quavering voice:

"Shaitan.... Shaitan...."

X stopped. His brows drew tightly together. He held the tortured one tenderly in his arms. "What did you say, old man?" he asked kindly.

"Shaitan. Shai—tan," the maniac wailed.

SHAITAN. A shiver coursed along the Agent's spine. He raised his eyes from the malformed face and jerked an apprehensive glance into the shadows. That name awoke terrible memories of things that had occurred years ago in a foreign land. In the days of the red revolt in Russia, when the astrakhan-capped Bolsheviki had terrorized all Asia with their massacres along the Mongolian border, the name Shaitan had brought shudders whenever uttered. Whether man or demon, none had ever known. But there were hundreds who had witnessed his cruelty, unequaled even in the days of the Spanish Inquisition.

Neither a fanatic nor a Bolshevist, a soldier nor a politician, Shaitan had made the most of what history offered. He had scourged humanity to gain gold for his own coffers. He had harnessed the power of one corner of a war-torn world for his own selfish purposes. And like a vulture over a battlefield, he had fattened upon the misfortune of others.

But Shaitan was a man of the East who had inherited the worst traits of various strains of blood mixed in his veins. How, then, had his name come upon the lips of this babbling wanderer of the Pennsylvania hills? Perhaps the deformed lips of the man may have accounted for his utterance of what seemed the name of Shaitan.

X picked up the tortured one, carried him to the car, and propped him up in the seat. The man was utterly exhausted, but his muscles never stopped twitching with the torment of the pain within him.

X reached into his pocket and brought out a small medical kit. He carefully charged a hypodermic syringe and gave the madman a stiff jolt of the drug. Soon, the muscular twitching stopped. For the first time in perhaps days, the madman was at rest. X got in behind the wheel, beside the slumped form with its horrible, malformed face, and drove on toward the city.

The dirt road along which he had been traveling abruptly

"None but a man too wicked to die could have received such a wound and lived," said the doctor.

joined a brick road at the edge of the city limits. But there was a wooden barrier across the road and a watchman waving a red lantern. On either side of the road were two square canvas tents lighted by electric lamps.

Agent X stopped the car and leaned out to speak to the watchman. "What's the matter? Bridge out?"

The watchman shook his head. "Quarantine. You'll have to go back. Nobody allowed to enter or leave Brownsboro. We've got the plague around here, or something worse. We don't want to spread it around."

X frowned. "The plague? What kind of plague?"

A tall man with snarled red hair, crooked nose and bitter lips joined the watchman. He peered at X with slits of eyes, and when he had stared rudely for a few moments, he asked: "What do you want?"

The Agent said quietly: "I'm from Washington, and I'm here on government business. Who are you?"

Stepping closer to the car, the tall man answered: "I'm Reed P. Kennedy, owner of the *Brownsboro Bugle,* greatest daily in western Pennsylvania. The paper, incidentally, is responsible for waking the people up to the fact that something must be done about this plague of madness."

"Plague of what?"

"Madness. We have had a number of cases. It is continually spreading. Sometimes, it means violent, choking death, but more frequently, men go mad."

"Hydrophobia?" asked the Secret Agent.

Reed P. Kennedy shook his head. "Nothing like that. Nothing that anyone knows anything about. No cure, but we're not going to pass it on to the rest of the world." He reached out his hand. "You have credentials, of course."

X produced the identification card he had taken from John Morris. Kennedy compared the small photo of John Morris with the face of the man behind the wheel of the ear. Thanks to the Agent's makeup mastery, photo and face corresponded exactly. Kennedy turned his head and called over his shoulder:

"Chief Hurd, will you step this way a moment?"

A HEAVY-JAWED man with close-clipped iron-gray hair and worried, squinting eyes, joined the newspaper publisher. Kennedy pointed to the card in his hand. "A secret service man," he said in a whisper. "Wants in. Has orders from Washington. I think you, as chief of police, had better attend to this."

The chief of police stuck out a large hand and smiled affably. "Mighty glad to know you, Mister Morris. And mighty glad you're here. Tell you, the responsibility on our shoulders is getting so heavy that we'd like to have some one to help us out."

"Not so fast there," Kennedy butted in. "We don't know that Mr. Morris has come here to help us."

"To be perfectly frank, I was brought here on another mission," X told them. "Of course, if there is anything I can do to help you while I am in town—"

Chief of Police Hurd seized Kennedy's arm. His heavy jaw dropped. He took a quick step backwards and pointed a fat forefinger at something in X's car. "He—he's got one of the mad ones in there. One of the mad ones must have escaped and he's picked him up. You'd better get out of there quick, Mr. Morris. That man's got the plague."

X frowned. "You mean this plague is something like—" he indicated the unconscious maniac beside him. "But that's absurd. This poor devil has been tortured. I found him staggering down the road, fighting with his own shadow—"

"That's it," Kennedy cut in. "That's the malady of madness. We can't let you in town, card or no card, unless you have a thorough physical examination. Dr. Davies, head of our health department, is in that tent. You'd better go see him."

Kennedy and Hurd backed away from the car while X opened the door and got out. They regarded the Agent with glances of apprehension as he walked toward the indicated tent.

"I say, 'No!'" a blustering voice roared from behind the flaps of the tent. "Mr. Garvey, what you ask is utterly impossible. At times like this, the health officer is law in this town. We can't have this thing spread. We haven't any means of coping with it and it certainly seems contagious."

"But my experiments. I'm working on something for the government. I can't have my work held up because a few people seem to have developed epilepsy or something of that nature. I must have supplies—"

"No! And that's final, Lorin Garvey. Under no consideration can you leave this city. Now—get out!"

THE FLAPS of the tent swirled furiously and a man plunged into the open, nearly knocking Agent X down. His blond hair was upstanding and his thin, colorless lips were forming silent oaths. He wore large, horn-rimmed, smoked-lensed glasses. He muttered a hurried apology and carried his appeal to Chief of Police Hurd. This was the first time Agent X had seen Lorin Garvey, the man he had been sent to guard. He watched the tall, stooped, scholarly figure of the scientist as Garvey approached the police chief.

Then X raised the flap of the tent and went inside. A bald man with a prolific growth of black, elevated eyebrows, stopped his worried pacing long enough to ask:

"Well, what do you want with me?"

X smiled. "I was under the impression that you wanted me. My name is Morris. I'm from Washington. Mr. Kennedy has my credentials. I'd be glad if you'd take a look at them."

Dr. Davies sighed, said something with his hands and shoulders, went to the door of the tent and called Kennedy. He took the card X had taken from Morris, glanced over it, and handed it to X.

"It would all be so much easier if we had less so-called help around here. Kennedy, owning a newspaper, thinks he has license to poke his disagreeable nose into everything." Then Davies returned his attention to the Secret Agent. As his eyes passed, almost enviously over the tall, square-shouldered body, he snapped: "As far as I know, there's nothing that can keep you from entering the city if you have orders from Washington. Let me warn you, however, that ours is a city with a curse of madness—"

Kennedy put his head through the tent flaps. "Look that man over, Davies. He has one of the victims of this staggering madness out in his car."

Dr. Davies frowned. "Will you kindly allow me to attend to my own business?" To X, he snapped: "Strip down to the waist, man." Then he trotted over to a table and procured a stethoscope.

X removed coat, shirt and undershirt, asking as he did so: "Have you any idea what can be the cause of this malady?"

"Filterable virus. Filterable virus," Davies replied with considerable assurance.

"Which means," X said with a smile, "that you really have no idea what is causing it. When a medical man is completely stumped, he consigns any new disease to the filterable virus scrap heap."

Davies grunted, yet the grunt was an admission. "We know this: the mad malady seems to affect the heart and lungs, sometimes causing death as soon as it strikes. Then again, the patient suffers such terrible agony that he becomes deranged. How's your heart, young man?" He started to apply the stethoscope when he noticed a jagged scar on the Agent's left side—a sear that bore a crude resemblance to the letter "X." He demanded: "What's that?"

"A bit of shrapnel landed there once upon a time," said X, quietly.

"Huh! Perfect wonder you're alive. Matter of fact, you ought to be dead." Davies listened to X's heart a moment. Then his right hand reached up abruptly and nipped X's cheek between thumb and first finger. X stepped back. His eyes darted to the doctor's fingers. There was a small piece of makeup material between thumb and forefinger.

Davies nodded shrewdly. "Watch for the man with the 'X' scar on his left side. Didn't you know that ever since the police discovered that the man disguised as Mark Brady who escaped from the

New York morgue some months ago, was Secret Agent X, that a means of positive identification of the mysterious Mr. X has been passed along to other members of the medical profession?" [21]

X had often feared that this scar would serve to identify him some day. But his face remained impassive when he asked: "Has it ever occurred to you that others might have a similar scar?"

"Never for a moment. None but a man too wicked to die could have received such a wound and lived. There is not the slightest doubt in my mind but that I have the singular pleasure of arresting—the most notorious criminal in the world today."

---

21 AUTHOR'S NOTE: The Agent's startling impersonation of Public Enemy Mark Brady, and the strange events that followed were related in the novel titled "Horror's Handclasp." During this impersonation, X, thought to be Brady, was taken to the morgue, a victim of a cataleptic trance which simulated death. Though he did not know it, up to the time of meeting Dr. Davies, the information that Agent X bore this identifying scar on his body, was immediately circulated among the members of the medical professions in hopes that sometime some doctor might stumble upon the Man of a Thousand Faces.

CHAPTER II

THE CITY ACCURSED

THE AGENT'S LEFT hand shot to Davies' throat, his fingers closing like steel jaws on the man's windpipe. His right fist lashed into a particularly sensitive spot beneath the doctor's heart. Such a blow when accompanied by sufficient force had the power to kill, but the Agent's masterful control of muscles enabled him to simply paralyze with it.

Davies' body stiffened. He fell forward like a fence post. X caught the doctor and held him up while his eyes darted about the tent for a place of concealment. The only possible place in which to put the doctor was a small steel cabinet.

X opened the door of the cabinet and found it contained one of the doctor's smocks and little else. He flung out the smock, stood Davies in the cabinet, and just managed to squeeze the door shut.

He hurriedly put on the smock over his own clothes, first removing his pocket makeup kit from his coat. Outside the tent, all was confusion—confusion that promised success to X's enterprise. Lorin Garvey had carried his appeal to the police chief. Hurd, Garvey and Kennedy could be heard loudly arguing the matter.

The Agent opened his makeup kit and began another miracle of transformation.[22] In the pocket of the smock, X found a surgeon's white skull cap. This, pressed tightly over his head would conceal the fact that he was not bald. He hastily pressed plastic volatile material from a tube and applied it to his face. Since Dr. Davies was light complexioned, little coloring material had to be added.

X's own brows were smoothed down and covered with the plas-

---

22   *AUTHOR'S NOTE: The Secret Agent's pocket makeup kit is complete in every detail. There are special pigments for simulating every skin tone. There are several neatly folded toupees, artificial eyebrows and mustaches. And in addition, his plastic volatile material with which he so skilfully fashions the contours of any face.*

tic material. He removed a pair of artificial eyebrows from the kit, went over to the cabinet and opened the door. Using Davies as a model, he pressed the artificial brows into place and arched them carefully.

He was then ready to start forming features from the heavy application of plastic material on his cheeks. But at that moment, X heard the tent flap rustle. His heart leaped into his throat. He turned, at the same time slamming the door of the cabinet. He sprang across the room toward the electric light hung temporarily from the top post of the tent.

His keen eyes found the bakelite connecting plug near the canvas wall of the tent. X's back was toward the door, he instinctively assumed the position that would to some extent enable him to simulate the doctor's drooping shoulders.

"That man Garvey," said a voice that X recognized as Kennedy's, "says he simply must get out of town. Can't you waive the rule, doctor?"

"Garvey be damned!" snapped Agent X, and his voice could not have been told from Davies'. And at the same time, he kicked out, caught the light connection with the toe of his right shoe, and broke it. The tent was instantly plunged into darkness. X did two things in a split-second's time. He leaped to the table and scooped up his pocket makeup kit. When he shoved this down into his pocket, his left hand brought out his pocket knife. He flickered it open, at the same time shouting:

"Agent X! He's escaping! That man who called himself Morris is a fake. Get him, Kennedy. Get the police in here. Secret Agent X. Makeup all over his face, I tell you! He must have turned out the lights."

And all that X was shouting was perfectly true, but it was uttered in the voice of Dr. Davies. Knife in hand, X sprang to one side of the tent and ripped a big slit in the canvas. Then he stepped back, pocketed the knife and drew out his flashlight with the same hand. He turned the beam in the direction of the slit he had made in the tent, shouted:

"Look! Just went through there. But he can't escape. The place is surrounded by police. Close in, everybody!"

X SET an admirable example, by stepping through the slit and running squarely into a policeman. "Did you see that man who called himself Morris?" he cried. "It's Agent X. Get him!"

There was immediate pandemonium. And among all those who hunted the darkness in search of Secret Agent X, apparently no one was more active than X himself. But he did his hunting in shadowy places where his skillful fingers, working blindly and entirely from memory, gradually modeled his plastic mask into a passable resemblance of the doctor's own features.

Then X scurried to the roadster that he had borrowed from John Morris. There he found very suspicious evidence of the hiding place of the man they hunted—a handkerchief he had used to keep the rumble seat door from locking and thus smothering the unconscious John Morris.

X beckoned to nearby police, gave whispered orders, had men surround the roadster with guns in their fists. Then, one finger pressed to his lips, X mounted the step plates and opened the rumble compartment. He turned the beam of his flashlight into the opening. The light ray fell upon the placid features of the real John Morris.

"Secret Agent X!" shouted the men about the car.

"Must have struck his head with the top of the door," X quickly supplied. "He's knocked out. I guess we effected a pretty smart capture here, Chief Hurd!"

Hurd raised John Morris's limp arms and clicked handcuffs on his wrists. "I'll have this crook under lock and key in no time," Hurd declared.

John Morris, X knew, was bound to cause him trouble if he remained at large. Jail was a very good place for the competent Morris while X went about his mysterious mission. Shortly after Hurd had taken the still unconscious secret service man away in his own car, X turned to Reed Kennedy saying:

"You're in charge here until I show up. My duty is to take the poor, staggering maniac, who came with Agent X, to the hospital."

"Just leave everything in my hands," said Kennedy.

X went over to Morris's car. The unfortunate victim of torture and the malady of madness, was still at peace under the influence of the drug X had administered. In the guise of Dr. Davies, X passed the barrier without further trouble and was driving at top speed toward the city when the pavement in front of him suddenly conjured up an oncoming car. The car, rocketing out of a side road, deliberately turned into his path.

INSTINCTIVELY, X spun the wheel to the right. There was a

*It was drop or
be dropped.*

scream of metal against metal as fenders clashed. X's car seemed
to leap into the air as it struck a culvert and bounded across a ditch.
As though in the grasp of a mighty giant, it was flung sideways
against a tree. Door hinges sprung. The sudden loss of momentum
as the car struck the tree flung X through the door. He had no sensation of striking the ground.

Completely stunned, he lay there without moving for nearly a
minute. Then gradually, his senses returned and he recalled that at
the moment the two cars had caromed off one another, he had got
a glimpse of the face of the man behind the wheel of the other car.

Or had he? It all seemed like a hideous nightmare. Yet the vague
impression of that face clung persistently to his memory. It was
hardly a face. There had been a veil of something like green silk—
and above it, the most diabolical pair of eyes he had ever seen. Eyes

that had gleamed with satanic, unholy light.

Agent X picked himself up and staggered toward the remains of the roadster. Through the twisted door, X saw the unfortunate victim of the mad malady. The man was dead. There was a deep gash in the center of his forehead. It might have been made by an axe, certainly by no portion of the wrecked car near at hand.

X's eyes narrowed. Had this been an accident? How easily it might have been cleverly plotted murder. And the murderer, the man in the other car whom X had instinctively saved by wrecking his own machine, could have so easily stopped long enough to dispose of the unfortunate man who was riding with Agent X.

It was possible that the murdered man had known something that he might have told in an interval of sanity. X remembered how, when he had first picked up the man, he had babbled about "Shaitan." Was it possible that the fiendish, clever criminal who had terrorized half of Asia was actually here in America?

Two cars had pulled up opposite the place of the accident. Men were hurrying toward Agent X. He anticipated any inquiries by immediately saying:

"This man has been killed. One of you take him to a hospital. They will notify the morgue. I'm Dr. Davies. Some one give me a lift into town."

The driver of one of the cars offered to assist him. X, now completely recovered from the crash, climbed into the car and told the driver to go to the corner of Twentieth and Elm Streets. This was on the edge of the city. X alighted, thanked the driver, and proceeded on foot. He thought to himself that he must have cut a very odd figure, walking down the street in a surgeon's cap and with a torn and soiled smock flapping about him. He was only a block from Lorin Garvey's big house, and this distance would give him an opportunity to repair his makeup.

A few moments later he passed through the imposing iron gates and hurried along the gracefully curved walk that led to the big square house of yellow brick. He crossed the wide porch and knocked in the authoritative manner that he thought befitted his impersonation of Dr. Davies.

The door opened.

"Good evening—" X began, only to stop and take a second look at the huge figure, crowded into butler's livery, that had opened the door. The butler's component parts seemed all in the form of cubes—square-headed, square-shouldered, and so marvelously equipped with solid muscle that his breadth belied his six feet of height. He was dark complexioned, with shaggy, black hair. The man was Harvey Bates, Secret Agent X's chief lieutenant.

THE AGENT did not reveal himself to Bates. He simply asked to see Lorin Garvey, saying that he was Dr. Davies.

Bates, who had somehow managed to worm himself into Garvey's household as butler, bowed and led X into a reception hall.

For several minutes, X was allowed to wait alone. Seated in a shadowy corner where dim light was kinder to his hastily applied makeup, X watched a door beneath the stairway opening quietly. He heard the rustle of silk, saw a short, flared, black skirt and the white, postage-stamp apron of a housemaid. The girl was evidently unaware of the Agent's presence. She closed the door quietly and turned around.

Agent X all but started from his chair as he beheld the girl's face in the revealing light from the hall lamp. She was darkly beautiful. Her narrow, velvety-lidded eyes were almost black and extraordinarily shrewd. High cheek bones accented a small, pointed chin. Her rouged lips suggested firm determination without in any way detracting from her beauty. Her name, as far as X knew, was Charlotta.

Nature had endowed her with brains as well as beauty. Her mastery of foreign languages and her love of adventure had caused her to seek her fortune in strange lands at an early age. She had served Russia in the early days of the war though she was American born. In the capacity of a spy she had remained connected with the Czar's government until the Russian army had become demoralized.

Agent X had met her when she had transferred her abilities to the French Intelligence Service. Their paths had crossed frequently. Wherever X had found adventure and intrigue, there he had found Charlotta.

She claimed no country as her own. She devoted her time to any service that promised money and adventure. She had always been an enigma to Agent X, and he instinctively mistrusted her. He wondered if the years had altered her character or whether even now she might not be employed by some foreign power to obtain the secret which Garvey so jealously guarded for the United States Government.

X allowed the woman to cross the room and go through the opposite door without attracting her attention. As soon as she was gone, he stood up and went directly into the living room which he had seen Bates enter. The big, square man was evidently just returning from announcing the arrival of the man he supposed to be Dr. Davies.

He looked at the odd figure in white, his eyes wide with surprise. "Mr. Garvey will see you soon," he said in close-clipped syllables.

"Bates," X whispered.

The big man jerked up his head. His eyes widened. "Beg pardon?" he said hesitantly.

"Bates, don't you recognize me?" X was now speaking in the voice which served to identify him to his lieutenant.

A STRANGE expression, that mingled devotion and delight, crossed Bates's countenance. In his eyes there was an almost worshipful glow. "You, sir!" he said hoarsely. He came forward quickly to eagerly grasp the Agent's extended hand. "Think it is all right?" he asked. "Didn't want to take too much on myself. Didn't know what you'd think."

"You couldn't be in a better position."

"Think there's a connection between Garvey's danger and the mad sickness?" Bates asked.

"It's too early to decide that definitely," X told him. "How far has this strange malady gone?"

"About ten cases and three deaths so far, sir."

"I see. Now about Charlotta—"

"Who, sir?"

"Charlotta," X repeated. "I mean the maid."

"Oh, Charlotta," Bates replied. He seemed to be tasting the name. "Why, that's *her* name. What about her?"

"She is a very dangerous woman," said X quietly.

Bates's heavy, black brows drew together. Yet there was something more than bewilderment reflected in his countenance. There was pain, too, and doubt.

"Charlotta?" again his tongue toyed with the name.

"Bates, I know how this woman has plotted, and how her beauty has confounded the best brains in Europe."

Bates shook his head slowly, almost sadly back and forth. "No, sir," he said huskily.

"She is as cunning as—" X stopped, his brow furrowed. "What do you mean, 'no, sir?'"

"Just—just that, sir," Bates said humbly. "She isn't, couldn't be, what you said." He still looked hurt and worried, but there was bulldog determination in the set of his square jaw. X pitied the man, thought he could imagine how Bates felt. He was thoroughly aware of Bates's unswerving loyalty to his chief. Yet somehow, some way, in the brief time that Bates and Charlotta had been together in the house, the clever spy had managed to gain some portion of Bates's affection.

"Bates," said X kindly but earnestly, "I may be mistaken, but I think I know this woman better than you do."

"No, sir," Bates said again. "She's good and beautiful and generous."

"How do you know?"

"I—just know. She couldn't be otherwise."

"She's an international spy, I tell you. How can such a woman be loyal if she serves one country one day and another the next?"

X thoughtfully regarded Bates. Then he spoke mildly. "I don't deny that she is beautiful. No one knows better than I the power of her enchantment. I have seen her make fools of generals, field marshals and members of nobility. I have seen that same beauty result in the destruction of an entire German battalion because of information she had gained through apparent innocent questioning of men who had become infatuated with her. I know her and I fear her. Surely that should mean something to you."

Bates swallowed with difficulty. "I hate to contradict. I hate to do anything or think anything that doesn't agree entirely with you, sir. But I would stake my life on it, that Charlotta is exactly what I think she is."

A SLOW, patient smile formed on the Agent's lips. "I understand," he said quietly.

"Then—then I'd better go, sir," Bates asked huskily.

"Go?"

"I mean leave. Better leave your services. I can't spy on Charlotta. And I couldn't have you think I wasn't doing my part."

X regarded Bates for several seconds before saying: "My orders did not instruct you to spy on Charlotta. Your job is to keep an eye on Garvey and see that no harm comes to him. That's your job. Stick to it."

Bates's eyes brightened. "Then you—you'll let me go on, doing what little I can? You'll—"

"Some one is coming."

Bates coughed, stepped back, bowed stiffly as the door behind him opened. "Mr. Garvey will see you in a moment, sir," Bates said.

It was Garvey who had entered the room. The man squinted at the light in spite of his smoke-lensed glasses. There was something almost spectral about him. His thin cheeks were so pale, his hair so blond, his lips so colorless that they were practically invisible. He looked steadily at Agent X.

"You wanted to see me, Dr. Davies?" he asked without the slightest hint of cordiality. "You have perhaps changed your mind about permitting me to leave the city for a day or two?"

"I wanted to see you, yes. As to your wanting to leave the city, I have already intimated that that was impossible."

"Very well." Garvey held the door of his study open. "Just step in here, please." And when Agent X had entered, Garvey waved him into a chair. "I resent very much these constant efforts of yours to pry into my affairs, Dr. Davies." He sat down on the desk and seemed tremendously interested in a hang-nail on his thumb. "I think if you were a little more subtle in your efforts to find out what I am doing, I could find it in my heart to like you a little better."

"Perhaps," said X pleasantly, still clinging to the impersonation of Davies' voice, "you will think better of me when you know more about me and why I am here." He reached into the pocket of his coat beneath the white smock and produced a sealed letter addressed to Lorin Garvey and which, X knew, was from K9, the Agent's Washington sponsor.

GARVEY took the letter, excused himself, opened and read it over quickly. Then he folded it and put it in his pocket. For a moment he continued picking at the hang-nail on his thumb. "I hardly understand this letter you have given me, Mister— Mister—"

X allowed the man to grope. "Suppose we let it go at that, Mr. Garvey. You understand my position. As the writer of that letter explains, I cannot reveal my true identity. Call me Davies, if you wish."

"But you are not Davies." Garvey tapped the note in his pocket. "This tells me that you are a special agent who has been sent to cope with the spy situation."

X nodded. "I am here to protect you. And, believe me, I can do a better job of it if you will frankly explain to me the reason for all this secrecy. What kind of a discovery have you made that is of such great importance to Washington?"

"Sorry," said Garvey. "I cannot confide in you as to the nature of the formula I am working on. Doubtless, at some later date, the official who chooses to call himself K9 will tell you of it. The point is that I am certain that I am surrounded by spies. I might go so far as to say that should my secret become public the world might never be the same again. Perhaps that will make it clear to you why I cannot trust you with it. Under the circumstances—"

Garvey stopped, turned his head quickly to the right. "What's that?" he asked sharply.

It was a mighty roar that might have come from the throats of a hundred men. It sounded right outside the Garvey house and mingled with it was the sound of marching feet. The flare of red torches tinted the drawn blinds of the study with a rosy glow.

X sprang up, went to the window and pulled back the blind. Lorin Garvey joined him. A motley army of men and women paraded down the street. Their faces were white and strained, their eyes bright with hatred and fear. And as they marched, they chanted:

"Kill Agent X! Kill the Master of Madness! Show him he can't make a madhouse of our town!"

Garvey asked: "What do they mean? Is the man known as X in this town?"

"Yes," said X quietly. "They seem to have the notion that he is the man behind this epidemic of madness. Where is the city jail?"

"Up Elm Street a little way. Why? Have they Agent X in jail?"

"I am afraid they are under that impression," replied X. He knew well what had happened. Chief of Police Hurd had not been able to keep his triumphant capture of Agent X a secret. Nor was there any particular reason why he should have kept it a secret. Then some ugly rumor had taken root that X was the chief cause of the plague of madness.

Garvey sighed. "I suppose because the people make the laws they think the laws belong to them and they can take them in their own hands whenever they want to. But a lynching is an ugly business."

"It's murder," said X. "I'll be back soon."

"Leaving?"

"A matter of urgent importance," X told him as he went through the door of the study. Urgent importance indeed! A man's life at stake. For in some cell of the city jail, John Morris was the hunted quarry of that furious mob. It was Agent X who had sent him there. So John Morris had to be saved from that mob.

CHAPTER III

MALADY OF MADNESS

AGENT X SPRINTED along the street in the direction of the city jail. Ahead, he could hear the roaring mob as it stormed the prison, demanding that the man they supposed to be Secret Agent X be delivered to them. How easily a lynching could be accomplished this night—with most of the police force out on quarantine duty.

The red brick jail building had an eight-foot wall around its shallow front court, but this had already been scaled, the guard knocked down, and the gate opened. The mob was pouring into the court as Agent X plunged into their midst. He fought like one possessed to gain the front line of the advancing mob. He gouged with his elbows. He cracked heads together. He dealt stunning blows. But always, at the top of his lungs, he shouted: "Lynch Agent X!" Apparently, he was the most vengeance-thirsty man among them.

X had not had time to make even a slight alteration in his makeup. To all appearances, he was Dr. Davies, one of the leading citizens. Many bystanders, who might have doubted the justice of lynch law, joined the mob when they saw the man they supposed to be Dr. Davies foremost among the mobsters.

Only a man of the Agent's supple strength and sudden movements could have worked his way from the rear of the mob to the very front by the time the jail-house doors were battered down. X was among the first into the entry way. He seized a guard who was trying to hold off the mob with a rifle which he was obviously afraid to use.

X took the man by the collar and sent him spinning to the floor of the turnkey's office. He stooped, picked the guard's pockets of keys, and was off again at the head of the pack that rushed from cell to cell until at last they came upon the one occupied by John Morris.

The secret service man was standing upright. Not the slightest sign of fear showed in his hazel eyes. There was no expression on his face except that of a bewildered man who was alert to his own dangerous position. He strode to the bars of his cage.

"So I am Agent X, am I?" he cried defiantly.

And the mob jeered and hooted and shook the bars. Some removed shoes to hurl at the man in the cell. All cursed him, called him Agent X, Master of Madness as well as every vile name they could lay tongue to.

Foremost in the mob that stormed the cell was Agent X. He battled his way to the cell door, the guard's keys in his hand and something else cleverly palmed in the same hand.

"Let Doc Davies through!" cried a man. "He's got the keys."

"Yes, let Davies through. That's the stuff, Doc!"

X got the key into the lock, but instead of turning it, he left it there and elbowed a little to one side. When the grating was opened, X knew that the man who opened it would be forced slightly back. This X dared not risk. The infuriated crowd could beat Morris to death in the cell before X could reach him. Other hands than X's were ready and eager to turn the key. As the cell door opened slightly, Agent X was the first to enter.

Morris went into a fighting crouch. He feinted with his right and hooked with his left, but X turned the blow aside, literally smothering any other blows that Morris attempted by crowding the secret service man back to the wall. X's left arm slipped around behind Morris. His hand came around so that thumb and forefinger could clip Morris's nostrils tightly together while the palm of his hand was firmly planted over the secret service man's mouth. At the same time, the tiny object palmed in his right hand dropped to the floor to be crushed beneath the feet of the mob.

X SIMPLY held Morris, protecting him with his own body while apparently struggling with him. And always, his left hand prevented Morris from breathing. The small round object that X had dropped was a glass vial containing a large quantity of X's anesthetizing gas, sealed under pressure. As soon as the vial was broken, the gas began to spread rapidly throughout the cell and the outer hall.

Men and women of the mob went limp, keeled over one another without even so much as a groan. Those who saw what appeared to be sudden death, tried to run, but the tightly jammed hall prevented rapid movement. The gas caught up with them and dropped them in their tracks.

Only X and the half-strangled Morris remained standing. Long practice had taught X just how long it required for a charge of his famous gas to dissipate. Its concentration gave it tremendous power and the pressure within the little bombs gave it a wide range. To Morris, it must have looked like nothing less than mass murder, though actually the gas was perfectly harmless.[23]

In another moment, X began maneuvering through the crowd of unconscious men and women. He dragged Morris along with him. When they had gained the hall, X thought it safe to breathe. He released his hold on Morris's nose and mouth and hurried the breathless man toward the side door. But on opening the door, X stopped suddenly.

Parked in the street was a long, sleek, black sedan. Its motor was idling. And near the car a strange and horrible drama was being enacted. One man, who had been lounging beside a telephone post, was suddenly seized with a violent fit of coughing that doubled him over. In another moment, he was down on the sidewalk, fighting for breath and struggling for life itself.

A few bystanders who were near at hand started to go to his aid. But even before they reached him, a marked change came over their faces. Muscles contorted as though they had suddenly been seized by intense pain. Some cried aloud, others shrieked in maddened voices. Some flung themselves about as though fighting with an invisible monster.

It was the plague of madness. Able-bodied, mentally alert men and women were instantly converted into insane puppets that shrieked and danced disjointedly, that rushed headlong into buildings and passing cars, that gibbered and chattered like monkeys. Others in the street, as yet unaffected, took to their heels, screaming in terror so that it was difficult to distinguish the madmen from the sane.

A uniformed chauffeur came out of a building across the street. He took in the situation in a single, frightened glance. He raced across the street, sprang into the sleek sedan, and drove away at top speed.

Still clutching John Morris by the arm, X hurried down the steps

---

23   *AUTHOR'S NOTE: Agent X has a hearty dislike for lethal weapons and seldom carries anything of the kind with him. Guns and knives, he believes, should be left to those investigators who lack resource and scientific knowledge.*

and onto the sidewalk. White-faced, terrified police, determined to do their duty if it cost them their lives, darted this way and that, trying to corral the mad ones and keep the dead and injured from being tramped on by the crowd. With his free hand, X reached out and seized a running man by the arm. "That car," he shouted, pointing down the street after the black sedan. "Know who owns it?"

"Reed Kennedy," called the man, jerking his arm free and running.

The danger seemed to have passed when the sedan left the curb. The crowd was gathering around the dead and maddened victims, to look on and be fascinated by the horrible, grotesque antics of the captive maniacs in the hands of the police.

Suddenly, with a quick, deceptive twist of his arm, John Morris broke free from the Agent's grasp. He took three backward steps, stood perfectly erect, and pointed at the Secret Agent. "I saw you do it," his lips curled venomously around the words. "The mob back there in the jail. You killed them all. You did it with gas—the same gas used here in the street not a moment ago. The mad malady is caused by gas and you are the man who is doing it. Police!" He turned his head, looked at the bewildered officers of the law who surrounded them. "Police, it is up to us to stamp out this so-called plague. It is gas, I tell you. Gas! I saw him use it in the jail. He dropped a bomb from his hand."

"That's right," a man spoke up. "They're all dead back there in the jail."

"But—but," a policeman stammered, "you've made some mistake. This man is Dr. Davies."

"That man is Secret Agent X!" a voice shrilled. And elbowing his way through the throng, came the real Dr. Davies.

The appearance of the head of the Board of Health put an end to all doubts. The crowd surged forward, eager to wipe out this man whom they supposed was menacing their very sanity. Foremost in the mob, were the police whose wealth of misinformation regarding Agent X had led them to believe that he was the most notorious criminal unhanged.

X's glance compassed the ever narrowing circle of humanity. Not a single break in the line of accusing eyes and the clenched, threatening fists. Revolvers were springing into the hands of the police. The slightest resistance meant a volley of leaden death from police guns. Yet to argue with a panic-scourged crowd was in itself stark madness. Nothing he could have said would have convinced them at that moment that he was not the cause of all their trouble. The one way out would plunge him deeper and deeper into dangerous waters, but it might, for a minute or so, offer him security. What came after that was in the hands of the gods.

CHAPTER IV

MURDER RACKET

"ONE PHONY MOVE, and let him have it!" one of the police chewed out of the corner of his mouth. "And get him through the head. He may be wearing a bullet-proof vest."

Secret Agent X raised his hands slowly above his head. "I shall make no resistance," he said quietly. "I am going to walk away from here and nobody will prevent me." A cunning smile twisted his lips. The fingers of his right hand straightened. In the crotch of his thumb he held a round, glass sphere as fragile as a bubble. It contained anesthetizing gas which, in the open air, was capable of knocking out only a few of the many who surrounded him.

"The gas!" husked John Morris. "I saw him use it." The secret service man stood his ground, but several in the crowd who heard his whispered words turned and fled.

X held his hand above his head, and yelled: "The gas of madness. You have seen its work. You cannot doubt but what I am able to kill you—or drive you all insane with it. Sorry I have to deprive you charming men and women of my company." And he backed slowly toward the rim of the circle.

The crowd fell back, the circle parted. Even police who had had their courage tempered by years of service, turned pale and backed away from Agent X—Agent X, the man whose capture or death would have made them nationally famous and enriched them with a sizable reward. But a man couldn't enjoy wealth if he was insane, and the terror of madness was far more potent than the fear of death.

"It—it's a bluff!" shouted Dr. Davies. He sprang into the clearing, started to pursue X.

A policeman caught him by the arm. "You want to land us all in the asylum because of your foolishness?" he demanded.

"A bluff!" shouted Davies. "You can't drive any one insane with gas. It's a disease, I say. A filterable virus."

Smiling at the doctor, X said: "Which is an admission that you don't know what causes the plague of madness. But John Morris knows and others know. Would you care for another demonstration, just for your benefit?" X poised the gas bomb as though to throw it. The crowd seemed to shout its terror from a single throat. Men and women ran pell-mell down the street. Only the police remained and they melted back before X's advance.

X gained the entrance of a narrow alley. He backed into it still holding the bomb aloft. "I am going to place the bomb in the alley," he told them. "Should any of you pursue me, you run the risk of stepping on it in the darkness. Good night to you all. We'll meet again." He stooped, seemed to be rolling something along the pavement, stood up and raced for the other end of the alley.

Not a man followed him, though actually X had returned the harmless gas bomb to his padded pocket from whence it had come. His plan had worked—but he had heaped a new price upon his head. Now every person in the city would believe that it was Secret Agent X who was the Master of Madness.

At the other end of the alley, X found himself on Elizabeth Street. A few blocks to the south was a temporary hideout which Bates had previously arranged for him. Uncertain as to his next step, X started for the hideout. There he could manage a complete change of clothes and makeup.

He had not walked more than half a block when a car purred up to the curb beside him and a hoarse voice said:

"Doc!"

X turned around. The car was a sedan. Its dome light was on and two men could be seen sitting in the back seat. One was a red-faced, bloated-looking person with lips that snarled back from immense, glistening gold teeth. A short, snub-nosed automatic was almost hidden in his fat fist. Beside him was a man with close-clipped hair and an exceedingly long upper lip. His right eyebrow was elevated far above its mate as though he was in the habit of wearing a monocle. His yellow-gloved hands were clasped on the head of a black walking-stick. He wore a black Van Dyke beard that, to X's trained eye, appeared false.

X immediately recognized the man with the stick. His name was Peter Knore. It was because of Knore that both X and John Morris had come to Brownsboro. Washington had good reason to believe that Knore was a spy in the employment of a powerful European nation. X slowly approached the black sedan.

THE BLOATED MAN jerked his head. "You get in, Doc, and no grumpin' about it. We got places to go and things to do."

"I—I—" X began hesitantly, though he fully intended to comply with the red-faced man's request. The impersonation of Dr. Davies seemed to lead from one adventure to another. It began to appear as though the head of the health department was scarcely the man his fellow citizens supposed him to be.

"I said no grumpin', Doc. This thing in my hand is a gun."

X shrugged, got into the car and sat down between Knore and the bloated man.

"You know where, Andy," said the man with the gun, as the car got under way. And not another word was said as they rolled on through the town, avoiding the well-kept streets, taking dark alleys until finally they came to the edge of a railroad cut near the outskirts. There was a little village of disreputable shacks. The car came to a halt in the yard behind the largest of these.

"Get out, Doc," said the man with the gun. "I got my pursuader on you all the time and I can plant a slug in your gizzard quicker than you can jerk out a man's appendix."

X was marched into the house at the end of the bloated man's gun. There were three hard-looking characters seated around the kitchen table playing some sort of a card game. They stood up, nodded at Peter Knore, and said, "Hello, Jo," to the florid man.

The man with the gun, X decided, was Jo Pyle, a local political grafter and racketeer mentioned in one of Bates's reports. Pyle held Brownsboro's small underworld in the palm of his hand.

Pyle slammed X down into a chair. "Now you *listen* for a change, Doc," he grated. "You know damned well you aren't giving us the front you should. How in hell can we make any money out of this insanity racket with you telling everybody there's no cure for the disease?"

X's mind worked rapidly. He spoke firmly in Dr. Davies' voice. "I said we hadn't found a cure as yet."

"Same damned thing," growled one of the men.

"We have found a cure," Pyle corrected. "That's the kind of hot air you're supposed to hand out. You don't know the cure, but a famous Venice doctor—"

"Viennese," Peter Knore corrected.

"Well, yeah. A famous doctor has found it. Dr. Knore, here. He's the guy. He's got an antiseptic—"

"Antitoxin," Knore corrected.

"Will you let me do the talking, Knore?" growled Pyle.

"*Doctor* Knore, is it?" X asked mockingly.

Knore coughed. "For the time being, yes."

X laughed. "And you're fleecing the public with a patent antitoxin composed of sugar water or something? You expect me to front a scheme like that for you while one man after another dies or goes completely insane?"

Pyle screwed his face up into a knot. "We got to go all over that again? You know what I said you'd get—if you didn't play our kind of cards?" Pyle seized X by the shoulder and dragged him to his feet. "Well, I'm handin' out a sample right now!" His big fist buried itself in the Agent's midsection.

Hard, trained abdominal muscles would have enabled X to take the blow without wincing. But he was playing the part of Dr. Davies. He doubled over, cursed, started to fall back in the chair.

Pyle caught him, held him up. "By hell, I'll teach you to listen when Jo Pyle speaks!" His gold teeth locked over his lower lip and he launched another battering-ram blow that sent X down so violently that the chair was broken and the Agent rolled to the floor.

"What you say now, Doc?" Pyle was jubilant.

X PULLED groggily to his feet. "You think," he choked out, "I'd disgrace my profession by subscribing to a crooked scheme like that? It's not the racket so much as the fact that it's tied up with murder. You think—"

Pyle charged across the room, hooked for X's chin. X turned his head slightly and Pyle's knuckles wiped across X's temple.

"If I have to pull the hide off you a piece at a time, you're going to kick in with us, Doc!" Pyle shouted. "Why, you cocksure—"

There was a knock at the door. Pyle ripped out his gun and turned it on X. "One funny move, one word, and I'll let you have it…. Knore, see who that is."

Peter Knore went to the door and opened it cautiously. "Charlotta," he whispered. "Come in, but quickly."

The woman spy came in, glanced haughtily around the room. Her eyes met X's coldly and shifted to Pyle where they became twin gimlets of contempt. "You poor fool. Trying to gain the doctor's co-operation by means of what you faintly imagine is torture, are you?" She turned to Peter Knore. "Peter, I want to—" Her eyes glinted, her small right foot stamped angrily. "Peter! Will you listen to me a moment?"

"Sure. What do you want?"

"Put a stop to this mauling of Dr. Davies. The doctor is a cultured man. He must be persuaded, not browbeaten."

"Ah, listen, lady," Pyle objected, "I offered the guy a cut on the profits. If that won't do it, I ought to be able to beat him into it."

"I didn't say persuade him with money," said Charlotta softly. "Fools' methods. Had you been in Russia at the time of the revolt, you would have known the meaning of the word 'persuasion.' Lock him up down below."

Pyle shrugged heavy shoulders. "Okeh, lady. Come on, you guys. Escort the doc to the basement and lock him up. But I ain't quittin' on him yet," he added as the three toughs braced X up with automatics and hurried him down the basement steps.

They flung him into a filthy hole, slammed a heavy wooden door, and slid an iron bar across it. No sooner was he alone than the apparently half-dead Agent X was on his feet, exploring his prison with his flashlight. The floor was packed earth and the walls were of cement block. There were no windows. Evidently the place had been originally intended as a fruit cellar.

HIS IMPERSONATION of the doctor had been carried off so well that Pyle had not thought to search him. X had devices and small tools in his pockets, under the doctor's smock, that would enable him to get out of the cell in a few moments' time. He could have quite easily prevented his imprisonment and managed his escape when Pyle had been mauling him, had he wanted to. But an opportunity such as this was not to be neglected. Pyle, Knore, Charlotta and the gang were tied up in the mystery of the insane sickness.

X went over to the door. A modern lock would have given him less trouble than the old-fashioned iron bar, for X always carried a master-key system that enabled him to unlock almost any standard lock. He took from a pocket tool case a long, gimletlike instrument which fitted into an extension handle. Its keen, tempered-steel point, when pushed through the crack between door and door frame, imbedded itself far enough in the iron to enable him to move the bar ever so slightly in the direction away from the socket.

As he was on the point of setting the tool for another move, the bar slipped across the door, snapping off the point of X's instrument. He stepped back, turned out his flash, and drew his gas pistol. The bar had moved because some one on the outside of the door had moved it.

The door opened very slowly, very quietly. There was a whisper of footsteps approaching him across the earthen floor. A low, musical voice whispered: "Where are you, Agent X?"

X took a quick breath. "Charlotta." He turned his flashlight on. The woman's face stood out of the dark background like a lovely cameo. She came nearer, smiling. She extended her hand, took his wrist in her white, fragile-looking fingers.

"Come," she said quickly. "I have them all out of the house looking for a prowler who is not here. You must hurry. I was afraid you did not remember me, Secret Agent X."

"It would be impossible to forget you, my lady," X said. "But how does it happen that you have penetrated my disguise?"

"It was in the crowd outside the jail," she told him. "There were two Dr. Davies. The one who was in trouble was bound to be Agent X. I think that none but you and I, in the whole world, has a genuine penchant for getting into trouble."

"And I'm not getting out of it so easily," X told her. "I must know more."

She dropped his wrist, faced him, her eyes steadily upon his. "You've never quite trusted me, Agent X. You need not now. But do not think too badly of me. I want only to find my mortal enemy."

"So?" said X skeptically. "And who is that?"

Charlotta's lips curled in an expression of intense hatred. "Shaitan!"

"Shaitan?" X echoed. "Is he here?"

She looked slightly puzzled. "You mean to say you didn't know that? I supposed that was why you were here. Why are you here, Agent X?"

"To guard Lorin Garvey against spies," he replied, regarding her narrowly.

Her red lips were tightly compressed for a moment. "I see. And you suppose that that is the reason that I am in Garvey's house?"

"What else would I suppose?"

Her eyes flashed. "You're wrong. The infallible Mr. X is wrong for once! I have but one objective—to see Shaitan in the hands of the authorities. Or see him dead. Better dead!" She seized both of the Agent's arms. "This nation is alive with spies. But spies are not as dangerous as Shaitan. He is the devil incarnate. He is here because the East is impoverished and war-ridden."

"You have seen him? What does he look like?"

SHE SHOOK her head. "I have not seen him any more than I have really seen you. He may be any one about us. Once, in Mongolia, he was pointed out to me by peasants who were afraid to even turn their eyes in his direction. He wears a green veil hiding all of his face except his eyes. His head is totally bald, his forehead a ponderous thing to hold all the evil behind it."

"And now, why are you in Garvey's house?"

"Because Garvey has some momentous, deadly discovery in his possession. Don't you see? Shaitan never stoops to ordinary crime. To establish himself in America, he must have a powerful weapon. What other reason would he have for coming here, than to steal Garvey's secret?"

"Are you certain he is here?"

Charlotta glanced hurriedly about her as though Shaitan himself lurked in some of the gloomy corners. "He is here," she whispered. "Once, in the night, I was awakened by a nightmare. I lay there in my bed, staring out at the darkness, and I saw two luminous eyes looking at me through the window. Then they were gone. I nearly screamed. Can you imagine Charlotta screaming?"

"I can't," said X. "But the eyes might have been part of your dream."

She shook her head slowly. "No. Once you have seen Shaitan, you will never forget those eyes. He is in this town and the citizens have good reason to tremble. He is a master of disguise, though hardly as great a master as you. He may be any one in this city."

"And why do you hate him?" X asked mildly.

"Because I have seen the scores of helpless men and women lying dead in the fields where he had them shot during the revolt. He killed them not for political reasons but because they refused to pay him tribute."

"Five hundred men," said X slowly, "died at the village of Spada during the late war. Five hundred Germans. If my memory is not fickle, a woman named Charlotta was the cause. Why this sudden hatred of murder?"

"Because that was not murder. That was war. Those Germans were not helpless. They could have saved themselves if they had been willing to surrender. Besides, you have no reason to criticize,

Agent X. You were more active in the Intelligence Service than I. The difference between our methods of operation is that you stole plans of fortification and the like. I stole men's affections."

"I was not criticizing," said X quietly. "I was simply trying to fathom you."

She laughed. "When a woman loses her mystery, she is no longer a woman." Then: "But forget the past. I am not a spy, though I seem unable to convince you. The war is over. No war really matters but the war of right against wrong. I am on your side, if you will have me. But I am against Shaitan, whether you will have me or not."

"And this little murder racket you are mixed up in—this business of driving men insane and then selling a fake cure—I suppose it pays the room and board while you're hunting this demon from Asia?"

"You refuse to take this matter seriously, Secret Agent X."

X SHOOK his head. "No, Charlotta. You are perfectly right about Shaitan being here. He wrecked my car tonight. The point I am making is this: Shaitan must be connected in some way with this malady of madness that is sweeping the town. And when I find you—"

"You didn't find me!" she interrupted sharply. "Have you never lied and deceived and acted to worm your way into a band of criminals for the sole purpose of gaining information? Of course you have! And that is why you found me with that fat fool, Jo Pyle, and that self-satisfied Peter Knore. I don't know but what they are connected with Shaitan. Either one of them might be Shaitan, for that matter. But if they are causing this disease of insanity, I do not know how they do it. You see—"

She stopped, listened a moment. "Some one coming into the house. Quickly, Agent X!" She seized X by the arm and led him through the door and toward the steps.

"Wait," X whispered. "They're coming in the front door. We can just make it through the back."

They tiptoed up the steps, X taking the lead, his gas pistol in his hand. He opened the back door and stepped out into the yard. Charlotta followed him a little way, then stopped him by catching his arm.

"You do trust me a little?" she whispered. Her small, lovely face was very close to his and moonlight lent intoxication to her beauty. "The old Charlotta was never very bad. A foolish girl who loved adventure even as you loved it. The new Charlotta is a better, wiser woman."

"And more beautiful."

"And a Charlotta with a very different objective. You'll try to trust her?"

"After what you have done tonight—I will try."

Charlotta pressed the Agent's hand. "I must go now."

"They are sure to know you released me," warned X.

She tossed her head. "Don't worry about me. I can handle men."

X thought of Harvey Bates, and heartily agreed with her. He hurried across the back lot, climbed into the car that had brought him to the house, and found the ignition key in place. He started the car, turned it into the lane, and sped back toward the center of the town.

He drove at once to the hideout Bates had pre-arranged for him. It was a large frame house, the owners of which were vacationing. They had been glad to rent it for a week or two.

There were a number of folded newspapers on the porch where the carrier had evidently left them by mistake. X gathered these up, unlocked the front door, and went in to inspect his headquarters.

As soon as he found that his elaborate wardrobe, necessary for his masterful impersonations, was in order, he sat down under a lamp and opened the newspapers. He was particularly anxious to learn all that he could concerning the history of the malady of madness in Brownsboro.

Reed Kennedy's *Brownsboro Bugle* seemed quite a complete little sheet and boasted a surprising circulation. After X had looked the paper over, he turned to the front page and let his eyes skate down one column after another. Suddenly, he stopped, his brow furrowing. In one column he read the following:

SPECIAL POLICE ARE RECRUITED

Kirn, Sweden:—Signs of new wealth in Latvia led Duke Ivan, Europe's incapacitated nabob, to willingly occupy Dorelle André's yacht sailing directly on North Tyrol. Dorelle expects creditors in event Viceroy employs yacht orderlies under restricted service. Enemy less victorious enters Strausburg. Ivan met ensign André navigating Baltic under seas in new Empire submarine service.

(Which may not mean a thing to you. But a want ad in the BROWNSBORO BUGLE will mean money in your pocket.)

Here, apparently, was an attempt on the part of the newspaper publisher to attract attention, by means of absurdities, to his appeal to patronize his want-ad section. If that had been the sole purpose of this squib, it was wholly successful. Yet something attracted Agent X beside the fact that the city mentioned, Kirn, was not in Sweden, and that geography would have to be altered considerably if anyone was going to sail a yacht on mountainous Tyrol. It was the fact that glaring out of the type, like a death's-head, were those three capital letters, D-I-E.

The more he looked at this bit of nonsense, the more certain he was that while the paragraph might not, as the parenthetical advertisement beneath stated, "mean anything to you," it was definitely intended to mean something to somebody. In another moment, he had out pencil and paper and was jotting down the first letters of every word in the paragraph in the order in which they came. When he had finished he had something that, to an expert cryptographer such as X was, was a little less puzzling:

SpARKSSonwillDIEintwoDAysdoNTDecieVeyoursElveSImean-
Business

This, when properly divided and spaced read:

Sparks's son will die in two days. Don't deceive yourselves. I mean business.

AGENT X glanced up at the top of the paper. It had been published just two days before. Today there had been murder, exactly as predicted in what was obviously a code message to some one. And among the murdered men should be some one who had been the son of a man named Sparks.

X reached for the phone and called the office of the *Bugle*. "Was some one by the name of Sparks killed today?" he asked as soon as the phone had been answered.

"Yes," came the reply. "Or perhaps we shouldn't say killed. Glen Sparks, son of one of our most prominent citizens, died as result of a sudden attack of the plague of madness. It occurred right out in front of the jail. Police are looking for Secret Agent X in connection with this trouble. There seems to be some difference of opinion as to the origin of this terrible disease that has come to our city. Read all about it in tomorrow's *Bugle*."

"Don't worry about that," X replied. "The *Bugle* is going to receive considerable attention from me from now on." He hung up, seized the paper issued on the day before, and hurriedly scanned the front sheet. If he could find any more predicted deaths, he might be able to prevent them, though what weapon he could use against this unseen menace of death and madness, he had not the slightest idea.

There they were, the three glaring, death's-head letters staring out of the column of one of yesterday's papers. He read:

DEAN OF RACING ACADEMY BATTLES EXTRADITION

Defense fought orders releasing Dean with illegal lottery letters. Dean Isaac Edwards today opened merciless oration regarding Robert Oliver's wild midnight indiscretions. Demanding new independence grants, he told Greensburg every thing that indicated new graft. Court lost order suspending entire reprieve.

(Which is nonsense simply to emphasize the horse-sense of selling through *Bugle* want-ads.)

X decoded the simple cipher as he read, using the first letter of each word as he had done before:

Dora Bedford will die tomorrow midnight. Getting closer.

Once again X called the office of the *Bugle*. This time he disguised his voice so that the inquiries might seem to come from different persons, "Who's Dora Bedford?" he asked. "Know her?"

The man at the night desk informed him that Dora Bedford was the daughter of Hale Bedford, one of the five millionaires who controlled most of the manufacturing in the city.

Agent X hung up, glanced at his wrist watch. He had exactly half an hour to change his disguise and drive over to the Bedford home before the scheduled time of Dora Bedford's death. And if death struck as it had in the case of Sparks's son, more than one would die.

X took a large makeup kit from the closet where Bates had stored it, opened a triple-folded mirror, and began to hastily alter his appearance. When he arose ten minutes later, he was a far younger man than he had appeared as Dr. Davies. A black, slicked-back toupee covered his own hair. His features were finely formed. A small black mustache put in place with spirit gum completed the facial alterations. He then changed to a tweed suit, taking care to transfer all his special equipment to its pockets.

Then he went to a garage behind the house where he found one of his own cars waiting for him. He backed it out and headed west. The Bedford mansion looked down on its less exalted neighbors from the top of Newton Hill near the edge of town. It was a longer trip across the city than X had supposed, and though he pushed the car to the limit, it was just striking midnight when X stopped in the drive in front of the house. He sprang from the car, started for the house, stopped suddenly, his heart jumping up against the roof of his mouth.

Parked beneath the porte-cochère was a second car—a small coupé carrying a New York license plate. The numbers on that plate were familiar to X and what they signified caused icy sweat to exude from every pore.

The coupé belonged to Betty Dale, lovely girl reporter and the Agent's best friend, who at the moment should have been safely at home in her cozy New York apartment.[24] But instead, she was somewhere within a house where unseen, unknown menace stalked with outstretched hands ready to kill.

---

24   AUTHOR'S NOTE: *Regular readers of these chronicles need no introduction to Betty Dale, charming companion of many of Secret Agent X's most perilous adventures. She has aided him frequently with information gathered through her newspaper work. Her goodness and beauty have been a constant inspiration to him and at times her cleverness has saved him from dangerous situations.*

CHAPTER V

THREE EYES OF SHAITAN

HAD SHE PERMITTED herself to admit it, Betty Dale's visit to Dora Bedford was but an excuse for her to be near Agent X. Her relation with the Agent had always been that of a dear friend, but as each new adventure brought her closer to the mysterious character of the real man behind the makeup, she found her regard growing into something more than friendship.

She had tried bravely to stifle this love for the man whose face she had never seen, even though she knew he returned her love. For she realized that sentiment could not be mixed with duty in the Herculean battle X waged against crime.

She had spent many hours lying awake in her bed, wondering where X could be, wondering if Death, whom he continually taunted, had caught up with him. When he had confided to her that he was going to Brownsboro she had immediately decided that she would somehow manage to be there, too, if her newspaper could spare her a few days.

"Better," she thought, "to lie awake at night in Brownsboro and at least have the consolation of being in the same city with him than to lie awake in New York, hundreds of miles away."

Though she had retired early, after her long drive, she was scarcely dozing by the time the first stroke of twelve boomed from a nearby steeple. She had just turned over with the firm resolve to stop worrying and get to sleep, when the sound of soft, whispering footsteps caused her eyelids to spring open. A white, ethereal form was moving stealthily from the door of the adjoining bedroom.

"Betty," a soft voice whispered tremulously, "are you asleep?" Betty sighed: "No, darling." She sat up, turned on the bed lamp to reveal in soft, rosy light the petite figure of Dora Bedford in négligée. The girl's oval face was white. Even her lips were pale. Her soft, brown eyes were very wide. She toyed nervously with one glossy, brown curl that hung down across her creamy shoulder.

"I'm a-afraid, Betty," she stammered.

"Afraid?" Betty laughed. "Of what?"

"A—mouse. I think there's a mouse in my room. Aren't you afraid of mice?"

"I've certainly no love for them," Betty replied. She got out of bed, thrust feet into slippers, and pulled a crêpe négligée over her shoulders.

Dora clutched her arm. "Listen!" she whispered.

In the next room there was the sound of tiny feet scampering across the floor. Hardly the sound that a mouse might make. Betty reached beneath her pillow and took out a small flashlight and a little automatic that Agent X had given her some time ago. She started into Dora's room, Dora behind her, hugging her closely around the waist.

Betty swung the flashlight beam around the room. The light glistened on two tiny, close-set eyes peering out at them from under the bed. Betty's heart jumped. Then she uttered a strained laugh as a comical little figure scarcely ten inches over all scampered across the room. "Why, it's just a little monkey!"

Dora's fingers clenched. "Oh, I'm going to scream! Who wants monkeys climbing in windows in the middle of the night? Even little ones. And look, there's a string tied to one of his legs. And—" Then Dora did scream shrilly. She pointed a white, quivering finger at the window.

Coiling down from the top of the sash was a glossy, serpent-like shape that dropped full length then raised its snakelike head toward the two girls.

THE DOOR of the bedroom was flung open. Betty's flashlight darted to the door, outlined the figure of a tall, square-shouldered man who wore a hat pulled down over his eyes. Betty fired a single shot. The man leaped forward, straight toward the window. "Stop that, Betty," he said in a crisp voice that was familiar to her.

"You!" Betty cried. "I shot—I shot at you!"

"And missed!" Secret Agent X called over his shoulder. He was at the window. The coils of the black snake were in his hands. He was twisting the serpentine form, kinking it, tying it in knots.

"Look out!" Dora cautioned shrilly. "It might bite you!"

"A rubber hose doesn't bite, Miss Rexford," X told her. "This one would be less dangerous if it did. The monkey threaded it into the room by means of the string fastened to the little beast's leg."

"But why?" Betty asked.

"Because some one is trying to kill Dora Bedford with gas—the gas that's been causing all the madness around town. It's a gas, and not a disease. This hose, dropped from the roof, was to direct that gas into this room. It would have killed Miss Bedford and probably driven everyone else in the house insane."

"And on the other end of that hose?" Betty ventured.

"The gas cylinders and the man behind it all. Step back from the window and keep back. I'm going up."

X sprang to the window sill, tested the strength of the hose for a moment, and swung out to climb hand over hand up the hose toward the overhanging eaves. He climbed swiftly, bracing his feet against the wall and pulling himself upwards with his arms. When he was within inches of the eaves, the hose suddenly slipped.

Where another man might have clung to the hose in panicky desperation, Agent X thought as he had been trained to think in those split-second intervals that meant the difference between life and death. No sooner had he felt the hose slipping, than he reached out with his right arm to its fullest extent. The tips of his fingers just caught on the eaves trough as the hose slipped to the ground.

X tightened his grip, got his left hand on the eaves trough, and slowly drew his body upwards. As his chin came up even with the eaves, he saw three eyes staring into his face. Two eyes that were faintly luminous and immeasurably evil glared over a flowing green veil. The third eye, chill and gray, sought the center of his forehead. That third eye of Shaitan's was the muzzle of a revolver.

X sent one quick glance downward. It was drop or be dropped.

FIVE DOOMED MEN

THIRTY FEET OF thin air separated Agent X from the ground. He swung in toward the house, kicked both feet against the wall, and released his grip. At almost the same instant, Shaitan's gun blasted. X felt the breeze of the bullet skimming the toupee he wore, as he lurched back and down, arms and legs clawing at nothing.

Something whipped across his back nearly doubling his supple body. His grasping fingers locked over thin strands of wire and for a moment he clung breathlessly to the network of electric and phone wires that led into the house. It was with the hope of landing on these wires that he had flung himself as far out from the house as possible. As he teetered up and down, he was thankful that the wires were both strong and well insulated.

He could hear feet scurrying across the tiles of the room above. Perhaps Shaitan thought that his bullet had found its mark. X swung himself along the wires until he reached the place where they entered the big garage. From there it was an easy matter to climb down wood lattice work to the ground.

By the time he had reached the house, all within were thoroughly aroused. Hale Bedford and the servant staff were all out on the lawn in various stages of dishabille and carrying hastily mustered weapons that ranged from carving knives to shotguns.

"What—what's all this nonsense?" demanded Hale Bedford as Agent X came up.

"You could find a much more appropriate name for it," said X dryly. He hurried around to the side of the house and there discovered the gardener's ladder reaching up from the sun room.

"Begging your pardon, sir," said a man who had donned his solicitous manner if not his servant livery, "but, as this gentleman says, it is hardly nonsense when one sees a man with a veil over his face running across the lawn. Which was exactly what I saw, sir."

"When was that?" X snapped.

"Just a bare minute ago, sir," replied the man. "I aimed with my shotgun and it was not till I pulled the trigger that I discovered I had forgot to attend to the loading."

"A slight oversight," X said. "Mr. Bedford, if you don't mind, suppose we go in the house a moment. You do not seem thoroughly awake to the fact that this was attempted murder."

"What stuff!" said Bedford, but he was willing enough to show X into the house.

Light found Hale Bedford a pleasant-faced, white-haired gentleman of perhaps fifty. In the living room they were joined by the two girls, Betty Dale and Dora Bedford. Dora, wide-eyed and flushed with excitement, told her father all that had happened. When she had finished, Hale Bedford looked at Agent X. "Have you ever been in my house before?" he asked.

X shook his head. "You are wondering how I found your daughter's room, perhaps. I was prowling around the house, saw a bedroom light turned on, and recognized Miss Dale as she passed by the lighted window. Miss Dale and I are old friends." He smiled at Betty.

"Well," said Bedford, "Miss Dale's friends are our friends." He turned to Betty Dale. "Won't you introduce the gentleman who seems to be made of such heroic stuff and a well-defined bump of imagination?"

Betty hesitated. It was entirely impossible for her to introduce X, for she had not the slightest idea who he was impersonating. X quickly supplied the wanted information, introducing himself as John Moss, the secret service man he had impersonated on first entering the city. It was a big risk to take, for his present makeup in no way resembled John Moss. But he felt that he would have to explain his prowling about the house, and the papers of John Moss, still in his possession, gave him something of an official position. He took out the papers belonging to Moss and flashed them in front of Bedford's eyes.

Bedford nodded. "But—er—just what brought you to our house tonight? What," he added, with a twinkle in his eyes, "besides Miss Dale?"

"Mr. Bedford," X said earnestly, "you are taking this matter far too lightly. The reason I came here tonight was that the murder of your daughter was predicted."

DORA BEDFORD began to cry. Her father put both arms around her. "Look here, Mr. Moss, I'll not have you coming around here and frightening my daughter with your astrology and predictions. Such things are utterly absurd."

Betty said: "Please listen to what Mr. Moss has to say. I've known him a long time and he is certainly not an alarmist."

"But for a stroke of good fortune," X said, "your daughter might now be dead and you might be insane."

"Oh, that!" Bedford scoffed. "I paid a thousand dollars for immunity from this malady for myself and my household. Did you know there was a serum developed by a Viennese doctor—"

X checked Bedford with a shake of the head. "You've handed over a thousand dollars for nothing, sir. That quack doctor happens to be a spy of international reputation. His name is Peter Knore. And if you had tweaked his Van Dyke beard, you would have discovered that it is as false as his so-called serum. This mad malady is the effect of a poison gas such as might have been introduced into your daughter's room last night. Have you last night's *Bugle* around here?"

"I think so," Bedford said. "Betty, will you run into my study like a good girl and see if you can find what Mr. Moss wants? I declare, Mr. Moss, this is the strangest thing I ever heard of. How can a gas affect the mind?"

"It doesn't, as I understand it. The gas kills outright when in sufficient concentration. I believe that when diluted considerably with air, it has the power of driving people insane simply because of the terrible pain it causes."

"Oh, Daddy," sobbed Dora Bedford. "I know Mr. Moss is right. Won't you do something? Call the police or something?"

"It's absurd," declared Bedford. "Why neither my daughter nor I have any enemies. No one kills people for the sheer love of it unless he's crazy."

"Definitely, Shaitan is not crazy," X told them.

"Shaitan?" Betty asked as she returned with the paper. "Is that the killer's name?"

X nodded. "And he's after something big. Selling quack serum strikes me as being pretty small potatoes for a man like Shaitan."

"Why don't you arrest him, then?" asked Bedford.

"Because, no one knows what he looks like." X took the paper out of Betty's hand and turned to the front page. He pointed out the nonsensical squib in the first column. Bedford read it over and laughed.

"Why, Reed P. Kennedy has been running things like that for years. They used to be quite amusing, but I must say his sense of humor isn't what it once was."

X agreed. "As a matter of fact, the man who wrote that, lost his sense of humor long ago. If you'll combine all the first letters in each word in that paragraph, you'll find something like this: 'Dora Bedford will die at midnight. Getting closer.' If that's funny, go right ahead and laugh."

Bedford's brow puckered. "It is rather queer. Still, it could be coincidence. A queer quirk of fate, you know."

"There's about as much fate connected with that as there is about tomorrow's sunrise!" X snapped. "I'm going to see that you're protected, whether you like it or not. There won't be another attempt before morning, inasmuch as the killer has no reason to suppose that his attempt wasn't successful. However, I'll see you soon."

Agent X beckoned Betty to follow him out into the hall. When they were alone, he said: "I don't suppose there will be another attempt tonight, as I said before, Betty. If I thought there would be, I wouldn't leave you here alone with the Bedfords. But in case anything should happen that even strikes you as queer, call Lorin Garvey's residence and insist upon speaking to the butler. The butler is Harvey Bates. At least, he will be until tomorrow when I shall transfer Bates to other quarters."

The girl nodded. "You'll be extremely careful, won't you? Somehow this constant threat of madness is worse than death."

X nodded, held her two hands a moment, and whispered good night. He thought he had never seen her so lovely, with her golden hair all in disarray and her deep blue eyes looking worriedly into his.

THE FOLLOWING morning, Agent X put in his appearance at the office of Reed P. Kennedy, publisher of the Brownsboro *Bugle*. He had adopted his most famous alias for this visit, one which should have made a definite impression on Kennedy. He appeared as a sandy-haired, commonplace looking man who wore a not too carefully pressed suit of gray material. On the card which he sent in to the publisher was engraved: "A.J. Martin, Associated Press."

Kennedy's mouth was less dour-looking than it had appeared

the night before. He gave the Agent an hearty hand clasp, rumpled his unruly hair and said: "Don't see how you got into the town without the quarantine catching you, Mr. Martin, but as one newspaperman to another, let me welcome you to our unfortunate city. There's plenty of copy right here in Brownsboro."

"That's exactly why I am here," X said quietly. He accepted Kennedy's proffered cigar and lighted it deliberately. Then he reached over and thumbed a stack of back copies of the *Bugle* arranged in a wire basket on the publisher's desk.

"What do you think of our paper, Mr. Martin?" Kennedy asked.

"It is accurate in every detail, Kennedy." X's eyes riveted on the publisher's face. "Especially is it accurate in the matter of prophecies." He pulled the paper which had announced the attempt on Dora Bedford's life from the stack and threw it down in front of Kennedy.

"What do you mean?" Kennedy squinted down at the paper, at column one where X's finger pointed. Then he looked up and grinned strangely. "Oh, you like my way of drumming up trade for the ad department, eh? I've been using drivel like that for years. And people read it. That's the funny part."

"Have you read this?" X asked.

"Of course. The only thing in the publication I write, so naturally I read it."

"Read it again, discounting every letter except the first letter in every word."

Kennedy squinted. "I don't understand."

"The first letter of every word. Spell it out. D-O-R-A, Dora and so on. Don't you get it? And you say you wrote it. 'Dora Bedford will die tomorrow midnight. Getting closer.'"

Kennedy whitened. "Good Lord! Is Hale Bedford's daughter dead?"

"But for the grace of God she would be!" X snapped. "Now, I'm waiting for an explanation. Quickly, please."

"Explanation?" Kennedy looked bewilderedly about as though searching for a place to hide. "Why—why there's no explanation. It's just one of those things. A—a coincidence."

"And I suppose it was a coincidence when the same column in your paper, which you have admitted writing, also predicted the death of Mr. Sparks's boy?" X hurried through the other papers on the desk and came upon one that was over a week old. He snatched it up. Read this:

FRENCH INVADERS VICTORIOUS

Each man entering Nantes dropped optional opponents making excellent disputes. Before entering Denmark, French officials regarded dispute settled. Perry, American rector, killed several French envoys right in street. Having antagonistic leanings, each captain killed many ancient Turks having easily won success.

(It appears our linotype machine is filled with mistakes today. But you can make no mistake lining up with our want-ad department to sell what you don't want and buy what you do.)

Kennedy laughed weakly. "Isn't it good? Missing word jumble, you know. We're offering a prize to anyone who can make sense out of it. All to create interest in our want ads."

X nodded. "You can just give me the prize. I've separated the meat from the bone in that paragraph above the parenthesis. It's the same sort of cipher. It reads: 'Five men doomed. Bedford, Sparks, Feris, Haleck, Mathews.' They are the five rich men who practically own this town."

"It—It's coincidence. Typographical errors. You know how things creep in," Kennedy stumbled on desperately.

"You omitted one possibility," X said dryly. "It might be spirit writing." He turned on his heel, went through the door and left Kennedy gasping. Mentally, Kennedy was a badly whipped man. He had good reason to be frightened. If he was in some way associated with the crimes, and there was no reason to doubt but what he was, he would be forced to make some counter move in his own defense. If he was but a lieutenant of Shaitan, he would have to get information to his chief.

X realized fully that nothing could be accomplished by third-degreeing Kennedy. If Kennedy was in reality Shaitan, he would never have admitted it and there was certainly no way of proving it. If Kennedy merely worked for Shaitan, Kennedy would know nothing more about his chief than would Agent X. By leaving Kennedy wondering what the mysterious Mr. Martin would do next, X felt that he had advanced well into the enemy's territory.

The Agent went immediately to Lorin Garvey's rambling house. This time, he was fully prepared to find out exactly what the nature of Garvey's secret was. Then, too, Bates must take up his duties elsewhere. Every move that Kennedy made would have to be watched and Bates was the man to do that.

IT WAS Bates who answered X's knock at Garvey's door. X placed a cautioning finger on his lips. The disguise associated with the Agent's alias of A.J. Martin was well known to Bates, so that no identifying sign was necessary. X stepped into the hall, took Bates by the arm and whispered:

"As a butler you're through. Your job is to watch Reed P. Kennedy, the newspaperman. His paper has been predicting these killings and Kennedy looks suspicious. Follow him everywhere. You understand?"

Bates nodded. "I just disappear?"

"From here? Yes. Is Charlotta still here?"

Bates nodded, flushed slightly.

"I just wanted to know. I thought perhaps you'd like to know that she helped me out of a tight fix last night. I may have to apologize to her some day."

X left Bates grinning widely, walked into the living room and to the door of Garvey's study. He knocked. A moment later, Lorin Garvey, wearing an acid-stained white apron, opened the door and came out. He looked X up and down.

X smiled. "Garvey, this is probably something of a surprise to you. I am the man sent by K9."

Garvey sucked in his pale lips until they were entirely out of sight. He stared thoughtfully at X through his thick-lensed, smoke-colored glasses. "I am afraid I don't quite understand your language," he said.

"It is well to be cautious," X told him. "This, however, will convince you of my identity. In his letter, K9 said: 'Dear Garvey: I am sending you with this letter the best possible protection—a man whose identity necessarily remains a secret but in whom you can place implicit trust.' I might add to further convince you, that K9 writes in blue ink and in an almost indecipherable back-hand."

Garvey smiled: "Very good. Won't you step in? Our conference was badly upset last night when you left so abruptly." He ushered X into the study, a room darkened by blinds. At one end, X could see the entrance to Garvey's laboratory. Garvey went over, closed the laboratory door and locked it. Then he switched on the electric lights and offered X a chair on the other side of his desk. He turned an elaborate electric clock with electric calendar so that both could see it. "I can spare you just about thirty minutes," he said. "Now, what are your questions?"

"I believe," X said slowly, "that you at least owe me your confidence. I cannot possibly protect your secret unless I know what I am to protect."

Garvey shook his head. "I am sorry. Any other questions?"

"You're being a fool, Garvey," X continued. "Perhaps I can convince you to confide in me by telling you what I already know. You are working on the development of a poison gas. It is suffocative, exceedingly deadly, and causing great pain even when greatly diluted with pure air. So great is this pain that if it does not kill a man outright, it can drive him insane." X leaned back in his chair and waited a moment while the cautious Garvey turned this over in his mind.

Finally, the scientist said: "Oddly enough, you have described the properties of this gas to perfection. How did you manage?"

"Chiefly a matter of guess work. You see, it occurred to me that I came here a little too late. Somebody else is in possession of your secret. Is that true?"

"Perhaps it is," Garvey confessed. "I have, of course, not been able to try my gas on human subjects. What you mean is that this present plague of madness is caused by a gas which might very well be the gas which I have discovered. It will interest you to know that shortly before I wrote to Washington, asking protection, my only laboratory assistant disappeared. That is what caused my first moments of alarm. Though I had not confided my secret to this man, it is possible that he managed to interpret notes I had locked in my safe. There was no evidence to lead me to believe that he had opened the safe, however."

X LEANED forward eagerly. "Can you tell me what this man looked like? Did he have a ponderous bald head and eyes that were slightly luminous? Eyes like Satan's, I might add."

"No-o," Garvey said slowly. "On the contrary, he looked so much like you do at the present moment that I am inclined to—"

Garvey's two hands suddenly went into action, in synchronous movements. His left hand darted out toward X's left arm, jabbing something that gleamed like a tiny sword straight into X's wrist. At the same time, his right hand produced a small, efficient-looking revolver. "Don't move," he said in a dull, dead tone.

The warning was superfluous. X could have hardly stirred a finger. Already his joints were beginning to feel cold and stiff. He stared apathetically at the hypodermic needle in Garvey's left hand.

"Your boasted knowledge of my gas was just a little too great," Garvey was saying. "Only one man could have that knowledge—

the man behind this damnable mad malady that has come to our city. *You* know about my gas because *you* use it. It isn't quite perfected, or at least wasn't when you stole my formula. You are here for additional information which you could not work out for yourself. You are the fiend out of hell known as Shaitan!"

But to Agent X there seemed a dozen Lorin Garvey's sitting in a circle that was whirling about him. A dozen pair of all but invisible lips were spouting absurdities. The light faded until there was no light at all. Then Garvey's voice was gone and there was nothing for Agent X but dark silence.

It was a long, dreamless sleep from which he finally awakened. His eyes lighted on the electric clock that was standing directly in front of him as it had been when he had gone into his drugged trance. The hands were approaching twelve. The calendar on the clock dial was beginning to shift. It was then nearly midnight. X had lost nearly fifteen precious hours because of Garvey's insane actions.

The Agent started to get out of the chair, but found himself too weak and too drowsy to move. He looked around the room. Lorin Garvey was there placidly smoking a pipe and looking owlishly at X. Near the door was Charlotta. She wasn't wearing her serving-maid's costume.

"I have discovered," Garvey said, "that my maid is not a maid at all but a young woman who has been searching the world over for you, Shaitan. She is almost as anxious to see you brought to justice as I am."

"More so," said Charlotta huskily.

"But before we turn you over to the authorities, we want to hear certain information from your lips. Are you working for any particular government at the present?"

X turned the question over in his half-drugged mind. Was he working for any government? Of course. "The United States," he answered slowly.

Charlotta frowned, looked at Garvey. "Are you certain that this serum of yours is what you think it is?"

"It has never failed before. It should be extremely effective with the subject still feeling the influence of the drug I administered."

Agent X thought he understood. With his resistance broken down by drugs, he might reveal secrets which were known only to himself and were of the utmost importance. He resolved to keep absolutely silent. But that was far easier to say than to do. For over an hour Charlotta and Garvey worked over him, plying him with questions, trying to obtain a confession, trying to get him to admit he was Shaitan, trying to get him to tell whom he had planned to kill next.

Garvey seemed to take a fiendish delight in trying out all the drugs on his shelf in an effort to break down X's resistance. Finally Garvey gave him morphine in such a large dose that it was necessary to pour large amounts of black coffee into him, then walk him back and forth across the study to keep him out of the morphine sleep that has no awakening.

Here was torment of the third degree in its most civilized form. It was little more than psychological torture with resistance scientifically worn away. But for all that, the Agent had more resistance than either Charlotta or Garvey. By two o'clock, they had given up. Then, in spite of all his efforts not to, Agent X went to sleep. He passed through a series of nightmares in which he was helplessly chained to a big rock and forced to watch Shaitan drive Betty Dale insane with fiendish tortures too terrible to describe.

CHAPTER VII

MILLION-DOLLAR MURDER

HARVEY BATES FELT that his new assignment had both advantages and disadvantages. He felt that while he remained in Garvey's house he had to look upon Charlotta with suspicious eyes and this was becoming more and more difficult for him to do. She seemed such a charming companion, so generous and good-natured.

Furthermore, she seemed to delight in doing thoughtful little things for him. Because he had felt guilty of spying on her, Bates was glad to get away from the house. Still, it was hard leaving her, just disappearing as he had been forced to do. He began to worry as to what she might think of him.

But devotion to Agent X made Bates throw himself into the task before him and in a few hours he had stumbled upon some rather curious information regarding Reed P. Kennedy. This information came from a member of the circulation department of the *Bugle* whom Bates met when he visited the plant under the pretense of getting information on linotype-room efficiency for a printer's journal.

The circulation man was very enthusiastic. Yes, the *Bugle* had statewide distribution, the man informed Bates; and that he shouldered the responsibility of seeing that all the out-of-town subscribers got their papers. "All except Mr. Franks, that is," he added.

Bates chewed the bit of his square-bowled pipe. "Who is Franks?" he asked casually.

"Oh, Mr. Franks is the newspaper skeleton," the circulation man said with a laugh.

Bates's black brows crimped together. "The what?"

"Skeleton. Mystery, you know. Some say that Mr. Franks is a prospective purchaser of the *Bugle*. He is a subscriber in Philadelphia, and I can't tell you much else about him. However, I am never allowed to distribute Mr. Franks's paper in the usual manner. Old Sour-puss—I mean Kennedy—will come into the press room and snatch up the first paper out of every issue. This he folds up and slaps a wrapper around it. It goes special delivery to Mr. Franks and the Old Man Sour-puss takes it to the post office himself."

Bates grunted, thumbed the glowing bowl of his pipe, and mentally made a note to see just what Mr. Kennedy did at the post office each day when he mailed the mysterious Mr. Franks his newspaper.

By two o'clock that afternoon, Bates was waiting in a taxi outside the *Bugle* press room. Ten minutes later, Reed Kennedy came out, rolling a freshly printed newspaper in a brown wrapper as he hurried to his car. Bates tapped the driver on the shoulder. "Kennedy," he said. "Follow."

The driver nodded, shifted gears and tailed Kennedy the distance of two blocks to the post office. Bates got out and went up the steps directly behind Kennedy. He took out an old envelope from the pocket of his coat and pretended to examine it closely before thrusting it into the mail chute. Kennedy went up to the stamp window and demanded a three and a special. Bates crowded in behind him, looked over his shoulder, and saw that the newspaper was addressed to Mr. R.W. Franks of Locust Street, Philadelphia.

Bates hurriedly bought a stamp, turned and strode down the corridor behind the publisher. Kennedy mailed the paper, went to a wall of lock-boxes, stooped to a big one on the bottom row, and looked through the little window.

Kennedy's face blanched perceptibly. His fingers were trembling so that he had to run the combination three times before he succeeded in getting the box open. The box contained a brown-wrapped square parcel that fitted so tightly that Kennedy had to tug and jerk to get it out. Even then, a portion of the paper was torn off getting it through the door.

Bates was close behind Kennedy. Kennedy left the door of his lock-box open and started to hurry away. Bates reached out a hand, dropped it on the publisher's shoulder. Kennedy turned as though he had been bitten. His long-lipped mouth was open, and his face had a slightly greenish cast.

"Left box open," Bates clipped.

"Ah—er—th-thanks." Kennedy turned to slam the box shut, and as he did so Bates got a glimpse of the package under his arm. It was marked as newspaper clippings and was simply addressed to

Box 518, and it bore a return address of some one in Philadelphia. Kennedy started at a stumbling, long-legged gait down the corridor. He had evidently lost his direction, for he was going out the door that was farthest away from his car.

Harvey Bates suddenly forgot to pull at his pipe, which dropped from between his lips to land in his right palm. The torn part of the big package under Kennedy's arm was plainly visible from behind and the contents partially exposed. Newspaper clippings? Well, not like any Bates had ever seen before. Those clippings were green in color. Not a special-edition newspaper green, but the green of newly printed paper money.

KENNEDY turned around at the moment, sent a frightened glance over his shoulder, and saw Harvey Bates bearing down upon him. Kennedy struck the post office door with his shoulder and went down the steps two at a time. Bates followed in long, ponderous strides. Kennedy guessed the direction of his car, guessed wrong and started to sprint. Realizing his mistake, he turned into what he evidently took for an alley but which was actually a narrow court running to the back of a business building.

The publisher realized his mistake even before Bates did. Unexpectedly, he turned, lowered his head, gripped his bundle as though it were a football and charged straight at Bates. Bates sidestepped. His left fist shot out, punched the bundle from beneath Kennedy's arm. Both stooped for the bundle at once.

Kennedy's right knee came up to catch Bates under the chin. Bates went over backwards, but he just managed to dig his fingers into the bundle of greenbacks. The back of his head struck against the foundation of the building. Partially stunned, he rolled over, holding the package closely, expecting Kennedy to make an effort to recover the money.

Bates's senses cleared quickly. He turned over, found Kennedy gone, and the money still in his possession. Bates ripped the package a little more and saw that it contained bills of every denomination from fives to hundreds. No great matter if Kennedy had momentarily escaped. Here was evidence that was undeniable. Bates got to his feet and started toward the opening of the blind alley.

When he was within five feet of the entrance, six men came running around the corner. Four of them were police. The others might be plain-clothes detectives. Bates hesitated a moment. Should he walk on, pretending not to notice them or double back and try to get through the back of the building that closed the alley? He decided that it would be impossible to walk past the six men and not show that the package he held contained money. He turned suddenly and ran as fast as his legs would carry him toward the back door of the building.

"Stop!" shouted an authoritative voice behind him. A gun spoke thunderously in the narrow alleyway. Bates heard the whine of the bullet. He reached out his hand to seize the door leading into the building. The door burst open. A revolver, a fist, a length of blue and gold-clad arm appeared. Bates looked up into the face of Police Chief Hurd.

"You're under arrest!" Hurd whipped out. "The charge is murder!"

THOUGH he had lost all conception of the passage of time, it was almost at the same moment in which Harvey Bates was arrested for murder that Agent X came out of his drugged sleep. He had been carried to an upstairs room and placed on a bed. Inactivity, the constant application of sedatives, had left the Agent's strength far below par. He tried to get off the bed, managed to put his feet on the floor, only to feel his knees give way.

He lay on the floor, numb fingers searching his pockets. If he but had his pocket medical kit he could easily prepare himself a powerful stimulant which would enable him to snap out of his present limp condition in less than ten minutes. But his pockets had evidently been emptied before he was brought to the bedroom.

He crawled on hands and knees to the door and shook the knob. Almost at once, a lock on the other side clicked. X rolled away from the door as it was opened. Charlotta stood there. There was a gun in her hand and contempt in her eyes.

"Well, Shaitan," she said softly. "Do you remember Charlotta?"

Agent X seized the door knob and dragged himself to his feet. The girl watched him narrowly. The gun was firm in her grasp.

"Garvey is going to phone the authorities in a few moments. You will soon see that the police have a way of making even you confess your crimes."

The Agent looked at her shrewdly with tired, somber eyes. "You really think I am Shaitan, Charlotta? Listen, do you remember the little village back of the Austrian line? You were trying to get across into Italy with special information and the Austrians were on your trail? You hadn't eaten for a long time. Then you met me and—"

Charlotta's indrawn breath whistled between her clenched

teeth. The gun dropped from her fingers. "You—you're Agent X! Whatever gave Garvey the notion you were Shaitan?"

"As a detective," X said, "Garvey may be perfectly sincere, but he's a washout. Because I knew something about the gas, he insisted I was Shaitan."

Charlotta nodded. "I see. Yet you didn't dare tell him you were Agent X, because Agent X is wanted by the police. Don't worry. I'll see that Garvey makes this mistake right."

"Can you manage it without telling who I am? I could have escaped a dozen times, had I the stuff he took from my pockets."

The girl smiled confidently. "I know right where he put your things. I'll get them in some way. Just try to be patient."

Charlotta was gone not more than five minutes. She again opened the door and came in breathless, her cheeks flushed. In her hands was a bundle done up in a small napkin. She opened it on the bed. Inside was the Agent's makeup kit, his gas pistol, pocket tool case, master keys, medical kit and glass gas bombs. He quickly returned his equipment to their proper places with the exception of the medical kit.

"You'll have to hurry," Charlotta told him. "Garvey's telephoning the police. That's how I managed to get your things."

X nodded. He filled a hypodermic syringe, rolled up his sleeve and injected the powerful stimulant. He packed his tiny vials of drugs back into the kit and returned it to his pocket. He took hold of Charlotta's arm and gave it a quick squeeze.

"Thanks," he said earnestly. "And I apologize for anything I might have done or said."

The door of the room opened. Some measure of the Agent's former strength had returned. His right hand went to his coat pocket and rested on the butt of his gas pistol. It was Lorin Garvey who entered.

"There—there's been a frightful mistake," he blurted. "You must be the man K9 mentioned. You can't be Shaitan. They've caught Shaitan. The whole thing's over. It was some sort of an extortion scheme. But the terrible part of it is that another man has been murdered."

"Who?" demanded X.

"A Mr. Bedford. Oh, you might have stopped it, had I not prevented you by my idiotic actions. He was killed last night at midnight." Lorin Garvey wrung his hands.

The blood arose in Secret Agent X's veins. He was thinking of Betty Dale. If Bedford had been killed by the gas, probably everyone else in the house had felt its effects. The gas either killed or maddened. Without another word to Garvey or Charlotta, X hurried from the house.

Lorin Garvey turned to his serving maid. "I think I understand how my secret got out," he said. "Who do you suppose Shaitan turned out to be?"

Charlotta shook her head. "Who?"

"The man who was my butler before he so strangely disappeared!"

X GOT his car and drove at once out to the Bedford property. He found the doors and the windows of the place thrown wide open. There was a police officer who got up as X crossed the lawn. The Agent flashed his Associated Press card. "Just got the news," he said. "Mind if I ask a few questions?"

"It's a little late for news, I'm afraid," said the officer. "Our local paper has scooped you. But ask away if you want."

"Anyone beside Mr. Bedford affected?" X asked.

"Sure. The whole outfit of them. Servants and the girl are all in the hospital with the mad sickness."

X's heart sank. "There was a young girl reporter visiting the Bedfords. Do you know anything of her condition?"

"I couldn't tell you."

"Mind if I go look through the house?"

"Well," the cop said slowly, "I was told not to let anybody in, but I suppose a newspaperman could go in if he didn't touch anything. I got the windows open to air the place, you see."

X nodded, hurried into the great, deserted house, ran up the broad, curving stairs and found the room that Betty Dale had used. He started to the closet to see if any of her clothes were there, stopped suddenly as he saw a piece of paper on the dresser. It was a typewritten note and X recognized the type as that of Betty's portable machine that always accompanied her wherever she went. The note read:

Dearest Dora—

I am suddenly called back to New York. Love, Betty.

Then Betty had escaped. She was safe in New York. Or was she?

So unlike her to run away, especially when she was at the location of a crime that promised good newspaper copy.

Puzzled and worried, X left the house to drive back to the center part of town. He parked in front of the City Administration Building not far from the jail. If Shaitan had been captured, no one was more anxious to know the details than X. He entered the building and turned into the office marked: *Chief of Police.* There a young officer wanted to know his business.

X showed the Associated Press card and asked to see Chief Hurd.

"Sorry," the young officer replied. "Chief Hurd is busy at the moment. He has important guests from out of town and will be occupied with them for some time. I have orders to admit none who were not invited to the conference."

The Secret Agent did not press his request further. He turned, re-entered the hall. Possibly he could get a glimpse of the captured Shaitan if he went to the jail. As he was about to leave the building, he saw John Morris entering the front door. X turned, fell in step beside Morris and said: "Your name Morris?"

The secret service man nodded.

"And you have been asked to attend a conference in Chief Hurd's office?"

"I have," Morris replied.

"Good!" X took hold of the man's arm, steered him down the hall to the door of a washroom.

IT WAS a totally unexpected move. Agent X kicked the door open with his foot and flung Morris bodily into the room.

As Morris folded backwards through the door, X followed him. Morris was on his feet in a moment, trying to draw his gun. But X closed in fast. His left fist whipped across Morris's right biceps, paralyzing the man's gun arm. Then his right lashed at Morris's chin. It was a perfect knockout punch.

Morris had hardly struck the floor before X had his pocket makeup materials out. It would be a quick easy change for both A.J. Martin and Morris were light-complexioned.

Five minutes later, the Agent stalked boldly into the hall, approached the guardian of Hurd's door and demanded admittance which was immediately accorded him. Hurd took hold of his arm and introduced him to the other men in the office, saying:

"This is John Morris, to whom the city of Brownsboro owes the deepest apology for having mistaken him for the notorious Mr. X."

X bowed to each man in turn. Lorin Garvey was there as well as Dr. Davies and Reed Kennedy. Four elderly gentlemen who sat somewhat apart and looked as though they wondered what this was all about, were then introduced as Mr. Sparks, Mr. Haleck, Mr. Feris and Mr. Mathews—the four who remained of the five men originally doomed by Shaitan.

"What is quite beyond us," said Haleck, speaking for his companions as well as himself, "is that up to this moment we hadn't the slightest idea that this Shaitan person intended to murder us. We have received no threats of any sort, yet you insist this is an extortion game."

Chief Hurd nodded. "It's a good bit different than anything of the sort I have come across." He motioned to a man who was sitting at the side of his desk. "This is Mr. George Franks of the Philadelphia Association of Life Insurance Companies. He can explain the racket better than I can."

FRANKS stood up, cleared his throat and began: "The insurance business is the real victim of this extortion racket—which, had it not been nipped in the bud, might have spread entirely across the country." He turned to Sparks, Haleck, Feris and Mathews, saying: "You four gentlemen have insurance policies which total about one million dollars, or a total of five million in life insurance, distributed among you. The policies are from six different firms. The reason why you were not molested by this fiendish Shaitan is that you were not immediately concerned in his original threat."

Franks cleared his throat again, then continued: "Shaitan demanded one million dollars to spare you five gentlemen. The money was to be raised by the six firms in our association. That was the threat as it originally appeared. We were inclined to take it all as a joke, since murder of five men is quite a large order and the fanciful name of Shaitan suggested that the writer of the threat note might be a little touched in his head.

"We ignored his threat. A few days later I received a note saying that I should watch the first column of the *Brownsboro Bugle* for proof of the fact that Shaitan was capable of carrying out exactly what he had threatened to do. It further stated that the message would be intended for our eyes alone and would be written in cipher, the key of which was given to me."

Agent X's eyes fastened on Reed Kennedy, as Franks went on:

"The first threat note coded into the paper was simply a repetition of the written note we had received, stating that five men were doomed. Four days later, my copy of the *Bugle* informed me that a member of Mr. Haleck's family was to die. And two days later, I am sorry to say, Mr. Haleck's son was killed in an inexplicable manner in the street. A number of persons in the street near him at the time were carried to the hospital, apparently converted into shrieking maniacs. How this was managed, I have just learned. Gas, of a deadly poisonous nature, had been stolen from Mr. Garvey's laboratory."

"Not the gas—the formula," Garvey corrected.

"How it was turned into the street," Franks went on, "we have yet to learn."

"It came—" X said quietly—"from beneath Reed P. Kennedy's car."

Kennedy sprang to his feet. "It's a lie!" he shouted. "You're accusing me of having a part in this killing? I have already confessed to Chief Hurd that I was forced by the most terrible threats from Shaitan to print this cipher message in my paper. I also confessed that Shaitan compelled me to act as his messenger in collecting the money the insurance companies mailed. But I have had no part in murder. I even hadn't the slightest notion that what I was doing was connected with murder."

"Then," said Agent X, his soft, compelling voice dominating every man in the room, "perhaps you were also compelled to devote your car and your chauffeur to the services of Shaitan. I was judging the method used in the Haleck case to be the same as that used in the murder of Sparks's son which I witnessed outside the jail last night."

KENNEDY sank into his chair and gnawed his lips. Finally, he nodded his head. "Twice, I received phone calls from Shaitan, whom I have never seen. Twice he told me to have my chauffeur drive to certain parts of the city, and to let the motor idle.... I lied a moment ago when I said I didn't know this was murder.

"I later discovered that some sort of a timed gas bomb had been connected to my car and this probably fed the gas out through the exhaust pipe while the motor was idling. I should have gone to the police then, but I was afraid. Shaitan had said he would torture me into madness if I went to the police. He said he would cut off my eyelids! Could anything out of hell have conceived a more terrible torture than that?"

"Probably not," said X. He retired in favor of Franks, the insurance man.

"That sort of thing continued," Franks explained. "Always, the murders got closer and closer to the five doomed men. We knew well that if these men's beneficiaries were to turn in their claims all at once, our companies would have been ruined."

"Why didn't you pay Shaitan's demands, then?" Dr. Davies asked. "Here you'll have to fork out your million for Bedford's death and still the murder may go on."

"No it won't," declared Chief Hurd. "We have captured Shaitan. He is in our jail. You see, the insurance company started sending him money in fifty thousand dollar installments. The first shipment of money, Shaitan was to be allowed to take from Kennedy. That was to make Shaitan bolder. The second shipment arrived, and Mr. Franks's detectives and our police were on the job. Shaitan pursued Kennedy in his eagerness to get the money, and I arrested Shaitan after a terrible fight."

"How," asked X, "did you know it was Shaitan? Mr. Kennedy has stated that he has never seen Shaitan. To my knowledge, no one has seen his true face."

"When a man makes a demand for money, then receives the money, it's a pretty good sign he was the man who made the original threat," Hurd stated. "Besides, this fellow acted suspicious. And he did have an opportunity to get hold of Mr. Garvey's gas patent or whatever it was. He was Mr. Garvey's butler."

Agent X sprang to his feet. "You mean—" He stopped. Then his voice softened. "You've made a very grave error," he said to Hurd. "According to your method of reasoning, Kennedy might just as well be Shaitan as this fellow you've arrested. I feel certain that if I were Mr. Haleck, or Mr. Feris, or any of the other threatened men, I would still consider myself doomed when an arrest was made on such flimsy evidence. I say with all assurance that you do *not* have Shaitan in jail at the present moment."

"Mighty good reasoning," said a voice from the door. All looked up to see two members of the police force standing in the doorway. Both had revolvers in their hands. "You see," one of the cops said, "Shaitan is in this room right now. His other name is Secret Agent X. We have just discovered the real John Morris locked in our washroom."

Agent X looked at the accusing circle of eyes turned on him, and at the police guns. His hands never approached his body. He merely brought them together and clasped them. Then he took a single step that brought him directly behind Chief Hurd's desk.

"Stand still!" rapped Hurd.

X smiled disarmingly. "One accusation is quite enough. I am satisfied to be called Agent X, for I must admit that I am—Secret Agent X. But I am not—Shaitan. Think a moment. Last night at the jail, an entire mob was rendered unconscious by a little gas bomb of mine. Of that mob, not a man or woman in it feels any the worse from the little gas attack I staged. Had I been Shaitan, it would have been just as easy for me to have killed them. You probably will never understand the motives behind my methods of investigation—"

X's voice never dropped. He had been speaking so softly, so confidently, that there was not a man in the room but what was completely absorbed in what he was saying. When he stopped speaking, his body was already in motion. Motion so swift, so precisely executed that he took everyone by complete surprise.

His right leg shot out with all the force of his powerful body behind it. His shoe planted against the desk, sent it rolling across the room straight toward the door. The two police saw it coming at them like a juggernaut, backed, shot at X—or rather at the place where X had been a moment before.

X had moved at the same moment he had kicked the desk. He dove headlong for the door, or rather for the desk that was jammed in the doorway. He landed on his side, felt two glass gas capsules, in his pocket, crush as the force of his leap sent him sliding across the top of the desk to somersault into the hall outside.

Then he was on his feet, running, holding his breath lest his own anesthetizing gas catch up with him. Probably those in Hurd's office would never know what had happened. X's hands had never approached his body. He had not so much as swung a fist, yet he had scored a perfect knockout.

In another moment he was in his car, roaring down the street.

CHAPTER VIII

CITY OF DEATH

THAT NIGHT, HARVEY BATES sat on his jail-house bunk and stared moodily at the floor. He wasn't at all satisfied, particularly with one Harvey Bates. He thought back over what had taken place that afternoon and tried to reason out just what Agent X would have done had he been in Bates's place. One thing was certain, Bates thought, X would never have permitted himself to be clapped into jail while the real murderer roamed the streets.

Bates heard footsteps in the corridor outside. He didn't look up. He wouldn't have cared to see anyone unless—unless that person was Charlotta. He looked up hopefully when he thought that it might be the girl, groaned and dropped his head when he saw it was only the young jailer.

"Oh, you still here?" the jailer said. He had been making that brilliant crack every half hour since Bates's imprisonment until the big man wanted to grind his teeth every time he heard it. "Well, do you want to see a woman?" asked the jailer.

Bates stood up suddenly. He had seen a familiar silhouette against the opposite wall of the hall. He crossed to the bars as Charlotta came up. A bright smile flashed across the girl's face. She seemed oblivious to the existence of the bars that separated them. Her body pressed flat against the bars, as close to him as she could get, she thrust her arms through the opening and managed, by standing on tiptoe to get them about his square shoulders.

"Gun under handkerchief, right hand," she whispered. Then she suddenly broke the embrace, pulled her right arm away so that her right hand passed over his left hand. Bates felt the handkerchief and the cool gun steel hidden by it. It was a perfectly executed move on Charlotta's part, but Bates was so completely right-handed as to be absolutely awkward with his left hand.

He dropped the gun. It clattered to the concrete floor. The young jailer shouted hoarsely and sprang forward. But Bates had already stooped, scooped up the gun with his right hand and thrust it between the bars.

"Unlock this door in a hurry," he ordered huskily. And he glowered down from his formidable height upon the jailer in such a manner that the jailer had not the slightest doubt but what Bates would shoot to kill if his order wasn't obeyed. The jailer took out keys, fitted one into the lock, turned it.

At that moment, the corridor suddenly became filled with men attracted by the jailer's shouts. Bates shouldered open the door, sprang into the corridor and turned the gun on the approaching guards. "Stop!" he whipped out. "I'll shoot." Pure bluff. Under no consideration would Bates have shot these men. But his threat was enough to halt them.

But at the same time, Charlotta uttered a warning cry. Bates turned halfway around as three men sprang at him from behind.

Bates struck out with his right hand. The muzzle of the automatic Charlotta had slipped him gashed the cheek of one of his attackers. He threw another to the ground with what appeared to be an exaggerated shrug of his shoulders. He danced out of a hail of blows from the third. Some one managed to get Bates by the wrist and twist the gun away from him. Bates plunged forward, dragging two men who had gripped him from behind. But he found he faced still another man—a seemingly slight man whose hair was iron-gray.

BATES swung for the gray head, found his wrist locked in a grip of steel. The gray-headed man yanked Bates toward him, twisted around and actually pulled Bates's body over his back and flung him to the floor. Because of this surprising move on the part of the gray-haired chief jailer, Bates found himself pressed to the floor by a mass of guards. They gripped his legs and arms and carried him back to the cell from which he had escaped.

The old jailer slammed the door. "That'll teach you, I guess," he said. "Now where'd that gun come from?"

The man who had brought Charlotta to the cell, pointed at the girl. "She must have brought it, sir."

The old jailer said: "Watch for the femme, as the French say. You fellows clear out. I want to talk to this young woman alone."

The younger guards had profound respect for the chief jailer after they had seen him throw a man who had looked as though he had a fair chance of knocking out the entire personnel of the city jail. They turned and retired down the hall, leaving the old jailer with Charlotta.

Charlotta held her head high and looked at the old jailer with contemptuous eyes. "Why don't you lock me up?" she asked.

There was a strange, amused smile on the old jailer's face. He said one word, quietly: "Charlotta."

Charlotta's eyes widened. On the other side of the cell door, Bates became suddenly animated. He pressed his face against the cage bars and regarded the jailer with such a devout look that the girl stared in amazement from the jailer to the imprisoned Bates.

"You, again!" she exclaimed softly. "But why—" she gestured bewilderedly and let her question dangle.

"Why should I aid you in liberating Bates?" X concluded. "Simply because there's not a rope in town that would hold him."

Agent X, for it was indeed he who had managed to throw the powerful Bates, produced keys and went over to Bates's cell.

"Then—then you two—work together?" asked Charlotta in amazement.

"Constantly," X told her. He unlocked the cell door and permitted Bates to step out.

"Thank you, sir," Bates said quietly. He took Charlotta's hand in his own big fingers. "And thank you."

"Save all that," X whispered. "As you've guessed, I was forced to knock out the chief jailer. He isn't very well hidden and I didn't hit him very hard. He's not particularly strong and I didn't want to hurt him. Any moment now, some one will find him and then there will be plenty of trouble. We can get out through the back way. I've a car all ready."

X LED the way down the hall and came to the chief jailer's office. He opened the door softly. Bates and Charlotta followed him into the jail kitchen and out on a little concrete platform where a small truck was backed up.

"Not exactly a luxuriant conveyance," he apologized, "but its appearance at the rear of the jail was less likely to arouse suspicion. A grocer down the street was careless enough to leave it unlocked. Remind me to see that he is well paid for his car in case we damage it, Bates."

The three of them crowded into the cab of the truck. X piloted it down the alley.

"I was frantic to get you out of jail," Charlotta said to Bates. "Some one has kidnaped Lorin Garvey."

"Frantic?" X interrupted. "With good reason! Are you sure of this, Charlotta?"

"Positive. He's gone. Simply vanished."

X uttered a prolonged whistle. "We'll have to work fast. If all those secrets of Garvey's brain fall into the wrong hands, there isn't a man or woman in the country that will be safe. He probably knows more about ultra-modern weapons than any other living man. You can appreciate what would happen if he was forced to turn over his knowledge to some criminal like Shaitan. Was there any sign of a clue left?"

"I don't know," the girl said. "As soon as I heard that Harvey was in jail, I got a gun and came over here."

"Then, I'll have to go to Lorin Garvey's house right away. Did you notify the police, Charlotta?"

"No," the girl replied, as X braked the truck in front of Garvey's house. "But it looks like some one is there now. I thought I saw a flashlight in the front room just now."

X got out, and Bates started to follow. The Agent stopped him. "Charlotta is a very capable woman, no doubt, but you'd better stay here and keep your eye on her. I'll whistle if I need you." Then X hurried off across the lawn, seeking the shadows, working with his makeup as he moved toward the house. He removed the gray toupee revealing his own natural hair. His skillful fingers smoothed out the wrinkles in the plastic material on his cheeks so that by the time he reached the house he had the appearance of a much younger man.

The front door was open. X walked into the dark hall, listened a moment to hear footsteps prowling about in the next room. X opened the door and slipped into the room. Footsteps stopped. Some one near at hand was breathing heavily.

"That you, Knore?" a voice whispered.

"Yes," X whispered back, recalling Peter Knore's voice as near as possible. He thought the speaker was Jo Pyle.

"Kelly got this safe open, but the damned thing is empty. You sure that Charlotta dame hasn't looted the place before we got a chance?"

Guided by the voice, X moved across the room. The toe of his shoe kicked into the leg of a chair. A flashlight snapped on, its white spot centering on the Agent. X had his gas gun in his hand. "Put 'em up!" he ordered.

The light went out. Somebody cursed. A flying body struck X thigh high. He went down under two hundred pounds of beef. Somehow he managed to keep his gun arm free from the heavy man's body-crushing grip. He brought the gun up in the palm of his right hand to slap his attacker across the side of the head with it. The man groaned and rolled over to the floor. X sprang up. Another voice whispered:

"You got him, Jo?"

"Sure," X said, imitating Jo Pyle's voice. "Turn your light on the floor."

THE MAN'S flash flicked on, found the mountainous form of Jo Pyle lying on the floor. But before the other man could so much as utter an exclamation of surprise, X stepped in and jammed his gas pistol into the man's ribs. "Got you," he whispered. "You even so much as take a deep breath, and I'll let you have it."

He took the flashlight from the man's unresisting fingers and turned it on the man's face. His captive was one of the local toughs X had previously met in the shanty down by the railroad tracks. "Is Peter Knore here?" X asked.

The man nodded glumly. "Somewhere. He fixed it so Jo and I would take all the risks. What is this? A pinch?"

"Where's Knore?"

X took the gun out of Kelly's ribs, tilted the barrel slightly, and pulled the trigger. A thin stream of harmless, anesthetizing gas spouted into Kelly's face. Completely surprised, he gulped it all in and wilted to the floor.

The Agent hurriedly searched the lower floor of the house. Things were turned inside-out in the laboratory and the study. There had been a most thorough search for something. But there was no sign of Peter Knore. X went up the steps, tiptoed down the hall, saw a glow-worm of light moving about in a bedroom. X stepped through the door. Again he resorted to the ruse of speaking in the voice of Jo Pyle. "Find anything, Knore?" he asked.

Knore cursed softly. "I thought I told you to stay downstairs."

"If you found that gas formula, Knore, I wanted to be in on it, see? Whatever you get out of it, you've got to split fifty-fifty."

Knore turned his light beam on the Agent. X sprang forward, thrust his gas pistol up in Knore's face. The gun was empty, but formidable-looking. His left arm went around and whipped out Knore's gun from the latter's hip pocket. He tossed it into a corner of the room. "Now," he said, "the truth." Danger flashed in X's eyes. He reached out and twitched Knore's Van Dyke beard. It came loose, nearly tearing part of Knore's skin away with it. Knore winced with pain.

"That's a starter," X told him. "What were you trying to do here?"

"You seem to have that information already," Knore said. "Why should I tell you?"

"You were looking for the formula to Garvey's poison gas, then? Yet you were apparently already in possession of the formula or at least some of the gas. Weren't you using it to kill and drive people insane with the idea of selling fake antitoxin to the wealthy for protection of what Dr. Davies thought was a disease of madness?" X knew this was not so, but his statement might scare the truth from Knore.

"That's not true," Knore denied. "Selling the fake serum was Pyle's idea. He was simply taking advantage of the plague of madness. I acted the part of the foreign doctor for him. I hadn't the slightest idea that the madness was caused by a gas."

"But you were looking for the gas formula? You wanted Garvey's secret for your own country?"

Peter Knore nodded. "What do you intend to do about it?"

AGENT X reached over to a table and turned on a lamp. He nodded toward a chair. "Sit down," he ordered. Knore sat down. With one eye on the man, Agent X hurriedly searched the room. Dresser drawers were wide open and the closet had been rifled. On the dresser was a hastily written note scrawled on the back of an envelope. It read:

> To the friend of K9. If you read this you will know that there is a small chance of saving my life. I have discovered that I am being deceived by a member of my household. I know that Shaitan will make an effort to kidnap or murder me tonight. Nothing can prevent it.
>
> (Signed) Lorin Garvey.

X crushed the piece of paper into his pocket and turned to Knore. "You knew Garvey was going to be kidnaped, didn't you?"

"No!"

"Why, then, did you pick tonight to search the house? You mean to say that you didn't know that Garvey wouldn't be here?"

"Whether Garvey was here or not, I had decided to make an effort to obtain the gas formula. Now that you know the truth, what do you intend to do?"

X wasn't at all sure that Knore had told him the truth. He strode over to the spy. "I'm going to do this!" He brought his right hand up fast, landing a blow with the gun barrel on the side of Knore's head. It was so perfectly timed and placed that the spy hadn't a chance to escape its stunning force. He sagged forward in the chair and tumbled to the floor unconscious. X went to Garvey's dresser. He picked up Garvey's hair brush and pulled out a single pale hair that clung to the bristles. This he carefully wrapped in paper before going downstairs.

In the hall below he called police headquarters. Without giving his name, he left a message for John Morris, saying that the spy, Peter Knore, was unconscious in the Garvey house together with two local toughs. He advised Morris and the police to act accordingly. Then he hurried from the house to join Bates and Charlotta.

"We're so near the end of the trail," he said, "and yet just far enough from the end that we can't quite touch the man we're after. You two better get in the back part of the truck. You don't stand in so well with the police after that jail break and we can't risk an argument with the law when every second counts."

Bates and Charlotta climbed over the back of the cab seat and into the truck. X got the motor started and drove at once to the hospital. Then he got out and told Bates and Charlotta to keep dark until he returned.

"What do you suppose X is going in there for?" Charlotta asked. She was standing in the back of the truck, peering out through a crack in the rear door. Bates joined her.

"Hard to say," Bates clipped.

"He always does queer things. Have you known him very long—I mean as well as anyone could know Agent X."

"Haven't known him more than a year," Bates told her, "though I've worked for him for a long time."

"And you've never seen his face?"

"No one sees his face."

Charlotta was silent a moment. Then: "What did you think when I came into the jail tonight and—" She stopped.

Out of the night came a hoarse shout: "Ex-tree! Ex-tree papah! Ex-tree!"

"What do you suppose that is?" Charlotta asked.

"Paper boy." Bates took out his pipe and lighted it. They listened to the newsboy as he came nearer. Bates pushed the back door of the truck a little farther open. "I'm going to find out."

CHARLOTTA'S hand went out to clutch at his sleeve. "No! Some one might see you. They still think you're Shaitan, you know."

"Too dark." Bates ignored her warning and sprang to the street. He hailed the newsboy, jingled coins in his pocket. The boy ran across the street. "What's up?" Bates asked as he pressed a dime into the boy's hand and took a paper.

"Rumor some guy will wipe out the town, sir. Terrible, ain't it?"

"Keep the change." Bates folded the paper.

"The chief of police and the mayor got a note from a guy with a funny name. Sounds something like Satan when you say it. He's the guy that wants to do the dirty work." The boy ran down the street, shouting out his sensational wares.

Bates got back in the truck, struck a match, while he and Charlotta bent over the paper. A black scare-head screamed:

SHAITAN STILL AT LARGE!

And further down, Bates read aloud: "It is rumored that Chief of Police Hurd has received a warning signed by Shaitan—"

The match went out. At that moment, Agent X leaped into the cab of the truck. Charlotta hurried forward to lean over the back of the seat where X was starting the motor.

"Shaitan will destroy the town," said the Agent.

"Just a rumor, sir," Bates put in calmly. "Can't go on these papers. Maybe just a scare."

"In the papers? Did they put out an extra edition?" X asked. "Let's see that paper a moment." Bates handed him the paper and X held it close to the dashlight of the truck. He read quickly. "Not much here. Maybe just a rumor, but I'm inclined to take it seriously. Shaitan has Garvey's gas. He *could* do exactly what he threatens to do. Charlotta and I know he *would* do it. We'll have to move!"

He started to nose the truck into the center of the street and opened it up. Two blocks west, he turned into Elm Street and headed for the City Administration Building. There were quite a few people going in and out the door as X sprang from the cab and ran up the steps.

"What's this I hear?" X asked of a man just leaving the building.

"About Shaitan? Just a threat. He can't do that, you know. We're getting up a volunteer organization to prevent panic. That fool Kennedy would sell his soul to put out an extra edition to scare folks crazy."

X went into the building and hurried straight for Kurd's office. There were so many other people going in and out that he knew he could pass unnoticed. George Franks, the insurance man, was there, as were Dr. Davies and the mayor.

"Most audacious nonsense I've ever seen," declared Davies, waving a paper above his head. "Why, killing everybody in the town wouldn't be anything but war. One man can't declare war on a city."

"It would be war with all the loss on one side—the city's side," Agent X said. He reached out and snatched the paper from Davies' hand.

"Here, what business is that of yours?" Dr. Davies cried out as he endeavored to retrieve the paper.

"It's the business of every man in the city," X said. He glanced down at the paper. On it was printed in pencil:

The original demand was one million dollars from the insurance people. Because you have been slow in paying and because the people of this city have tried to interfere with my plans, I agree to spare Brownsboro only on the condition that you pay the original demand plus one half of all the money in the city treasury. Lorin Garvey is completely in my power and will be compelled to aid me if I have to wipe out all life in the city. A red lantern on top of the Administration Building will be your signal to agreement. Better pay me and have your lives in exchange, than die and thus enable me to loot your city anyway.

(Signed) Shaitan.

P.S. Any attempt on the part of Secret Agent X to interfere with my plans will result in the immediate death of Betty Dale.

With cold, numb fingers, X handed the paper back to Dr. Davies. He pushed back through the crowd without feeling the elbows that jostled him. Betty in the hands of a man who had terrorized Asia where life is cheap and pain the heritage of every man and woman! The city threatened with destruction while the city officials treated the whole matter as an impossibility. With Garvey's gas in his hands, Shaitan had reduced the impossible to the probable.

CHAPTER IX

CAVERN OF TERROR

"WHAT NEWS?" ASKED Bates and Charlotta together as X came out to the truck.

"The worst," X said hoarsely. "Shaitan has given his ultimatum, to a people he has already tied hand and foot. There is not the slightest doubt but what he has a quantity of Garvey's gas and is prepared to use it. If I don't move against him, there'll not be a living or sane creature in this town. If I do move against him—" He shook his head despondently. He walked around the track, stood in the middle of the street, moistened his finger and held it above his head for a moment.

"From the west, sir," Bates said.

X nodded his agreement and got in beneath the wheel of the truck.

"What do you mean, 'from the west?'" asked Charlotta.

"The wind," X explained. "If Shaitan intends to wipe out the town with gas, he'll have to discharge that gas to the west of the city so that the poison will be carried across the town. That means that somewhere among those black hills to the west of town, Shaitan is waiting to turn loose his cloud of madness and death."

"What would he gain?" Bates asked.

"The sheer pleasure of destroying," Charlotta said, with a shudder. "The man is a fiend."

"A very clever fiend," X said. "Not averse to killing, but not a man to kill without motive. When the gas has swept the town, Shaitan will come down and loot the banks. Then, Brownsboro will act as an example for other cities he will threaten afterwards. Only there isn't going to be any afterwards for Shaitan. I've got to stop this."

X drove on, his jaw set doggedly, his eyes staring straight ahead. They passed the great Bedford house, standing dark and deserted, a monument to the cruelty of Shaitan. They drove out to the old turnpike and jounced into a rutty lane that led on toward the hills—black hills, frowning with the wrath of Shaitan. The moon, hanging above the ragged horizon, was as placid and pale as the face of a corpse.

X took out his watch. It was ten-thirty. An hour and a half in which to search through country with a thousand hiding places. And then, if he was successful in finding Shaitan, what could he do to keep the fiend from killing Betty? What could he do against the terrible gas?

X slammed on the brakes, turned almost angrily on Bates and Charlotta who sat silently beside him. He had forgot them entirely, so engrossed had he been with his own problems. "I'm getting out here," he announced. "You two drive back to town. Do all you can to get the people to get in cars and evacuate the city. And if they won't move, see that by midnight you're miles away from here. I can't be responsible for getting you into a jam like this."

CHARLOTTA smiled slightly. She reached over and took Bates's hand. "Is there anything about us that reminds you of a couple of washouts?"

"You think we'd let you go on alone?" Bates asked.

"You must go back," X insisted. "Don't think I'm not grateful for your offer, but I can't jeopardize you in this way."

"There's only one way you can stop us," Bates said. "A shot of anesthetizing gas. And with that stuff in us, we won't do much running when Shaitan turns on his gas."

X sighed. "For once, I'm sorry for devotion." He started the car jogging up the lane that was climbing steadily into the hills.

A little farther on, the car refused to climb another foot. They got out and plunged into the thick underbrush to work wearily upward toward the highest peak in the range. X knew that it was like looking for a needle in a haystack, but he kept carefully on, using his flashlight sparingly. The brush thinned out after they had mounted a few hundred feet. There was considerable more rock formation and less foundation for vegetation. Suddenly, Charlotta uttered a little cry. X whipped around, sent his flashlight beam streaking in her direction. The girl held up a little scrap of cloth.

X sprang to her side. "Let's see that!" He snatched the piece of cloth from her hand and held it close to the light. It was a piece of silk from a woman's dress, possibly Betty's, though he had never seen the material before that he remembered.

"A piece torn from the hem of a woman's skirt," Charlotta told him.

X started fanning the flashlight around in all directions, searching for more bits of cloth until his eyes ached. "Keep your eyes open for more. It may mark the trail to Shaitan's hiding place. Let's go on."

"Looks like another up ahead," Bates whispered.

X broke into a run that carried him far ahead of the others. He stooped, picked up the second piece of cloth. It matched the first. They hurried forward as the bits of cloth marked the trail. At last, they found a piece fully six inches long dangling from a thorny bush. And there was nothing farther. Just beyond the bush, a rocky wall towered high above them. And there was no break in the wall in either direction that they could see.

Cautiously, X parted the bushes and scarcely suppressed an exultant cry. Beyond was the mouth of a cave.

"Charlotta behind me," he whispered. "Bates at the rear. Now forward and keep quiet. We haven't a ghost of a chance if Shaitan hears us coming."

Once within, X risked one searching gleam from his flashlight. The ceiling of the natural rocky corridor was far beyond the reach of his light. Ahead the floor was smooth and without any treacherous openings that X could discover. X moved on rapidly, groping his way, fearing to use the light any more than was necessary. The passage turned and climbed. Beneath his feet he felt a soft carpet of dust. He stopped, turned the light down toward the floor. Footprints in the dust—large, round-toed prints and beside them, the mark of small, pointed-toed shoes.

X's heart pounded. He was near Betty, he felt certain. So near and yet so far away. He couldn't take his eyes off that small footprint. He regarded it almost worshipfully. "Bates," he called, "Charlotta. They came this way."

Footsteps hurried along the passage behind him. In another moment, he would hear Charlotta's eager young voice questioning—

Something struck the Agent's head with terrific force. It was as though an explosion had taken place within his brain. Blinking light fluttered and flashed like angry lightning before his eyes. He knew he was going under—under the black curtain of oblivion. Had Charlotta played them false? Had she struck that blow? Or had both Bates and Charlotta fallen into the iniquitous hands of Shaitan?

YELLOW lantern light tinged the rocky walls of the cavern chamber by the time X opened his eyes. His magnificent physical condition enabled him to recover quickly from a blow that would have left another man with an achy, fuzzy head for a long time.

This was not the same part of the cavern in which the blow that had laid him out had been struck. It was a large, rough chamber closed at one end and with a low, rough doorway at the other. There was no door, nothing to prevent X from making his escape. He picked himself up and started for the door.

"Wait," a voice from somewhere near at hand murmured.

X turned around, saw no one.

"Above your head. Always, above your head, you will find Shaitan, Agent X."

X raised his eyes to where the rocky roof came together in a wedge-shaped formation. Dimly outlined in the light from the lantern, X could see a face. The features were indistinct, yet X was as certain that he knew what they looked like as if he could see them clearly.

"I will not detain you, Agent X," went on the whispering voice from the man above him. "I am too familiar with your marvelous escapes to try and detain you—with iron bars and doors, that is. However, I should like to warn you that the chamber just beyond this is dangerous. In the first place, there is only a narrow ledge around its outer rim and the floor is something of a bottomless pit.

"However, you would not have much difficulty in getting across the ledge were it not for the fact that the room is filled with poison gas—the gas of madness and death. Madness, if you breathe only a little of it—madness from the terrible pain it causes. Death, of course, if you get a good whiff. I don't want you to do anything you would later regret, you know.

"Do you know what time it is? Probably not, since I have taken your watch. There was some of that harmless anesthetizing vapor concealed under the crystal, wasn't there? At any rate, it is twenty minutes before midnight. I have learned that the people of Brownsboro are taking out gas masks from the national guard headquarters and distributing them. That is a waste of time, since Garvey's gas will penetrate any of the ordinary filters."

"You fully intend to go through with this scheme?" X asked calmly.

"I do. Cylinders of gas are mounted up here on a rocky ledge. The elevation and wind are both in my favor. On the stroke of twelve, I turn Death loose. I do not know what will become of you, but I rather imagine you'll starve to death or else plunge into that death chamber next to you. But before I go, I am sending you a present. Please open it at once."

A flat paper covered package dropped down through the opening. And the face of Shaitan had disappeared. The parcel landed almost at X's feet. He picked it up, broke the strings and unwrapped it. It was a piece of polished metal eight inches square. Agent X held it up, frowned in bewilderment at it.

And out of the gloom, looking up at him, frowning back, he saw his face. His *own* face. The unmasked face of Secret Agent X! Shaitan's hellish laughter sounded in the distance. "I know the man behind the mask now, Secret Agent X," Shaitan called back.

X slapped the pockets of his coat. All of his special equipment had been removed. His bullet-proof vest was gone. Nothing remained to him except that small secret compartment in the heel of his shoe. There he had secreted enough plastic material for a single disguise, and a small hypodermic needle loaded with a powerful narcotic. But what good would such flimsy weapons do him?

Footsteps along the rocky floor. X did not turn his head. He simply raised the metal mirror a little. In its polished surface he beheld the vision for which his eyes had hungered. Betty Dale, her dress in tatters, but apparently unharmed. X shoved the mirror hurriedly under his shirt. He turned slowly.

The girl came forward hesitatingly. In her large blue eyes was an almost heavenly light. Her red lips were smiling, yet quivering. Three feet away from him, she stopped. Her eyes devoured every inch of his face. The Agent's heart seemed to occupy the whole of his throat and was thumping so that he could hardly breathe. Forgot for the moment was the doom that hung over Brownsboro, over civilization for that matter. Agent X was wondering very humanly if Betty was disappointed at meeting him face to face for the first time.

BETTY DALE could neither move nor speak. At last she saw the face she had dreamed about—the true face of Agent X. She saw and longed to touch the soft waves of his dark-brown hair. His forehead was high, wondrously intellectual-looking. His eyes, beneath level brows, were the same eyes she had so frequently seen peering kindly from behind his many masks; there, too, she read of wisdom and generosity. They were eyes that spoke of the immense soul of the man. Eyes with driving power in their steel-gray depths. His nose wasn't too large. His lips had a ghost of a smile lingering at their corners. His jaw was square and aggressive.

In all, he was a good bit younger-looking than she had imagined. Yet, no; when he turned his head ever so slightly, the boyishness was gone and he appeared as a mature man of the world.

A joyful sob trembled in Betty's throat. She threw herself forward into the arms that ached for her, that held her with the strength of steel hands, yet were warmed with deepest emotion. She raised her head. Her eyes shimmered. Her lips parted.

"I knew long, long ago this would happen," he said in a deep, husky voice. "And long ago I knew that once I spoke to you with my real lips nothing in the world could keep my lips from yours."

For moments, their lips were locked. And while the fire of their own lives burned brighter than ever before, the city at their feet waited in breathless anticipation for the smothering cloud of madness that Shaitan had promised them. Suddenly, X seemed to realize what he was doing. He gently released the girl, whispered breathlessly: "Brownsboro. Shaitan."

"But—but what can you do? We're prisoners here together. There's no escape."

X jerked his head toward the doorway. "That room. I've got to chance getting across it. It may be too far. But I've got to try, Betty."

"No—no. You can't. You'll be killed!" She ran after him toward Death's door, seized him with small, strong fingers. "I couldn't bear it. Not after this—this, our one moment in a lifetime."

Gently, he took her wrists and pressed her arms to her sides. "You'd never forgive me, Betty, if fifty thousand people died because you and I were selfish."

"If you go into that room—I'll go with you!" she sobbed.

And X knew that she would. Nothing could prevent her from following him to hell itself. He dropped to the floor. Immediately, she was beside him.

"What are you going to do?" she demanded. "Is there no other way out except that room?"

X seized the heel of his right shoe and gave it a quick twist. A slot was revealed in the back of the heel and from this he took the tiny hypodermic needle. "My one weapon, Betty," he said. He pushed the plunger of the syringe a little way down, releasing some of the precious drug on the floor. His one weapon, and he was going to use it on the one he loved the best! He stood up.

"Kiss me once again, Betty. Quickly, dear." And as their arms entwined, he thrust the point of the needle into the flesh of her forearm. A scream of terror, as she realized his purpose, came from Betty's lips. Even as her body wilted to the floor, her fingers clutched at him. He broke away, staggered backwards to the door.

Agent X had given Betty only a small amount of the drug, enough to keep her unconscious for five minutes at the most. The narcotic, while powerful, had no bad after effects so that when she regained consciousness her senses were clear—painfully clear. She found herself alone in the cavern. The shadows, the silence filled her small body with terror. She stood up. Her frightened eyes turned toward the doorway. In the next room was Death, and there Agent X had gone. With a short, sharp cry, she started to run toward the doorway. Life without him seemed an impossibility.

There came a low, rumbling sound from the rear of the rock room. Betty stopped, turned around. Her eyes widened. Her hands crawled up toward her throat as if to strangle the scream that was forming there.

A huge stone at the end of the room was slowly rolling inward.

CHAPTER X

MAD EYES

WHEN X, BATES, and Charlotta had entered the rocky passageway, the Secret Agent had moved quite a bit more rapidly than either of his two companions were able to move. They had gone not more than a hundred feet along the passage before Harvey Bates, who was at the rear, had a premonition that they were being followed.

Without a word that might have alarmed Charlotta, he turned, went back around the last corner they had passed, and listened a moment. Somewhere, he was sure he heard footsteps. He produced a box of safety matches, struck a spark of light that never blossomed into flame.

Instantly, a noose of rope dropped to his shoulders and was yanked tight about his throat as his body was actually lifted from the floor only to be dropped a second later. Half strangled, Bates tore at the rope with both hands. Something sprang out of the dark. There was a brief flash of light from an electric torch, and a hard-toed shoe kicked out and caught Bates in the side of the head. The big man flattened to the floor. His senses had left him.

A few seconds later, Charlotta came to a stop. Directly ahead she saw the Agent's flashlight wink. But where was Harvey Bates? She called him in a voice that whispered and that was immediately choked off by the thin fingers of two hands that reached out for her. Those thin fingers tightened, tightened until every beat of her heart boomed in her ears and a faintly illuminated red cloud floated before her eyes.

When the cloud was gone, when she had once again regained consciousness, strong arms were about her and a husky voice was calling her name. She opened her eyes, saw, by yellow lantern light, that she was in the arms of Harvey Bates.

"Thank heaven!" Bates whispered fervently. "I was afraid—afraid—" And what he feared seemed too terrible to talk about. Bates was sitting on a rough, stone floor, his back braced against a great boulder. He had drawn the unconscious Charlotta up into a sitting position so that her head rested upon his shoulder. For frantic seconds, he had been attempting to revive her.

Charlotta made no effort to move. She felt very tired, but very comfortable and safe in this big, square man's arms. Ever since her early teens there had been men about, wanting to caress her. But there was something about this man's sometimes awkward touch that thrilled her. He was always so gentle and kind. Never presumptuous.

At last she began to wonder where they were. The lantern in the center of the room showed that the place was apparently without doors. No, there was a small opening in a rocky ceiling fifteen feet above their heads. The place was a sort of pit.

"How did we get here?" she asked. She felt Bates's big shoulders shrug. "Guess we were both knocked out. Some one dropped a rope over my head."

"The Punjab lasso," Charlotta said. "A weapon that Shaitan sometimes used in the east. In Mongolia, a peasant once pointed out a Soyot herdsman hanging to the limb of a tree. Shaitan had passed that night, the peasant explained to me. Shaitan has always struck from behind. He never fights if the odds are equal. That is why I hate him as I have never hated anyone. It's a wonder he didn't hang you."

"Would you have cared much? I mean—" Bates coughed.

"Very much," she whispered earnestly. She uttered a little laugh, sat up straight, and looked around. "How are we going to get out of here? What has become of X? And look! Had you noticed that both of us have lost our shoes? Why's that?"

"Don't know," Bates said. "Doesn't look—"

"Shsh—"

Bates looked at Charlotta. The warning hiss had not come from her lips. A crumb of rock was dislodged from above and dropped to the floor. They looked up, saw a wood ladder that was being pushed through the opening in the roof.

"It's X," Bates whispered. "Never fails. The one man who never misses."

BATES and Charlotta got to their feet. The ladder was resting on the floor, the opening in the roof now easily accessible. Bates sprang to the lower round of the ladder. Instantly, he uttered a sharp cry of pain and fell back to the floor. Charlotta dropped beside him. "Your hands, dear!" she cried anxiously. "You've been cut!"

Bates didn't need to be told that. His hands were drenched with his own blood. His feet, too, were severely cut. He looked up toward the top of the ladder and could just distinguish something resembling a human face in the gloom. A hellish chuckle sounded from the opening.

"Shaitan!" gasped Charlotta.

"Shaitan!" the voice mocked. "How do you like my ladder? Razor edges all along the rounds and side pieces. One way I had of torturing Garvey. I saved the ladder especially for you, Charlotta. My dear girl, if I remember properly, you have a very healthy appetite. There will be a sumptuous feast spread out for you at the top of the ladder. Each day I trust your appetite will improve. Tantalus knew no greater torment."

"I might have known," Charlotta said bitterly. "Satan incarnate!"

Shaitan laughed. "Well, you *would* follow me halfway around the earth, you know. Now that you have met me, I hope you are not disappointed. Sorry I must leave. Secret Agent X, you might like to know, is in a similar fix—he and the blonde reporter. The night I went to erase Bedford, Betty Dale was foolish enough to try and stop me. When I overcame her, she said that Agent X would see that I got my just deserts, from which I surmised that she was a particular friend of the Agent and therefore valuable alive.

"It seems that after all I am the only successful prophet. In as much as I have predicted the destruction of Brownsboro, I will have to go about my business. Happy days!" The face in the opening was gone.

"The beast," whispered Charlotta, her fine eyes narrow and burning with hate. "The cowardly beast!" She turned to Bates. "Are you badly hurt?"

Bates shook his head. "Blades are sharp, but not very long." He stood up somewhat painfully and began moving about the prison. After he had made the circuit once, he walked around again. There seemed no possible way out except up the ladder of knives. He leaned back against a big boulder and looked around the room.

"It's moving!" Charlotta whispered. "That rock you're leaning against moved. You pushed it a little!"

Bates turned around, braced his shoulder against the rock and pushed. The boulder inched back into the rocky wall. Beyond, he could see a crooked thread of light. He pushed again. The rock moved easier. Here was an exit that Shaitan had overlooked. Just as he gave the rock a final heave that rolled it clear of the opening, some one on the other side screamed. Bates ducked his head and passed through the opening.

He found himself in a natural rock room very similar to the one in which he and Charlotta had been confined. Standing in the center of the room, her hands raised to her throat, was Betty Dale.

BETTY uttered a long sigh and suddenly broke into tears. Charlotta ducked through the opening and was at her side in an instant. "You poor darling!" she whispered. "Who are you? How did you get in this terrible place?"

"Betty Dale," Bates explained to Charlotta. "Friend of the chief. Where is Agent X?"

"In there," Betty sobbed. "The room of death. It's filled with the gas. He went through there, trying to save a lot of people who would like to see him hanged!"

"If he did that," Bates said gravely, "it was because he felt it his duty."

"I know it," Betty choked. "But wh-what's happened to him?"

Charlotta snapped her fingers. "Wait. I'm getting an idea. You stop crying, honey. I know that X man. As Harvey says, he never misses."

Bates wasn't quite so confident. If X had gained his freedom, why hadn't he come to their aid?

Betty dried her eyes. "Sorry," she choked out. "I never washed out like this before. But it was different this time. Right after I had really seen him, to have him go like—like a dream." She smiled weakly. "Go on, Harvey Bates. I'm ready for anything. I'll find him somehow, some way."

"Sure," Bates agreed. They would find him, but this time, perhaps— Bates shook the gloomy thought out of his head. He turned to Charlotta. "Idea mature?"

"We'll go back from whence we just came," said Charlotta, "and go right up the ladder. Turn it up the other way, you know, so the blades of the knives will point downwards!"

"Beautiful!" Bates exclaimed.

Charlotta forced a laugh. She put her arm around Betty and led her toward the opening. "All the brains weren't given to the men, were they?"

They went back into the stone pit and Bates approached the ladder. He took hold gingerly at the under side and tried to move it. "Fastened above," he said glumly.

"Nor all the muscles given to the men," Charlotta said. "Come, Betty, the three of us can move this. The three of us have *got* to move it!"

Bates got under the ladder and braced his shoulders against it. The girl took hold beneath the round. "One, two, three, heave!" Bates grunted out. And the ladder moved, dislodged the rock that had retained its top, and tore loose from the opening. Bates drew the ladder down, inverted it, and replaced it. Then he climbed up, put his head through the opening and looked around. "All right," he called back. "Bring the lantern." He waited at the top of the ladder to extend a helping hand to Betty and Charlotta.

Bates pointed down the passage. "Some one's got a light down that way. Big, electric light. Easy, now." He took the lantern from Charlotta's hand and led the way toward the source of light. Far in the distance, the steeple clock in the city began to chime out the midnight hour—the zero hour for Brownsboro.

They had moved about twenty feet from the opening when Bates stumbled over his shoes and Charlotta's piled together in the passage. He hastily stepped into his oxfords and helped Charlotta on with her slippers. Then they went on toward the white light.

Fifteen feet from the end of the passage, they heard a high-pitched, insane laugh. A tall, staggering figure lurched from the shadows. It zig-zagged along the natural corridor, bumping into things, fighting with its own shadow, laughing, shouting, screaming. Long strides brought Bates to the staggering maniac. There was something familiar about the screaming, contorted face. The madman almost fell into Bates's arms and then began a feeble, pointless battle.

Betty and Charlotta came running up. Betty took one look at the madman. She knew that brown, wavy hair. She knew those gray eyes: in spite of the makeup that was smeared on the man's face, she knew it was Agent X. She uttered a faint cry and fell back in Charlotta's arms, sobbing out:

"It's Agent X!"

And the staggering thing with the flying arms looked at Bates and giggled idiotically. Bates dropped the lantern, seized his beloved chief, and stared in horror into dull, mad eyes. "Good Lord!" he whispered. "Stark insane!" And gripping the struggling form he went to the mouth of the passage while Charlotta helped the grief-stricken Betty along behind.

They were on a rocky ledge overlooking the city. A powerful electric lantern illuminated the ledge where six big gas cylinders were mounted. Standing with his hand on the valve, counting the strokes of the distant clock, was the tall figure of Shaitan, his features covered with a gas mask.

SHAITAN turned, yanked a heavy automatic from his belt. His other hand left the valve and went to lift the bottom of the gas mask. "Put up your hands, all of you. Your hands, do you hear! Release that staggering idiot!"

Reluctantly, Bates released X. The maddened Agent dashed headlong to the edge of the cliff. Betty screamed, hid her face on Charlotta's shoulder as X slipped from the narrow ledge, fell, but somehow managed to catch himself and drag himself to safety. Then he staggered back across the ledge, fighting with nothing, falling over his own feet.

Shaitan covered them with his gun. Bates was cursing slowly and methodically. In his dark eyes a terrible rage was smoldering.

"I warned Mr. X," Shaitan said lightly. "He *would* try to prevent the inevitable. Too bad he didn't get enough of the gas to kill him outright." Shaitan dropped the bottom of his mask into place, still keeping the gun turned on Bates and the two girls. Agent X wasn't worth watching. He was lunging at the rock wall, clawing at it, trying to climb its perpendicular face, all the time uttering a meaningless babble. Shaitan's hand went to the main gas valve.

"Here!" Bates called out sharply. "Not going to do that!" He took a step forward. He knew what X would have done at that moment if he had been able. He would have risked anything to keep Shaitan from loosing death upon the city below.

Shaitan reached over and swung one of the flexible gas vents so that it pointed across the ledge. He lifted the bottom of his mask again. "Another step like that and I'll let you sample the gas!" he warned.

"You're not going to turn that valve!" Bates said slowly. He was steeling himself for the effort he was going to have to make. He wondered how long it would take him to die with a bullet in his body; wondered if there was going to be time for him to save the city and the two girls whose lives depended entirely upon his actions. He ground his teeth together and sprang forward. Shaitan raised his automatic.

But at that moment, the insane Agent X did the most insane thing of all. His right hand darted in under his shirt and brought out the metal mirror Shaitan had thrown to him when X had been in the rocky prison. Shaitan pulled the trigger of his gun, but at the same time he involuntarily dashed his left hand across his eyes.

The bullet intended for Bates went wild. Shaitan couldn't have hoped to aim, blinded as he was by the reflected rays of his own lantern directed into his eyes by the mirror in X's hands.

THE AGENT'S mad staggering had brought him much closer to Shaitan than the latter had realized. And in that moment when the reflection from the mirror had blinded Shaitan, X regained his sanity. He pounced upon Shaitan with the ferocity of a lion. His right hand went up, seized Shaitan's gun, and twisted it from his grasp. At the same time, his left fist drove upwards to catch the killer on the point of the chin.

Shaitan sagged back against the wall of stone, where breathless and furious, he glared from the gas mask lenses into the cold, hollow eye of his own gun. And never had Shaitan seen a more sane man that the one who held that gun.

A joyful sob from Betty Dale as she realized that all this madness on X's part had been but acting that had made misdirection and cunning deceit possible. He had won again against terrible odds with no more formidable weapons than his wits, a mirror, and his fists. Betty would have rushed to him had not Charlotta detained her.

X never took his eyes off the treacherous Shaitan as he spoke rapidly to his friends. "Sorry I had to make the mad act so realistic. Had to make Shaitan realize you were all desperately afraid I had gone mad from the gas in that death chamber. When we met in the passage, we were too near Shaitan's ears to risk any conversation. I got through the gas chamber by holding my breath, for something of a record time, I believe. But holding my breath for long intervals when I use my anesthetizing gas keeps me in practice for that sort of thing.

"Charlotta, Shaitan doesn't look like such a terrible monster when he's robbed of his weapons, does he? But he has a wonderful brain. None but a criminal genius could have lone-wolfed this whole scheme. He hadn't a soul helping him except Kennedy who had been forced to act as his messenger."

X went over closer to the cowering killer. "Bates and Charlotta are going to feel disappointed when I remove this man's gas mask," he said. "But if it's any consolation, I felt about the same way. To think that the only man who had a perfect alibi the night Bedford was murdered should turn out to be the killer was quite a shock to me. But when I realized that *I* was the very man who would have been the witness to say that he *couldn't* have killed Bedford, very nearly made me crazy, as I must have appeared a moment ago. What time was it Charlotta, when you and Lorin Garvey were trying to get me to confess that I was Shaitan?"

"About noon," said the girl. "Why?"

"Simply that, had you told me it was noon or had I thought to ask, the alibi wouldn't have worked and we would have had the murderer right on the spot. Not for one minute did the man whom we knew as Lorin Garvey suppose that I was Shaitan. But he managed to drug me, keep me only about half conscious in a room where I could not see daylight. The only way I had of telling the passage of time was by watching the electric clock in Garvey's study.

"It was one of those calendar clocks. At midnight, the date on the calendar changes automatically. What Garvey did was simply set the clock up twelve hours so that the calendar changed at noon instead of midnight. In my doped condition, I had no conception of the time that had passed.

"What Garvey did was to make me think he and I were together at midnight when it was really noon. Then, after I had been doped so that I would sleep for about fifteen hours, Garvey just waited until midnight to kill Bedford."

AGENT X reached out and pulled the gas mask away from the face of the man they had known as Lorin Garvey. "You were very smart all the way through," X said. "That gag about your assistant stealing the formula for the gas was just a bluff. The only thing that tripped you up, that gave your identity away, was so ridiculously simple that any school boy would have discovered it. I doubt very much if you could spell the word 'deceive' correctly this very minute."

The killer's pale lips peeled back in a snarl.

"I noted," X explained, "that in the code messages you used to try and extort money from the insurance people, the word 'deceive' was misspelled. You had simply twisted the 'i' and the 'e'—a very common error. That, of course, told me nothing. But when you kidnaped yourself for the purpose of explaining your own disappearance, you left a note addressed to me, saying that Shaitan was going to get you. Even that might have got by me if it hadn't been that once more I saw the word 'deceive' spelled 'decieve.' And to that message, you had signed the name, Lorin Garvey."

"You mean to tell me that I was in Garvey's house all that time and didn't know that he was the killer?" demanded Charlotta.

"Just that, only it's a little worse. You had been hunting Shaitan all over the world. You were waiting in Garvey's house for Shaitan to make his appearance, when all the time the man you thought to be Garvey was really Shaitan. Shaitan arrived at Garvey's laboratory long before Peter Knore, who also was anxious to get Garvey's gas formula. Shaitan arrived before John Morris or you or Bates or I could get there. He tortured Garvey into revealing the formula. One of the things he did to the real Garvey was cut off his eyelids— an old Oriental torture, as you know, Charlotta.

"Then, because I had picked up the real Garvey, by that time a disfigured, wandering maniac, Shaitan feared that Garvey's reasoning power might return long enough so that Garvey could give me some information. So Shaitan staged an automobile accident which resulted in a period of unconsciousness for me. In that time, he completed his work on Garvey and killed him. The real Garvey had probably been mad for weeks. And he has been dead for three days.

"Tonight, I stopped at the hospital morgue. Microscopic comparison of hair from Garvey's corpse, then unidentified, with a hair taken from Garvey's hair brush, told me that the mad unknown had been the real Garvey. Then this man here, who has called himself Garvey, is Shaitan—the bald Shaitan."

X reached out, snatched the pale toupee from the killer's head to reveal the high, domelike pate of Shaitan. He pulled the smoke-lensed glasses from the man's eyes. The catlike, faintly luminous eyes of Shaitan lashed their beams of hatred across X's face.

With a terrible cry, Shaitan sprang at X's throat. His long fingernails gashed X's flesh. X reeled backwards, almost to the edge of the cliff. Bates sprang to aid his chief, but even as Bates reached out, he saw one of the struggling figures outlined against the sky. Arms and legs were beating the air as the lank figure shot off into space. A terrible, ascending shriek made the night hideous with its awful sound and awoke every echo in the black hills. Then a dull, thumping sound far below. Then silence.

On the edge of the cliff, X straightened up and drew a long breath. Shaitan had seen the Agent's real face, but he would boast of that only in hell.

"I must show you the jiu-jitsu stunt sometime," X said calmly to Bates. "The same one I got you with in the Brownsboro jail."

They started back toward the spot where they had left the truck, winding their way slowly along the rocky trail, X and Betty in front and Charlotta and Bates behind. Down in the valley, lights were going out all over Brownsboro. The crisis had passed. Midnight had sounded and yet the air was pure to breathe. The citizens would say that Shaitan had been bluffing when he threatened to destroy fifty thousand of them at a time.

"They'll never know," Betty sighed. "They'll never know how close they came to death, nor will they know the man who saved them. Not as I know him, anyway."

X laughed. For the first time in many days it was a happy, boyish laugh. "You really wouldn't want them to know, would you?"

Betty shook her head. "I'd be frightfully jealous if anyone besides me knew. Sometimes, I think I was even jealous of your mirror." Her head tilted back, her red lips smiling.

"Darling," he whispered.

Some fifty feet behind them, Charlotta stopped. In the moonlight, she saw Agent X holding Betty tenderly in his arms.

"Matter?" asked Bates.

"I think your chief sets you some very good examples," she said slowly.

Bates nodded. "Finest man in the world—" He stopped, stared ahead. He faced Charlotta and saw the invitation on her lips. "That? Example I'd do mighty well to follow, eh?"

"What do you think?" Charlotta asked.

BOOK XXX

DEATH'S FROZEN FORMULA

Why did those strange human derelicts patronize
newsreel-movie showings and immediately leave
the theatres with evil, mysterious intent? That was
the veiled enigma Agent X had to pierce—while
unfathomable gusts of hell's killing cold trapped
X and Betty Dale in a murder maelstrom.

CHAPTER I

DEATH DANCE

A **RAGGED AWNING** of faded striped stuff fluttered dismally above the doorway of the Juana Diaz Wine Shop. It was bitter cold in the street. In the shop, a guitar whanged a nasal accompaniment to the rich baritone voice that sought to forget the chill of the wind in a song of warmer climes. November was not for the dark-eyed, olive-skinned natives of the Puerto Rican and Spanish quarter just north of Central Park.

A taxi turned off to Fifth Avenue at 111th Street and came to a stop in front of the Juana Diaz. Its fare was a woman. What could be seen of her face and figure indicated that a more searching light might have revealed great beauty.

There was something indefinably strange about the woman— something beside the fact that her stockings, though of the sheerest chiffon, did not match. It was obvious that she had dressed in haste and without a moment's thought. Her jaunty sport hat clashed with the formal sable evening wrap she wore.

The woman had trouble separating one bill from the thick wad in her pocketbook. Finally, she had the driver help himself to his pay and tip. Then her trembling fingers dropped the pocketbook on the running board of the taxi.

"You want to hang on to that, lady," said the driver as he picked up the purse.

The woman stared at her purse as though she had never seen it, then clasped it tightly and ran up the street. Halfway up in the next block, she stopped.

From across the street came the sound of music ground harshly from a phonograph. The woman stood on the corner and clung to a steel telegraph post. She uttered a strained, anxious laugh and crossed the street to the somber, gray-fronted dwelling from which

The masked man muttered at the cigarette-smoking Agent X: "Keep back..."

the music came. On worn, narrow stone steps she paused.

"Must not forget the mask," she whispered, and then she opened her purse and searched in its depths for a small black packet of silk. This she unrolled to reveal a domino mask to which was attached a length of elastic.

She fastened the mask over her face. She found the bell-pull, gave it a jerk so that the bell within jangled hysterically.

The brass mail flap in the gray door clinked as though cautious eyes had examined the woman on the steps carefully. The door was opened, and the light of an amber-shaded lamp fell upon the exotically beautiful figure of a second woman.

THE WOMAN who sought admittance had dressed without thought or sense of harmony, but the woman in the doorway had omitted nothing from her toilet that would lend her charm. Hers

*Here was a thrill for
the jaded appetites
of the dopesters.*

was a dark, secret beauty that warmed to gay colors and daring costumes. Her dark, soft skin had a faint yellowish cast that suggested mixed bloods. Her lips were warm and scarlet, her eyes cold and sea-green.

The woman on the steps swayed slightly forward. "Zerna," she breathed, "I'm desperate. Help me!"

Contempt rather than compassion curved the vivid lips of the woman called Zerna. "Get a grip on yourself, my dear," said she in a strident voice, as she helped the caller into the house.

A man came running down the street, sprang to the narrow steps before the gray-fronted house. He thumped the door furiously and, noticing the bell for the first time, pulled and pushed it until time the woman called Zerna reappeared.

"My wife," the man gasped. "I saw her go in here. I will not have—" He stopped, noticed for the first time that he was speaking to an exceedingly beautiful woman.

Zerna smiled. "Oh, really, haven't you made a mistake? The young lady who just entered has no husband."

The man shook his head. "I beg your pardon. That woman was my wife. I must see her at once. This is a matter of the utmost importance."

A man in the stiff, black garb of a servant appeared directly behind the woman called Zerna. There was something in the dredge-engine cut of his jaw that suggested that his dress was the only humble thing about him.

"This gent making trouble, m'am?" he asked.

Zerna frowned slightly and shook her head. She addressed the anxious man on the steps. "Your name, please."

"Colrich—Mr. Fred Colrich. The woman who just entered this house is Mrs. Colrich. I demand to be taken to my wife at once."

"I am very sorry, Mr. Colrich," said Zerna, "but there is no one here by that name. I know the young woman who just came in very well."

"And that's that," added the servant. He slammed the door in Colrich's face.

INSIDE the house with the gray door, the phonograph continued to scratch out its music in tireless accompaniment to the shuffling of dancing feet. All the dancers wore small black masks. There were débutantes and wealthy club men. There were street women and potential thugs. It was an odd democracy of the best and the worst in society, joined here by a single link—dope.

Dope stared from the slots of their little black masks, through pupils dilated with cocaine or contracted with morphine. Dope spoke wordlessly from their twitching lips.

Round and round the floor, the couples moved beneath the dim light of tawdry lamps placed on old tables around the sides of the room. And over and above them all hung an aura of indescribable evil. Terror, too, was there, and death; and the darker tragedy of minds going mad, drug-chained to nightmares.

Perhaps the most incongruous couple on the floor was the woman in her sable furs and her partner. Her black mask was spotted with hot, frantic tears and now and again her shoulders would shake with a sniffling sob. Her partner was a withered youth, who whispered to himself, laughed shrilly, smirked continuously.

A man in evening clothes, his face completely masked, stepped from a doorway and spied the weeping woman and her partner.

As they wheeled gracelessly within his reach, the man in evening clothes reached out and tapped the woman on the shoulder. She jerked a glance at the man, and instantly her lips twitched into a smile. She all but threw her partner from her, seized the arm of the man in evening clothes, and said: "Thank heaven! I couldn't have lived a moment more!"

The man said nothing. He led the woman in furs across the room and through a small door which he closed after them. The woman in furs jerked off her mask and hat, and with trembling fingers pushed tangled hair back from her waxy brow. Her face was a ghastly mockery of former beauty. She threw herself into a chair, only to spring to her feet a moment later to welcome the exotically beautiful Zerna as the latter entered the room.

"Give it to me, Zerna," she said.

Zerna took the woman coldly by one wrist and forced her back into the chair. "Your husband was here, Mrs. Colrich. That won't do, you know."

The dope-starved woman bit her quivering lower lip. "I couldn't help it. You've got to put me somewhere where my husband can't find me. But you've got to give me a shot first. I'm dying for a shot."

Zerna's green eyes regarded Mrs. Colrich dispassionately. "How does it happen you haven't paid your club dues?"

Mrs. Colrich knotted her fingers. "I haven't the money, I've told you again and again! Oh, why won't you let me have a shot! I can buy that. I've enough in my purse. But I can't get any more money from my husband."

Mrs. Colrich seized Zerna's hand in a tight, desperate fist. "Listen, Zerna," she pleaded in whisper, "I'll do anything. Give me a shot, and I'll try once more to get money from Fred. And if I can't do that, I'll do something else. Isn't there something else I could do? Some work, or something? All those people out there aren't rich, yet they get their stuff regularly." The distracted woman began to weep bitterly.

ZERNA looked incapable of helping anyone but herself. Her green eyes were unflickering. Suddenly she slapped her fingers briskly across Mrs. Colrich's face. "Oh, come out of it!" she said sharply. Then she turned, and with hip-swaying steps, approached the door. She knocked twice.

The man in evening clothes entered the room and looked querulously into Zerna's now stormy eyes. Zerna tossed a gesture toward the all but hysterical Mrs. Colrich. "She's finished. Sell you the Brooklyn Bridge or her soul for a shot of hop. You'd better write *finis* on her page."

The man in evening clothes had scarcely turned toward the unfortunate Mrs. Colrich before the latter sprang from her chair and threw her arms around the man. She spoke through locked teeth:

"Listen—I don't know who you are. But you've got to give me a shot before I die. I've got money for the shot, but I haven't got the two thousand dollars. I'll—"

The phone on the desk jangled. The man put a hand across Mrs. Colrich's mouth. "Pardon me," he said mockingly. Then, still holding back Mrs. Colrich's hasty words, he raised the phone with the other hand. "Shoot," he said. Then he listened, eyes in his black mask flickering.

After a moment, he uttered a short, dry laugh. "Secret Agent X? Sure, I've heard of him. I heard of Santa Claus, too. Listen, you take a headache pill and quit worrying. One more man on our trail isn't going to make any difference, even if his name is Secret Agent X. We got the whole police force guessing, haven't we?... Then, ride on the breeze, buddy." He hung up and released Mrs. Colrich.

"Sorry, Ruth Colrich," he said, "but I can't do a thing for you. You don't pay club dues, you don't get in on the club privileges."

For a moment, some of her old strength of character returned to Ruth Colrich. Beneath the pitiful face that dope had made, there was a ghost of her old pride as she said: "I am going to turn myself over to the police. I'm going to tell them everything."

The man in evening clothes lighted a cigarette. "Sure," he said quietly.

Then he went to a door at the other side of the room, threw it wide open. "This way out, Mrs. Colrich."

Ruth Colrich started for the door, only to stop three feet from it. A quivering extended on down through her body. "No," she said tonelessly, "it isn't true. You won't—"

She stopped, locked a scream in her throat by cramming a fist against her lips. The thing that she had seen in the shadows stepped into the room. It was man-height. It was man-shaped. But long black hair covered it from head to foot. Weird, saucerlike eyes stared from its hairy head.

Ruth Colrich's fingers peeled away from her lips. "Wh-what is this?" she stammered. "What does it mean?"

The man in evening clothes laughed. "It means that you or no-body else is going to do any blabbing."

Two long, hairy arms reached out and seized Mrs. Colrich. The woman's face was flattened against a mighty, fur-covered chest so that her screams were stifled. Then the monstrous thing carried the struggling woman into the darkness.

The man in evening clothes shrugged and rejoined the danc-ers. He sought out Zerna. "Whoop things up a little," he said. "The more noise, the better."

IN AN entirely different section of the city, a rather remarkable man paused near the front of the Paragon Theatre and knocked the ashes from the cubical bowl of his pipe. A black overcoat tented shoulders so immense and square that few would have supposed that this man topped six feet in height. The same right angles so much in evidence about his body also governed the shape of his head and face. Atop his square head he had no protection against the chill blast, except his thick, shaggy, black hair. His name was Harvey Bates, and he occupied a unique position among the men who fight the nation's battle against crime. Harvey Bates was chief assistant to that mysterious man of many faces, Secret Agent X.

When he had reloaded his pipe with shag-cut tobacco and tamped it well with a square-ended thumb, he paced by the front of the theatre for perhaps the twentieth time that evening and came to a stop near the mouth of the alley just beyond. There he leaned against the corner of the building and listened to footsteps of some one coming up the alley.

"*His* footsteps?" Bates wondered. Even when he faced Agent X, Bates could not be certain of his identity—not until X spoke in a certain one of his thousand voices.

"Bates!" *The* voice. It was a mere whisper from the tall man whose face was hidden by the shadows of the alley.

Then from the same tall man who stood at Bates's elbow came a second voice, entirely different from the one that just whispered Bates's name: "I beg your pardon, but have you a match?"

Bates produced a box of matches. The man of mystery scratched one into flame and held it at the tip of his cigarette. There was nothing remarkable about his face, or rather the complex combina-tion of plastic makeup material, clever pigments, and hidden face-plates that served him as a face. As he now appeared, Secret Agent X would have been lost in a crowd of three unless you happened to pay particular attention to his eyes. They were the cool gray of steel with a suggestion of compelling, hypnotic power flickering in their depths.

"Anything to report, Bates?" Secret Agent X asked softly as he returned the matches to his lieutenant.

"Yes, sir," Bates clipped. "Certain that in the past ten minutes, five persons entering the theatre were drug addicts. They entered only a few minutes before the newsreel." It was a long speech for Bates to make, and he paused a moment before asking: "Why do the hopheads have this unusual appetite for movies, sir? What's the connection?"

Secret Agent X shook his head. "Maybe there is a connection, a dope connection. An usher could pass the stuff out in the dark." The Agent flipped his cigarette toward the gutter. "You may go to the Princess Theatre and check on it in the same manner, Bates. I'm going in here. This begins to look like a rather nasty business."

Agent X walked briskly to the ticket window, obtained a ticket and entered the theatre. His gray eyes darted right and left and centered upon a smartly uniformed usher. Agent X snapped his fingers and beckoned to the usher.

The usher crossed quickly to where X was standing and touched his round, red cap. "Help you, sir?"

A strange sort of smile curled one side of the Agent's mouth. "Very much, I believe," he said quietly. "Will you step into the lavatory just a moment? I really believe you'll do nicely." And he nipped the elbow of the young man and steered him toward the lavatory.

As soon as they were alone, Agent X opened his wallet and produced a twenty-dollar bill. "Will this be sufficient pay for several hours in the arms of Morpheus, my friend?"

The eyes of the young man grew wide. "Beg pardon, sir?"

A chuckle from the Agent. He pressed the twenty dollars into the young man's hand, and at the same time, his left hand removed a cigarette lighter from his vest pocket. "You see this, son?" He held the lighter very close to the young man's nose.

"Yes, sir."

The Agent touched a secret lever on the side of the cigarette lighter. There was a slight hiss. A jet of misty vapor darted from the lighter. The usher's mouth was open, but his cry died in his throat as he pitched forward into the arms of Secret Agent X.[25]

---

25 AUTHOR'S NOTE: *Secret Agent X has no use for lethal weapons of any sort. He prefers to rely upon his fists and wits and a few unique defensive weapons, of which the most*

LESS THAN five minutes later, a miracle of transformation had taken place. Agent X emerged from the lavatory wearing the usher's natty uniform. It fitted him to perfection, for he had purposely chosen an usher whose figure resembled his own. But what was more remarkable was the amazing change in the Agent's face.

Beneath his deft fingertips, plastic volatile makeup material had been shaped into the exact contours of the usher's face. Coloring had been exactly duplicated.

The agent crossed the foyer, opened the door leading to the center aisle, and glanced across the dark theatre. On the screen, the newsreel had just ended. His eyes as yet unused to the dark, X did not see the man who suddenly bobbed from his seat, near the back of the theatre, and all but knocked the Agent over in his haste to leave.

X turned and followed the man into the foyer. The man glanced anxiously over his shoulder, and X had an opportunity of glimpsing his face. The waxy skin, odd eyes, and twitching facial muscles told the tragic story at once. The man was a dope addict.

Agent X watched the man go on his staggering way, and hardly had the door closed behind him, then a man and woman hurried from the theatre. And there was not the slightest doubt that they too knew the evil pleasures of dope. X was on the point of following them, when a fourth drug disciple came hurrying from the theatre.

This was no mere coincidence. There was definite reason and planning behind the moves of these addicts. Agent X was on the point of stopping this last hophead, when he felt a tug at his elbow. He turned to look down into the face of a mild-eyed, anxious-faced man whose expensively tailored clothes had been badly soiled.

"Usher, you must find Dr. Daniel Wicker for me at once. But for the love of heaven, don't make a fuss about it. He's in the theatre, I know. And you must tell him that Mrs. Colrich needs him immediately."

X regarded the worried man gravely. Only one sort of person ever urgently needed Dr. Daniel Wicker. Dr. Daniel Wicker was the owner of a sanitarium devoted solely to the cure of drug patients.

---

useful is anesthetizing gas of his own invention and which is extremely effective at close range. This gas is supplied him in small cartridges, which may be fired from his cigarette lighter, and larger and heavier cartridges which fit his powerful gas pistol. The same gas is contained in the gas bombs he carries, which are capable of rendering a whole roomful of people unconscious.

X bowed slightly. "Certainly, sir. And what name shall I give Dr. Wicker?"

"I am Mr. Fred Colrich. And you must get Dr. Wicker for Mrs. Colrich at once."

All the hypnotic power of X's eyes came into being as he held Colrich's gaze.

"Come this way, please," X said in quiet voice, and led Colrich across the foyer and into a small smoking room. Colrich dropped wearily into a chair.

"Now, Mr. Colrich, something seems to be troubling you. Your wife, eh?" X was speaking very quietly and gazing steadily into Colrich's eyes. "What seems to be the matter?"

"I don't know exactly," Colrich confided. "I followed her tonight. She went to the Princess Theatre just across the street at about eight o'clock. I thought nothing of that. She seems so restless. She left the Princess not ten minutes after she had entered. Then she got into a taxi. I followed her to a particularly unpleasant quarter of the city and to a house, the address of which I have in my pocket." Colrich slapped the breast pocket of his coat. "I can't bring the police in on this, you understand."

Colrich stood up. A bewildered frown furrowed his brow. "Who are you, sir? I seem— Why, you're just an usher—and you've been trying to pry into my affairs."

Colrich's right fist shot unexpectedly to the Agent's chin. It was a feather-weight blow, but it took X completely by surprise. He backed to the wall, leading Colrich in close before he sent a short, jolting left to a point directly above Colrich's heart.

It was a blow that might have killed, had not the Agent's superb muscular control reined it in at exactly the right moment. Colrich's eyes rolled back, and he sagged to the floor.

X glanced quickly around the smoking room. That had been a desperate stroke, entered into with the lightning-like decision that characterized all of the Agent's actions. Here was a rare opportunity to obtain inside information on a dope syndicate that was beginning to assume alarming proportions.

AGENT X had seen in Colrich a possible opening through which to strike at the insidious dope monster. If he could manage an impersonation of Colrich, to gain the confidence of Dr. Wicker, there was a chance that he might learn something about the distributing point of the drug syndicate. For Mrs. Colrich was a drug addict. There could be no other reason for Fred Colrich wanting Dr. Wicker to attend her.

His course decided upon, X hurriedly ripped off the usher's uniform which he had put on over his own clothes. As he moved, he practiced imitating Colrich's voice and characteristic facial expressions. It would be a rather difficult change, for Colrich was a decided blond and the Agent's present makeup simulated a dark complexion.

From the inside pocket of his coat, X took out a compact makeup kit, containing his special plastic volatile compound and basic pigments. He knelt beside Colrich, was studying the man's features intently, when he heard the sound of voices just outside the smoking room door.

"I tell you Dr. Wicker, this investigation will give the Paragon a bad name," came a deep voice from the other side of the door. "I believe that your suspicions are entirely unfounded. Suppose that a few cocaine addicts *have* been seen in the Paragon. There is no possible way in which we can prevent them from entering. We are not medical men, to judge whether or not our patrons use narcotics."

"Er—Mr. Nixon, we of the Anti-Vice League are not confining our investigation to any one theatre."

Agent X recognized the slow, thoughtful manner of speaking that characterized Dr. Wicker. But there was absolutely no time for the Secret Agent to eavesdrop. There was no means of leaving the smoking room while Wicker and Nixon, owner of the Paragon Theatre, chose to stand directly outside the door. Nor did the little room offer any place of concealment save a small corner behind an overstuffed chair. Should the two men decide to enter the smoking room....

The rattle of the door knob galvanized Agent X into action. He grabbed his makeup kit and pocketed it. He lifted the unconscious Colrich in his arms, held him upright with one hand while his other hand snatched a scrap of paper from Colrich's breast pocket. Then he lifted Colrich over the back of the large chair in the corner and let him fall to the floor.

X sprang away from the chair and snatched the jet-black toupee, which was part of his disguise as the usher, from his head. His features remained unaltered. Even as the door of the smoking room was opening, X picked up the usher's uniform and threw it into the corner on top of Colrich. Agent X ran his fingers through his own wavy brown hair and turned around.

The first to enter, Dr. Wicker, was a man whose face ran heavily to jowls. His nose was flat and large-pored. His eyes twinkled from pockets of fat. With Dr. Wicker was white-haired, soft-spoken Samuel Arvin, beloved philanthropist and head of the Anti-Vice League. His soothing voice and benevolent words were directed at the somewhat ruffled Walter Nixon.

"My dear Mr. Nixon, I sincerely hope we have not given you the impression that your theatre, or its management, has anything to do with this ugly narcotic business."

The teeth of Nixon's undershot lower jaw sought to gnaw his black mustache. "That would be absurd. I am interested simply in what the patrons of this theatre will say if—" Nixon's dark eyes strayed to Agent X.

At that moment, a boisterous voice from the doorway called: "Hold it, gentlemen—and look like three conferees, if you can!"

THERE was the sudden lightning of a flashlight bulb. Nixon's shoulders gave a startled twist. He cursed softly and turned toward the door, as a cherubic-faced young man, wearing a battered hat on the back of his head, walked triumphantly into the room with a camera under his arm. He was followed by a golden-haired, blue-eyed girl, who produced notebook and pencil and immediately attacked Samuel Arvin with a dazzling smile.

"Let's have a story on the dope roundup, Mr. Arvin. Or *is* this a dope roundup?"

Dr. Wicker cleared his throat noisily. "I thought I told you reporters to stop following us around." His puffy fingers were picking bits of imaginary lint from his vest.

"There isn't any story, Miss Dale," Nixon whipped out angrily. "And if Stien develops that picture he just took, there'll be war."

Stien, the newspaper photographer, chuckled while he mothered his battered camera. "Why not give us the story straight? Who is this gentleman?" He looked directly at Agent X. "Another dope chaser?"

"I could strangle you!" Nixon was muttering as he watched the photographer anxiously.

Agent X had eyes only for the golden-haired Betty Dale who had been so insistent upon getting a story from Samuel Arvin. She was standing in such a position that, with the slightest movement of her eyes to the right, she would be able to see the unconscious Fred

Colrich where he lay in a heap behind the chair. If she saw Colrich, she would naturally cry out. And if she cried out, she would unthinkingly betray her best friend.[26]

Agent X was in a most precarious position, caught in the very act of changing his disguise. He was crushing his black toupee into as small a compass as possible in his right fist. The discovery of the unconscious Fred Colrich would instantly precipitate trouble.

There was only one way in which X could prevent this disaster: he must clearly identify himself to the girl, without revealing himself to the others within the room.

---

26   AUTHOR'S NOTE: All followers of the Agent's exploits are familiar with Betty Dale, reporter on the Herald, and X's companion through many perilous adventures. Of all living persons, Betty Dale alone has seen the real face of Secret Agent X. Betty Dale, more than any other person, knows the courage, kindliness, and resourcefulness of the Man of a Thousand Faces.

CHAPTER II

THE CHILL OF DEATH

BETTY DALE TURNED her head. Instantly her eyes fell upon that portion of the unconscious Colrich that was visible from her position, her lips parted and formed a half-uttered word of alarm.

And at that moment, Agent X was seized with a spasm of coughing. All the power in his compelling glance was exerted in attracting Betty Dale's attention. As the girl's wide blue eyes met his steady gaze, he folded his hands, extended his forefingers so that they crossed to form the letter "X."

Sudden realization that she had all but betrayed the very person dearest to her, almost started a cry from Betty's lips. Then she hurried across the room and settled herself in the very chair behind which Colrich was hidden. She leaned far to the right. It was so marked an effort to hide the Agent's secret, that X feared she would call the attention of everyone present to the hidden man.

Agent X's eyes roved from one to the other of the men in the room. "Which of you is Dr. Wicker?" he asked. "I have a very urgent message for Dr. Wicker."

Wicker cleared his throat. His puffy hands were busy with the upstanding lock of black hair at the back of his head. "I am Dr. Wicker."

X took a step toward the famous doctor, but Walter Nixon detained him a moment, one hand on the Agent's arm. He gnawed his upper lips a moment, looking at X from head to toe. "I beg your pardon, but there is something familiar about you. Who're you?"

"James Nelson," replied X promptly, using the first name that popped into his head. Then he turned to Wicker. "I have a message from Mr. Fred Colrich. It is very important that you see his wife at once. I understand that she is in some sort of trouble at this address." X took out the piece of paper he had slipped from Colrich's pocket. "Colrich followed her and asked me to see you."

Wicker looked at the address and scowled at it. Gordon Stien, the newspaperman, took a hasty glance over Wicker's shoulder. He whistled softly. "Nice neighborhood for people like the Colriches to be visiting. There's a story around here somewhere."

Agent X was watching the door of the smoking room. It was open a crack. The more he watched the door, the more certain he became that some one was listening.

X took two steps that brought him nearer the door. "Dr. Wicker," he said, "may I urge you not to ignore the message I just gave you?" And as he said that, X reached out and swung open the door of the smoking room. A very surprised and embarrassed man turned scarlet in the face, took one step backwards and began to stammer an apology.

Sam Arvin's eyes lighted up as he observed the hollow-cheeked, blond-haired man in the doorway. "Rister! Come in, won't you?"

THE MAN in the doorway smiled in a sickly fashion and came forward eagerly to clasp Arvin's extended hand.

"You've met Morgan Rister, haven't you, gentlemen? Dr. Wicker has, I know. Mr. Nixon, I know the name of Rister is familiar to you. He is the manufacturer of commercial oxygen, acetylene, and similar gases of great importance. In addition, he is secretly associated with our Anti-Vice League."

"Really, Arvin, you overwhelm me," Rister said, keeping his eyes in constant motion. "I really had no idea of meeting you here."

Walter Nixon, who had been staring through the open door, turned suddenly to Agent X. "I've just noticed that one of my ushers is missing, a man who resembles you remarkably."

X smiled. "Unfortunately, the business of lending assistance to Mrs. Colrich prevents me from doubling for your usher, Mr. Nixon, though I must admit a secret yearning to wear one of those dashing uniforms." He backed to the door, sought Dr. Wicker over the heads of the newly arrived Rister and Mr. Arvin. "Doctor, if you will, I really believe that Mr. Colrich would appreciate your coming to see his wife at once."

"Yes, yes," agreed Wicker gruffly. "Coming, Arvin. Er—we may find something that would, er— You understand?"

Arvin nodded. "Coming at once." And, linking arms with Rister, he followed Dr. Wicker from the room.

X shoved the gun against her arm.

Betty Dale waited patiently until all were out of the room, then, with a deep sigh, she hastened toward the door. Agent X was there, waiting for her. He stepped into the room and closed the door partway behind him. He slipped one arm about Betty's waist, and held her so for a moment, searching the depths of her eyes, marveling at the devotion he saw there.

"Betty," he whispered. "Betty. How can I ever thank you?"

"Thank me? Thank me when I all but gave your plan away? Who is that man behind the chair?"

"The man is Colrich. I was caught, or would have been if it hadn't been for you. I don't know what it means, exactly. This sudden increase in dope traffic is terrible and far reaching. We must stop it. I must warn you that you've put yourself in danger again on my account."

"I love it," she whispered.

"I know. But, Betty, when they find Colrich, they'll know something queer went on here tonight. Nixon has half an idea right now that I am his usher's double. It won't be a very long jump from that to discover that I am Agent X—and that you aided me. I'm not thinking only of the danger this might expose you to from the criminals behind this gigantic scheme, I'm thinking of what the police might do to you if they learned that you are my one close friend." [27]

"I'll be careful," she said earnestly. "I'll take care of myself."

"Always," he whispered, "take care of yourself for me." And he hurriedly left the smoking room to join Dr. Wicker and Arvin, who were waiting in the foyer.

Dr. Wicker was dangling his watch. "Er—Mr. Nelson, if you will give us that address, I am sure that Mr. Arvin and I can take care of this little matter satisfactorily."

"I am certain of it, Doctor," replied X pleasantly. "However, I have known the Colriches for years and am quite as anxious to help in this difficulty as you are." This was decidedly untrue, but Wicker and Arvin evidently suspected nothing, for they permitted him to join them without further demur. They left the theatre and crossed the sidewalk to the curb.

A taxi swung in near them. The driver opened the door, so that the brilliant light from the front of the theatre fell across his homely features. His nose was a lean hook, his shoe-button eyes set close together. A cigarette was pasted to his doleful, long upper lip. He stared obliquely at the slip of paper X held out to him.

"Know that address?" X demanded.

"Right!" The taxi driver had a thin, raucous voice. "Took one fare there already tonight."

X sprang into the seat beside Arvin and Dr. Wicker. He glanced through the rear window in time to see Gordon Stien and Betty Dale scrambling into a second cab, undoubtedly with the idea of following them.

The Agent leaned over the driver's seat as the cab started. "Was

---

27 AUTHOR'S NOTE: *The Agent's highly advanced and daring tactics employed in his battle against crime are greatly misunderstood by the police. X has secret sanction from an official of importance in Washington, but because of the very nature of his work, he has never even been able to trust the police with information regarding this official support. So unorthodox are X's methods, so frequently do they carry him outside the law, that he is thought to be a clever criminal. Inspector Burks has accused X of every crime on the calendar and has sworn not to rest until he has seen X strapped to the electric chair.*

your other fare a man or a woman?" he asked.

"Woman," replied the driver. "A queer dame. Picked her up in front of the Princess Theatre at about ten after eight."

"What do you mean—queer?" X persisted.

"Oh, dressed funny. Looked like she was gettin' away with some swell dame's fur rigging. She was nervous, too. Dropped her pocketbook, and I could have had the whole works, for all she would have known. I gives her back the wallet, see. Honest Ham Esler, they call me."

Dr. Wicker leaned forward interestedly. His puffy fingers were fiddling with the brim of his hat. "Furs, you said, driver?"

"Sure—classy furs."

Wicker exploded: "Ruth Colrich has the finest sables in the city! A present from her husband. Poor Fred!" The doctor's twinkling eyes glanced at X. "Where did you leave Fred Colrich?"

It was far wiser to ignore that question. X nudged the taxi driver. "Speed it up, Ham Esler. There's a cab following us. Think you can lose them?"

Esler grunted. "Watch my dust!"

AT THAT moment, in the room off the dance floor that was a part of the gray-fronted house in the Spanish quarter, the woman called Zerna was standing in front of a mirror retouching her perfect lips with rouge.

The house was silent. Zerna was on the point of leaving when the telephone jangled. Deliberately she stepped to the table and picked up the phone. "Yes?"

A man's voice came over the phone: "Move, Zerna. Secret Agent X is on the way."

"Oh, cool off," Zerna replied insolently. "The guests cleared out five minutes ago, and were plenty satisfied with the brand of hop we hand out. When X gets here, there won't be a thing except the stiff. Not unless—" A look of cunning crept into Zerna's eyes. "Say, chief, why don't you tell what you've just told me to Inspector Burks down at police headquarters. Just a tip to the cops on the side, see, and we'll be rid of this X guy for all times."

She replaced the phone, picked up the smoldering butt of a black Puerto Rican cigarette, and ground it out in the ash tray. She glanced once more, critically, at herself in the mirror, and left the house....

The house with the gray front was totally dark when X and

his party arrived. Arvin looked anxiously from the cab window. "You're certain this is the place, driver?" he asked timidly.

Esler turned and thumbed at his chest. "Listen, I got a map of New York for a brain. Never-lost Esler! When I say that's your house, why that's your house."

Dr. Wicker thrust a bill into the driver's hand. "You'd better wait," he said, before he joined X and Arvin.

The Secret Agent took the lead, mounted the narrow steps, and took hold of the bell-pull. Its very jangle proclaimed the house empty. He found the door unlocked.

"You're perfectly sure this is all right?" asked Arvin.

"Not at all," said X quietly, thrusting himself in front of Dr. Wicker as the latter would have pushed his way into the house. He flicked on the tiny beam of his pen-size flashlight and sent it darting about the large room into which they had passed. Rugs had been rolled up and furniture pushed back. A phonograph stood at one end of the room.

"Seems to have been some sort of a harmless dance," Wicker suggested.

"Yes," replied X thoughtfully. "Yet a dance closing comparatively early in the evening. A dance held in a private dwelling; yet immediately after the party is over, the house is empty."

He crossed the room that had been used for dancing and pushed open a door to reveal a smaller room adjoining the first. He turned on the light switch.

"Desk, chairs, telephone," X mused aloud. "Air heavy with cigarette smoke." He crossed the room to heavy green curtains that hid another door. He pushed back one side of the curtains and touched the doorknob. "Odd," he muttered. "This knob is icy-cold. Come here, gentlemen."

Arvin pushed Dr. Wicker ahead of him as the pair came nearer to where X was standing. Arvin said: "I suppose you know this amounts to house-breaking, young man?"

X ignored Arvin. "Do you notice a chill draft coming from beneath this door?"

Wicker, nervously fingering the buckle of his overcoat, informed them that it was a chill night. Agent X turned the cold doorknob and opened the door.

"B-r-r-r!" Arvin shuddered. "Feels like a refrigerator."

Agent X found the light switch on the side of the door and

pressed it on. There was no visible occupant. Furniture in the room looked as though it was covered with white mold. As X moved around the chilly apartment, his coat sleeve knocked a fountain pen from a small walnut secretary. The pen crumbled to bits as it struck the floor. Soundlessly, the Secret Agent rounded a love seat and came to a stop. Then slowly his lips formed the words: "Look, gentlemen. Here is where the cold comes from."

As Wicker and Arvin were timidly approaching, a merry whistle sounded from another part of the house. Some one boisterously shouted: "The old duffers tried to fox us, Betty. We'll get a story now or tell the cops they're burglarizing."

The cherubic countenance of Gordon Stien appeared in the doorway. Almost at once, his smile faded as he regarded the anxious faces of the three men huddled about the love seat. "Cripes!" he whispered.

Stien hurried forward, took one look over the back of the love seat. His eyes suddenly threatened to pop out on his cheeks.

"And that," said Sam Arvin, like a man in a dream, "was once Ruth Colrich."

THE BODY of Ruth Colrich, stripped of its furs, was stretched out behind the love seat. The flesh was blue-black, brittle in appearance. And from the body rose a cloud of chill, condensed mist.

"Frozen to death," whispered Dr. Wicker.

"Yes," X added. "Killed with cold. Those fingers—why, a good hard snap would break them off. This is murder."

"Wow, what a picture!" exploded Stien. "Betty, here's a scoop to end scoops!"

Betty Dale, accustomed as she was to horror that came to her in her life as a reporter, turned deathly pale as she viewed the blue-black corpse of Mrs. Colrich. She turned quickly away and centered all of her attention on her notebook.

In the other room, Arvin could be heard phoning the police. Agent X knew that if he was to pick up clues, he must work fast. While Dr. Wicker's eyes were busy in a cursory examination of the body, X picked up Mrs. Colrich's purse and carried it to a table near the door. There, beneath the light of table lamp, he turned the purse inside out.

There was no money. Calling cards engraved with *Mr. and Mrs. Fred Colrich,* brought a curious, heavy feeling to the Agent's heart as he thought of the helpless husband who must have recently discovered that his wife was heading for the gutter via the dope route. There were also two cheap marihuana cigarettes and an empty hypodermic syringe in the bag. X picked up the hypodermic syringe with his left hand. Closer examination of the instrument might reveal important evidence. X glanced quickly around the room.

Betty Dale was grimly taking notes with a stubby pencil. Stien had just closed his camera with a triumphant snap.

"Could sell these plates to any newspaper in town for five C!" the photographer shouted. "The good old *Herald* ought to give me a raise." He made a dive for the door and was brought to a sudden stop by a ham of a fist that shot out to his face. The big knuckles nipped Stien's nose and pinched until the reporter yelped.

"You're not going any place, picture clicker," said a gruff voice, exceedingly familiar to Agent X. It was the voice of Inspector John Burks of the Homicide Office. Instantly on the defensive, X moved nearer the curtained doorway as the six feet of red beef and brawn that was John Burks came padding into the room.

Burks didn't look toward the corpse. He simply reached out and seized the man nearest him by the chin. And that man was Agent X.

The Agent understood perfectly why Burks had pinched Stien's nose. Burks knew that Secret Agent X, his old enemy, was in that room. And he was determined to find out which of the men was X by a simple method of trial and error. Stien had passed that test— the test that X could not pass.

X's right hand jabbed toward the pocket where he kept his gas pistol. But Burks had been forewarned and was consequently forearmed. The barrel of Burks's gun jammed up just beneath X's chin.

"Move a muscle, and this slug travels up through the roof of your mouth, Agent X. I'm one jump ahead of you this time. A good pinch shows up that putty you use for a face every time!"

Sergeant Keegan and others of Burks's crew surrounded the Agent. Keegan's deft fingers were going through X's pockets like a vacuum sweeper. Nothing would be left him but his flats and his wits—nothing except the hypodermic needle he had taken from Mrs. Colrich's purse and which he now held in his left hand.

Across the room, X saw Betty Dale, standing very straight, her blue eyes anxious and her notebook clasped close to her breast. Agent X smiled slightly. The game wasn't up yet. One chance in a hundred remained to him....

CHAPTER III

FACELESS HORROR

INSPECTOR JOHN BURKS had achieved a triumph. He had every advantage, his opponent stripped of all those amazing devices that had so frequently helped him to fool the police. But as he stood in front of the curtained door, his gun muzzle an inch or so from the Agent, he unwittingly gave X a powerful weapon. Inspector Burks was too confident. So it was that he did not notice what X's left hand was doing.

At the moment when Burks, face flushed with pride, glanced about the room to make certain that X could not possibly escape, the Agent began the execution of his surprising scheme.

His left arm went up underneath the curtains, so that his hand was directly over the small of the inspector's back. In his left hand, he held the hypodermic syringe, entirely empty, which he had taken from Mrs. Colrich's purse.

X knew perfectly well that the point of a needle might well be mistaken for the point of a knife. He also knew what powerful weapons are suggestion and surprise. To achieve surprise, he simply thrust the hypodermic needle through the curtain and into Burks's back. And for suggestion, a voice actually seemed to come from the room beyond the curtain: "Drop that gun, or I knife you!"

It was ventriloquism, an art in which Agent X was an adept. Never for a moment did X suppose that the courageous inspector would drop his gun.

Burks cursed, sprang forward, wheeled, and fired directly at the non-existent man on the other side of the curtain. And scarcely had the slug roared from the revolver, before X's right hand dropped like a striking falcon to Burks's gun wrist.

It was all over in a moment—a powerful wrench with his wrist, a knee-kick upward to Burks's arm, and Agent X was in possession of a serviceable accurate police special.

In spite of his dislike for lethal weapons, few persons could shoot with more deadly accuracy than Secret Agent X. The gun was half raised, lying easily in his palm, when Sergeant Keegan drew his gun. The revolver in X's hand bucked, and then there was no longer a gun in Keegan's hand. It had been knocked two feet behind him and had all but taken the sergeant's fingers along with it.

X shouldered the furious Burks away from the door, so that the inspector came under the threatening sweep of the revolver. The Agent was standing, stooped slightly forward, his gray eyes promising certain hell for the man who so much as raised a finger. On his lips was smiling mockery. "It should be written in the police primer, my friends, that it is far more dangerous to park in front of a curtain than a fireplug!" And with that he sprang backwards through the door.

Burks's whistle screamed. There was an instantaneous scuffle outside the front door. X knocked over the lamp in the office, sprang into the dance hall, and shot out the light that burned there—even as the front door opened and police in uniform streamed into the room.

X took to the stairs, ran noisily up half a flight and vaulted over the bannister to land soundlessly at the side of the stairway. Police flashlights pointed toward the steps. There were hoarse orders from Burks. Six coppers started pell-mell up the steps. Several more guarded the front door.

IN THE DARK, X crept around the stairway and started up the steps a second time, following the footsteps of police, who undoubtedly believed they were following him. X slipped into a closet a moment after a searching police light had explored that closet and found it empty. And when he heard the police thudding down the steps, he slipped out and went to the back of the hall, where a door led out onto an open stairway.

He opened the door cautiously and squeezed out on the stairway. Then he ran down into the backyard to cross it and enter the alley at about the time the police decided they should surround the house.

But there was further trouble in the alley. Three police were jamming one end of it, and there was a car at the other end. X considered the car the lesser of the two dangers.

When he had reached the nose of the car, the headlights suddenly came on and the motor whirred. X sprang just out of line of the searching light beams, leaped to the running board, and shoved the gun against the driver's arm. Suddenly, his right arm went limp. "Well, Betty!" he breathed.

"Hurry!" Betty whispered. "I was going to get this car around in front to pick you up as you came out, but I guess you moved too fast for me. Get in back. I've a slumbering passenger."

"So I see!" X opened the back door of the sedan and got in as Betty threw the car in reverse and backed out of the alley. There was a man in the front seat. His head was all but on Betty's shoulder. X reached over, hooked his hands beneath the arms of the man in the front seat and hauled him into the back seat. He turned the beam of his small flashlight on the man's face.

He was a man about forty years of age, a man with tan, thick-looking skin and faded hair that was graying about the temples. He had a mouth that looked as though it were made for keeping secrets. There was a bruise on his temple.

The Agent's gray eyes twinkled. "Betty! You knocked him out with your slipper. What for?"

"I thought you needed a car. Besides, I don't like him anyway. He's on a rival paper, and he doesn't know the meaning of the word 'ethics.' His name is Steve Wyer. I asked to borrow his car, and he said nothing doing."

"You say his name is Wyer," X puzzled. "Queer. His face is familiar. How long has he been in newspaper work?"

Betty shrugged. "I've known him for at least a year. By the way, where can I drive you?"

"The Paragon Theatre. No, on second thought, I wouldn't dare show up there looking like this. About three blocks north of the theatre would be better. I've a hideout there." [28]

The Agent turned so that he could see the girl's delicate profile in flashes of passing light. His left arm dropped across her shoulders. "Betty," he said very gravely, "you can't go on like this. You mean far too much to me. I can't have you getting yourself into danger."

---

28   AUTHOR'S NOTE: *In his dangerous work, Agent X requires many hideouts located at strategic points throughout the city. There he keeps complete wardrobes and makeup outfits, as well as compact radio transmitters for communicating with Harvey Bates and other members of his vast group of secret operatives. These hideouts are rented under many aliases, and as long as he is in New York, X is never very far from one of these safety stations.*

Beneath his arm, the Agent felt Betty's shoulder muscles tense. A cry of terror screamed from her lips: "That face—"

THE STEERING wheel twisted from Betty's grasp. The car careened across the street, struck the curb, and stopped with its radiator against a fireplug only because X had had presence of mind enough to drag back on the emergency brake. "Betty!" X's anxious eyes sought the girl's pale face.

"A—a thing, watching us through the rear window—a black, goggle-eyed monster!"

"Don't move from the car!" he whispered tensely as he kicked open the door.

As he rounded the car, Inspector Burks's gun in his hand, X saw a shadowy form running soundlessly up the street. He raised the revolver and held his fire as the weird shape twisted to the left and plunged into an alley.

The Agent's long legs enabled him to gain yards on the fleeting shadow. He turned the corner of the alley and saw, in the light that passed from a window at the rear of a dwelling, a monstrous shape, a thing of long, thick fur.

X shouted a warning and again raised the gun. This time he shot and then instantly stopped, stood still, and stared, his gun hanging limply at his side.

In the alley, where the hairy monster had been, a swirling cloud of vapor, blue-white in the dim light, spread its ghostly fingers across the alley. The echo of the shot died. The night wind had suddenly become freezing cold, like a blast from the arctic ice fields.

Gradually, the blue-white mist cleared, and Agent X ventured forward toward a tiny black blot in the center of the alley. He turned his flashlight on the black object, and an exclamation whispered from his lips. The huddled, dead thing on the pavement was a black cat. It had been frozen instantly into a furry statue.

X hurried to rejoin Betty, but on gaining the street, he saw a police officer standing beside the all-but-wrecked car. The crash had evidently brought Wyer to his senses, for he was sitting on the running board, rubbing his head and trying to explain something that he didn't know anything about.

Agent X heard a soft whistle from a dark doorway near at hand. He went toward the door and caught a glimpse of Betty's white face. The girl was putting on the slipper she had used so effectively against Wyer and at the same time she was watching Wyer and the policeman.

X stepped into the doorway beside her. "I know that friend of yours. I can't think of his name. Maybe it really is Wyer. But when I saw him last, he was mixed up in a particularly odorous blackmail racket in London."

"I don't like him, anyway," Betty whispered. "I got out of the car when he started coming around. But that monster—what was it?"

Agent X put both hands on her shoulder. "I don't know yet, Betty. But do you remember, back there in the Paragon Theatre, when I caught a Mr. Morgan Rister snooping at the smoking room door?"

"Yes. But that—that *thing* wasn't Rister."

"That 'thing,' as you call it, was what killed Mrs. Colrich. What I saw just now brought home to me the terrible gravity of your position. Rister could have easily seen your little act to try and conceal the unconscious Colrich. He didn't leave the theatre when we did. He could quite easily have interpreted your actions as an effort to protect and assist me, as soon as Colrich was discovered. And I am absolutely certain of Rister's connection with this criminal gang."

And while Wyer and the cop were engaged in their argument, X took Betty by the arm and led her quickly from the doorway. "I've a car in a garage about six blocks up this way," he told her. "Then I'm taking you to your apartment. Watch out for Mr. Wyer. He's in a nice spot to make trouble for you."

Betty shook her golden curls bewilderedly. "And what has the Paragon Theatre to do with this?"

"I wish I knew. Do you realize, Betty, that at least five dope fiends were among the audience at the Paragon tonight and that those dopesters spent their money for ten minutes of newsreel. That's all they were interested in. They left as soon as the newsreel was over. It doesn't make sense."

IT WAS after eleven o'clock before the Agent had seen Betty safely in her apartment, obtained material for a new disguise, and arrived at the Paragon Theatre. Secret Agent X had become the ruddy-faced, roaring Inspector John Burks himself.[29]

In Burks's characteristic manner, X stamped into the theatre just as the patrons were leaving. He went to the lounge off the balcony, and from there, to Mr. Nixon's office. He drummed authoritatively

---

29   AUTHOR'S NOTE: Once he has used a disguise, X can duplicate that same disguise without resorting to a living model from which to work. He has impersonated Burks frequently, as well as other important officials of the city. Even the police commissioner himself has not escaped the Agent's marvelous mimicry.

on the door with his knuckles, and was immediately admitted by Nixon himself.

X poked a finger at the theatre owner. "Your name's Nixon, isn't it?"

Nixon gnawed at his upper lip and admitted the fact with a nod.

X growled: "What I want to know is if you've a Mr. Colrich here. We just got hold of this notorious Mr. X, who has now admitted knocking Mr. Colrich out and concealing him somewhere in your theatre. Have you found Colrich?"

Nixon smiled and brushed his mustache with a knuckle. "Mr. Colrich is in my private office at this moment, recovering from the attack of this criminal you mentioned. Do you want to see him?"

"Do I?" snorted X. And for an answer, he strode to the door of the office indicated by Nixon.

It was difficult for Agent X to look upon Fred Colrich with anything but sympathetic eyes. Colrich was lolling in one of Nixon's leather chairs, still feeling the influence of the knockout blow X had handed him. Life hadn't been kind to Fred Colrich. The discovery of his wife's vice had probably driven him to desperation. But there was an even greater blow in store for him. As he regarded Colrich, Agent X regretted that he was to be the man to strike that blow.

Colrich blinked with bloodshot eyes at the man whom he doubtless supposed to be Inspector Burks. He sat up a little straighter.

A couple of strides brought X to Colrich's chair. He helped himself from Nixon's cigar humidor and sat down on Nixon's desk.

"What do you want?" asked Colrich.

"Now don't take that attitude," X pleaded. "What I'm trying to do is save a lot of men and women from a hell that somebody's fixing for them." X leaned forward suddenly. "You know what I mean, Colrich," he said hoarsely. "The hell that dope digs! I know you don't want to talk about your wife—but you've got to help us, Colrich. If you've got the slightest idea where your wife has obtained dope, speak up, man. We've got to stop this thing—you and I together!"

Colrich's lips tightened for a moment. Then he said: "I haven't the remotest idea to what you refer. I further object to your mentioning my wife's name in connection with narcotics. My wife has had a nervous breakdown—"

"My eye!" X exploded. "Listen, Colrich, if you don't give a damn for the poor drug-chained devils, you'll give a damn for your own skin. You'll talk, or I'll take you up on a charge of aiding and abetting your own wife's murder!"

That was the blow X had hated to strike. But it was the only way he could get Colrich to talk.

AT FIRST, the man was completely floored. He seemed to shrink inches. He trembled from head to foot. Then suddenly the lion in him asserted itself. He sprang to his feet, color racing back into his face.

"Damn you!" Colrich shouted, his trembling fists menacing the Agent. "It's the fault of every damned, bungling policeman. You get your murderers soon enough, but you don't take up men like James Starbuck!"

James Starbuck. The name was familiar to X, as well as the character of the man it represented. Starbuck was a worthless, wealthy rounder; a man whose attraction for women had led to the crackup of many a home. In all probability it was Starbuck who had led Mrs. Colrich into dope's dark alleys.

"Murderers, gunmen, you get them all!" Colrich raved. "But when some rotter introduces a man's wife to dope, you sit still and do nothing. And that isn't all; I've been paying out money to keep this thing quiet, and now it will all come out in the papers."

"So you've been paying blackmail, have you?" X prompted.

"Yes. Every other day I would get little printed slips of paper. The whole ghastly mess would be set up in newspaper type and pasted to a letter headed: 'This is how it will look in headlines.' Of course, that was just a threat. The story didn't break into the papers. But now it will."

Little printed slips in newspaper type! X suppressed an exclamation of triumph. Betty Dale's newspaper enemy, the man named Steve Wyer, fitted into the picture perfectly. That was the exact method Wyer had used in London several years ago.

"Listen, Colrich," he said earnestly, "this isn't going to get into the papers if I can prevent it. You help us, and we'll help you. Do you know where your wife got her dope?"

"No, I don't. I only know that she used every pretense to get large sums of money from me—four and five thousand dollars at a clip. Any excuse would do. Sometimes it would be charity of some sort, and then again it would be some sort of a trip which she never took."

X wondered if it could be possible that Wyer had been black-mailing Mrs. Colrich as well as her husband.

The phone on Nixon's desk rang. Agent X scooped it up and immediately a gruff, but carrying voice issued from the receiver: "Is Mr. Nixon there?"

Secret Agent X drew a long breath and put the phone down without saying a word. The voice at the other end of the telephone line was that of Inspector Burks himself. Had X answered in any other voice than that of Burks, he would have immediately given himself away to Colrich. And if he had answered in Burks' voice, he would have simply told Burks that the latter was speaking to Agent X. It was a nerve-wracking situation.

"You tell me about this Starbuck, Colrich," he said. "If he's done anything, we'll put him away where he can't do any more damage."

Colrich shook his head hopelessly. "You can't do anything with Starbuck. He's a slippery lizard. I knew that he had been taking my wife to lunch now and then. I didn't think anything of it; I'm broad minded. I just didn't know Starbuck. But I've learned since then that the man takes dope in one form or another."

The phone rang again. X paid no attention, until the second ringing was suddenly interrupted. Then he knew that some one *had* answered that call. Some one, using an extension to the phone in Nixon's office, was now listening to the voice of Inspector John Burks—Nixon, of course. Nixon was in the outer office.

X picked up the phone in time to hear Burks roar: "The hell I am, Nixon! I know where I am. And if there's another man in your office who looks like me, you hold him until I get there. He's Agent X, and he's all tied up in the most ungodly murder I've run across in a lifetime!"

Agent dropped the phone as though it were hot. He had to move and think with something approaching the speed of light, to get out of this jam. The investigation was taking form. He could see his next move clearly—impersonate Starbuck and force his way in on the dope distribution. If Starbuck took dope, which he undoubtedly did, Starbuck would furnish the link between X and the criminal group. Then there was the blackmail angle. Whether dope and blackmail were connected in this crime, was a question that he might answer soon....

CHAPTER IV

NEWSREEL NEMESIS

SECRET AGENT X lunged toward the door of the office and shouldered it open. "Don't draw that gun, Nixon!" he cried, as he moved like a human projectile across the outer office.

But Nixon had drawn his gun. The phone in one hand, a little automatic in the other, he cried no warning to X, but shot twice in rapid succession. Both of the slugs thudded into X's chest. He fell forward across the desk, to seize Nixon's gun arm and bring it down swiftly against the edge of the desk.

The Agent's bullet-proof vest had stopped the shots, yet their very impact had doubled him over with pain. Even after Nixon had dropped his gun, X clung to the manager's arm. Then he straightened, dragged Nixon halfway across the desk, and slammed a knockout blow to the side of Nixon's head.

X opened the door, slammed it behind him, and hurried from the theatre. Burks had undoubtedly heard most of the scuffle through the phone Nixon had dropped. The police signal system would have the Paragon surrounded in a few minutes—men with orders to arrest anyone who resembled John Burks.

X hurried across the street toward the Princess Theatre, from which Harvey Bates had just emerged. He strode up to his big, square-cut operative. A touch on the arm, and Bates jerked his head around. There was a look of alarm in the big man's black eyes. He never knew when the police were going to connect him with Agent X and take him up for questioning.

The eyes of Agent X were twinkling as he said in one of his voices which was familiar to Bates: "This isn't a pinch, Bates."

There was a long sigh of relief from Harvey Bates. "Fooled me again, sir," he said crisply.

X chuckled. "Is your car around here somewhere? Inspector

Burks objects strenuously to this sort of masquerading."

"Just around the corner, sir. Learned something at the Princess."

"Let's have it," said X as they strode along toward Bates's car.

"Same thing. Hopheads go there, too. But just for a few minutes."

"Yes. One of them left the Princess Theatre tonight, about ten minutes after eight," X told Bates grimly. "It was a woman. She'll never go again. She was murdered in a particularly horrible fashion."

"Eight-ten," Bates mused. He pulled a scrap of paper from his pocket and glanced at notes scrawled across it. "That was at the end of the newsreel."

"Newsreels again. Bates, there's something about these movies that we're not getting next to. Did you notice anything that could be construed as a dope connection?"

Bates shook his dark, shaggy head.

THE FOLLOWING evening, Mr. James Starbuck lounged in his luxurious apartment overlooking the Hudson. His jaded eyes were on a stack of photographs in the lap of his satin lounging robe. They were photographs of women—women whose hearts beat faster at the sound of his voice or at a glimpse of his handsome face.

James Starbuck was alone, yet he was not startled when he heard the front door of his apartment open softly. Several of his feminine friends were free to come and go as they chose.

The living room door opened slowly. But Starbuck betrayed no sign of alarm, although his visitor was a tall man whose odd, steely eyes so completely dominated his face that Starbuck scarcely noticed his other features. Had Starbuck known them to be the eyes of Secret Agent X, he might have lost some of his composure.

Agent X closed the living room door behind him. He had entered the apartment, without invitation, by means of one of his master keys. As he faced Starbuck, his right hand was thrust suggestively into his trouser pocket where his powerful gas pistol rested.

"You know why I've come, Starbuck?" he asked in a husky voice that was not his own.

"Haven't the foggiest," replied Starbuck without raising his head. "A holdup, what?"

X shook his head slowly. "I know that you use narcotics, Starbuck. Never mind how I know, it's my business to find out such things. But I haven't found out quite enough; do you understand?"

"Won't do you a particle of good," said Starbuck easily. "I've paid my last bit of blackmail money to your stinkin' organization."

"You're grossly mistaken, Starbuck. I am not here to blackmail you."

"Well, of course not. Call it 'club dues' if you want. It's still blackmail. I'm through, understand?"

"Not with me," said X. "I've come here with one purpose in mind—to get information. Where do you get your dope?"

Starbuck smiled. "Don't use any. If you're trying to under-sell some one, you'd better go elsewhere."

X dropped a hand on Starbuck's satin-covered shoulder. The ends of his fingers bit deep into Starbuck's flesh. But the man in the chair scarcely winced.

"Listen," said X sternly, "I'm going to find out where you get your dope; where you *got* your dope, since you insist you don't use it now. I'm after the higher-ups who sell the stuff."

Starbuck smiled insolently. "Go to it. I still think you're one of the gang. If you can get me to talk, then—according to your code—you'll have enough evidence to have me murdered. Go on with your blackmail, if that's what you're up to, but spare me your third degree. I won't talk, because I'm not a fool."

The apartment buzzer sounded. Starbuck slid out of his chair. "Excuse me. Some of the people who come here have enough manners to ring before coming through the door."

X followed Starbuck over to where the speaking tube was set in the wall and listened closely while Starbuck lazily answered.

"This is Zerna, Jim," came a strident, feminine voice from the tube. From his position, X could hear every word.

Starbuck glanced at X. "So you're coming in pairs, are you?"

And that gave X his cue for action. If Starbuck believed that X was a member of the gang, then, from what Starbuck had just said, it was a certainty that the woman at the other end of the tube *was* associated with the dope gang.

THE AGENT'S fingers were like hooks of steel as they reached out to clamp over Starbuck's throat. He pulled Starbuck back and put his own lips near the tube. And from those lips came, in perfect impersonation of Starbuck's languid drawl: "Come up in ten minutes, Zerna. Just finished a tub; I'm not quite decent, you know."

He closed the tube, and still gripping Starbuck's throat, forced the man back into the bedroom and threw him on the bed. Starbuck lay flat on his back, fingering his throat. Even Starbuck's icy nerves were shaken by the deadly earnestness of the Agent. For the first time in his life, Starbuck had met a man who was fighting desperately and entirely without a selfish motive.

X slipped a hypodermic needle from a leather case. While his hands were busy with it, his eyes harnessed the man on the bed. But when Starbuck saw the glint of that needle, he uttered an oath and flung himself from the bed.

"I've had enough dope!" Starbuck shouted. At the same time, he tried to knock the syringe from X's hand. His left thumped twice over X's heart, but he might as well have battered at a stone wall.

Once again, X had him by the throat and was forcing his squirming body back to the bed. The point of the hypodermic needle pricked Starbuck's throat. The clubman's struggles stopped almost at once. He sighed, and his whole body relaxed in a harmless, drugged sleep.

X turned to a mirror and opened his pocket makeup kit. He quickly removed plastic material and pigments from his face, and fastened metal plates over his cheek bones before applying new makeup. Thus he simulated Starbuck's prominent cheek bones.

The rest of the work on his face was the sheerest artistry. His slender, graceful fingers pinched and patted the plastic material, while his eyes darted from Starbuck's face to the mirror and back again.

When he was satisfied with the effect, he traded a red toupee for a sleek, black one which, when correctly combed, looked very much like Starbuck's glossy hair. A few drops of a liquid in each eye gave him a darker appearance. Agent X had only to change his coat for Starbuck's dressing gown to be ready to receive the woman to whom he had talked over the speaking tube.

A final glance in the mirror, then he left the bedroom for the living room. Just on the other side of the door, he paused.

A LONG, ivory hand with tapering fingers hung over the arm of one of Starbuck's huge chairs. Those ivory fingers held a slender black cigarette from which a gray wisp of smoke eddied into the air.

"I found the door unlocked and walked in, Jim," said the same strident voice X had heard over the speaking tube. "You don't mind?"

"Not in the least, Zerna," said X, adopting Starbuck's honeyed tone. He sauntered around the chair and looked down at the striking, beautiful ivory-hued face of Zerna. "I am highly delighted."

"Yeah?" Zerna elevated her eyebrows. "Save that honey for some one not so hard to get, Jim. Why haven't you been coming to my parties?"

X smiled Starbuck's half-smile. "Perhaps I haven't been coming because you are so 'hard to get,' as you say."

Zerna laughed harshly. "I am more interested in the fact that you haven't been paying your club dues. Those dues are used in a good cause, you know. They keep certain unpleasant pictures of James Starbuck out of the newspapers. A person does such strange things when he's a little bit hopped, you know."

Zerna stood up, flashing her cold smile. "That's all, Jim." She started toward the door.

"Just a minute." X caught the woman's hand and found it cold and firm. "I don't want those pictures to get in the papers. What's the price? Do I bring the money to you?"

X knew in asking those questions he was taking a desperate chance. If Starbuck had been paying "club dues," as the blackmail money was evidently called, Starbuck would have known the particulars. But Zerna did not act in the least surprised at X's ignorance.

"You can pay the two thousand dollars tonight and save yourself a penalty charge," she told him. "If you were to step out from the front of the Princess Theatre, in about an hour, and get into a Blue Streak Cab bearing Number Twenty-six on the door, you could drop the money in behind the back seat." And with that she left the apartment.

No sooner had the door closed, than X sprang to the phone and dialed a number. The phone was answered immediately by Harvey Bates, whom X had stationed in a hideout less than a block away.

"Bates, there's a woman coming out of the Crestview—an exotic beauty. Dark hair and eyes, ivory skin, lips you can't miss. She wears a scarlet dress and black furs. Get on her trail, and stick!"

He hung up and hurried into the bedroom to select evening clothes from Starbuck's extensive wardrobe. He was steadily nosing into the fog of mystery. The sale of dope was of secondary importance to the criminals. Once they had introduced a wealthy person into the ways of vice, pictures were evidently taken which could be used for blackmail.

As soon as he had dressed, X left the apartment, walked around the block to the point where he had parked his car. With no minutes to waste, he drove rapidly in the direction of the Princess and Paragon theatres.

THE SECRET AGENT parked his car about six blocks from the theatre and proceeded on foot the rest of the way, arriving at the Princess about five minutes before the appointed time. In his pocket was a neat package of bills amounting to two thousand dollars, money that he had picked up at the hideout near Starbuck's apartment.[30]

A moment later, a blue taxicab pulled up in front of the theatre, and X saw Number 26 lettered in gold on the door. He noticed also the lone face and close-set eyes of the driver. The man behind the wheel was Hank Esler, who had driven Mrs. Colrich to her rendezvous with the cold that killed.

X got into the cab and settled back on the right-hand side of the rear seat. Esler turned around and eyed X from beneath the shiny bill of his cap. "Where to, sir?"

"Go to the corner, turn east and go six blocks," X told him, for it was there that he had parked his own car. If Esler was connected with the dope crowd, and there seemed little doubt of that, X intended to follow Esler and see what became of the blackmail money.

As soon as the cab had pulled away from beneath the lights of the theatre, X reached into his coat pocket, produced the pack of twenty hundred-dollar bills, and pushed it down the back seat cushions. A few minutes later, he alighted from the cab, paid his fare, and went across the street to where his own supercharged car was parked.

X waited only long enough for the taxi to swing around the corner. Then he sprang into his car. Esler had started out fast, and might have slipped completely out of sight. But as X swung his car around the corner on two wheels, he had to brake quickly; for Esler's cab was directly ahead of him, rolling along at a moderate rate of speed.

Two blocks farther on, Esler's cab pulled to the curb. X turned his into a driveway and watched the cab driver get out and raise the engine hood. X got out of his car and approached quietly on foot to a point where he could watch Esler from behind a clump of

---

30 AUTHOR'S NOTE: As far as is known, Agent X is not a man of great personal wealth. He has, however, an inexhaustible fund of money, placed at his disposal by certain wealthy and public-spirited men, through the Agent's official sponsor at Washington.

evergreens planted at the corner of some one's front yard.

The taxi driver tinkered with something beneath the hood, cursing aloud. Then he went to the back door of the cab, and X could see him taking the back cushion out. All this motor trouble was pretense, then, on Esler's part.

"Well I'll be damned!" X heard Esler explode. The taxi driver sprang from the back of the cab. In his hand was the paper-wrapped package of bills that X had put behind the seat. Esler held the package beneath the front lamps of his cab and ripped off a portion of the paper.

X watched Esler tuck the package of bills under his arm and strike out on foot. X stepped from his hiding place and followed at a discreet distance. Esler rounded the corner and continued briskly along. Directly ahead, X saw the lights of a precinct police station. And then the Secret Agent saw the whole scheme....

STANDING out in front of the precinct station, no doubt trying to look the part of a police reporter was Betty Dale's newspaper rival, Steve Wyer, who was no doubt directing the blackmail scheme. Esler would secretly pass the bills to Wyer. That seemed to be the idea, for Esler was walking toward where Wyer was standing.

But no; Esler passed within five feet of Wyer, ran up the steps, and entered the station. X lengthened his stride, reached the steps, and followed Esler. At the door of the station, he stopped. Inside, he could hear Esler whistling tunelessly. Then he heard Esler say:

"Howdy, Sarge. Honest Ham Esler, that's me. Last night a lady tried to lose her pocketbook in my cab, and I give it back to her. Tonight, some swell gent, who looked like he'd put perfume behind his ears, gets into my cab—and what do you think happens? Well, I'd been havin' trouble with my carburetor. When I got out, after takin' this swell to where he wants to go, and went to get pliers to fix that carburetor jet, I finds this under the back seat. It's dough, Sarge!"

For once in his life, Agent X was utterly bewildered. Why had Zerna told him to put the money in Esler's cab, if Esler wasn't the man to collect it? And who could have collected it if not Esler?

X turned and looked back toward the street. Steve Wyer was no longer lounging near the steps. Well, if the ex-blackmailer had anything to do with the crime, now was as good a time as any to find out just what his connection was.

The Agent ran down the steps and looked up and down the

street. He saw Wyer walking rapidly. X broke into a run, only to
slow down at the corner as Wyer entered the door of a small apartment building. X followed, paused in the vestibule to note Wyer's
name on a card above the mailbox assigned to a second floor apartment.

A shrill, unearthly cry knifed the silence. It rose to a quivering
pinnacle and died in a short, choked gasp.

But even before it had been silenced, Agent X was legging it
up the steps. As he sprang into the upper hall, something lurched
out of a door—a white, ghostly thing that seemed to crackle in its
joints. The thing fell into the Agent's arms. The very touch of it
against his flesh brought burning agony.

X sidestepped and allowed the thing to fall stiffly to the floor.
White vapor was condensing in a cloud about the body of a man.
That stiff, lifeless, frozen form had been Steve Wyer, not more than
five minutes ago. The flesh about Wyer's face looked as though it
had been burned, it was that black and crackled. And burned it
had been, by a cold so intense as to be actually corrosive to human flesh. Even had a man's body been able to withstand such a
temperature, his nervous system could have never stood the shock.

X dragged his eyes from the frozen horror. At the other end of the
hall, something was moving, swiftly and quietly. The Agent gripped
his gas pistol, wondering what chance it would have against the
cold that could kill. He tiptoed down the hall and peered around a
right-angle turn. A chill draught waved the curtains in front of an
open window. X stepped to the window and looked out on a fire
escape. A black and monstrous shape was padding swiftly down
the iron steps.

X got out on the fire escape. The black monster was a perfect
target, but entirely out of range of the Agent's anesthetizing gas.

The thing gained the alley pavement. X vaulted over the iron
railing of the fire escape, and dropped. Instantly, he was aware that
he was followed. He turned his head. Six men were moving swiftly
down the alley in his direction.

In the uncertain light from the apartment house windows, X detected the glint of gun steel. Ahead of him, the black monster was
hurrying along on soft, animal-like feet. X ignored the men who
were closing in behind him. He sprinted after the black, hairy form.

Then, at the opposite end of the alley, the Agent saw another
group of men coming toward him. They, too, were armed. Suddenly, X realized why Zerna had showed no surprise at his not know-

ing the usual method of paying the blackmail money. Somehow, some way, she had known all along that she was addressing Secret Agent X, rather than James Starbuck. Yet his disguise had been perfection itself.

The Agent had been completely outwitted. These men were closing in upon him, were the hopheaded gunmen who served the master brain of the dope gang. They were not out to kill Starbuck, for Starbuck was still blackmail material. They were out to get Secret Agent X.

X understood now why Wyer had been killed. Wyer had been blackmailing Colrich, for the method used was unmistakably Wyer's. The dope gang had resented this muscling in on their prospective victim. So Wyer's death had been scheduled and executed with brilliant daring. And the same master brain that had planned Wyer's death was now out to remove his chief opponent, Secret Agent X.

Not twenty feet ahead of him, X saw the black, hairy monster disappear into a dense pool of darkness. X gripped his gas pistol and stepped into that same shadowy corner, fully expecting to encounter the monster. But the hairy thing was gone.

X's groping fingers encountered a doorknob. Here was a way out of an alley that cleverness had converted into a death trap. But what a choice he must make—beyond the door lurked the thing that killed with cold: out in the alley were slot-eyed, dope-keyed gunmen, ready to riddle him with shot.

Agent X hesitated only a moment. Then he opened the hidden door in front of him.

CHAPTER V

HOUSE OF THE DAMNED

AS SOON AS he had received the telephone message from Agent X, Harvey Bates had hurried from the apartment where he had been awaiting his chief's orders. He was only about half a block away from the stylish Crestview where James Starbuck lived.

When he had reached the street door, Bates saw the woman in red, who was undoubtedly Zerna, coming toward him and not more than a rod from the door. He proceeded with deliberation, pausing to stuff the square bowl of his pipe and get it glowing before he left the building. He saw Zerna walking rapidly ahead of him. The woman gained the corner, looked both ways, and stopped. She stood at the curb, tapping her foot impatiently.

Bates got into his car, which he had parked in front of the apartment. It was obvious that the woman was waiting for a private auto to come and pick her up, for she completely ignored a taxi that rolled slowly by.

Perhaps two minutes passed before a big green car stopped at the corner. The woman got in beside the driver, and the green car rolled on down Amsterdam Avenue. Bates kicked his motor into life and followed.

Bates kept about a block behind the green car, which continued for a distance of about twelve blocks before it cut to the left and angled for a mile or more deep into the east side of town. The green auto came to a stop in the middle of a rather shabby block. Bates jerked his car around the corner and stopped.

The green conveyance was parked in front of a once-grand brick dwelling. From the corner, Bates watched the woman alight and hurry into the house. The green car rolled on into the night.

Bates proceeded on foot until he was opposite the building Zerna had entered. It was one of those old houses that had been worked over into an apartment building. Without a moment's hesitation, Bates walked slowly up the six stone steps to the door, took hold of the knob, and looked into the shadowy vestibule. His heavy black brows drew together in a scowl.

Just beyond the door, a man lay flat on his face, one arm extended above his head, an automatic loose in his motionless fingers.

Cautiously, Bates opened the door. Had the woman simply stepped over this body? Hardly. It was some sort of a trick.

Bates took a quick stride and planted his heel on the wrist of the man on the floor. The man was suddenly very much alive. He uttered a sharp cry of pain.

"'Possum, eh?" Bates clipped. He stooped to pull the gun from the man's helpless fingers, but he never touched the weapon. The chill nose of a revolver was jammed into the back of Bates's neck. "Don't try it!" a man's voice threatened.

Bates stood up slowly. His eyes shifted slowly around the little room. Two men coming through the outer door held automatics in their hands. There was evidently another directly behind Bates. A fourth armed man and the woman stood in the inner doorway. Bates was completely rimmed by guns. And on Zerna's lips was taunting laughter.

The decoy corpse on the floor got to his feet, picked up his gun, and prodded Bates with the muzzle. "Up the steps, big boy," he growled.

Hands on hips, Zerna jeered: "Sap! How do you like the reception, Mr. Bates? The brains behind our gang think ten jumps ahead of X. They knew X would impersonate Starbuck. Right now, Mr. X is in as tight a fix as he'll ever be. The telephone wires leading from Starbuck's apartment were tapped. When your chief sent out his order for you to follow me, the boys were wise."

Bates growled inwardly as the ring of gunmen closed, forcing him toward the steps and toward he knew not what fate. But greater than the anxiety over his own safety, was his fear that the gang had managed to trap Agent X. Zerna did not appear to be a woman who threatened idly.

ZERNA had not exaggerated when she had said X was in a tight spot. No one knew that better than X as he stepped into the dark where lurked the monster that killed with cold.

Quietly, he closed the door behind him. He listened without breathing for a moment, then took a step forward. Still no sound, no threat of danger. The Agent's hand stole into his vest pocket, where his pen flashlight was clipped. But before he could pull out the flashlight, a shuffling sound put him instantly on his guard. His right hand dropped toward his gas pistol, but before he had a chance to grasp it, something lurched into him.

Instantly, X found himself caught in a typhoon of bestial fury. The unseen, hairy monster lashed out with arms and legs, kicking and striking, driving the Agent back against the door. Here was blind fighting, with many a wasted blow, when a false move from either man or monster might have decided the victory.

X lashed out with powerhouse blows. Twice his fist sank deep into fur and flesh, without doing any apparent damage. The big, hairy form again pressed him to the wall. Clumsy fingers sought his throat, but got him by the shoulder.

The black monster threw itself suddenly backwards to the floor, bringing X down on top of it. It was like wrestling with a bear that possessed the wit and agility of a man. Once, X was certain that his two hands were locked about the thing's throat. Then, with an unexpected roll to the side, the monster broke that hold and was back on its shuffling feet.

The Secret Agent sprang up, ready for any trouble the black monster might cause—anything but the freezing death. X knew no defense against that. Then something came hurtling out of the darkness and struck X squarely in the chest.

The missile had weight and speed. It caught X off balance, beat the breath out of him, threw him to the floor. As his empty lungs sobbed for breath, a door opened on the other side of the room, and for a moment, X saw the fleeing form of the black monster against the gray light of the night.

X picked himself up, got his flashlight from his pocket, and turned it on the floor. The thing that had been thrown so effectively at him was a metal cylinder a little over a foot in length.

The Agent took the strange weapon and examined it closely. The metal casing seemed for protection. The walls were heavily insulated, and there was an empty glass container inside, not unlike the flask of a vacuum bottle. Some sort of a copper connection had been hastily removed from one end of the cylinder.

Agent X nodded slowly. It was then, as he thought, the weapon that killed with cold was probably gas in the liquid form, compressed until its temperature was something approaching absolute zero. Possibly the stuff was ordinary liquid oxygen, such as is prepared commercially.

Such was the weapon carried by the hairy monster. It accounted for the horrible deaths of Mrs. Colrich and Wyer. It accounted for the death of the unfortunate cat that had appeared in the alley the night before. X understood that, when he had shot at the escaping monster on the previous night, the slug from his gun had struck the tank of liquid gas the monster carried. The gas had been suddenly dissipated, freezing to death anything within its path.

But liquid gas required special equipment for its preparation. It was not cheap stuff. Morgan Rister manufactured commercial gases. He would have the necessary equipment. Definitely, Rister was connected with the gang in some way. The Agent's next move would be to go to Rister and force him, in some manner, to speak.

X crossed the basement room, where he had sought sanctuary from the gunmen in the alley, and went out the same door through which the hairy monster had made his exit. A flight of steps led upward to the street level. X paused a moment to get his bearings.

He was approximately four blocks from one of his hideouts. He would go there at once and get rid of the Starbuck disguise. The disguise seemed actually to have marked him for murder. Some one was thinking ahead of Agent X, anticipating his every move.

As X was passing under a street lamp at the next corner, a crackling voice called: "Jimmy, old boy!"

X turned his head, saw a ragged figure stagger out of a doorway and come toward him with hand outstretched. Mechanically, X shook hands with the giggling, ragged man who seemed so delighted to see him. Then, as the light struck the man's face, X became immediately interested in this apparent intimate of James Starbuck.

The man's face was thin and waxy appearing. His eyes were unmistakably those of a dope addict.

THE MAN in rags slapped X on the back, linked arms with him, and started to walk him down the street. "How come you haven't been around to any of Zerna's parties, Jimmy?" the dopester asked.

Here was X's chance to pick up information for which he was willing to play the game as far as his limited knowledge would permit. "Didn't know where to go, that's all," he replied.

The ragged man laughed. "Why, don't you go to the movies any more?"

Movies again. X was back to the original question: what had movies, and especially newsreels, to do with the workings of the dope syndicate?

"Tell you what I'll do," the hophead volunteered. "You just come along with me. Zerna's putting on another brawl tonight."

Agent X agreed instantly. Here was a chance to get in on one of Zerna's orgies. As to his disguise, nothing could be more perfect for such a venture than the disguise he was wearing. It had once failed him so obviously that his opponents would never suppose he would try it again. And in the presence of this man, who had been an intimate of Starbuck's, there was no reason in the world why anyone should suppose that X was not the man he appeared to be.

"Is the place very far from here?" X asked.

"Sure—quite a ways. Maybe you can find the price of a taxi, huh?"

"I can do better than a taxi," X told him. "I've got a car up here in a garage."

"Swell! Say, you're a pal!" The hophead staggered up against X and instantly recoiled. "Say, Jimmy," he said seriously, "you ain't packing a rod?"

Evidently the man had felt the gas gun bulking in X's pocket. "Sure," X admitted. "Why not?"

"Why not? Don't you remember, nobody with a weapon can get in? They got some sort of an electric-eye machine sitting at the side of the door. You better get rid of that gat before you try to crash Zerna's joint."

If he entered Zerna's drug depot tonight, he must do so without weapons, or, at least, any metallic weapons that could be detected by an electronic beam. It was a long chance he was taking, he fully realized. But when he thought of the drug-sick man beside him and of the hundreds of other lives that had been ruined, that might yet be ruined, by the insidious syndicate of drug merchants and blackmailers, X decided that the chance he took would be worth it.

IT WAS shortly after eight o'clock that night when some one beat a rapid tattoo on the door of Betty Dale's apartment. The girl got up from her typewriter where she had been working. Mindful of the warning that Agent X had given her, she opened the door a cautious crack and looked out.

"Oh, Gordon!" she laughed. "Come in. But what's happened to your eye?"

Gordon Stien needed no second invitation. He popped into the room with: "I ran into a door. Have you a nice slice of beef steak?"

Stien went over to a mirror and examined a black and puffy right eye. In the glass, he could see Betty laughing at him. Stien made a face at her. "Cut it out. Get into your going-out rags. Where in hell do you think we're going?"

"I don't know where you're going, but I'm staying here."

Stien pleaded: "Ah, listen here. Betty, don't let it be said that I got this shiner in vain." He jumped to the door. "I brought the evidence with me. Take a squint into the hall."

Betty went to the door and looked out into the hall. Her rapidly indrawn breath had the ghost of a scream in it. A man lay face down on the floor beside Betty's door. He didn't show any signs of life.

Stien pulled the girl back into the apartment. "I did it with my little hatchet. And what kind of a bird do you think that is out there? A snow bird, by gosh! I mauled all the stuff out of him, see. That's how come the eye. But I got all the stuff out of him about the dope parties. There's a female named Zerna who gives these parties. She moves after each party, as I get it, so the cops can't catch up with her. It's at these parties that the dope is given out."

"Wait a minute," Betty said. "Let me knock out some of this on the typewriter."

Stien grabbed her arm. "Listen, you bit of mellow sweetness, if you think you've got a story now, wait until after tonight. I know where this dope party is being given. I know how we can get in. Everybody wears masks, so I got a couple of masks. I told you I really pulverized that snow bird in the hall. We're set to get in on a real story, if you're game."

"If I'm game!" Betty mocked. "Wait till I change my clothes." And she hurried into the bedroom.

A few minutes later, they were off in Stien's car. At the end of a forty-five minute drive, they entered a shabby, narrow street and Stien slowed down, watching the house numbers carefully. "Here we are, Betty," he said in a whisper. "It's that house we just passed. Get into this mask." He handed the girl a little roll of black silk.

THEY got out of the car and hurried back to a brick dwelling, the identical house to which Harvey Bates had followed Zerna. Stien rang the bell and produced a small card, which he informed Betty, was a pass he had obtained from the dope. The door was opened by a servant who looked like an ex-pug. He glanced at the card in Stien's hand, nodded his head, and allowed them to enter.

They entered a long room that had been cleared for dancing.

A radio was going full blast. Men and women were dancing in a crazy, graceless, abandoned manner. It looked like a drunken brawl to Betty, one in which the cream of society was churned with the bluest of the milk. Hardly had she entered the room before she was seized in the arms of a masked man, who whirled her about the room in a mad, frenzied fashion.

Then a man, sedately clad in evening clothes, cut in, took Betty's arm and led her to the other side of the room. "We want to speak to you, Miss Dale," he said.

Betty saw that this man's face was completely covered, distinguishing him from the others in the room who wore only domino masks. He held her arm in a grip she could not break, led her into a room apart from the noisy dance floor.

There were a number of dope-eyed thugs lounging about the room, the man in evening clothes motioned one of them out of a chair and offered the chair to Betty.

"There is nothing to be alarmed about, Miss Dale," he said gently. "We are simply anxious that you know exactly where you stand. You have the peculiar honor of being a friend of Secret Agent X. This we know, because one of our operatives saw you making an effort, the other night, to aid Mr. X in the smoking room of the Paragon Theatre. Since that time, we have outguessed Mr. X on every occasion. We guessed, for instance, that after he had talked to Colrich, he would impersonate James Starbuck. So, earlier this evening, we arranged a trap for your Secret Agent.

The man in the mask paused, seeming to enjoy the fearful suspense his last statement was creating in the mind of Betty Dale. "Unfortunately," he sighed, "the Agent gave us the slip. Our one fear is that he has managed to crash this party tonight, even as you did. You, who know him, shall point him out to us tonight."

"I—I—" began Betty.

The man held up his hand. "Wait. Will you step this way?" He went to a door at the end of the room and opened it.

Betty glanced around. Two of the doped thugs stood beside her, ready to see that the masked man's demands were carried out. She got somewhat unsteadily to her feet and walked to the door. There she stopped, a scream choking in her throat.

THE ROOM beyond was dimly lighted. Three hairy monsters with great, glassy eyes, sulked in the shadows. In the center of the room sat Harvey Bates. His legs and body were tied to a chair. His hands were held palms up on a wood table by means of straps and staples. Metal supports held curious metal cylinders above each hand.

"You know this man, Miss Dale?" the masked man asked. And when Betty did not reply, he nodded his head. "Of course you do. His name is Bates, and he is a friend of Agent X. Those cylinders above his hands contain liquid air, a fluid that, when dropped on human flesh, produces far worse burns than acid, and far more pain than hot coals."

One of the black, furry monsters advanced, touched a stop-cock at the bottom of one of the cylinders. A tiny stream of blue-white liquid splashed into the palm of Bates's right hand.

Bates turned deathly pale. He bit his lower lip until his large, square teeth were stained with blood. The liquid gas fumed into misty vapor and was gone, but the palm of Bates's hand was black and stiff.

"Keep lips closed, Betty," Bates said hoarsely.

Betty shook her head. Her blue eyes glistened with compassionate tears. She turned to the masked man. "Stop it. Oh, you can't be so brutal!"

"I think we can," said the masked man. "*You* can stop this torment—if you go into the dance room and point out Agent X."

Betty thought a moment. Unless X so willed it, she had no more chance of pointing him out than the masked man himself. Yet somehow, she must stop this tormenting of Harvey Bates. Without the slightest idea what her next move would be Betty nodded her agreement.

"Betty," said Bates hoarsely, "you couldn't do a thing like that!"

Betty flashed Bates a quick smile. He was right. She couldn't betray X, even if she wanted to. She did not know, even, that X was in the house.

CHAPTER VI

MYSTERY WOMEN

BEFORE THEY ENTERED the house where Zerna's dope party was in full swing, Agent X removed all metallic weapons from his pocket and left them in the car. The same servant who had admitted Gordon Stien and Betty Dale, a few moments before, allowed Agent X and his companion to enter. The Agent's keen eyes compassed the room where the strange dance was being held.

Mingling with the crowd, X saw the hostess, Zerna, in her bizarre and colorful gown. She would dance first into one man's arms and then into another. X saw how deftly she slipped packets of dope into the hands of her partners. There was also a man in the crowd who was handing out dope to the women in the same manner.

It was all very cleverly done. There was nothing to excite police interference. Furthermore, it seemed that these parties were never held twice in the same building.

X was about to choose a partner from among the women, so that he might not appear too conspicuous, when a masked woman all but threw herself into his arms.

"Jimmee! Jimmee, darling!" She seized his arms and pulled them about her slender waist. "Where have you been keeping yourself, naughty boy?" The Agent searched the dope-dilated eyes revealed through the slots in the mask. This unknown woman was obviously acquainted with James Starbuck—intimately.

X smiled mechanically. "How did you recognize me?" he whispered.

The woman drew a long breath. "Oh, darling, what a question!" She looped the handle of her evening bag over her arm, grasped X's hand, dropped her head upon his shoulder. "How good to feel your arms about me again! Hold me tight, Jimmee." And as they began to dance, the woman was weeping softly.

Agent X had only pity for the woman in his arms. Already her vice had left its tracks upon that portion of her face visible beneath the mask. Whether her evident passion for James Starbuck was real or simply infatuation stimulated by dope, he did not know.

Their dance was not long. Another man seized the woman and dragged her from X's arms to whirl her about the room in dizzy, drunken circles, while she hysterically called out: "Jimmee, dear!"

X was about to search for another partner when he noticed that the mystery woman who had insisted he was Starbuck, had dropped her bag at his feet when she had been dragged from his arms. X picked up the bag, slipped it into his pocket, and turned into a little room at the side of the dance hall.

He closed the door behind him. He hoped that examination of the bag would help him identify the woman, but he dared not risk being caught in the act. There was another door at the opposite side of the room. He crossed to it and opened it a little way. It led into a closet, entirely dark save for a shaft of light that passed through a rough hole in the plaster.

This hole looked out upon the dance hall. Beside it was a camera mounted on a tripod. It was evidently from such a secret place as this that the gang obtained pictures later used to blackmail the wealthy dope addicts.

X returned to a table that centered the room and turned the contents of the bag out on its surface. There was a large wad of bills, a jeweled compact, a card case and a many-folded sheet of paper.

THE CARD case was empty, but the inner flap of it had been engraved with the name: *Sylvia Rister.*

The Agent's eyes narrowed. Sylvia Rister was Morgan Rister's wife. If Rister was really associated with the gang, surely he wouldn't have permitted his wife to take dope. If he wasn't in with the criminals, where were they obtaining the liquid gas they used for a weapon?

X next turned his attention to the folded piece of paper. On opening it, he discovered that it was a complete metropolitan map of New York.

Why would Mrs. Rister, a resident of the city for years, be carrying a map like this one? X flattened the map out on the table and studied it for a minute.

There were thirty-one circles, all having a common center,

drawn on the face of the map in fine lines of India ink.

X folded the map and put it in his pocket. With the idea of returning Mrs. Rister's bag, he left the room and was halfway across the dance floor, when the radio was turned off. The sudden silence fell like a blow upon the drug addicts. They stopped their dancing, clung to their partners, and looked around the room as though they expected something terrible to happen.

"Absolute silence!" Zerna's strident voice demanded.

She was standing at one end of the room, her hard, chill eyes flickering from one masked face to another.

"There is a traitor among you," Zerna said.

Instantly, there arose an excited murmur among the guests, but Zerna stamped her foot and put an end to that. "Because," she said, "there is a traitor here, all must remove their masks at once."

For a moment, no one moved. Zerna repeated

X swung over the sill and dropped to the ground.

her demand. Still, no faces were bared.

The Agent's pulse quickened. Had his deception been discovered? How could his disguise have been penetrated? Then it suddenly occurred to him that there was one bold stroke he might use to divert suspicion from himself.

He quickly raised his right hand and jerked off his mask. Surely, the first man in the group to expose his face would be the last suspected of being the traitor.

One by one masks were removed. The Secret Agent was shocked as he recognized many people from the best families in the city, among other dope addicts. Half the crowd seemed to have come from the wealthy class. They, no doubt, paid "club dues" to prevent their vice being made public. Others in the group were obviously the lowest in the criminal scale. Probably, their "club dues" were paid in services of unlawful nature.

Zerna looked from one face to another. "We believe that Secret Agent X is among those present," she said. "We have a way of proving this, of course."

She clapped her hands. A door at the side of the room opened, and, to X's horror, Betty Dale was led into the room.

Betty Dale was actually almost beside herself with terror. She knew why she had been brought here. She was to point out Secret Agent X. Actually, she had no more idea which of those present was the Agent. Yet to save Harvey Bates from torture, she had to point. And what if her wild guess should prove correct?

Betty closed her eyes for a moment, bit her lip. Then she raised a trembling forefinger and pointed straight at the back of the man next to her. "That is Secret Agent X," she said firmly.

CHAPTER VII

THE BETRAYAL

BETTY DID NOT raise her eyes to meet those of the man
to whom she had pointed, until she heard him curse. There
was something so familiar about the ring of his voice that the girl's
heart skipped a beat. She looked up quickly, then, into the goggling
eyes of Gordon Stien.

"Betty," the newspaperman gasped, "this is a hell of a gag!"

Three men immediately fell upon Gordon Stien. Some one
cried: "The girl's giving it to you straight. She came with that guy."

The hophead criminals dragged the struggling, kicking Stien toward the door through which Betty had come. Stien was shouting:

"Of all the rotten deals a man ever got from a woman, this is it!
Me, Agent X? What a laugh! Why—"

Then the sound of Stien's voice was muffled by the closing of
a door.

It was obvious to Agent X that Betty Dale was on the brink of
complete collapse because her grabbing in the dark had resulted
in the plight of her fellow reporter. X had no idea what motive had
been behind Betty's action, but he greatly feared that she had been
tormented in some way.

No sooner had the criminals seized Stien, than X began moving toward the doomed reporter. It was utterly impossible for the
Secret Agent to stand back and allow some one else to take punishment that had been designed for him.

Behind the cover of excitement caused by Betty's startling
disclosure, Agent X got to the door through which Stien and his
guards had passed. When he was certain that no one was watching,
he cautiously opened the door and stepped into the room beyond.

The room was dimly lighted. Evidently Stien had been taken to
another part of the house. X started across the room, but came to

an abrupt stop. Directly in front of him, bound to a chair and table, was the great, square-shouldered form of Harvey Bates. X sprang to his operative. "Have you out in a second, Bates," he rapped in the voice by which Bates could recognize him.

"You, chief!" Bates gasped. "Miss Dale—"

"I know. We must get her out of here. And Stien is on the spot—the spot where I'm supposed to be. Can't have that, you know." The Agent's capable fingers unknotted ropes and loosened straps.

"Any plans, sir?" Bates whispered.

X shook his head. "We'll plan as we move. Here—" X pulled a package of cigarettes from his pocket and shook out three or four on the table together with a paper of matches. "After they've burned about half an inch, a tear gas cartridge inside the cigarette goes off. Only weapons I have that wouldn't have been detected. Can you manage them with that nasty burn on your hand?"

Bates nodded. "Burn's nothing," he insisted stoutly. "Liquid air."

X held up a warning finger. "Some one coming," he whispered. Hastily, he pulled the straps back over Bates's wrists, but did not hook them. He winked cheerfully at his lieutenant and sprang across the room to crowd himself into a small, open closet.

THE DOOR opened, and Gordon Stien was brought into the room by four of the hophead criminals. The young man had admirable courage. There was a scornful smile forming on his lips as he was taken toward the door of the dance hall.

One of the criminals carried a shiny cylinder, undoubtedly one of the guns used to project the deadly liquid gas. Probably, the criminals had decided to make an example of this man they supposed to be Agent X.

"Better lock that door after you," said one of the hopheads, when Stien and his guards had entered the dance hall.

From his hiding place, X noticed that the key was on the inside of the door. One of the four guards came back into the room for the key. Once he had obtained it and locked the door, X would have no chance of getting to Stien's rescue.

The hophead had his back toward the closet where X hid. The door leading into the dance hall was partway open. Nothing but quick, silent action could turn aside the fate in store for Stien.

X sprang like a panther. His leap carried him to within two feet of the man at the door. His left arm shot out, his hand slapping over the mouth of the hophead. His right fist pounded up to the back of the man's neck at the base of the brain.

The man went limp, fell into the door with a thumping sound that made X hold his breath. Only the excitement in the dance hall prevented those near the door from noticing the noise.

X pulled the unconscious hophead to one side. Harvey Bates sprang to his chief's aid. Together, they knelt beside the hophead and quickly searched his pockets. X found an automatic and passed it over to Bates.

"I'm going in there and start something," he said grimly. "Stien won't be in any danger after I prove to that mob that he isn't Agent X. I can probably get as far as the middle of the room before they'll even notice me. When I start trouble, you come in to cover the crowd while I get Miss Dale out of this hole. Use tear gas where you can. Shoot only as a last resort."

"Ready for anything," Bates said eagerly.

X stepped to the door and slipped into the dance hall. Two of the doped killers were holding Stien in a chair in the very center of the room. Nearby, stood the man with the gas cylinder. The man in evening clothes, the only one in the room whose face remained covered, was saying: "And as a warning to others in this room, we have decided that you shall all witness the death of this Secret Agent X."

Here was a new thrill for the jaded appetites of the dopesters. Some greeted the announcement with shouts and others with pleasureful shudders.

Betty Dale was terrified beyond speech, beyond tears. Her face was ash gray. Her fingers were knotting and unknotting themselves. Here was murder of her own making. And she knew no way to prevent it.

Agent X calmly jabbed a cigarette between his lips and lit it. With a slight smile on his lips, he walked briskly toward the center of the room. Virtually weaponless. Agent X risked everything to save the life of the man in the chair.

The masked man muttered at the cigarette-smoking Agent X: "Keep back, Starbuck," he growled.

AGENT X's face never changed. The smile seemed frozen there. He moved on until he was directly behind the man with the gas cylinder.

The two hopheads who held Stien never look their eyes from the Agent's face. Then, with a lightning-like motion, X's right hand passed over his face and removed his cigarette, at the same time pressing and twisting the plastic material that covered his face. When his right hand dropped to his side, those quick alterations in his features had told their story—a story that instantly marked him for death.

Fingers, eyes pointed. Then voices exclaimed: "There's Agent X!"

The man with the gas cylinder swung around. The back of his right hand came in contact with the point of X's cigarette. At the same time, X seized the cylinder of gas and wrenched it from the man's grasp.

The two hopheads had released Stien. The reporter was legging for the door. Heedless of the gas cylinder with which X threatened them, the hopheads sprang at Agent X, who squirmed out of their reach and moved toward Betty Dale. His long fingers flipped the smoldering cigarette into the midst of the hopheads. There was a faint pop and white clouds of choking, blinding tear gas broke from the cigarette.

Across the room, Harvey Bates appeared. He was moving backwards toward Betty Dale, threatening the mob with his gun. He, too, had one of the tear gas cigarettes going, and this he flipped into the center of the excited throng.

"Toward the front door, Betty!" X sang out. Then he broke into a run to follow the girl and Bates. Only one man stood in their way—the masked man in evening clothes. He stood directly in front of the door, legs wide spread, an automatic in his hand. The eyes in the slots of his mask met those of X.

"Another inch," he warned, "and I'll kill that girl!"

X dared not count the cost of his next move. There was but one way out for Bates and Betty. The man in the doorway had to be removed, for it was only a matter of moments before the dazed and surprised mob would sufficiently recover from the tear gas to close in. X raised the gas cylinder and stepped directly between Betty and the masked man.

The masked man's gun spouted flame and thunder. Slugs that were like twin battering-rams plumped into X's bullet-proof vest. The Agent's knees felt like jelly. A red cloud of pain filmed his vision. Yet an almost super-human will kept him upright to shield the body of the girl he loved.

He staggered on, straight into the blazing gat in the man's hand. The gas cylinder hacked down once. The masked man melted to the floor. X tripped over him, fell flat on his face, and lay there a moment, grasping at his wavering senses.

Bates seized X beneath the arms and pulled him to his feet. X saw Betty's pale, anxious face close to his. His lips twisted into a wry grin. "I'm all right," he worked out through clenched teeth. "The bullet-proof vest takes death out of the bullets but leaves the wallop. Let's go. The car's out in front."

Still clinging to the gas cylinder with one hand, X hurried Betty through the front door of the building. From near at hand came the skirl of a police whistle. The sound of the shooting had evidently attracted the cops.

"Move!" X urged. His old strength back again in his well-conditioned body, he lifted Betty in his arms, strode to the car, and put her in the front seat. Bates slipped in under the wheel, kicked over the motor, and as X sprang into the back seat, the car rocketed from the curb.

CHAPTER VIII

SECRET CIRCLES

X LEANED OVER the front seat, his head between Bates and Betty. "No time for chatter. We're making progress for the first time since this investigation began. These are orders to you, Betty, and to you, Bates."

"Yes?" the girl said eagerly. "What can I do?"

"Keep away from everybody, Betty," X said earnestly. "I mean *everybody*. While this gang exists, you're not safe a minute. These criminals know they can strike at me through you. Our best bet is to trap the whole mob in some way." X drew out the map he had taken from Mrs. Rister's purse, and tossed it into Bates's lap.

"There are thirty-one circles on that map, Bates. Your job, as soon as you have seen Betty safely home, is to find the center of those circles. Communicate with me through G.H.Q." X took hold of the door handle of the car. "Stop in the center of the next block," he ordered.

"What are you going to do?" Betty asked anxiously as X got out in front of the entrance of a gloomy lodging house.

X smiled kindly. "Much, I hope. We've got to wipe this mob out." Then he added beneath his breath: "Before it wipes us out." He hurried into the lodging house, where, on the third floor, he had rented a modest room under one of his many aliases.

In this hideout, he briefly examined the gas cylinder he had taken from the hophead. When at last he put it aside, there was a strange, troubled look in his eyes. As he began working on a change of disguise, he thought back over the evening's adventure. Many things that had been fogged with mystery began to stand out clearly. He understood now that the danger threatening Betty Dale was even greater than he had anticipated.

When he left the hideout a little later, he was a man who looked at home in his shabby surroundings. His face was a hard, vicious mask, with thin lips, a fist-flattened nose, and a killer's squinted eyes.

A rattling old car that looked incapable of the speed he goaded from it, was the conveyance that took him across Manhattan to the beautiful West End Avenue home of Morgan Rister.

A servant informed the Agent that Mr. Rister wasn't at home, and X dealt the man a flat-handed blow to the chest that sent him reeling back from the door. Then X came through the door fast enough to catch the servant by the coat lapel and keep him from falling over backwards.

"I'm goin' to see Rister, yah understand?" he said nasally. "And you ain't stoppin' me, yah understand?"

A door opened, and an anxious voice asked: "What is the trouble here?"

X looked over the servant's shoulder to see Morgan Rister, his pale hair rumpled, his face colorless above the black satin collar of his dressing gown.

An unpleasant grin spread across the ugly mask of makeup that covered X's face. "Aw, me and James was playin' knock-knock. I gotta little business to transact with you, Rister."

"Very well." Rister's voice became limp. His hand trembled as he opened the door and ushered X into his study.

"Sit down, Rister," X said. "Guess you know why I'm here. It's your lady, again. You wouldn't want it to get out about her and Jim Starbuck and these dope parties, would you?"

Rister said nothing. His eyes had a frightened gleam.

"Sure, you wouldn't, Mr. Rister. Your lady oughtn't to hang out at the joints she does. I seen her tonight with about two shots of dope under her skin. How much for hush?"

"I'm paying you enough," Rister snapped. "I've shelled out money to you for the protection of my wife's name. And I've furnished your boss the gas he asked for. I'm through. If I had known you were going to use the stuff for murder, you wouldn't have had it."

"That's fine, Mr. Rister!"

RISTER'S jaw dropped. He stared in utter amazement at the man before him. The voice that had just spoken to him seemed to be that of an entirely different person. Agent X's hand darted into the pocket of his baggy trousers and produced a neatly counterfeited police badge.

Rister slapped his perspiring brow, gasped like a man plunged suddenly into icy water. "I've been talking to a police detective."

X came nearer and put his hand on Rister's shoulder. "That's the idea. We knew down at headquarters about your wife. We had an idea that the liquid stash the gang used to freeze Mrs. Colrich came from your plant. We just wanted to be sure."

"Wh-what are you going to do with me?" asked Rister.

"Well, I could take you down to headquarters as an accessory to the Ruth Colrich murder. You tell me all you know about the gang, who runs it, and where they get their dope—and maybe I'll give you a break."

Rister shook his head and stared blankly at the wall. "I can't help you. I know nothing of these people. They simply had some pictures of my wife. Not very pleasant pictures. They had been blackmailing her with them. Then they turned on me. I didn't actually give them the gas. I made it easy for them to steal it."

X had been studying Rister closely. The unfortunate man was perfectly sincere, he was certain. Probably, his eavesdropping at the door of the smoking room in the Paragon Theatre had been an effort to hear if Wicker and Arvin were talking about his wife in conjunction with the dope parties.

X took Rister's hand in his own and gave it a grasp that seemed to transmit new energy into the man's body. "Good night, Rister—and good luck!"

Agent X left the Rister home and drove for several blocks until he came to a drug store. He went in, found a telephone pay station, and called a number that was listed in no telephone book. It was the telephone of Harvey Bates's office, the general headquarters for the Agent's crime-fighting machine.

To his surprise, it was Bates himself who answered the phone. The Agent's voice at once slipped to the familiar tone that Bates would recognize.

"Any results from the map, Bates?" And as he listened to what Bates told him, his brow became deeply furrowed. "Impossible! Have you made those measurements carefully?" He was silent for a moment, staring thoughtfully at the wall of the telephone booth. Finally, he said: "Meet me at the office of A.J. Martin in one hour. Bring the map." [31]

---

31 AUTHOR'S NOTE: A.J. Martin, representative of the Associated Press, is the Agent's most useful alias. Under that name he maintains a downtown office where many of his

Though it was after midnight and traffic had thinned out, it was nearly an hour before X arrived at the office he maintained in the name of A.J. Martin. He had not changed his disguise.

Bates as usual was punctual. As soon as he had arrived and had stopped marveling at his chief's present appearance, he brought out the map, a flexible steel rule, and drafting instruments.

"Want you to check my measurements, sir. Think I'm right. Be glad to find out," Bates clipped.

X spread the map on the top of the desk. There were thumb-tack marks in the extreme corners. He measured the distance between these. Then, with the rule and instruments, he found the common centers of the circles. He nodded his head slowly.

"You're a hundred per cent right. The center of those circles is in the estate of Samuel Arvin, head of the Anti-Vice League. But before we accuse Arvin of anything, we ought to take another look at newsreels. Arvin may have nothing to do with this business, but newsreels and this map have. I'm going to the movies tomorrow. And before you go, Bates, here's something to think about. The gas cylinder I picked up tonight contained nothing more potent than ice water."

Bates frowned. "Something colder than that was used on me," he said with a shudder.

"Yes!" X smiled. "Used on *you*. Think it over. It's important."

AGENT X attended the first matinee at the Paragon Theatre the following afternoon. He was disguised as a well-known member of the narcotic squad, a guise that brought Walter Nixon, the operator of the theatre, across the lobby with a troubled frown on his forehead. Just as X was about to enter the aisle. Nixon tapped him on the arm.

"Will you step over here a moment, Sergeant?" he whispered.

X was agreeable. "What's on your mind, Nixon?" he asked.

Nixon gnawed his lip and said nothing until he had drawn X away from the patrons who were entering the theatre. Then he said irritably: "How long is this going to keep up? It seems to me that there are police or members of the Anti-Vice League here at every performance. I think the patrons are beginning to notice it. I demand to know just what you expect to find here at the Paragon."

---

secret records are kept. His press credentials are genuine, giving him the privilege of entering many doors that would otherwise be closed to him.

"We're looking for dope," X said. "The reason the investigation continues is that we have been unable to find any dope here or at other theatres. You should be thankful of that, Nixon, instead of crabbing about it."

"It's very annoying," Nixon persisted.

When he left the theatre, ten minutes later, Agent X thought he was on the track of an important discovery. He had seen only the newsreel, and while his eyes had not left the screen, in the darkness his hands had been busy with pencil and paper. He went immediately from the Paragon to the Princess Theatre directly across the street.

Again, he left as soon as the newsreel had been shown, and his heart was pounding madly with excitement, because of his discovery. While he was as certain about it all as he was about tomorrow's sunrise, he nevertheless went to one of the downtown theatres and once again checked on the newsreel. Then he went directly to the office of A.J. Martin, phoned Harvey Bates and Jim Hobart.[32]

It was, of course, as A.J. Martin that he welcomed redheaded Jim Hobart and Harvey Bates. Though the two friends of the Agent had met, they had never worked together on a case before; and both were a bit reticent, fearful, no doubt, of betraying some of the Agent's secrets.

X SPREAD the map he had found in Mrs. Rister's bag out on the desk once more, and beside it he put a narrow slip of paper on which he had scribbled an odd list of letters and numbers. His gray eyes were twinkling, his lean lips smiling as he asked: "Did either of you ever see that particular newsreel known as 'Photo-News?'"

Bates nodded.

Hobart said: "Sure, Mr. Martin—a lot of times."

"Then I need not go into detail as to how the title, 'Photo-News' is thrown on the screen. You will remember that the word 'news' is spread pretty well across the screen, three stars separating each letter. Now, for just a scrap of history. I'm sure you both know the origin of the word 'news?'"

Hobart said: "It came from the directions, north, east, west, and

---

32   AUTHOR'S NOTE: Jim Hobart, famous director of the Hobart Detective Agency, is an old friend of Agent X whom he knows only as A.J. Martin. It was the helpful assistance of A.J. Martin that had established Hobart in his successful business and Hobart is devoted to his mentor, willing to fill strange requests at once and without asking too many questions.

south as represented by their abbreviations, N, E, W, and S. Isn't that right?"

"Exactly right. And when I found a slight, apparent flaw in the film, which cast a black mark on the screen above the letter 'S' in the trade-mark, and found that same flaw on every Photo-News film shown at every theatre I visited today, I began to think it meant something. And so it does."

Harvey Bates grunted. The Agent looked at him and smiled. "What's on your mind, Bates?" he asked.

"A direction. I noticed that flaw on the film before. It was in a different place, though. Never paid any attention to it."

"No one would pay any attention to it," X went on, "for without this map, it means nothing. However, if we take a rule and a compass, get the directions down on the map, then draw a line from the center of the thirty-one circles in the direction indicated so subtlely by the newsreel, that line will intersect all of the thirty-one circles."

"Now, which circle are we going to use? Simply pick out the day of the month, is my guess. This is the ninth, so we consider the ninth circle. Note that a line passing through the circles due south from the common point, which we know to be Arvin's backyard, intersects circle nine at East Eighteenth Street and at just about the place where Zerna held her dope party last night."

"I'm still in the dark, Mr. Martin," said Hobart, his freckled face screwed into a puzzled mask.

"It is simply a subtle way of informing the dopesters where they will meet and obtain their dope ration," X explained. "Serial numbers, faked on the film, indicate the exact time and exact address. All a dope addict has to do to establish his connection is to drop into any theatre showing Photo-News, get the direction, draw a line on his map, and go to the proper address at the proper time.

"It's no wonder the police have made no headway. The whole dope syndicate is constantly on the move. Zerna throws parties in houses or apartments that she rents. But is it Zerna who figured all this out? I doubt it. She's hardly that brainy.

"The point I'm making is this: now that we know how it is done, we can direct that mob into a trap of our own making!"

"Right, sir!" Bates clipped. His square face beamed in absolute admiration of his chief.

"Pull on a moment," said the more skeptical Hobart. "How's that to be done?"

"I've learned," X said, "that the Eastern Film Agency distributes next week's Photo-News films tomorrow morning. Tonight, with the aid of one of Bates's staff photographers, we tamper with those films so as to direct the whole gang into our trap. I'll need you and Bates, and some of your best men, to watch the film agency. See that no one else tampers with those films after we have made our changes. That clear?"

Bates and Hobart nodded.

"Then at midnight tonight, you'll be on Forty-ninth Street near the film agency. I have a little job to attend to before then."

The "little job" X had mentioned, concerned Mr. Hamilton Esler of the Blue Streak Cab Company. "Honest Ham," Esler might be— and certainly appeared to be, after turning over the money which X, as Starbuck, had placed in the back of Esler's cab. But after all, if Esler was associated with the blackmail dope-gang, he would have known ahead of time that the supposed Starbuck was really Agent X. It would have been well worth the money he had turned over to the police to be alibied in the eyes of Secret Agent X.

SHORTLY after Bates and Hobart had left the A.J. Martin office, X walked in the door of the office of the Blue Streak Cab Company. Esler, owner of the small string of cabs, was sitting with his feet on the desk. A commonplace man in appearance was Mr. A.J. Martin, yet Esler's black eyes examined his visitor searchingly.

Agent X pulled out his card, which represented him as a member of the Associated Press. "Looking for a little human interest angle on the recent death of Mrs. Colrich," he said to Esler. "I understand that you were the man who drove her to the quarter where she was murdered. Suppose you give me a line on how she was dressed and how she acted."

"Why, sure, Mr. Martin," Esler agreed. "You see a lot of funny stuff, driving around in a cab. Wonder to me some of you news-hawks don't go in for taxi-wheeling. It was like this...."

For the next ten minutes, X apparently listened to Esler's accurate account concerning Mrs. Colrich. Actually, his eyes were busy, roving around the office. His gaze got as far as Esler's desk, and there it stopped. There were thumb-tack marks on the surface of the desk—marks that immediately awakened the Agent's interest.

A few minutes later, when Esler excused himself to go out to the curb to give a message to one of his drivers, X slipped a steel tape measure from his pocket and calculated the distance between the four groups of thumb-tack marks which roughly represented the four corners of a square. A fifth group of pricks was somewhere near the center of this square. X reeled his tape and put it into his pocket. Then he went out to the curb where Esler stood.

"Do you know where Montgomery Mansion is?" he asked.

Esler thought a moment. "Oh, that old wreck of a stone building in the north end? You can hardly see over the weeds in the yard in the summer. Sure, I know that joint."

X took a roll of bills from his pocket and peeled out a twenty. "This will convince you I really want to go there," he said quietly.

HALF an hour later, the cab stopped in front of a dark, deserted house of stone that rambled across several unkept lots. Montgomery Mansion was a once-grand manor where Agent X had hidden one of the most complete crime laboratories in the country.

"You must be going to call on the rats, mister," Esler said, as he regarded the old house distastefully.

"Yes? Well, I brought the rat with me," X said quietly. At the same time, he pressed the muzzle of his gas gun into Esler's back. "Get out," he said. "And take it easy. My nerves are just a little unstrung tonight."

"What the hell?" gasped Esler. "Is this a stickup?"

"Oh, no, this is a finish. It's about the last thing that happens to a man of your stamp before they turn on the juice in the electric chair."

And across the sunken flags and through the old doorway, Agent X prodded the taxi driver. Through rooms of darkness, across creaking floors, X guided Esler. He forced the man down basement steps. He unlocked a steel door that looked as though it belonged on a bank vault. He thrust Esler into a room beyond, switched on lights, and followed. He closed and locked the heavy door behind them.

"You've got fox-brains," said X. "But when you drew thirty-one circles on a lot of maps of this city, the thumb-tacks, in the corners of the maps, left their marks on your desk. The needle point of the drawing-compass used to make the circles, also left marks. Knowing the measurements of the maps, and also where the center of those thirty-one circles was, I simply compared the known measurements with those indicated by the marks on your desk. Hamilton Esler, the maps which drug addicts carry in order to locate their dope connections, were fixed up by you in your office!"

"Who are you?" Esler asked hoarsely.

X smiled grimly. "I am the man you've always managed to keep two jumps ahead of."

"Secret Agent X," Esler pronounced slowly, fearfully.

"As good a guess as anyone will ever make," X admitted. "I am the man who looked like James Starbuck the other night when I rode in your taxi. You knew I wasn't Starbuck that night, for Zerna had no doubt warned you that I was simply impersonating Starbuck. My death was scheduled for that night. Your mob followed the cab, intending to kill me. But it seems I bear a charmed life. Even you were afraid I might escape. So you arranged a perfect alibi.

"Acting my part as Starbuck, as yet ignorant of the fact that my disguise had been penetrated, I put a stack of supposed blackmail money under the seat of your taxi. Knowing that I would watch to see what became of the money, you handed it over to the police. Thus you squashed any theories I might have had concerning your tie-up with your organization."

X slipped a black leather case from his pocket, snapped it open with one hand, and took out a loaded hypodermic syringe.

"What are you going to do?" Esler's voice was no longer steady.

"I am going to turn out your light for a time, my friend," X said. "Your day as a field general is over."

Step by step, Esler moved back toward the wall of the room. His eyes flitted from the hypodermic syringe to the Agent's gas pistol. When his back touched the wall, he lunged suddenly forward in an insane effort to jump the Agent's gun.

The hypodermic needle darted out like the fang of a serpent and buried itself in the flesh of Esler's throat. Esler's arms fanned the air wildly, feebly. Then, with a long sigh, he melted to the floor.

X was beside him in a moment, his keen eyes intent upon Esler's face. He nodded his head slowly. How could he better direct the dope gang into a snare than by disguising himself as the criminals' leader? He took out his pocket makeup kit and opened it on the floor. Henceforth, until the entire gang was behind bars, he resolved to look and act the part of Hamilton Esler.

CHAPTER IX

TRIPLE-TRAP SUMMONS

IT WAS IN the disguise of Hamilton Esler that Agent X set out to meet Bates's photographic expert that night. In this disguise, there was always a chance that he might run into some members of Esler's gang who would unknowingly drop important information.

At exactly midnight, X and the photographic expert approached the film distributing office. As they entered the alley at the corner of the building, X held up an arm, checking the man at his side.

"Wait," he whispered. "Some one is at the back door of the place. It may be a janitor or a watchman." Or, he thought to himself, it might be one of the gang, coming to make changes in the newsreels in order to inform his servants of their next meeting place. It was a ticklish situation. If he tried to hold the prowler up with a gun and the man turned out to be a watchman, it would be necessary to knock the man out. The watchman's absence would simply attract attention, not only to the police but also to the criminals.

The man beside X was a photographer, unused to night prowling of this sort. He was ill at ease, certainly, or at that moment he would not have lurched into an ash can.

Immediately, there was a scuffling of feet in the alley near the back door of the building. Agent X's right hand shot down to his trouser pocket and pulled out a small, round ball. He threw it with all his strength at the corner of the building. It was a magnesium flash bomb, such as X had frequently employed to create a moment of surprise when making some of his daring escapes. Tonight, he employed it with a different objective in mind.

The bomb struck the side of the building and burst. For an instant, the vicinity of the back door of the building was illuminated in the lightning-like flash. But the illumination lasted only for an instant, and X had not succeeded in seeing the running man's face.

However, there was something about his back, the sudden jerk of his shoulders, that was familiar. Agent X immediately broke into a run in a desperate effort to overtake the man.

But the prowler had a long lead. At the mouth of the alley, a car was waiting, its motor idling. The fleeing man sprang into the car, which accelerated down the street. X shrank back into the shadows. The men in the car must not see his face.

A moment later, X had rejoined the photographer. They entered the building together and quickly located the files where the newsreels that were to be distributed on the morrow were kept. Agent X spread a sheet of paper out on a table. On the paper, he had drawn an excellent facsimile of the trade-mark of Photo-News, and the flaws he wanted inserted between the "N" and "E" were clearly indicated, as well as the alterations in serial numbers.

He did not bother to explain the purpose of these alterations to the expert. Actually, these changes would direct the dopesters to a large, deserted warehouse near the Oak Point railway yards on the river front.

As soon as he had made his instructions clear, X left the man to his work. Near the corner of the building, he was met by Harvey Bates who was awaiting orders.

"Surround the place, Bates," X directed. "The alterations are being made, and your man must not be interrupted. The criminals may send a man to try and make changes, understand, since films go out to the theatres in the morning. Needless to say, you've got to prevent this. Our scheme may go haywire, but we've got to try it."

"Sure—everything will be okeh, sir," Bates said.

But Agent X, walking off alone in the dark, was not so optimistic.

X SPENT the following day in Esler's taxicab office, actually living the part of his disguise. But it was a day of anxiety and disappointment. The trap had been set for midnight that night. Had it a chance of succeeding? Had some master brain discovered his designs?

Hamilton Esler, he knew, was but one of the men behind the huge vice machine. Others, whom X suspected, were still at large.

Late that night, X left the taxi office and went to a pay telephone station, from which he called Betty Dale's apartment; but there was no answer to his ringing. He called the office of the *Herald* and learned that Betty Dale had gone with Gordon Stien, early that morning, to cover an out-of-town assignment.

X slammed up the receiver and left the booth. Why hadn't Betty heeded his warning? And it was not like her to leave town without leaving word with him.

In desperation, he took Esler's cab and drove to her apartment, hoping to find a note there from the girl. But there was nothing except a cold emptiness about the place.

His plan, his trap—it *had* to work now. Some sixth sense warned him that Betty was actually in the gang's power. Only by capturing a part of that pack of human wolves could he hope to pick up the trail of the girl.

Ten minutes before midnight, X slewed the taxi around the corner at Cabot and Oak Point Avenue. Instinctively, he knew that the shadows around the nearby warehouse were peopled with masked, hopheaded killers. As he brought the cab to a halt, he sensed motion all about him—men slinking in the shadows. Was he to lead them into the warehouse where Bates, Hobart and their men waited to subdue the gang with threatening guns and tear gas, or was he caught in his own web?

X got out of the cab. A man came shuffling along the sidewalk, head lowered and hands in his pockets. X waited. The man came up and flicked the beam of a flashlight on X's face. X saw that the man with the light was masked. But he was a dope fiend, no doubt of that. Had the others, the real leaders of the gang obeyed his newsreel summons?

"What's the job, chief?" the man whispered.

X commanded: "Bring the rest of the boys. We're going into that warehouse. There're some crated silks and furs inside. I got the whole job mapped out. There ain't a copper for blocks around here."

The masked man put his fingers to his lips and sounded a soft, owl-like whistle.

They came out of the darkness, the masked men with killer's eyes. There were perhaps a score of them. They surrounded the Agent, waiting impatiently for his directions.

"Don't draw no gats," X whispered. "This is a cinch, I says."

He led the way to the door of the warehouse and took hold of the latch. Was it merely imagination, or was that metal latch colder than the air that surrounded it? After all, it was a cold night. He lifted the latch.

THE DOOR swung suddenly out of X's hands. He sprang back,

reached for his gas gun. But his hand remained poised in mid-air as a stiffened form pitched forward to his feet. A cold draft, like that from an immense refrigerator came from the door of the warehouse.

"Cripes!" a man at X's elbow whispered. "The freezing death! Who is this guy?" and he pointed at the frozen man on the ground.

X took but one glance at the man on the ground. The man was one of Harvey Bates's best operatives. Then Bates and Hobart, inside the warehouse....

"Hey, Ham!" came Zerna's strident voice. She was elbowing through the crowd of criminals behind Agent X. "Ham, you gotta do something. They got no right to treat a woman that way!" Zerna reached X, seized his arm and shook him.

"What woman?" X demanded, his heart drumming dully against his ribs.

"Why, Betty Dale!" And at that instant, Zerna flashed the brilliant beam of a flashlight on X's face.

X knew he was caught. While his lips quickly said, "Why the hell should I care what they do with Betty Dale," he had been counting on the darkness to mask the anxiety that must have showed in his eyes. Zerna had been expecting something of the sort, and for that reason had flashed on her light at that moment.

But if Zerna had noticed that pained expression on the Agent's face, she concealed her knowledge cleverly. "Maybe you don't, Ham, but when I see those devils makin' a dope fiend out of an innocent girl like her, I get mad."

"Where is this girl you're so anxious about?" asked X. He was walking into a trap. He wanted to walk into a trap.

"Out on the yacht," Zerna said. "They're going to make a hop-head out of her. I'll take you out in the launch."

In spite of pangs of fear for Betty Dale that knifed his heart, X managed to comply to Zerna's request without the slightest indication of anxiety. There was no doubt in his mind but that Zerna had spoken the truth for the first time in a long while. Betty Dale was in the hands of the criminals. And they would use the Agent's love for her as a powerful weapon to gain their own ends.

CHAPTER X

TWO MINUTES TO DEATH

AGENT X LEFT the masked dopesters, without a word of explanation, and followed Zerna down to the river front and out onto the pier to join the woman, where a motor launch was tied. Zerna pushed ahead of him, climbed down the ladder, and got in under the wheel of the boat. X untied the painter, and as the motor started, sprang from the pier.

Zerna handled the speedy craft well, while X pretended to relax on the leather-upholstered seat beside her. Once away into midstream, Zerna pushed the throttle to the limit, and the boat seemed to skim along on the mist that pressed close to the surface of the water.

Zerna's green eyes seemed to possess catlike ability to see in darkness. She handled the boat with a recklessness born of desperation. But X knew that she was desperate, not because of any feeling for Betty Dale, but because she knew she was utterly alone with her worst enemy—Secret Agent X.

They had passed Fort Schuyler and had entered the deeper waters of the Sound. Zerna cut the speed of the craft somewhat and piped a shrill blast on the whistle. Her signal was immediately answered by a deeper note coming from near at hand. A little farther on, X made out the white, ghostly form of a steam yacht riding at anchor with a smaller gasoline cruiser in tow.

The right hand of Agent X had been busy in his pocket. He drew it out now as the steam yacht signaled again. Zerna's hand went out to touch the button that operated the electrical whistle of the launch, but the Agent's left hand darted forward and closed over her wrist. It seemed almost that he could feel her pulse jump as his fingers touched her.

"No," said X softly. And as he spoke, his right hand, holding a hypodermic syringe, joined its mate.

A frightened oath whispered across Zerna's lips as the needle entered her flesh. She struggled briefly against the hold the powerful narcotic was taking, then subsided in the Agent's arms.

X cut the ignition switch and allowed the boat to drift in the direction of the yacht. Then he climbed over the cockpit and slipped silently into the icy water.

Long, powerful strokes brought Agent X to the stern of the boat. He caught the rope that towed the gasoline cruiser and climbed hand over hand up the rail of the yacht. In another moment, he was moving along the dark deck, his water-soaked clothing making a telltale swishing sound.

A FLASHLIGHT cut a clean swath through the darkness and centered on the Agent's face. X staggered forward to fall, from pretended exhaustion, into a man's arms.

"Agent X!" X whispered hoarsely. "Is he here? He's impersonating me. He rounded up the gang some way, I think. I just escaped, swam out here to warn you guys."

A masked man came within the rays of the flashlight held in the hands of the man who was supporting X. "Yes," said the masked man quietly, "Agent X is here; right on deck, as a matter of fact. One of the crew picked out Zerna's launch with the searchlight. It's drifting at the stern. Zerna seems to be sleeping in it!"

X pulled quickly from the grasp of the man who had been supporting him. His hand started toward the pocket where his gas was concealed, but stopped halfway. In the dim light, black monstrous shapes loomed menacingly, surrounded the Agent with gleaming cylinders of the cold that killed.

"Don't move, Secret Agent X," said the masked man. "We prefer not to kill you at the present moment." The masked man came through the circle of hairy monsters, stepped boldly up to X and began to search his pockets. But his grasping fingers never reached the Agent's gas pistol. X's left fist cracked up to the point of the masked face's chin, while his right snatched out his gas gun. It was a certainty that the cold-killers would not open up their deadly liquid gas as long as one of their own bosses would have shared the same fate as Agent X. As the masked man collapsed on the deck, the ring of hairy monsters closed in. Yet as long as X kept near the unconscious masked man, he knew that he was safe from the killing cold.

*X darted for Zerna
with the needle.*

He fired the full charge of his gas pistol at the heads of those monster men. But, evidently, because they were amply protected against the effects of their own weapon, the Agent's anesthetizing gas seemed to have little effect. It was a hand to hand scuffle from there on.

The hairy men tried to smash X's skull half a dozen times with hasty blows from the metal cylinders in their hands. But their weapons were too heavy to easily follow the weaving, bobbing form of Agent X as every one of his supple muscles was brought into play in swift, deft dodges and in lightning bolt punches that flattened two of the hairy forms on the deck before the fight was well started.

Suddenly, a door in the wall of the cabin opened. The blaze of unexpected light caused X to glance toward it. A hoarse, pained cry ripped from his throat as he saw within the cabin something that made him immediately unconscious of personal danger.

Lying on a bunk in the cabin, her clothes twisted and wrinkled from continual tossing, her golden hair disheveled and snarled, was

Betty Dale. Muscles of her arms and legs twitched convulsively. Her lips moved, whispering, babbling about the nightmare-things that peopled a dope dream.

Instantly, the Agent's arms were pinned behind him by the furry monsters that had taken immediate advantage of his shock. Hands rifled his pockets, removed all his special devices and tossed them over the rail. A man stepped from the cabin where Betty Dale lay. He, too, wore a mask over his face.

"Miss Dale's future is not a particularly bright one," said the masked man. "Our dealings with dope have taught us that no matter how fine a character a woman may be before she acquires the habit, she eventually ends in the gutter. It is our hope that your affection is so great that you will not permit this thing to go farther."

THE HEART of Agent X seemed encased in ice. Better far that they had killed Betty outright than that they should subject her to slow degradation of body and soul in this manner.

"Name your price," he said dully.

"Very well," said the man in the mask. "First of all, let me compliment you on discovering our secret communication method depending upon newsreels and Esler's map. The trap you designed for us was a failure only because of one tiny error: you made the mistake of supposing that Hamilton Esler was the only leader of our organization. Naturally, when we discovered that the newsreel had been altered, we suspected you of doing the tampering, because our *real* director had not changed the films.

"Our killers arrived at the warehouse long before your men. And under the threat of the killing cold, they surrendered—after our men had made an example of one of your men. Both the redheaded detective, and the big, square-shouldered man named Bates, are locked in the hold of this boat, together with their eleven living operatives. The presence of Bates told us that you were the man behind the trap, since we were already familiar with Bates because of our eavesdropping on the orders you gave him when you were in James Starbuck's apartment."

"Get to the point," said X.

"Very well. You and your men are to die. There is no alternative. But it is within your power to save Betty Dale from a life that is worse than death. You seem to be a man of great financial resources. You may purchase Betty Dale's life for a check made payable to Hamilton Esler in the amount of fifty thousand dollars. In addition, you will tell us where you have hidden Esler. Betty Dale will be liberated immediately when the check is paid. *But,* if you do not pay, I swear to drag her through every hell conceivable."

"I see," said X. "Nevertheless, I should like some time to think this over."

"Certainly," the masked man agreed. To the fur-clad men: "Lock him in the hold until he decides."

A MINUTE later, X found himself in a cramped little room in the hold of the boat, chained by the left wrist to the steel wall. Just outside the door of the room, one of the fur-clad killers was on guard.

A look at these black hairy monsters beneath electric light showed the Agent that they were men wearing fur suits, hoods, and masks which evidently protected them from the freezing death they dealt. A small opening at the bottom of the masks enabled them to speak, but could be immediately closed when they went to work with their gas. These masks not only protected their faces, but also their lungs. Too much oxygen, such as was rapidly liberated from the frigid, liquid air was quite as harmful as too little: it was actually capable of burning up the lungs, if breathed in too great quantities.

X had not required time to think over the ultimatum he had been handed by the criminals. He would have gladly paid the price they asked to save Betty Dale. He had been simply stalling for time in hope of seeing some way to save Bates, Hobart and their companions as well.

No sooner had he found himself alone than his right hand pulled out his watch and snapped the gold chain attached to it. Then he put the watch behind him, pressed it against the wall, and opened the back of the case with his thumbnail. Though his watch was the size of an ordinary pocket watch, the actual movement was no larger than that of a lady's wrist watch. The rest of the room in the case was occupied by a coiled ribbon-saw of the finest steel.

With this keen tool in his possession, X went to work on the chain attached to his left wrist. The softer metal yielded quickly before the tiny teeth of the saw and twenty minutes later, he was free. He then dropped watch and saw on the floor and called to his guard.

The fur-clad man came into the room and approached X fearlessly, for the Agent held his left arm behind him as though it were still chained to the wall. Through the thick glass lenses in the man's mask, X saw his little black eyes, the pupils constricted to mere needle points. As he had expected, these servants of the gang were kept kill-crazy with liberal rations of dope. The man would make an excellent tool in the clever plan that was rapidly forming in X's brain.

"How much money would it take to buy you?" X asked. "Would a couple of grand fix things up so I could get away from here?"

The man laughed harshly through the mouth opening in the fur mask. "Don't act crazy! I know the guys I'm working for, see. They'd dope-starve me, see? I'd go nuts."

X had asked this question for but one purpose, to hear the man's voice. Suddenly he lunged forward from the wall. The fingers of his right hand were talons of steel, striking at the man's throat. At the same time his left arm swung around in a powerful haymaker, the single remaining iron link on his wrist catching the guard at the side of his fur-clad head. In spite of the protection his headgear offered, the guard dropped to the floor with scarcely a groan.

X dropped at the man's side, quickly found the fasteners that buckled the fur garment in place. He removed the suit, hood, mask and heavy, gauntlet gloves and laid them aside. Then he slipped out of the taxi driver's uniform that was part of his disguise as Esler, put on the fur suit and hood, and then dressed the unconscious guard in Esler's uniform.

Taking the makeup material from his own face was a task that required time and steady nerves, for he wanted to remove it and at the same time keep it as nearly intact as possible. For a moment, the light saw what no living person save Betty Dale had seen—the real face of Agent X, hidden, a moment later, by the fur mask that was part of the guard's uniform. Then, with infinite care, he replaced the plastic makeup material on the face of the guard, shaping it to conform with new facial contours.

The guard did not now resemble Hamilton Esler as closely as X had, but after all, that was not what X had tried to achieve. He wanted to be able to pass the guard off as Secret Agent X.

THE MAN already showed signs of reviving, and X braced him against the wall, held his head between his two hands, and stared steadily at the man's eyes. Never had the tremendous will power of the Agent been called upon for a greater test of hypnotism.[33]

---

33 AUTHOR'S NOTE: As it has often been stated, Agent X is a master of hypnotism. Science tells us that drug addicts are excellent subjects for hypnosis because their habit greatly lowers their resistance to suggestion from a more powerful mind. The daring plan which X put into execution at this critical moment would not have been possible had his

As the guard's eyes met those of X, the Agent repeated in a soft, compelling voice: "You are Agent X. You are Agent X. When anyone asks you who you are, you will tell them that you are Agent X. But you are also Elisha Pond because Agent X is Elisha Pond. When you sign a check you will sign it with the name Elisha Pond. Why?"

"Because," repeated the man mechanically, "I am Agent X. And when I sign a check, I sign it Elisha Pond." [34]

X smiled to himself. The plastic mind of the dope fiend was completely in his possession. As long as he remained in the same room with the man, he would be able to dictate his every action.

As soon as he was sure of his subject, X got to his feet, went to the door, where, in the voice of the guard, he shouted for help at the top of his lungs. As soon as he heard footsteps on the steel stairs leading down into the hold, he pivoted, went back to the guard, and lifted the helpless man in his arms—only to throw him down again as soon as he was certain that some one had entered the room behind him.

X turned around. Two men wearing black masks, several members of the crew, and three of the fur-clad cold-killers had crowded into the room. X pointed to the man on the floor. Through the opening in the fur mask he wore, he said: "The devil tried a getaway, chief. Look, he had a saw in his watch. He cut clear through the chain and tried to rush me."

One of the masked men nodded his head. "He was just stalling for time. He'll make his decision at once." He pulled a check and fountain pen from his pocket. The check was made out for $50,000 and lacked only the signature. The masked man held the check out to the hypnotized guard. "Will you sign this?"

The guard's dopey eyes were glued on those of Agent X. "I will sign it," he said tonelessly. "I will sign it with the name Elisha Pond."

"Why?" demanded the masked man. "Elisha Pond is an old coot with plenty of dough, but you're Agent X."

"I am Agent X," repeated the guard. "But I sign checks Elisha Pond. Agent X is Elisha Pond."

"Sure," said the other masked man, "that makes sense. You

---

hypnotic subject not been a slave to drugs.

34 AUTHOR'S NOTE: It is in the name of Elisha Pond that Agent X draws upon the huge fund of money placed at his disposal for use in his war against crime.

wouldn't expect Agent X to sign his own name to a check, would you? He'd be spotted by all the police in New York if he did. This Pond guy must be just one of the Agent's phoney names."

The other masked man was inclined to be skeptical. "Maybe you're right; but how come Agent X's voice sounds just like the voice of this guy?" And he indicated the real Agent X who masqueraded in the guard's fur uniform.

"Sure, boss, don't cha get it?" X hurriedly filled in. "X can talk like anybody. Wasn't he talkin' just like Esler when he came aboard?"

The masked man nodded. "You're right. What's the difference, just so he signs the check." He handed check and pen to the guard. The masked man would soon discover the difference if he ever had the opportunity of trying to cash that check. The handwriting in the signature would certainly not be that of Elisha Pond.

X slipped unnoticed from the room and hurried up to the cabin above, passing members of the crew unnoticed because of the fur garb he wore.

BETTY'S cabin door was a flimsy thing beneath the bucking shoulder of Agent X. As he rushed headlong into the cabin, the girl awoke suddenly from her drugged sleep, saw the Agent's fur-clad form, and opened her mouth to scream.

X clapped a furry glove over her mouth. "Betty!" he whispered tensely in the voice by which she knew him. And as recognition gleamed in the girl's eyes, his hand dropped from her mouth.

"You! Darling!" she fairly shouted. The drug had excited her to such an extent that she had lost all sense of restraint. She threw her arms about the Agent and sobbed hysterically.

"Betty, you must control yourself," he whispered and took hold of her shoulders and shook her. She stopped her laughing and crying, and stared at him with strange, wondering eyes. "Betty, there isn't a moment to lose. You must think straight!"

Betty's lips quivered as she complained: "Y—you're so cross!"

X shook his head sadly. The poor girl had lost all sense of proportion. "Listen, dear," and his voice became infinitely tender, "there's a motor boat drifting astern. There's an unconscious woman in it. I want you to get into that boat. I'll help you down to the water and you'll have to swim to it. Can you do that?"

Betty laughed. "With you I can do anything."

"No, I can't go with you. Bates and Hobart and the others are locked in the hold."

"I won't leave, then. You can't send me away, because I won't leave!" she all but screamed. And again came a fit of hysterical weeping.

There was nothing to do, X knew, but take her into the hold with him. He quieted her, promising that she should go wherever he went. "But you must be quiet, do you understand?"

"Still as a mouse," she agreed, nestling her head on his shoulder.

X went to the door of the cabin and looked out. The deck was clear. He beckoned Betty to join him. Together they tiptoed toward the companionway leading down into the hold. The Agent's heart was in his mouth. At any moment Betty might do something impulsive that would spoil their every chance.

At the bottom of the steps, X could hear the masked men questioning the guard whom they evidently still believed to be Agent X. They were demanding that he tell them where Esler could be found. The hoax could not last for much longer. But still, the hold would be the last place they would look for Agent X.

X held Betty in his arms, keeping his gloved hand over her mouth to prevent her from uttering so much as a whisper as they stole past the door of the room where X had been confined. Then they were again in the friendly darkness, moving quietly toward a yellow spark of light. They passed the door of the engine room. Then, directly ahead X saw that the light came from a globe screwed above a door. In front of that door, one of the fur-clad men mounted guard.

Still holding Betty tightly, X approached the guard. "The boss wants the girl down here with the others," he said.

The guard at the door asked no questions, but produced a key and fitted it into the lock. He swung the door open. X, standing directly behind the man, raised his left foot and planted a powerful kick in the small of the man's back, so that he sprawled head first into the room. And before the man could utter a cry, X landed directly on top of him, seized him by the throat, and choked him into silence.

X looked around the room. Harvey Bates, Jim Hobart and their eleven men were in the center of the room, lashed into a huge bundle around a wooden post that rose from the floor to the ceiling. X drew Betty into the room, closed the door, and set to work on the ropes and gags that held the men in motionless silence.

A THIRD masked man had joined the other two in the cabin where the criminals were impatiently questioning the man they supposed to be Secret Agent X. It was this man that X had knocked out almost as soon as he had boarded the yacht. He looked on a moment while his companions shook the supposed X by the shoulders and roared:

"You've not told us where to find Esler! Where's Esler?"

The dull-witted guard, still under the influence of the hypnotic trance, merely shook his head. "I am Agent X," he said. "I sign my name Elisha Pond."

The third masked man snarled an oath. "The man's crazy. How sure are you he's Agent X?"

He went over to the supposed X and gouged makeup material from the man's face.

"Why, you poor fools, he's tricked you. This is Jeris, one of our own men. Agent X has escaped, hell knows how!"

"Search the boat!" cried one. "Up on deck. He'll be with the girl." And they raced pell-mell for the companionway. On deck, they turned out the entire crew in a frantic search.

For five frantic minutes, they searched. Then the three masked men met at the stern of the boat. "Listen," one of them whispered, "the engineer says there isn't a guard down there where we had Bates and the others. Agent X and the girl must both be down in the hold, trying to get the others free. Our best move is to wipe out the whole group."

"That's the stuff," one of the others agreed. "Pump liquid air at 'em."

"Sure. Get down through the hatch at the stern. The one at the prow is locked, and the key's been lost for months. Bottle them up with the cold that kills."

DOWN in the hold. Agent X's deft fingers were flying, untying knots and pulling gags. Betty, too, worked with furious, dope-keyed energy. She gnawed at knots with her teeth, skinned her fingers on the coarse hemp.

"Not a word," X cautioned as he liberated Bates. "Everyone quiet. We're outnumbered by about three to one. You free the others, Bates." He turned to Betty. "Wait here. I'll be back in a moment. I'm just going to look out the door."

The Agent left the room and went back along the way he had come, but at the end of the companionway he stopped. There was a man on the steps—one of the fur-clad killers. Another man was passing down cylinders of deadly liquid gas.

It was impossible to mistake the purpose of the fur-clad killers. They held the vantage point that X had hoped to hold—the companionway. They had corked the one opening in the bottle.

X turned and ran quietly back to join the others. Not great need for quiet. All the gang members, and the crew, had been called out of the hold, which belonged to fourteen men and one woman—and death.

As soon as he gained the prison room, X called Hobart and Bates to the door.

"What are the chances?" Hobart asked eagerly.

The Agent shook his head slightly. "None, that way," he whispered.

"There's a stairway leading up to a hatch at the other end of the room where we were tied," Hobart told him.

"Locked," Bates clipped. "Don't think it's guarded."

"One of my men is an ex-burglar," Hobart said. "If we weren't so damned empty-handed—"

X interrupted: "Where is he?" Hobart called one of his operatives over to the door, and X addressed the man:

"How long would it take you to noiselessly open that hatch, if you had tools?"

The man grinned. "Sort of out of practice at that sort of thing. I could do it in ten minutes before Mr. Hobart sort of reformed me."

"Come. There ought to be something in the engine room you can use."

X hurried the man back to the engine room, there to hurriedly pick up a center punch, cold chisel, hammer and pliers. X found a jar of matches and some oil-soaked waste. These he stuffed into his pockets. Then he picked up all the pipe wrenches he could see. Good weapons, too—these....

Thus equipped, the Agent and the ex-burglar hurried toward the room where they were to make their last stand against the doped killers. Even as they reached the door, they could hear shuffling footsteps coming along the passage behind them. X closed the door of the room. It locked only from the outside, but by main force they might be able to hold it for a while.

"Talk, everybody," X urged. "Move around and make a lot of noise. We've got to cover the sound of the man working on the lock of the other hatch. If the gang gets wise, it will be just as easy for them to attack us from that point also."

He went to the door and opened it just a crack, so that he could look out. One of the black-clad killers was in sight, saw the door open, and raised his deadly cylinder. A stream of the hissing, blue-white liquid slapped against the door. Only the fur suit the Agent wore protected him. Some of the liquid got in under the door, and the temperature of the room dropped degrees almost at once.

For a slow torturing death, the mob had only to turn their weapon on the door. Half of the danger of the stuff lay in the fact that it could make the air in the room too rich in oxygen, actually burning up tender lung cells.

"How much longer to break that lock?" X called huskily.

"Two minutes, that's all."

THE KILLERS were massing outside the door. It would take just two seconds for them to break into the room, and less than thirty seconds to turn everyone in the room into frozen statues of horror.

X turned to Bates. "Promise me," he whispered, "to guard Betty Dale with your life."

"Of course. But what are you going to do, sir?"

"Never mind," X said sternly. "Protect that girl."

Secret Agent X reached into his pocket and took out the ball of oil-soaked cotton waste and the jar of matches. He had obtained these in the engine room, knowing that in a case of emergency one man could hold back the cold that killed, could destroy it—at a price. Agent X was ready to pay that price.

The liquid, oxygen gas was in itself uninflammable. But since all combustion depended upon the presence of oxygen, that combustion was much more rapid and intense when the surrounding space was saturated with oxygen. In his own laboratory, X had seen a heated piece of iron burst into white hot flames in the presence of a small quantity of liquid oxygen. He was ready to repeat that experiment tonight on a larger scale with human lives at stake.

He had only to carry the fire to the very origin of the freezing death to turn that portion of the ship's hold into a veritable blast furnace. It would cut off the criminal advance with a sheet of flame. It would rob the killing cold of its teeth by uniting the oxygen with combustible materials. And when the blast came—Agent X pushed the ugly thought from his mind.

Behind the furry mask, he smiled. Betty Dale, Hobart, Bates and the others would have their chance. That thought alone spurred him on to do what he must do.

CHAPTER XI

INVITATION TO HELL

BETTY DALE HAD seen Bates and the Agent talking near the door. As X took the ball of waste from his pocket, she came forward to join him. "What are you going to do?" she asked anxiously.

X did not look at the girl. He dared not to risk the pangs of a final good-bye. Instead, he answered her cheerfully: "I am going to plug up a little opening, that's all."

X raised his hand and closed the furry mouth-opening of his mask. Then he opened the door a crack. Outside, some twenty feet from the door, were half a dozen of the fur-clad killers. Each held a cylinder of freezing death in his gloved hands. Then, at a signal from their leader, they moved suddenly forward toward the door.

Agent X sprang out to meet them. His surprise appearance brought the line of killers at a momentary stop. But even as they released six solid streams of the blue-white, hissing stuff, X struck a match and lit the waste. Holding the flaming stuff at arm's length, he rushed headlong toward the killers and flung the burning waste into their very midst.

There was a dull roar, and white-hot flame rose in an all-consuming sheet from floor to ceiling.

Betty Dale screamed, sprang toward the door. But the strong hands of Harvey Bates seized her.

"Let me go!" she screamed. She turned, beat at Bates's chest with her small fists. Bates's arms were like bands of steel about her. He scarcely saw the desperate fury in her face as she struggled to throw herself into that white-hot inferno. Bates's eyes were dimmed. He was never to forget that heroic figure, silhouetted against that wall of flame.

Almost the first thing the blast had touched had been the fur-clad form of Agent X. Bates had seen that mighty figure flung backwards. He had seen the Agent's arms fly upwards to shield his eyes from the stunning brilliance of the fire. He had seen that figure lurch forward into the fire, a figure that was itself a writhing mass of flame.

Had he been able to project his sight beyond the searing curtain of fire that blocked the criminal attack, he would have seen that same flaming figure, fighting its way toward the companionway, staggering up the steps to reach the deck rail. Then he would have seen a human meteor dive from the side of the boat to be immediately extinguished as the black water closed over it, leaving only a little cloud of steam to mark the spot where Agent X had disappeared.

A TRIUMPHANT shout from Jim Hobart: "The lock's broken. Come on! Up on deck. Grab a wrench, you. Let's move!"

Bates held the struggling, sobbing girl in his arms as he moved back toward the steps with the others.

"He'll be all right," he muttered in the girl's ear. But Bates could not lend the ring of conviction to his words.

He lifted the girl in his arms as they gained the deck. The flames had sought out the wood framework of the central portion of the cabin, and the surface of the water was tinged blood-red by the tongues of fire.

A group of criminals, taken entirely by surprise, came around the corner of the cabin. But they had scarcely time to draw their guns before Hobart's men were upon them, beating them to the deck with lusty blows from their pipe wrenches.

Vigilant patrol boats and other craft were looming out of the rose-tinted fog, coming to the aid of the burning vessel. Some of the criminals were deserting in a lifeboat. Others fought with Hobart's men for the possession of a second lifeboat. But Bates had all he could do to hold Betty Dale. Help was so near that before the fire on the yacht began to creep their way, they would all be safely away. It was escape that the courage and quick-thinking of a single man had provided. But at what a price!

Thinking only of Betty's safety, Bates carried the girl as far away from the actual fighting as possible. But as he reached the other corner of the cabin, a fear-mad killer almost bumped into him. The man had a gun. He raised it, laughed insanely. Instinctively, Bates threw Betty behind him.

A bullet from the mad killer's gun lanced through Bates's left arm. Bates's big right hand closed on the man's gun wrist, and with a powerful twist, brought the man's right arm up almost to his shoulder blades in a hammerlock hold that brought a shriek of agony from the killer. The man dropped his gun, slipped from Bates's grasp, and dived for the rail.

Bates never noticed whether that crazy killer went over the rail or not. He turned around. To his horror, he found that Betty was gone.

THE GIRL who loved Secret Agent X had taken the opportunity offered by the criminal's attack, to slip from behind Bates's shielding body. Free from his protection, she had run swiftly down the deck, past the blazing cabin, and to the other end of the boat. She had but one objective—get to Agent X.

Golden hair flying, eyesight blurred from clouds of smoke through which she had passed, Betty seized the arm of the first man she met.

"Where is he?" she gasped out. "I must find Agent X. Where is he?"

The man laughed harshly as he tore out of her grasp. "Gone to hell, where the rest of us will go, if we don't get off this damned tub. He dived over the rail in a mass of flames, sister. I'd look for a new man if I were you!"

Blindly, her hands found the rail. She stared fixedly at the flame-tinged water. She blinked back tears to see three shadowy forms drop one at a time into the gasoline cruiser tied to the stern. A flare of ruddy light found the face of one of the men. That face was covered by a black mask.

Not far from the cruiser, Zerna's small launch drifted. Betty looked from the cruiser to the launch. Her two fists clenched. In her slim body a new strength was born. She would carry on the great work that *he* had been unable to finish....

In the forty-foot cruiser, one of the three masked men untied the rope that connected the smaller boat to the yacht. Another tinkered with the engine.

"It couldn't have ended better," said the third man. "We can make a clean getaway. We have realized nearly a million dollars in the racket."

"We needn't quit," said the man in the prow as he cast off from the yacht. "I have some of the best blackmail pictures in the lot right here in my pocket." He took a leather case from the inside of his pocket, patted it affectionately, and returned it to his pocket.

The engine popped, broke into a steady murmur. One of the masked men took the wheel, reversed the screws, and backed the cruiser away from the burning yacht. Then he turned the prow of the boat due east across the Sound. They had not gone a hundred feet before they sighted a motor launch coming straight toward them.

"It's Zerna," said one of the men. "She's following us."

"Take her aboard," replied one of the others. "After all, she's been on the level with us."

The man at the wheel cut down on the throttle a little. "It looks as though she were trying to ram us. No, she switched off the motor. She's going to bump. Stand by to give her a hand."

A small anchor at the end of a line was flung from the launch to land in the cockpit of the cruiser. The masked man who was leaning forward to steady Zerna's boat, muttered an oath. "Zerna didn't throw that anchor. Zerna's doubled over in the cockpit. Looks like another woman."

They saw the woman beside Zerna stand upright, step to the edge of the cockpit, and spring to the deck of the cruiser.

"Look out!" cried one of the men. "She's got a gun."

"Put up your hands, gentlemen," said Betty Dale, her voice as steady as Zerna's gun in her hand. "Agent X taught me to shoot straight."

Three pairs of hands stretched above three masked faces. Betty nodded her approval. "Move just a little closer together, please, so that I will have less trouble shooting you if it comes to that. I am going to signal the police."

But Betty was watching their hands, when she should have been watching the feet of the man to her left. He braced the sole of his shoe against the anchor Betty had tossed aboard. With a suddenness that took the girl completely by surprise, he sent the anchor sliding across the deck. Betty saw it coming, tried to jump aside, tangled with the rope attached to the anchor, and fell to the deck.

They were upon her in a moment. Cruel hands wrested the gun from her. Cruel fingers shackled her wrists together. A hand clamped over her mouth.

"Now, Betty Dale," one of the masked men whispered, "you wanted to be with Agent X. You'll get your chance! Get that anchor and rope, one of you fellows. The girl goes over the rail, see?"

ANOTHER masked man reached for the rope and started to pull it over the rail into the cruiser. It seemed to be stuck on something. The man went to the edge of the deck, knelt to untangle the rope. But for two ticks of a watch he was unable to move.

Sticking out of the water, clinging to the rope that reached from Zerna's launch to the cruiser, was a black, withered-looking hand. Then a black, gleaming, goggle-eyed head bobbed to the surface.

The man at the rail uttered an alarmed oath, tried to scramble backwards from the rail and at the same time drew his gun. But the black monster from the water jerked itself to their deck and rolled into the masked man. There was a frantic tangling of arms and legs. The masked man raised his gun toward the monster's black head. But instantly that withered-looking hand clamped over the man's wrist and turned the muzzle of the gun skyward.

The black talon of the monster from the water wrested the weapon free. His grotesque head turned slightly. His goggling eyes saw the other two masked men forcing Betty Dale back toward the rail. The monster raised the gun, fired once.

The single shot clipped one of the masked men in the leg. He tumbled to the deck. The other released the girl and stepped back toward the tiny cabin of the cruiser.

Betty Dale, from where she crouched near the rail, watched the dripping, grotesque figure herd the three masked men into the cabin of the cruiser and follow them to the hatch. The girl got to her feet and came timidly toward the strange man who had saved her. What if *he* had not died?

A police boat siren wailed, and the bright beam of its searchlight slit the blackness.

"Cruiser ahoy!" came the cry from the patrol boat. "What's going on there?"

The strange man with the gun turned his head and called back: "This is Detective Sergeant Keegan of the Homicide Office. Come alongside!"

Betty's arm, half-raised to touch the man in the strange garb, dropped limply to her side. She backed to the stern as the police cruiser swept alongside. As Keegan entered the cabin, he called out to the men getting in from the patrol boat:

"Get that girl out of that launch this cruiser is towing. It's Zerna, the dope peddler. Some of you come in here while I talk with these mugs. Miss Dale, you stick around for a story."

KEEGAN stepped to where the three masked men were backed against the wall. Silently he frisked them. He produced the flat leather case from the pocket of one of the men and flipped it open. He nodded his hooded head. "This is good evidence of the black-mail racket, Mr. Gordon Stien!"

The masked man thus addressed shrank back against the wall. Keegan reached out his gloved hand and pulled aside the mask that had covered Stien's pop-eyed, chubby face.

"Just as Esler handled the field work of the gang," he said, "Stien snapped indecent pictures of the doped victims with hidden cameras set up at Zerna's dope parties." Keegan handed the folder of pictures to one of the cops from the boat. "Give those to Burks."

His goggle-covered eyes turned on Stien. "The other night at Zerna's party, you were to be killed because Miss Dale had pointed you out as Agent X. Actually, this was not only an opportunity for you to alibi yourself, but also you knew that Agent X would never stand by and see an innocent man suffer for his own deeds. By appealing to his human qualities, you hoped to force X to reveal himself. The gas cylinder which was to be used for your 'execution,' contained nothing but water. You were taking no chances. Agent X discovered that and understood at once that you were associated with the gang. It was you, Stien, who were responsible for Betty Dale's capture by the dope gang, for she trusted you. She was later drugged in an effort to extort money from Agent X."

"But who are the other two birds?" asked a patrolman.

"One at a time," was the reply. "The man next to Stien is Dr. Samuel Wicker. Just pull off the mask, won't you?"

The patrolman jerked off the mask of the second of the two villains. Dr. Wicker's jowls wobbled with wrath. "A damned lie!" he roared.

"The lying was on your side, Wicker. You pretended to cure dope addicts while you actually supplied the gang with drugs from your own pharmacy. Dope legitimately supplied to the Wicker Sanitarium for the tapering-off type of dope cure, who resold to the addicts who were victims of this gang's scheming.

"We now have three points to a compass, do you see? Esler might represent the east; Stien, the south; Wicker, the west. I really believe that they got their idea for their clever method of communicating from the fact that their own initials could be found at the four points of the compass. Esler did the field work, Stien was chief blackmailer, and Wicker supplied the dope. But there had to be a head man. Behind that remaining mask, you will find the handsome visage of Mr. Walter Nixon!"

Nixon jerked off his own mask. His small black mustache was bristling. "All right. Let's hear some more of that wild tale, Sergeant Keegan. And you might explain why you're wearing that crazy garb!"

"Later, perhaps. Mr. Nixon was not a difficult person to spot. He has a strange peculiarity. Whenever a flashlight picture is taken, he twitches his shoulders as though some one had slammed him across the back. The other night, when Secret Agent X saw Nixon trying to enter the film distributing office, he tossed a simple flash bomb in Nixon's direction. Though he did not see Nixon's face, X noticed that peculiar twitching of the shoulders as Nixon ran down the alley.

"Then again, it was Nixon who kept thinking one jump ahead of Agent X. When Agent X made alterations in the news films in order to attempt to direct the gang into a trap, Nixon got wise almost at once. Why? Simply because Nixon himself was the man who altered those films, and he knew there was trickery somewhere. Again, when Agent X was impersonating Inspector Burks, and questioning Mr. Colrich in Nixon's office, Nixon was the only one who could have overheard what Colrich said about Starbuck having led Mrs. Colrich astray. A moment later, when he picked up a phone call from the real Inspector Burks, he knew the Burks in his office was Agent X and that X's next logical step would be to go to Starbuck and question him in regard to Mrs. Colrich's murder.

"So Nixon had the wires to Starbuck's apartment tapped, sent Zerna to do spy duty. When Agent X impersonated Starbuck, the whole gang was all set to kill Agent X."

Nixon sneered. "That's very clever, but how is it that you know all this?"

"Agent X told me this before he died."

"That's a lie!" Nixon whipped out. He pointed a finger at the accusing figure in front of him. "I'll tell you how he knows all that. He's Secret Agent X. That garb he's wearing is one of the cold protection suits our men wore—" Nixon stopped, turned deathly pale. "I mean, I—I—"

"Yeah," said one of the cops, "we get exactly what you mean. You've just let yourself in for the chair and dragged your buddies right along with you. Every cop in the city knows that Mrs. Colrich and Steve Wyer were killed with liquid air. Now, you've just admitted the job. Maybe this guy is Agent X. We'll take him up if he is, but that isn't going to help you any, Nixon. If this guy is Agent X, he's done a sweet job of rounding up a mob of worse than murderers." The cop turned to his men. "Handcuffs for three. No, make it four. Agent X, after a job like that, I don't care about taking you in, but duty is duty."

NEAR the door, Betty Dale was quivering like a leaf. Was there a chance that this strange man, who wore one of the cold-killers' fur garments with the hair singed off, was really Agent X? Could he have gotten through that wall of flame, even though that protecting garment was on fire, and plunged into the Sound?

Keegan's harsh voice laughed at them all. "Don't be nuts! Agent X is dead. I saw him burned. He just gave me the information, that's all."

Nixon gesticulated wildly with his handcuffed hands. "Take off that hood. You'll see! He's got his face covered with that mask to hide it. All his makeup material is gone. I threw it into the Sound myself together with his weapons."

Hoping against hope, Betty Dale crowded her way into the group of police surrounding the man in the black garb and his three captives. The officer in charge of the patrol boat reached out and unfastened the black leather hood of the man who insisted he was Sergeant Keegan. Then he pulled off the leather mask with its thick-lensed goggles. Betty uttered a pitiful little scream and buried her face in her hands.

Sure enough, behind the mask was the face of Detective Sergeant Keegan.

Keegan grinned triumphantly at the men about him. He gestured at the three captives. "The arrest was made on your territory," he told the cop. "You're responsible for delivering them safely, together with the evidence. They're dangerous. When a dope addict got to the point where he or she was of no further service to the gang, that addict was disposed of. That was why they killed Ruth Colrich. Of course, Steve Wyer was killed because he was muscling-in on the blackmail racket by sticking Colrich on the grounds of threatening to reveal Mrs. Colrich's vice."

Keegan started back on deck, stopped in the doorway, and added: "If you see Burks before I do, tell him I'll deliver Mr. Esler, the fourth member of the gang tomorrow morning. I'm a little tired, and I'm sure Miss Dale is. Maybe, if she'll let me take her back in

Zerna's launch, I can give her more details about the story she'll write for the paper."

"Thanks," Betty husked. "You're very kind." She allowed the detective to lead her to the deck where the unconscious Zerna was stretched out. Keegan pulled Zerna's launch near the cruiser and helped the girl in. Then he cast off and started the motor.

Betty sat silently in the cockpit beside him, looking steadily at the cruel, black water. She felt Sergeant Keegan's arm drop about her shoulder. "Please don't," she said huskily. But the arm remained just where it was, pressing her a little closer. She heard Keegan's voice talking, but she didn't look at him. He was saying:

"It was cruel, wasn't it, to stand there and talk about Agent X's death."

"You—you knew then?"

"I've known for a long time what Agent X thought of you, Betty. That's why I said it was cruel to stand there and talk about his death. I couldn't help it. You understand, don't you? Or have you forgotten that, in a little compartment in the heel of his shoe, Secret Agent X always carries a tiny tube of makeup material big enough for an emergency disguise?

"Agent X didn't die, Betty. The fire couldn't quite burn through that suit of fur before he struck the water. And Agent X is quite a swimmer. He clung to the side of the cruiser long enough to remove that little tube of makeup from the compartment in his heel. Then he did a quick, but quite convincing job of making himself look like Keegan."

"Oh, darling—" And if Betty had anything else to say, the words were lost in joyous sobs as she clung close.

The lips of Agent X were very close to her ear whispering: "Agent X couldn't die, knowing that you were waiting for him, dear...."

In the prow of one of the patrol boats that had picked up the doped killers of the criminal crew, as well as the operatives of Agent X, Harvey Bates stood looking out across the water. The burning yacht cast ruddy reflections upon the water. Police searchlights created strange, gargantuan shadows. He was listening intently, and there was a tight feeling in his throat as he heard a weird, eerie whistle from somewhere in the darkness.

"Thank heaven!" Bates choked out. For he knew that whistle could have come from the lips of but one person. It was the mysterious musical signature of the mysterious Secret Agent himself.

BOOK XXXI

THE MURDER BRAIN

Weird white crosses were splashed upon the sidewalks
of a terror-ridden city. And under each cross lay a
man murdered without a motive. Agent X, the man
of a thousand faces, set out to meet the murder
master whose face was known only to the dead.

CHAPTER I

MURDER EPIDEMIC

IT WASN'T A pleasant room. A filmy light-globe wired into an old, brass gas fixture lent a nauseous shade to the blue-kalsomined walls. An iron bedstead shed enamel as a birch tree does its bark. There was a telephone on a table of woven fiber.

At the table, a man faced the wall, oblivious to its ugliness. He pulled the phone up under his jutting chin and called Rector 2-3520 in a voice that was crisply impatient. Three fingers of his right hand tap-danced on the table top. Foley Square and the United States Court House were thirty long seconds away, even for a man with the magic of the telephone at his command.

"Jackson speaking," said the man in the dingy room at last. "I must speak to Special Agent Weston, immediately."

He finger-danced some more, squirmed restlessly in the hard-bottomed chair. Then his voice lashed out at the transmitter:

"Jackson to report. I leave immediately for Bedford Street to meet Agent Parker at the corner of Commerce. Another white-cross killing has been scheduled."

G-man Henry Jackson clamped the receiver to its hook and pushed the phone away from him. As he did so, the polished metal shell of the transmitter caught a black and particularly ominous reflection. The reflection was that of a man. Either the nickel shell of the phone was distorting the image a great deal, or this man was about as large a specimen as Jackson had ever encountered.

Enormous square shoulders seemed on the point of pushing through his black coat. He wore no hat. Only his unruly black hair prevented his head from being a complete cube. His jaw resembled the foremost portion of a steamshovel. The stem of a square-bowled pipe parted the level line of his lips. The rest of his face was hidden by a black mask.

Bates waded in, and the man holding the girl flashed a knife.

It was remarkable how perfectly-relaxed G-man Jackson appeared to be. It was even more remarkable how quickly his lax fingers snatched up at his under-arm gun. But he was just not quite quick enough.

The cube-headed man was standing exactly in the center of the door behind Jackson. He had not stirred a muscle. But some one else had, and Jackson had never in his life encountered anything like the muscles of the slender hand and arm that shot over his shoulder to seize his gun wrist.

Jackson shook his head, a habit he had when he found himself in a bad spot. Two men had slipped into the room while he had been phoning—the masked man who looked as though he had been constructed with the aid of a steel square, and this slighter person whose body seemed a curious combination of the irresistible force and the immovable object. No small part of this second intruder's

power lay in the depths of his gray eyes. His eyes didn't stare; they anchored the G-man's attention to such an extent that several seconds clicked by before Jackson noticed that the man's face consisted of something besides eyes.

It took the G-man just a little off balance, that face of the man with the gray eyes. The cheeks looked hollow and pale. The chin receded slightly. The thin lips spoke only with their corners:

"Nix on the roscoe, G-man."

The black-masked man loomed larger in the nickel shell of the phone. His square-ended fingers went inside the G-man's coat, produced the gun Jackson would have given a year of his life to reach. Then the gray-eyed one's grip relaxed, and Jackson turned slowly to face his two unwelcomed visitors.

THE GRAY-EYED man held a gun that closely resembled a heavy automatic. The masked man had carelessly tossed the G-man's gun aside. There was nothing formidable about the masked intruder except his size, and even that was somehow dwarfed by the cyclonic energy that seemed stored in the lean length of his companion. Having felt the latter's muscles once, Jackson regarded the man with an infinite amount of respect. Still, he managed a brazen:

"What the hell do you call this?"

"The phone," the gray-eyed man snagged from the corner of his mouth, "should be so that you could keep an eye on the door. Remember that in the future."

Jackson worked his lips into a grin. "Consoling to know I'm to have a future."

The gray-eyed one laughed queerly. "I didn't say whether the lesson was intended for your use in this world or another one. My guess is that here is where you fade out of the picture."

The black gun in Gray-eyes' hand tilted up a little, and Jackson was painfully conscious of its steely stare. Yet those who serve the Department of Justice receive much tempering in the fire of danger. Jackson knew suddenly that he was going to try to jump that gun.

The G-man hurled himself straight at the man with the gun, but its owner wasn't a tangible opponent. There was suddenly nothing in the world for Jackson but a cloud of vapor that spurted from the weapon and blotted out everything before the G-man's eyes. Jackson fell forward into the waiting arms of the man whose face belonged to some underworld rat, but whose eyes were those of Secret Agent X.[35]

"Take his legs, Bates," Agent X said sharply to the man in the black mask. "We haven't a second to throw away. I am afraid I lost too much time already, talking to Jackson; but I wanted to make sure of his voice."

"Right," clipped Bates. He dropped his pipe into the palm of his

---

35   *AUTHOR'S NOTE: Followers of Agent X know that he has developed impersonation to the point of perfection. A plastic volatile material of his own composition, enables him to adopt the features of any man. Yet even this and other special makeup devices would be of little use without the masterful dramatic powers of the man himself. Keen perception of details, flawless mimicry, and natural ability all combine to make him "The Man of a Thousand Faces." Though he is crime's most dreaded foe, he seldom resorts to lethal weapons, preferring his gas pistol, loaded with a powerful anesthetic, to revolver or automatic.*

hand and assisted the Agent in carrying Jackson into the adjoining bathroom. Then the door was closed on X and the G-man.

Harvey Bates, the Secret Agent's trusted lieutenant, knew that when the door opened again, the white-faced underworld rat, who had accompanied him to the G-man's hideout, would exist only in memory. Agent X would become another personality, a man with a new face and a new voice.

Never would Harvey Bates cease to marvel at the impersonations of his chief. Never would he stop wondering about the true appearance of this man of mystery. Yet for all his natural curiosity, an almost reverential respect for his employer prevented Bates from asking questions. He was satisfied with knowing that Agent X had but one objective—to carry the war against crime to its just conclusion or to die in the attempt.

After an incredibly short interval, G-man Henry Jackson stepped from the bathroom. Anyone of average perception would have supposed that the man wearing Jackson's clothes, Jackson's features, and speaking with Jackson's voice, was G-man Jackson. Even Bates, who had seen such transformations many times before, could not suppress a gasp of astonishment at the new appearance of Secret Agent X. A faint flicker of amusement lighted the piercing eyes of Agent X. Then it was gone, and the eyes were once more the windows of a keen, cool-thinking brain.

"You will remain here," said Agent X, speaking in Henry Jackson's voice. "When Jackson regains consciousness, pump him for every bit of information you can get. Find out where he got his tip on this scheduled killing. Find out, if you can, just what these white-cross killings mean. There's an epidemic of them, and I don't mind admitting that I'm in the dark as to the motive."

"You, sir?" Bates asked.

Used to interpreting Bates's laconic speech, X answered as he went through the door: "I'm keeping Jackson's appointment for him, at the corner of Commerce and Bedford."

A TAXI rolled with slow uncertainty up Bedford Street. The fare, a man in a silk hat, leaned forward and craned his white-scarfed neck as if in an effort to find some familiar building. At last, he impatiently ordered the driver to a halt, got out, paid his fare, and continued up the street on foot.

A shabbily-dressed man shuffled along the street toward the man in the top-hat, who stopped him and asked pleasantly: "Could you tell me where J.O. Smith resides? I am looking for Mr. Smith and have no more definite address than Bedford Street."

The shabby man all but snickered. Possibly he was drunk. He pointed toward the next corner. "You'll find what you're lookin' for right up there."

The man in the silk hat thanked the other and continued toward the corner. The shabby man turned and cat-footed along behind him. When the man in the topper was almost at the corner, the shabby fellow uttered a shrill whistle.

Men came out of the shadow. Men seemed to grow out of the pavement. The silk-hatted man stopped, turned dazedly about. "What do you want?" he demanded firmly.

Yellow light from the street lamp, mirrored in gun steel, spoke more eloquently than words. These men were killers. The night was suddenly hideous with their murderous racket. Gun flame flared on the white face of the man who was their prey. The man who had worn the silk hat spun around on one foot, his arms jerking up toward his chest. Then he slithered to the pavement and twitched beneath a second barrage of lead. These men made sure.

Two of the killers knelt beside the victim a moment, reached across the sprawled body. Then one crawled around the body once, sprang up, and threw something white into the gutter. Just as he rejoined his fellow murderers, a car squealed around the corner on two wheels. A searchlight beam fingered toward the huddle of gunmen. One of the killers shot out the lamp. Before the echo of the shot was lost, some one uttered a hoarse cry: "Feds!"

Two men sprang from the car. A panicky flurry of lead from the killers, as they scrambled in retreat up the alley, smashed into the G-men's car. The foremost of the two men winced, clutched at his arm. "Nicked me, Jackson," he said, tensely. "We're not too late to give them what it takes."

"Okeh, Parker!" It was the voice of Jackson, but it came from the lips of Secret Agent X. He sprinted ahead of Parker to the entrance of the alley. The whine of shots greeted him. He sprang back against a wall, dragging Parker with him.

Somewhere, police whistles were shrieking frantically. He could see the band of killers halfway down the alley. They had stopped, and the reason was apparent a moment later.

At the opposite end of the alley, a car had drawn up. A machine gun voiced a preliminary stutter. More Feds. Special Agent Weston had sent reinforcements, acting on Henry Jackson's report.

Agent X gripped Parker's arm. "Hell's going to bust. We're going to be on the receiving end of things. There's only one way out for the rats—right through us."

Across the alley from where they crouched, some shadow-shrouded person stumbled into an ash barrel. Parker's wound must have been giving him fits, for he shot, indiscriminately and without warning, at the sound. Parker's shots drew fire. Between two ash cans, a yellow, pinched face was flared by the flame from the muzzle of an automatic.

Parker jerked forward, tearing himself madly from the Agent's fingers, stretched to detain him. Parker pitched face down to the alley pavement. The toes of his shoes made ugly, scratching sounds as his legs twitched convulsively.

X sent one glance up the alley. The killers were coming in his direction on the run, lashed into a stampede by machine gun slugs that rattled and ricocheted through the night. X crouched, sprang to Parker's side and flattened himself beside the G-man. Parker's breath was coming in crackling gasps. He was trying to talk, garbling something about, "Get Lewey Cassino."

A lead slug mashed the brick, scant inches from X's head. X flopped toward the ash cans where he had seen the lean face of the gunman who had pumped lead into Parker. He wormed his way between the cans, stopped, peered out into the alley. The gunmen were covering themselves well, scattering in a sort of guerrilla warfare maneuver. They would shoot it out with the reinforcement of Feds Weston had sent out.

A long sign rustled somewhere in the dark cranny behind the ash cans. X hauled himself farther back into the shadows and planted his hand squarely in the middle of a heaving chest. Hot fingers groped and hooked over X's wrist.

"The Feds," a voice whispered. "Tell Squid and the Brain I got a Fed before he—he—" A short, hacking cough racked the chest beneath X's hand. Then came the quivering breath of a dying man.

His eyes more used to the gloom, X saw that he and Parker's killer were back against the foundation of a building. A swinging coal-cellar door was within a few feet of the dying man's feet. A slight opening at the bottom of the door told X that it was not hooked. He reached out and pulled the door open. Already, in his alert mind, a brilliant plan was forming.

He inched through the opening in the basement of the building, found a footing on top of the coal, seized the gunman's legs, and dragged the man in after him. Any sound he made was masked by the gun battle in the alley and street outside.

THE AGENT pulled out his compact flashlight and turned it on the face of the man who had run into one of Parker's flying slugs. The face was narrow, the cheeks and chin all one sickly shade of yellow. Blood fringed the full, sensuous lips. The squinting eyes stared glassily into the light without wincing. Dying, this man was as any other to Agent X and he could look upon him only with compassion. Living, he would have hounded him to the edge of the earth; for Lewey Cassino was a desperado long wanted by the government men. He had packed a gun for Wolf Hollis, until federal men removed Hollis from the Public Enemy list.

X propped his flashlight up between chunks of coal, got out his compact makeup kit, and set to work. He had met Lewey Cassino once before. He knew some of the gunman's characteristics. Of Lewey's present connections, he knew nothing except that he was a member of a band of ruthless killers who marked their victims in a peculiar fashion. As Lewey Cassino, Agent X might learn much of the scheme behind what the newspapers called the white-cross killings. As Lewey Cassino, he would be on the inside of a murder machine that was rolling on and on like a juggernaut, killing without apparent motive.

Moments later, when the crackle of gun fire became less incessant, X crawled from his hiding place, the living replica of the dead man he had left in the basement. He must hurry on where Lewey had left off, but with an entirely different objective.

X took in the situation at a glance. Three gunmen were backing in his direction, exchanging a few wild, scattered shots with the hunting Feds. At the end of the alley, a car was ready, purring softly, waiting to carry the killers to safety. When that car left, it must carry Agent X with it—into the criminal hideout itself.

It was the most dangerous impersonation he had ever attempted, for Lewey Cassino was to have been shot on sight by the G-men. And if his disguise failed, he could hope for no mercy from the criminals. But it would not fail. The most convincing part of his makeup was yet to be added. X pulled from his pocket the automatic he had taken from Lewey Cassino. He pressed the muzzle against the fleshy part of his arm and pulled the trigger.

Agent X reeled directly into one of the three gunmen. Hands clutched at him. A rusty voice whispered: "Lewey, old pal! They got you?"

"Damn near it!" X gasped. The pain of the self-inflicted wound lent a convincing quiver to his voice. "Give us a hand, quick!"

"Sure, Lewey," said the gunman. "Never went back on a pal yet. That's Squid's car out there. Hang on, pal!" He seized X about the waist and half carried him to the waiting car.

After the last shot had been fired in the direction of the zig-zagging car that was carrying Agent X and four criminals away from the scene of slaughter, Federal men under the direction of Special Agent Weston, took stock. Besides Parker, two other G-men were dead. Another was in a screaming ambulance, racing with death. Others had minor wounds.

Two of the criminals had fallen. The rest had escaped, either in the car or on foot. Two criminals against possibly four gallant government men. Weston shook his sandy head gravely. Too high a price had been paid for two rats' skins.

Weston went around to Bedford Street, where a knot of morbid onlookers were being held back by city police. Weston knew in advance what he would find in the center of that group of people— the body of a man, crossed out, in the literal sense of the term. For the man in the silk hat had carried half a dozen slugs with him to the pavement.

Entirely surrounding the body, was a circle, hastily drawn in white paint by means of a small tennis-court marker which the police found in the gutter. A white cross was drawn in the same manner through the center of the circle and, consequently, across the body of the man.

Another white-cross killing. Here was the sign of sudden death, frequently applied by the City Safety Council to mark the spot of a motor tragedy. But here the sign was employed to mark sudden death at the hands of a maniac-mob—an epidemic of murder.

"It's Randolph Corlears, the mouthpiece," a policeman said to Weston. "He recently went into partnership with Charles McAdam—a criminal law firm, it was. When they bump mouthpieces, it looks like the old gang-war to me."

Weston shook his head. "That's a good theory, but it don't apply to other white-cross killings. It's as though some one had loosed a whole asylum full of criminally insane on the streets of New York and instilled a single monomania into the whole gang." Weston's face was grim and haggard. "And that is just about as unsound a theory as yours, officer."

CHAPTER II

UNDERCOVER GAMBLE

A ONE-TIME SPEAKEASY in an East Side basement, because of its fortifications, was admirably suited to the purposes of Mr. Murphy. Men who came to see Mr. Murphy—called "Squid" because there was something reminiscent of a devilfish's tentacles about Murphy's lean arms and continually squirming fingers—frequently needed the protection of steel doors and hidden traps.

Watching Squid Murphy pace the floor, was a woman. She was blonde, her hair clipped and combed as a man's. She wore a sleazy, cheap imitation of a dress some movie queen had introduced two years ago. She chain-smoked cigarettes and ground them out on the floor with the toe of a badly cracked gilt slipper. Her name was Sally Vergane. She had been a queen in her own right—gun-toting moll of the infamous Wolf Hollis.

Squid Murphy swung on the woman suddenly, took her rounded chin in his lean fingers, and rocked her head gently back and forth. His fishy eyes seemed to see straight through her.

"Cut it," he said hoarsely. "Cut looking at me like that. I got enough on my mind, without you starin' me into the bughouse."

"What mind?" Sally Vergane sneered. "If Wolf Hollis was alive and runnin' this outfit, he'd be out there with the punks, takin' the same dangers they're takin'."

"And getting hisself rubbed out, don't forget," said Squid. "Besides, I ain't runnin' this mob. I got to answer to the Brain. The answer's got to be good. If the boys don't plug this Corlears guy and do a swell job of it, the Brain loses his hundred grand, we miss our cut, and the Brain gives me hell."

Squid Murphy's normally dark face paled at the thought. "Are you nuts? Sometimes, I guess you are. Listen, when the Brain stepped in where Wolf Hollis got off, and took over the runnin' of this gang, I told him I didn't like the idea of me never seein' him. I don't like guys who prowl around in the dark. I had a flashlight, see? Next time he showed up, turnin' the lights off as he came, I put the flashlight on him. What I saw gave me the creeps. He had on a black hood that covered his whole head and face. He had eyes like the Devil himself—just slanting slots in the black cloth. He had a silenced gun in each hand—"

Lights in the room snapped out. There was something ominous in even the pop of the switch, something that choked Murphy into silence and forced a small scream from Sally Vergane as she threw herself into Murphy's arms.

"Shut up!" Murphy snapped. "It's the Brain."

A door squeaked open. A voice that was a thick and muffled monotone said: "Randolph Corlears is dead."

Murphy sighed audibly. "Sure boss," he bragged. "Didn't I say I'd bring it off okeh?"

"You did," boomed the Brain, "and you're a damned liar. It wasn't okeh. Two seconds after the job was done, the place was swarming with federal men. There's a leak in your organization, Murphy. I hold you responsible. You'll kill the man who squawked to the G-men or I'll fire you. Know the way I fire a man?"

"Uh huh," grunted Murphy from a dry mouth.

"In a box with six handles. That's the only way, Murphy."

Footsteps in the darkness were followed by the closing of a door and the click of a light switch. In the light, Squid Murphy looked down into Sally Vergane's face. The girl's rouged lips curled insolently. "Who powdered your puss, Squid?" For Murphy looked as though he was quite ready to be shipped in the Brain's six-handled box.

Murphy pushed the girl away from him. She put a cigarette in her lips, where it quivered, unlighted. "Sometimes," she said, in a far-away voice, "that Brain reminds me of Wolf Hollis; when he gets mad like that, I mean."

"Nuts!" Murphy croaked. "The Feds cornered Hollis in an upstate farmhouse. After they'd shot the joint full of holes and tossed tear gas, Wolf set the dump on fire. Must have figured he'd rather burn with his own matches than in the chair."

"Still," Sally said, "I feel sometimes like Wolf is near me. But he's got to be dead, or he'd come to me; wouldn't he, Squid?"

THE DOOR of the basement room banged open. Four men came

in, with a fifth who was half supported by one of the others. Squid Murphy slid his hands into his pockets where his fingers squirmed. His mouth became all but lipless. He looked the men up and down.

"Feds," he said slowly. "You had to run in with the Feds. You got Corlears and then, because things weren't excitin' enough for you, you yells for the Feds. Where'n hell's the rest of you?"

One of the gunmen walked over to the table and tossed down his gun. His hands were a little shaky. "Don't try to be funny, Squid. Somebody passed the Feds a tip-off. They were out after Lefty and Lewey. Now they'll be gunning for the whole mob, 'cause at least two of the G-boys got shot to hell. Couple of our gang got it. The rest is comin' back here—if they can get back."

"Lefty!" rapped Squid Murphy.

The big, blond, dish-faced rodman who supported the wounded Agent X, blinked at Squid Murphy. Murphy went over and seized Agent X by the collar. X rolled his eyelids back a little and stared blankly at Murphy.

"Lewey Cassino!" Murphy sneered. "Wolf Hollis's right-hand man, and you collect lead from one of Uncle Sam's boy scouts. Losin' your grip, fella."

X managed a sickly grin. "I sent the Fed who plugged me all the way, though. That's something, Squid."

Murphy took out his right hand and jammed a thumb into the ribs of the man called Lefty. "You get the hell out of here with your colicky baby. What'd you bring him here for? I said any of you worms that got stepped on by the Feds, stayed on the spot."

Lefty rasped: "Lewey ain't dyin'. He needs a doc. What if I'd left him there and the Feds had worked him over and he had squawked?"

Murphy's eyes narrowed. "Maybe he's squawked already. Some-body has." He seized X by the throat and squeezed until the Agent choked out a plea for mercy. Squid laughed. "He wouldn't have the guts to squeal with the Brain runnin' things. You get him out of here, Lefty. Get him a doc. If he checks in, that's okeh. But you can't leave him here and no doc in. The rest of you guys," Murphy swung on the other three gunmen, "I gotta give you hell."

As he leaned heavily on Lefty and groaned along up the dark stone steps to the dingy street outside, an ironical smile twisted the lips of Secret Agent X. So far so good. His impersonation of Lewey Cassino had passed Squid Murphy's careful scrutiny. The slight wound in his arm precluded any idea that his apparent agony was not genuine.

He had learned that Squid Murphy's gang consisted of the old Wolf Hollis crowd, to which had been added a number of young punks who were getting a kick out of killing. The G-men were out to mop up the remains of the Hollis crowd. Possibly the federal agents knew as little about the motive behind the white-cross murders as did Agent X.

But because he had passed Squid Murphy, was not reason to believe that smooth sailing lay ahead. Lefty Laughlin, who was at the moment struggling to get X into a car, was obviously Lewey Cassino's best friend. Friendship in the underworld usually had an eggshell thinness, but even so Lefty probably knew much of Lewey Cassino that X didn't know. The tiniest slip might give the Secret Agent away.

About seven blocks from where X had been introduced to Squid Murphy, Lefty Laughlin had a bed behind a door that could be locked. He carried X up a flight of narrow stairs that light and broom had never invaded, stretched X out on the bed, and pulled off the Agent's shoes. Fists on hips, Lefty regarded X solemnly. "You got to have a doc."

X rolled his head on a pillow that crackled with the straw inside it. "I'm doin' fine," he insisted. Here was another danger. Members of the medical profession the country over knew how to identify Agent X. There was an old shrapnel wound, which he had received during the war, which had left a scar that had taken the form of a jagged letter "X." [36]

"I said you was goin' to have a doc." Lefty reached over and took the automatic from X's pocket. "Just in case you try something screwy," he said as he left the room.

Then would have been a good time to beat a hasty retreat, but it was such situations that Agent X enjoyed most. Furthermore, he was determined to stop the white-cross killings. That couldn't be accomplished by running away.

Less than five minutes elapsed before the door of the room opened. X's eyes were closed. He was groaning and rolling around on the bed, muttering as though in delirium. He recognized Lefty's voice, as the latter indicated the patient. And he recognized something else—a rank, strangling odor of pipe tobacco of nauseating

---

36   AUTHOR'S NOTE: *The Agent's methods of investigation differ so widely from the orthodox routine of the police department, that the police of New York believe him to be a desperate criminal. Inspector Burks, of the Homicide Department, has even slated the Agent for murder.*

strength. Agent X knew of but one man who smoked such tobacco and still miraculously kept his health. The smoke had to be from Dr. Stuart Ormand's pipe. Through lowered lids, X stole a glance at the man with the foul-smelling, under-slung pipe.

Dr. Ormand was six feet of man in his prime. He had a well-developed, determined jaw, square teeth, and steady, courageous eyes behind glistening, rimless glasses. His hair was a rippling of silver. Not only was Dr. Stuart Ormand a capable, conscientious physician, but he was a criminal psychologist and amateur detective of no mean reputation. His book, *Potential Murderers,* which dealt with the type of persons who, given motive and opportunity, commit murder, was supplementary reading in police schools. Had Lefty Laughlin searched all over Manhattan, he couldn't have found a physician less apt to help a wounded criminal, than Dr. Stuart Ormand.

Ormand was clever. He was cool. If he discovered the fact that the man on the bed was not Lewey Cassino, he would know what to do. If he discovered that X was not nearly so bad off as he appeared to be, he would very probably reveal this deception to Lefty. Whatever happened, Agent X was in a bad spot.

But when the blow-up came, what would happen to Dr. Ormand? Without regard for his own predicament, the Agent's chief concern was to see the doctor safely through trouble. For there wasn't a chance in the world that this bulldog of a medico would submit to any of Laughlin's bullying.

CHAPTER III

G-GUN SERENADE

THOUGH HE WAS a man of infinite patience, Harvey Bates was also a man of action. His instructions, from Agent X, had been to obtain what information he could from the unconscious G-man Jackson. Inasmuch as the effect of a dose of X's gas sometimes required hours to wear off, it looked very much as though Bates's immediate future was to be filled chiefly with pipe smoke and waiting.

He removed the mask he had worn on entering the G-man's room, mopped his large, wholesome face with his handkerchief, and sat down. Presently it occurred to him that he might serve his chief by snooping about a little.

There was almost nothing in the room to connect it with an agent of Uncle Sam, for Jackson was a careful man and an intelligent investigator. Except for the far-flung secret organization which X operated through Harvey Bates, the Agent would probably never have known that a G-man named Jackson was getting tips in regard to scheduled white-cross killings.

But when Bates searched a wallet that X had left beside the G-man, he discovered a slip of pasteboard on which Jackson had recorded the tip. Information, Jackson had scribbled, told that Randolph Corlears was to have been the victim and also the approximate time and place in which the murder was to occur. Most of this information, Bates had overheard when Jackson was reporting to his chief. But at the top of the pasteboard card was a telephone number which had obviously been written some time before the other information, judging by the way the penciling was smudged. Was it possible that this telephone number was the source of Jackson's information? Decidedly, it was a hunch worth working on.

Bates went from the bathroom to the phone and called a number which was listed in no telephone directory, in order that its absolute secrecy might be assured. In a few seconds he was talking with one of his own operatives. Bates asked for information relating to the telephone number the G-man had written on the cardboard. When he had that information, Bates leaned back in his chair, stuffed his pipe with extreme care, and lighted it deliberately. Here was a mystery, indeed.

The phone number on the G-man's memorandum was that of a woman who had been making history in the tabloids lately. Pamela Dean was the particular passion of enough wealthy business men to make front-page news seven days out of the week. About the only government agent who might have been able to afford

Across the table lay the man's limp body. And shafting from the light beam that revealed him came the mysterious cross and circle—the sign of sudden death.

Pamela Dean's charming company was the director of the mint, Bates decided, and G-man Henry Jackson's salary was rather lean, considering the dangers his duties compelled him to face. It looked very much as though Bates's hunch was founded on fact. Though the connection between a Gold Coast pet and the underworld was just a bit hazy.

Nevertheless, Bates decided to pay a call on Pamela Dean. Bates secured the gold Department of Justice badge from Jackson's wallet, locked the G-man in the bathroom, and left the dingy room to taxi to the west end of town, where Pamela Dean's apartment overlooked the river.

A French maid was eloquent in regard to Miss Dean's absence, but the gold badge Bates had appropriated worked its magic. He was permitted to wait for forty-five minutes before Pamela Dean appeared.

She was breath-taking. The blue stuff of which her gown was fashioned had been particularly created to match her eyes. Her skin had a dark, warm flush. Her hair was a deep-brown and wavy. Her lips bore a warmer welcome than Bates had any reason to expect, and when he grasped her outstretched hand, he was painfully conscious of the immensity of his own powerful digits.

"Any friend of Mr. Jackson is a friend of mine," she said generously, in a voice that would have guaranteed her radio appeal even in the absence of television.

The French maid brought cocktails. Bates tasted his and set it aside. Here was a situation which Agent X would have met magnificently, but which Bates feared greatly he might fumble. He felt that Pamela Dean's blue eyes fronted a brain that could think circles around his. There was not a particle of use in his edging into the subject foremost in his mind.

"Gave my friend, Jackson, a tip tonight?" he boomed.

Pamela Dean pursed her lips and examined polished fingernails. "About what?" she asked guardedly.

"Mr. Corlears' scheduled death," Bates plunged—too deeply, he realized in another moment. For the girl was back with:

"And were you in time to prevent this—this horrible tragedy?"

And that was a question best detoured. "Your tips have always been useful," he said. "Wonder if you've got more?"

Pamela Dean stood up, took graceful steps to the window, seemed to meditate upon the darkness and the flicker of distant lights, returned, and lighted a cigarette.

"You realize that I am in a position of grave danger," she said. "Yet I have voluntarily given you information which has been useful to you. Mr. Jackson has been fair enough in promising that he would not attempt to learn the source of that information. He was simply satisfied with its authenticity, as you must be. Yes, I have more information, not fully developed at this time."

She paused, her eyes seemed to fathom the unfathomable. "The sign of sudden death hovers over the business house directed by Aaron Malthus. It is utterly impossible for me to elaborate on that statement, for the simple reason that I know nothing further." She smiled quickly. "It may help you, if you make the most of it. I promise more news just as soon as I can obtain it. Trust me, as I have trusted you."

And Harvey Bates left the apartment filled with the desire to trust Pamela Dean to the fullest; and at the same time, he was troubled by a wholly inexplicable something.

Perhaps that something was the deadly scrutiny of the eye of an automatic which appeared in a slightly raised window on the ground floor of the building as Bates wandered out on the sidewalk....

AGENT X came out of his faked delirium, to lie on his back and stare, dull-eyed, at Dr. Stuart Ormand. The doctor folded his arms, contentedly inhaled the poisonous fumes from his pipe, and challenged Lefty Laughlin with his eyes.

The dish-faced Laughlin was standing near the bed, his automatic in his hand. "You're goin' to get busy on my pal, Doc. You're goin' to fix up that wound of his or get one in your own belly— which you won't get over in a hurry."

Dr. Ormand laughed coolly. "Do you know what I think? I think, if I may resort to the vernacular, that you are some sort of a punk. I haven't any intention of aiding your companion, even though it were a matter of life and death, which it isn't."

Agent X reached up toward Laughlin's gun. "Let me plug the guy, Lefty," he said. But his ruse to get hold of Lefty's gun didn't work. Lefty back-stepped. Teeth on edge, he said:

"You got any idea who we are, Doc?"

Ormand nodded. "You are Lefty Laughlin. The man on the bed is Lewey Cassino. Both of you gentlemen were formerly associated with Wolf Hollis; probably the only reason why you are now considered public enemies. I don't think you're quite that important."

X sat on the edge of the bed and jammed his feet into his shoes. "I'm goin' to croak that guy, Lefty," he declared. "I like to be respected."

There came a rapid tattoo of knuckles on the door of the room. Dr. Ormand smiled. "The law, no doubt."

"No doubt!" Lefty jeered. "Happens to be one of Squid Murphy's boys."

He backed to the door, so that he could keep an eye on Ormand. He unlatched the door and pulled it open. One of the younger toughs X had seen in Murphy's place, came into the room. He was out of breath and pale.

"Lam," he jerked at Lefty. "It's that damned leak again. This joint is surrounded by Feds again. We got a chance over the roof, but—" He looked at Ormand, who seemed bent on smoking out everybody in the building. "What's that?" the tough asked, nodding at Ormand.

Lefty didn't answer. He swung on Agent X. "Can you stagger along, pal? We gotta move. You get that, or has that slug scrambled the old brain? G-men outside, see?"

X nodded. "I'll make out okeh. We sock this doc and leave him here."

"Like hell!" Lefty snarled. "He goes along for our protection. The G-men shoot, but not if there's a chance of hitting somebody on their side of the fence." He got at the back of Dr. Ormand and jabbed his gun into his spine. "Pocket that stove, Doc. That soft coal you smoke makes me dizzy."

The young hood grabbed the pipe and jammed it into the doctor's pocket. "You're a sap, Lefty," he said, and brought out a gun from Ormand's pocket, a gun which the doctor would surely have drawn had he been permitted to pocket his pipe himself.

They left the room, the young tough in the lead, then Agent X, walking unsteadily. Lefty and his hostage brought up the rear. They started toward the stair. The young tough stopped, turned around. His face was white. A creak of the steps had warned him that the federal agents had entered the building. The young tough darted around his companions, and led toward the end of the hall. There was a window there that opened on well-soaped grooves. They clanked out on a fire escape.

"Try anything funny, Doc," Lefty warned, "and from here on, you're just a grease spot on the alley pavement." To X he said: "Step on it, Lewey."

X faked a groan and stumbled up a flight of iron skeleton steps to a small platform. A simple iron ladder extended to the attic windows. This was evidently loose in its staples, for the young tough was sliding it up two feet farther to hang its hooked upper extremities over the eaves.

The wound in X's arm had stopped bleeding. He had taken particular pains to inflict it in such a spot that it would not hamper his movements. Still, he climbed the swaying iron ladder using one arm only. If fortune permitted him to carry his impersonation further, he did not want to do anything that would arouse suspicion in the future.

They gained the roof, where asphalt surfacing absorbed every light ray, and the starry sky hung oppressively low. They moved toward the western edge of the roof, Lefty goading the doctor on and whispering threats. The young tough was keyed up with hop. He heard the squeak of an opening skylight even before Agent X realized that some one in the building had divined their routes of escape.

As the skylight bobbed up, the young tough swung around with a vicious oath. Over the sill of the skylight, a G-man whipped out a shot. The young tough kicked out, landed a heel somewhere in the Fed's face. The G-man doubled over backwards and thumped and rolled down the steps. The skylight covering fell back. Up through the opening, came a warning cry. G-men on the floor below heard their companion's shot.

The young tough cursed, pivoted, and caught X by the coat front. "Lewey, you and me have got to swing that fire-escape ladder up here on the roof. We'll use it to bridge the gap to the next building. If we can hold back the Feds until the ladder is in place, we got a clean getaway. You, Lefty, sand that guy near the skylight. When the Feds start up those steps give the guy the works and dump him through the opening."

IT WAS good strategy, X realized. The body of Dr. Ormand, for the doctor would surely be a corpse by the time Lefty "gave him the works," would fill the narrow stairway and demand immediate attention from the Feds. Even a ten-second delay might mean the difference between safety and a hazardous battle with the G-men. But it was the sort of strategy X could not permit.

X turned with surprising speed, seized Lefty's gun. "Gimme that, pal. I don't like the way this doc parts his hair. If there's goin' to be any bumping to do, I ought to do it. With one arm I won't be any use movin' that ladder."

"Lewey's right," the young tough said. And Laughlin relinquished his gun to Agent X. Lefty and the other crook started back for the fire-escape ladder. X drove the muzzle of Lefty's automatic into the doctor's midsection and pushed him back so that his heels struck the edge of the skylight.

"You're a sap, Cassino," whispered Dr. Ormand. "You can't get by with anything like this."

"Shut up, Ormand!"

"You know me?"

"Who don't? Everybody but Lefty. He would pick a guy like you. When I tilt this gat toward the sky and let it blow, you jump back down the skylight. Do you get it? I'm not exactly what I seem to be."

"What's this? Sort of a death-bed conversion, Cassino?"

"Never mind. You're not going to get killed. I'm letting you off. In return, you can delay the G-men by feeding them a line." For X still hoped that by sticking with Lefty Laughlin, he would eventually get inside information regarding the white-cross killings.

But at the very moment when the federal men could be heard running along the hall below, Dr. Ormand went into action. His left hand shot out to X's gun wrist. His right rammed in just below X's ribs. It was a good punch. It had steam and surprise.

X staggered back a step. Ormand got the automatic. But before he could turn the gun around, X's right hand had brushed upwards to a vest pocket, curled into a fist, and lashed out toward Dr. Ormand's face. He pulled the punch short and at the same time flicked a secret catch on the cigarette lighter he had procured from his pocket.[37]

G-men were at the foot of the narrow steps leading to the skylight, and in another moment, so was Dr. Ormand. The anesthetizing gas took immediate effect. A gentle push was all that was required to topple him over the edge of the skylight.

X turned around, lost a precious second trying to see where Lefty and the other crook had gone. Apparently they had either deserted him entirely or supposed he knew the route they intended to take, for they were nowhere in sight.

---

37 *AUTHOR'S NOTE: This cigarette lighter is one of the Agent's most surprising weapons. There is a compartment in it which holds a single cartridge of his anesthetizing gas.*

A G-man had evidently hurdled the form of the unconscious doctor and was running up the steps. It was only a matter of seconds before the roof would be swarming with federal agents, any one of whom would have found a fine feather for his cap if he could bring back Lewey Cassino dead. And there wasn't a chance in the world of X convincing these manhunters that he was not Public Enemy Cassino.

CHAPTER IV

HIDDEN DEATH

A G-MAN BOBBED through the opening in the roof. As X legged toward the eaves he shot a glance over his shoulder in time to catch the full effect of the G-man's flashlight beam.

"It's Cassino!" shouted the Fed, and opened up with his automatic.

X zig-zagged to the left and got a fan-tail ventilator between himself and his pursuers. The G-man sieved the sheet-metal of the ventilator with bullets. Still he saw the man he supposed to be Cassino covering the roof like a rabbit.

The G-man broke into a run, two of his companions directly behind him. The Feds were sure of their quarry, for the running man was dashing toward the edge of the building. Either the supposed Cassino would fall three stories to the ground below, or lose his nerve in the last minute.

Between the buildings was a gap of twelve feet, possibly more. There was no way that the Agent could estimate the distance in the dark. He knew only that when his toes touched the eaves trough he would jump with every ounce of strength he could goad from his muscles.

Sheet metal drummed beneath his shoes. The eaves—he must jump, perhaps into eternity. He hurled himself forward into midair that shrilled in his ears no less keenly than the bullets which followed him. His right toe caught the eaves trough of the second building. He lost balance and, for a moment, all sense of direction; every route seemed to lead downward into a bottomless pit. His body smacked flat against the flat roof surface of the second building.

He gulped in breath, dragged his dangling legs out of emptiness, regained his feet, and raced across the roof, entirely at a loss as to what he should do next. He scurried for a skylight that loomed as large as a tent. Behind it, he had a moment's security in which to plot his future course.

The G-man who had first gained the skylight, after X had thrown Dr. Ormand down the stair, came to the edge of the roof. He must have decided that if a rat like Lewey Cassino could make such a jump, he, too, could make it. But his leap was poorly timed. It was but a matter of luck that fingers of his air-thrashing arms hooked over the eaves of the next building.

The other G-men came to a stop at the edge of the roof to stare in horror at their kicking companion who swung from the eaves of the building across the way. Forgot, for the moment, was Lewey Cassino.

"Hang on, Dick!" called one of the men. "We'll give you a hand." He swung his flashlight around, spotted the iron ladder which was bridged across the space between the two buildings. He ran to it, moved it along until it all but touched the fingers of the hanging man. Then he crossed to the other building, his companion following to give assistance to the man who hung on the eaves.

Glass smashed and tinkled frostily. The G-man's attention was instantly shifted toward the skylight where the supposed Lewey Cassino had disappeared.

The Fed called something to his buddies and then sprinted toward the skylight. A large section of the glass had been kicked out, and, somewhere in the darkness below, the G-man could hear heavy footsteps pounding along the hallway.

The G-man dropped through the opening in the skylight, struck the floor of the hall below. He required a second before his eyes became used to the greater darkness. Then he spotted the stair rail, ran to it, and down the first flight of steps. At the second landing, he leaned over the rail to see a man running down the hall below. The G-man vaulted the stair railing, dropped into the hall, to land within a yard of his quarry. His long arms sprang out straight to collar his man.

But the man he had collared jerked around, roared: "What the hell?" He sent a jolting left into the G-man's middle that flattened the Fed against the wall. The G-man took a long breath, when he could, and blinked at the man he had been pursuing—a man with a round, red face that mirrored an irate expression.

"Aren't you Inspector John Burks of the City Homicide Department?" asked the G-man, a bit lamely.

"Am I?" roared the red-faced person. "You've got me there, brother. For a moment I thought I was a tackling dummy. You make a practice of dropping from ceilings and trying to neck everybody you meet?"

The G-man fumbled in his pocket, produced his gold badge and flashed it. "Sorry, Inspector. A man just broke through the skylight on the roof and ran down these steps. There was only one man in sight. You just happened to be that man. I'm looking for Lewey Cassino."

"Cassino?" bellowed the inspector. "Why didn't you say so? I'd like to lay my hands on him myself. Where'd he go?"

"He vanished."

"Can't be done," the red-faced man interrupted. "If you can get men to guard the back door, I'll take the front. Nobody passed me in the hall, and nobody is going to pass me at the front door. If Cassino is alive, he's in this building."

There was no deceit in what the red-faced man had said. He, and he alone, knew that Lewey Cassino was dead, lying in some one's coal cellar. For the red-faced man whom the federal agent had addressed as Inspector Burks, was none other than Secret Agent X.[38]

THE TIME required for the G-men to rescue their companion had been sufficient for Agent X to make a hasty change in his makeup while hiding behind the skylight. The impersonation of Burks was one which he could manage from memory and which offered him comparative safety. It was true that his makeup would not have withstood close scrutiny, for he had adopted it in great haste. But there was no reason for the G-man to examine him closely.

Instead of mounting guard at the door of the building, Agent X walked briskly off into the night. So far, the impersonation of Lewey Cassino had resulted only in constant trouble for him. He had resolved to drop it for the time being, for he had lost all track of Lefty Laughlin and his white-faced companion. As far as the mysterious killings which were marked by a circle and cross were concerned, X was exactly in the same position he had been in at the start of the investigation.

Why should men be gunned down without apparent discrimination? Why, above all, should the victims be literally crossed out

---

38 AUTHOR'S NOTE: Agent X has so frequently impersonated Inspector Burks, that he can adopt the inspector's features at will, working from memory, even though he is in the dark at the time.

by white paint, drawn in a design used by members of the Safety Council to designate fatal automobile accidents? On the face of it, it appeared that some one person was possessed with a vengeful monomania—a person who had lost a loved one in a motor accident and was determined to square accounts by dealing death right and left.

But some *one* person wasn't doing the killing. These unfortunate victims of the sign of sudden death were set upon by mobs of gunmen. Vengeance of the mob type had to have some sort of motive. And here there seemed no sort of motive, whatsoever.

OBLIVIOUS to the fact that he was being sighted by killers over a gun that rested on the window sill of the apartment house where Pamela Dean lived, Harvey Bates paused a moment to rekindle his pipe. The head of his match, however, never touched the side of its box. Out of the night came a short, sharp, woman's scream.

Harvey Bates dropped the match and sprinted toward the corner of the apartment building from whence the cry came. The sound of his heavy shoes on the pavement muffled the *plop* of a silenced gun, but not the mosquito-buzz of the bullet. Bates didn't turn around. He knew he was being shot at, but also knew the wisdom of not pausing to discover from whence that shot came, and thus probably making a corpse of himself. He zig-zagged toward the opening of an alley where was the sound of a scuffle.

A woman was punching and kicking at a man who was doing his best to detain her and muffle her cries. As Bates waded into the war, the man released the woman, flashed a knife, and sprang at Bates. It was too dark in the alley to see anything but the ominous flash of the knife. Bates caught the man's wrist as the knife plunged downward, employed a deft twist that Agent X had taught him, and heard the knife clank to the pavement.

The man, perhaps for the first time, took a good look at the silhouette of Harvey Bates. Only fear could have given him the strength to break Bates's grip. Then he wheeled around and raced up the alley.

Bates would have pursued the man, had it not been for the two small hands that clutched at his coat and the familiar ring of the feminine voice that was thanking him.

"Miss Dale!" gasped Bates. He took the girl's arm and hurried her back to the sidewalk where lamplight enabled him to see a sweet, girlish face, flushed prettily from the struggle, and framed by unruly golden hair.

Bates's immediate task was apparent. Betty Dale, girl reporter on the *Herald,* was a far closer friend to Agent X than even Bates. Bates knew, from previous adventures, that the Secret Agent would have given up his own life rather than have any harm come to Betty. Therefore, Bates argued, his first duty toward X was to get Betty Dale to a place of safety at once.

"Harvey Bates!" exclaimed the girl delightedly. "I—"

"No time," he clipped. His grip on her arm tightened, and he hurried her possessively off down the street, put her in his car, and drove for three blocks before uttering a word.

"Is this a kidnaping?" Betty demanded. "I was on the threshold of the greatest human-interest story of my short and eventful career. Where's the fire?"

Bates jerked his head. "Back there."

Betty sighed. There were times when a little third-degreeing of Harvey Bates would have been justifiable. "All right. If you won't, I will. I've been trying to follow Sally Vergane. Remember—Wolf Hollis's old girl friend? There's a heart tug in every word she utters, if she ever utters anything I can print. I lost her trail half a dozen times this evening, then actually saw her enter that apartment back there, by the side door. I was on the point of following, when that gorilla came at me. If you're not busy, suppose we go back and you help me find Sally?"

"Busy," said Bates.

"Doing what?"

"Getting you to your flat. Then, maybe, go back for the murderer."

"Whose murderer?"

"Mine, almost." And Bates lapsed into the silence he had reluctantly left. Ten minutes later, he drew up in front of the apartment house where Betty Dale lived.

There was a man in Betty's apartment. He was sitting in a chair, facing the door. The girl jerked back in surprise and stood poised on toe-tips a second.

"Why, Inspector Burks!" she gasped.[39]

---

39 AUTHOR'S NOTE: *Though Betty Dale is a police reporter, she has every reason to feel uneasy when some member of the police force pays particular attention to her. Betty Dale is the only living person to have seen the real face of Secret Agent X, and she lives in constant fear of the fact that some day police may learn of her connection with X and attempt to force her to betray the Agent into their hands.*

BATES pushed his big, protecting body in front of the girl and measured the red-faced man in the chair. The inspector stood up, uttered a short, whimsical laugh, such as no one had ever heard from the lips of Inspector Burks. Betty Dale peered around Bates, an odd, expectant light in her merry blue eyes. Fingers of the red-faced man crossed to form a letter "X," one of the secret signs X had arranged to use in identifying himself to Betty.

"You!" Relief and sheer joy combined in the single word as Betty crowded past Bates into the room. No less surprised than Betty, Bates came through the doorway and closed the panel behind him. Agent X clasped both of Betty's hands. His gray eyes smiled warmly.

"I've a job for you," he said.

"I'm glad. What is it?"

"I'd like you to get next to Sally Vergane. What's so surprising about that?"

Betty looked at Harvey Bates. "I was trying to get next to Sally Vergane, but he wouldn't let me."

"By the way, Bates," X said, mildly reproachful, "where is G-man Henry Jackson?"

"Same place—locked up. Been working on a lead I got from him." And, thrifty with words, Bates told how he had gone to Pamela Dean's and obtained information regarding the scheduled murder in the firm headed by Aaron Malthus. Then he told of Betty's plight and the silenced bullet that some one had tried to plant in his back.

"Aaron Malthus," X muttered. "Again, there's nothing consistent about the murder mob's choice of victims. Some have money; some haven't. Aaron Malthus is one for the 'haven't' side. He, and several others, are engaged in an investment business that happens to be in a bad way. 'Queer.' "

"But what about Sally Vergane?" Betty asked. "Why should she be going into a ritzy apartment building like that? What's the connection?"

X sighed. "Certainly not enough answers to go around, are there?"

"Better get back to my post, sir?" Bates queried.

X nodded. "And before you go, just give me Jackson's badge and credentials. I may want to use them later. Keep Jackson under dope. Keep an eye on the Dean dame without getting yourself scorched by any more silenced bullets. You did a good job tonight."

Bates flushed, became interested in the toes of his shoes, and clumsily left the room.

"What are you going to do?"

"There's only one move for me—go to Aaron Malthus. I'll have to hang around his place as a plumber or something until I get a chance to step into his shoes."

Betty paled. "You mean that, knowing that the white cross is threatening Malthus, you—you'd impersonate him?"

X slipped an arm around the girl's shoulders. "Now, Betty," he said with a smile, "it's rather a necessary risk; don't you see? There's not a single other angle to work from."

"All right," said Betty meekly. She had long since learned that X's will was unalterable. "Then you want me to work on the Sally Vergane angle?"

"If you can do so in safety, Betty. If you could meet her in some public place and just pump her, as though you were getting a newspaper story. Watch out for anything she may say about Wolf Hollis. The man is officially dead. Still, I wonder."

"So do I. That charred body found in the house Hollis burned down over his ears—it was identified as Hollis's simply by the ring on the finger of the corpse. There might have been some one else in the house with Hollis."

X nodded. He liked watching the girl's intelligent, expressive face; he liked hearing her talk. But there would be time for all that later on, he hoped. He kissed her gently. "Take care of yourself," he whispered, and hurriedly left the apartment.

There was work to be done. Aaron Malthus, or some member of his company, was in danger. It was up to X to discover who was actually threatened by the insidious sign of death. Then, if he could shift the danger to his own capable shoulders by stepping into the threatened man's shoes, the Brain, Squid Murphy, or whoever headed the maniac murder-group would find a more worthy opponent when it came time to cross out another victim.

CHAPTER V

DEATH BARGAINS

THE FOLLOWING EVENING, Squid Murphy sidled into a booth in an untidy ravioli restaurant. On the other side of the table, her heels hooked on the round of a chair, was Sally Vergane. The thick platter of food in front of her was untouched.

Squid watched her with fishy eyes. "How come you don't eat when you're out with me?" he demanded unpleasantly.

Sally smiled hatefully. "Maybe it's because I'm so nuts about you I lose my appetite."

"It's as good food as Wolf Hollis ever fed you, ain't it?"

Sally's eyelids drooped wearily. "Yeah—the grub's as good.... What you been doin', Squid?"

Murphy plucked a cigarette and played with it between squirming fingers. "Linin' up the job for the Brain."

"But you got no line on the Brain, himself, have you?"

Murphy massaged his jaw and shook his head. "Why should I? Ain't I satisfied? It's good for the bank account to do as the Brain says. Good for the health, too."

Sally leaned across the table. Her blue eyes burned brightly, earnestly. "Listen, Squid, you gotta do something for me. I got a notion who the Brain is. You gotta find out for sure. It's burnin' me up, see? I think the Brain is Wolf Hollis. And if he is, and he don't come around to me any more, he's got a new girl. Wolf Hollis always had to have a girl. He was no good without one. It's killing me, just thinking of it. I love that guy, Squid. Even if he's got another girl, I'd love him. I just want to know."

Squid laughed. "Wolf Hollis is neckin' angels, if anybody. He's dead. I watched the house burn where they cornered him. When the Feds say a guy is dead, he's dead."

"All right. If the Brain isn't Wolf Hollis, how'd he get at the head of this mob? A guy without a name, who never shows his face, couldn't just come and say he was goin' to boss the toughest mob in town."

"I get you," Squid agreed. "Tell you something—the Brain was a friend of Wolf Hollis. The Brain's got a slip of paper with a note from Hollis, saying that if anything happened to Wolf the Brain was to take things over. That satisfied me and the boys. It's good enough for—"

Squid touched Sally's hand and nodded toward the door. "Here's where I get off, kid. See that blonde who came in the door?" Sally mirrored the doorway in a cheap vanity and nodded. "Well," Murphy continued, "she's a sob sister from the *Herald*. She's been trailin' you lately. Money says she wants a heart throb from you for her paper. Don't give no reporter the lifted snoot. They'll get suspicious. Act down and out and glad to grieve for Wolf Hollis, but watch your step. This *Herald* kid has a brain in that bonnet."

And as Betty Dale started down the aisle between the restaurant booths, Squid Murphy slipped out unseen....

AARON MALTHUS sat in his study awaiting dinner guests. He was a dark man, gray-templed, and with lumpy features. His leathery eyelids were nearly closed; yet he was not relaxed. His jaw muscles worked like an irregular pulse. Before the dark curtain of his mind a plain, oak chair equipped with straps and electrodes, and a curious metal cap persisted in harnessing his attention. Perhaps Aaron Malthus had never fully realized before that he was a murderer.

French windows opened a mere crack. A black-gloved hand slid through the opening and along the wall to press a light switch. In utter blackness, Malthus gasped a breath that whistled between clenched teeth. The French windows opened and closed.

"I am here, Mr. Malthus," said a muffled voice.

"Who—the Brain?" gasped Malthus. He jerked his chair around so that he could face the origin of the voice.

"Yes," said a muffled voice. "You have been trying to contact me through Murphy. So I am here. What is it you want?"

"I—I can't go through with this—this awful thing!" Malthus sobbed out. "You've got to stop it!"

"No, I fail to understand."

"Then, whether you understand or not, the deal is off. I'd rather starve."

"It is not as easy as that, Mr. Malthus," the voice continued monotonously. "One may not stop an avalanche with a feather."

"I—I'll be a murderer if this goes on. You *must* stop it!" Malthus choked. "If you persist, I'll see Ingram tonight. I'll have him cancel the policy. Ingram will be here tonight."

"I see," said the Brain. "Now that you feel like a murderer, Mr. Malthus, has it occurred to you that it is better to feel like a murderer than like a murder victim?"

Silence for a moment—then Malthus's hoarse voice: "Yes, damn it!"

"And you remember, according to the terms of our contract, one-half the proceeds come to me. That being thoroughly understood, I need not remain longer. Good night."

And in dark silence, the Brain left the way he had come.

Malthus stumbled across the room, peered through the French windows, and saw not a sign of the mysterious visitor.

"After all," he mused, "perhaps two hundred thousand dollars is worth it. At least, the bogey of bankruptcy will stop haunting me."

It was the cuisine of Aaron Malthus's chef, rather than the personality of their host, that made men eager to attend Malthus's bachelor dinners. Shortly after the departure of the Brain, the guests began to arrive. Aaron Malthus greeted Dr. Stuart Ormand with mechanical graciousness. Ormand gave Malthus's hand a vigorous pumping, all the time puffing clouds of his noxious tobacco smoke into Malthus's face.

Men liked Ormand in spite of his pipe and its sturdy mixture of perique and Algerian tobaccos. Ormand carried his bedside manner into social life, mingling with the guests, showing interest in their most trivial grievances, and seldom talking about himself.

In addition to Dr. Ormand, there was Thomas Ingram, a small, birdlike man who hopped about and made himself noxious by selling things—anything from his own particular brand of cigarettes to a new headache remedy that, in his opinion, far surpassed anything he had yet tried. Thomas Ingram was a successful life-insurance underwriter.

With Ingram came Major Sidney Hatfield, an Australian by birth, who had traveled the world over, played soldier-of-fortune, and was at present in some mysterious way connected with Ingram's insurance firm.

Then there was McAdam, partner of the murdered Corlears; McAdam who was fat and porky-pink, who wore a frozen smile because his mouth was somewhat cramped with excessively large false teeth.

It was to such a dinner that Agent X came, at least as far as the front hall. He wore the disguise that had started his adventure with the sign of sudden death—the impersonation of Henry Jackson, crack agent of the F.B.I.

A servant seated X in a hall chair beside a screen of Chinese metal work and told him that he would ask if Mr. Malthus could see him. X had waited perhaps five minutes when catlike footsteps attracted his attention. The footsteps ended abruptly, as though their owner were listening intently for some one he feared might have followed him.

Just on the other side of the screen, the cat-footing man stopped. There was the distinct click of a telephone receiver being lifted from its hook, followed by the ratcheting of a telephone dial.

Long silence, and Agent X stood up in order to peer through the intricate piercing in the top of the Chinese screen.

"Hello," a man's voice whispered.

Elbow and shoulder rammed the screen and sent it toppling backwards. The man at the phone had turned at just the wrong moment and had detected the gleam of the Agent's spying eye. The whisperer had moved, quickly and violently, but not quite fast enough to trap Agent X under the fallen screen. X had sprung clear of the screen and now stood facing the whisperer, a man of about thirty-five years of age, blond and handsome except for a badly broken nose. And the man was in the act of drawing a gun.

X sprang across the Chinese screen, met the man's gun wrist with his left hand. A short, chopping blow to the man's biceps left the fingers that held the gun numb and unresisting. X pulled the small automatic from the man's hand and stepped back.

"Now," he said quietly, "what is this?"

The broken-nosed man gulped, reached over and returned the telephone hand-set to its cradle. He said nothing.

AT THAT moment, Aaron Malthus, Dr. Ormand and Malthus's other guests trooped into the hall, attracted, evidently, by the clang of the fallen screen. Malthus looked from X to the man with the broken nose. "Birr," he said to the latter, "what does this mean?" Then he addressed X: "You are Mr. Jackson?"

X nodded. "And who, may I ask, is this china-shop bull who goes around wrecking your bric-a-brac and attempting to shoot your callers?"

"Birr, did you attempt to shoot Mr. Jackson? Birr, Mr. Jackson, is my secretary. He has never exhibited any of these strains of insanity before. Nelson Birr, did you hear me addressing you? What does this mean?"

"I heard you," said Birr unpleasantly. "I regret any damage to the Chinese screen. There is a possibility that I acted hastily." He turned to X and stuck out his hand. "May I have my gun? I have a permit to carry such weapons, something which is quite possible you have not."

"True," said X dryly. He returned the gun to Birr. If he was to accomplish his ends, it might be best if he appeared as little like an investigator as possible. He turned to Malthus. "May I see you a moment, Mr. Malthus, alone, if you please."

"Certainly," agreed Malthus. He waved his hand to Birr. His guests had already discreetly retired to the other room.

Agent X took out Jackson's wallet from his own pocket, and also the federal man's badge. Aaron Malthus's dark skin became suddenly pale. Muscles at the corners of his unpleasant mouth twitched. "F-from the—Department of Justice," he stammered dully.

"Exactly." X returned wallet and badge to his pocket. "I would very much like to attend your dinner party."

"Wh-what for? I mean, of course you're welcome. But really, I've read of these G-men, but never expected to meet one face to face."

It was hardly face to face, X thought as he said: "I do not want to alarm you, Mr. Malthus, but there is the possibility that you are in something of a tight spot."

"You—you mean something might happen—to me?"

"Now, don't alarm yourself in the least." Malthus was heading for a nervous crackup, the Agent thought. "Just permit me to be one of your guests tonight. Is that agreeable?"

"Of course. I-I—" Malthus closed his mouth very tight. Then he waved his hand toward the room where the others had disappeared. X bowed slightly and joined Malthus's guests.

"What is this I hear about you having a run-in with cops and robbers, Dr. Ormand?" inquired Charles McAdam as he seated himself in a chair. Dr. Ormand's eyes and rimless glasses scintillated in the warm yellow light. "Oh, nothing at all." He puffed contentedly at his foul, under-slung pipe.

"Particularly reticent about the encounter, isn't he?" Ingram twitted. He looked at Major Sidney Hatfield and winked.

"Perhaps he was on the wrong side of the legal line," Hatfield boomed jovially. Then he noticed Agent X and stiffened slightly.

Malthus introduced X lamely as "an old friend of my mother," which, because of the youthful face X wore, probably seemed a bit strange to all present.

X kept an eye on Birr, the secretary. Birr was restless, but it was a more ponderous restlessness than that displayed by the birdlike Ingram.

"Tell us about it, Ormand," Ingram insisted. Then he begged that X have one of his cigarettes—"positively the finest weed on the market today."

"Well, I was simply called to the aid of a man who had been wounded," Ormand explained. "'Called' is hardly the word, when you stop to consider that the man who called me was a person known as Lefty Laughlin and the patient was Lewey Cassino." He slowly and modestly related the encounter he had had the previous night.

Agent X hoped fervently that Ormand did not notice that he, Agent X, carried his left arm a little stiffly because of the self-inflicted wound.

While Ormand was concluding his story, X saw that Birr, the secretary, had again slipped from the room. The Agent turned quietly and reentered the hall, to catch Birr just as the latter was again lifting the phone.

Birr put the phone down as though it weighed a ton. His blond skin flamed.

Then hell broke loose.

THE SOUND was something like the explosion of a pack of firecrackers, except that it was louder and more startling and somehow foreboding. Birr heard the sound, turned pale, and cursed. Agent X heard it and sprang toward the front door. Malthus's guests heard it and tried to get through the hall door in a body.

Major Hatfield was heard to shout idiotically enough: "That's gun fire!"

They trooped out of the house. Malthus brought up the rear, murmuring words that were halfway between prayer and blasphemy. On the front lawn, Agent X looked right and left, saw a black car sweep around the corner on two wheels. Nelson Birr had his gun out and would have fired at the careening car had not X checked him.

In the street, not far from the approach walk in front of the Malthus house, something showed like a ghost on the pavement—the body of a man, X saw, as he ran up. The corpse was encircled with a ring of white paint. A white cross quartered the circle and passed over the center of the body. There was a gory mess of blood and white paint on the breast of the man's dinner jacket.

A policeman came up, his whistle shrilling. His call brought another who ran back to the corner call box to contact the Homicide Department. Agent X showed his, or rather Jackson's, card to the police officer. The patrolman welcomed the assistance of a federal man, for he admitted that death of this nature was something that had not occurred on his beat before.

X knelt beside the body, looked at it without touching it. The man had been middle-aged, gray, and respectable-looking. He had dressed carefully, though his dinner kit was a trifle shabby.

"By thunder, Malthus," Ingram exclaimed, "that's your what's-his-name!"

Agent X looked at the faces about him. Ingram was sputtery, Major Hatfield as immobile as a wooden Indian. McAdam was regarding Malthus strangely, and the fixed smile his false teeth made was somehow ghastly at a murder scene. Dr. Ormand was looking on with professional interest, placidly puffing his pipe. Birr was red and white by turns; his fingers seemed trying to squeeze assurance from the little automatic he carried. Aaron Malthus looked as though he sought a nice spot in which to faint.

"Know this man, Malthus?" X demanded.

"He—why, yes—of course I know him. Known him for years."

"Then, why in hell don't you speak up?" demanded one of the cops.

"He's one of my partners," Malthus explained. "His name is John Phelps. And what my firm will do without poor Phelps, I don't know."

"If you ask me," Ingram said, "mine's the firm that will suffer."

A police car pulled to the curb, and Inspector John Burks tramped out, followed by four of his men. Agent X was immediately on his guard, for no one was better acquainted with X's many tricks than Inspector John Burks. X turned his head slightly to watch the approaching police. His attention, however, leaped to the tall man who walked beside Burks. Then X quickly turned his head away. He stood up, muscles tense, and moved sidewise in

Burks's direction.

For the man beside Burks was not of the city police force. Impossible as it might seem, Burks's companion was G-man Henry Jackson, himself.

CHAPTER VI

DEAD MAN'S TRAP

THERE WAS NO immediate explanation of what happened. The Agent's movements were just a little too swift for the human eye to grasp the details. Every muscle in his lithe body seemed to explode in a bombshell of energy that left everyone breathless and baffled.

X turned on G-man Henry Jackson with the savagery of a tiger. His left fist, clutched tightly over something, jabbed for Jackson's body and swerved sharply as though the punch had missed its mark. At the same time, his right hand went to the G-man's collar, seized collar and tie-knot. He dragged Jackson's body forward until their two heads all but touched, then thrust out his jaw and cried: "Got you, faker!"

McAdam pointed a shaky finger at X and the G-man and shouted: "Two of them!"

Burks saw double, too; but knowing of the Agent's mastery in the art of impersonation, he knew that one of the two Jacksons was certainly X.

Jackson tried a punch that X skillfully thwarted and then returned with interest. Burks, and one of his men, stepped in and separated the two. That last punch of the Agent's had not been without definite purpose. His hard, lean fist had driven all the breath out of Jackson and rendered the G-man speechless. So it was that X got in the first words, spat out furiously in perfect imitation of Jackson's voice:

"Let me get that guy! He's Agent X. He and a big fellow wearing a mask attacked me, laid me out someway, and stole my credentials and badge. The big guy kept me locked up in the bathroom. I'd be there yet, if I hadn't managed to put over a fast one."

Jackson, after catching his breath, said: "That's my story, you crook!"

"And you're stuck with it," Jackson's voice echoed from the lips of Agent X. X tore away from the detective and would have started the battle afresh had not Inspector Burks been in the way. Even then, he got a well-concealed chuckle out of landing a hefty blow on the inspector's chest. The detective had X under control again, or thought he did.

"Search the pair of them," Burks ordered. "This guy," indicating Jackson, "just told me the same story in my office. These Feds are good, but they don't know as much about handling Mr. X as I do."

"Don't be so damned sure, inspector," X said. "Turn him over to me, and I'll give you a first-class demonstration of what handling means."

Jackson pointed furiously at X. "That's my suit he's got on. Any credentials you find on him are mine, and don't you believe otherwise. He stole my papers and badge."

And as the search progressed, Jackson forgot to talk. Makeup kit, a small tool kit, gas gun, and similar equipment, came from the pockets of the suit X was wearing. Jackson even looked as though he thought perhaps he shouldn't have mentioned the stealing of his clothes at all.

Burks asked, "Who stole what credentials and badge, my lad?" and thrust a wallet and a gold button under Jackson's nose. "Those, I'll have you know, I just took out of *your* pocket. Yet you told me *he* stole them!"

Jackson was beginning to feel a trifle dizzy. The badge and wallet were his. How they had appeared in his pocket, he couldn't quite grasp. Had he thought about that first punch which X had brushed his body, he might have understood. That first punch X had handed out had been for but one purpose—to plant the stolen wallet and badge on their original owner.

Burks took charge of Jackson himself. "Keep a gun on the other guy's head," he warned the detective who had taken charge of X. "One of these boys is Agent X. And Agent X wears some kind of a screwy, bullet-proof vest that's as good as a charmed life, almost. Get them into the house, and I'll damned soon find out which of them is Mr. X."

"I thought, Inspector," said Major Hatfield, "that this was a murder investigation."

"Huh?" grunted Burks. "Who d'yah think you are, mister?"

"Er, I happen to be connected with a certain life-insurance company as an investigator, and—" Hatfield began.

"Then you can confine your brilliance to shedding light on the poor widow's sorrows." Burks snapped.

"But," Dr. Ormand objected, "you can't leave a body in the street like that."

"Oh, hello, Ormand," said Burks, with slightly more respect than he deemed necessary in speaking to Hatfield. "The dead man can't run away. Agent X can, as I have good reason to know."

So the entire party was marched back into the Malthus house, where X and Jackson were forced back against the oak paneling of the staircase. X was standing beside the table on which the telephone lay. He contemplated the instrument as a possible weapon. He had never been more thoroughly cleaned out than by the detective who had just frisked him. Things began to take a more serious light.

Of the two "twins," the innocent appeared by far the guiltiest. Inspector Burks approached Jackson, an unpleasant grin on his broad face. He reached up and pinched the end of Jackson's nose. Jackson grunted:

"Ah, grow up, Inspector."

Burks, less sure of himself, applied a fingernail to Jackson's cheek. But he scraped off more skin than makeup. He knew instantly that he had drawn blank; that the other "Jackson" was Agent X. He wheeled on X, started to say something, but stood there, his powerful lower jaw sagging, and blood crowding his cheeks.

SECRET AGENT X held a flat, serviceable automatic in his hand. His gray eyes were mere steely points as they sighted over the weapon. Hands went up, police gun dropped beneath the menace of that gun and the cool-thinking man behind it. A mocking smile, that seemed especially for Inspector Burks, curved X's lips as he backed from the room and out of the house. Then he wheeled and ran like a hare to disappear in the shadows.

The mystery man was gone, and Burks knew well enough that X would change his disguise en route, to become just another man among millions.

"But," roared Burks, "where in hell did he get that gun? He was picked clean, yet right under my nose he snatches a gun out of empty air. By damn, the man's clever!"

The only man who was more surprised than Inspector Burks was Agent X, himself. He didn't know where that automatic had come from. He had detected the slight movement of something on the telephone table beside him. He had glanced down and seen a copy of a current magazine which had not been there a moment before. Furthermore, there was a large bulge in the magazine, as though its covers concealed some comparatively large object. Surreptitiously lifting the magazine front, his exploring fingers had closed on an automatic. A piece of paper had been clipped around the butt with a rubber band, and this he did not examine until he was safe in a nearby hideout—one of the many places of sanctuary he maintained throughout the city.

On the paper was written in a scrawl of black ink: "Good luck to the cleverest criminologist of us all."

The brief message was signed with the unmistakable signature of Dr. Stuart Ormand.

Only one conclusion could be drawn from this note. Dr. Ormand, himself a criminologist, had recognized the fact that Agent X deserved notoriety of another sort than the type city police records gave him.

Flattering as Dr. Ormand's opinion was, X dismissed the matter immediately, turned to his telephone, and called the headquarters of the secret organization maintained for him by Harvey Bates. It was Bates himself who answered, a rather crestfallen Bates who had to tell of how, when he had bent over to give G-man Jackson an additional shot of dope, the G-man had come out of a faked coma and struck Bates on the head. There had been a struggle in which the partially stunned Bates had allowed the G-man to give him the slip.

"Don't worry about that," X said kindly. "I guess there are enough mistakes made in this world for us all to have a share in them."

Bates further reported that Betty Dale had just called up. At the moment, she was getting Sally Vergane's life story over a table at the Milan Café.

X hung up, changed his clothes, replenished his pockets with makeup kit and other special devices, and once more adopted the disguise of Lewey Cassino that he had employed on the night before.

He took a taxi to within a block of the café Bates had mentioned. He got to the sidewalk, after a cautious look in all directions, pulled his hat well over his eyes, and hurried toward the café. As Lewey Cassino, he would not know a moment's safety until he again had the protection of Squid Murphy.

He saw Sally Vergane come out of the café. The girl turned, came down the street toward X. She carried her head high and looked neither toward the loafers, who eyed her up and down, nor toward the cars that cruised in close to the gutters of the narrow street. As soon as she had passed, X wheeled and followed her, fell into step beside her, and nipped the elbow of her coat.

"Sally," he whispered, "it's me, Lewey Cassino. I gotta get out of circulation quick. The cops—"

"Don't tell me, sap," she said with frosty quietness. "G-guys have practically camped on my doorsill, askin' for you. We're probably tailed now. Quick! I got a car around the corner."

"That's the stuff, baby." X gave the girl's arm a quick squeeze. She gave him a contemptuous glance and said: "Don't get ideas. I'm doin' this for Wolf Hollis on account of what you was to Wolf."

SALLY opened the door of a wire-wheeled junker, got in, and left the door open for the supposed Lewey. X got in beside her, and she drove recklessly and in silence straight to the old speakeasy that Squid Murphy had remodeled for his own purpose. She steered the junker around back of the building, turned it into a garage with a steel roller door, got out, and closed the door and locked it.

"You probably got something comin' your way from Squid," she warned him. "Lefty tried to tell him how you held off the G-men while Lefty and Doxie made their getaway. Squid says one man couldn't keep off a pack of Feds unless he was in cahoots with them some way. Squid thinks you've been singin' to the Feds. So you better think up some Irish balm to hand Squid."

"I'll handle him," X promised. "He ain't the big noise he sounds like."

They went through a system of electrically operated doors until they at last arrived at the sanctum where Squid Murphy's fishy eyes examined them through a shuttered opening before they were admitted.

Sally Vergane walked through the door. Agent X was pulled into the room, with Squid Murphy's fingers clawing at his coat front. Eight of Murphy's mobsmen were in the room. None of them had anything but icy glances for Lewey Cassino.

"Where in hell've you been?" demanded Murphy. He hauled the unresisting Agent so that he could stick his nose up into his face.

"Duckin' the Feds," X explained. "I was tryin' to get back here, but I didn't want to bring a squad of G-men behind me."

"You don't like G-men, I guess. Not much! How much dough they been payin' you for squealin', rat?"

"Nuts! If I got close enough to a G-man to squeal, it'd be with my last breath. Me squeal? You're nuts!"

Squid Murphy backed away. "We're goin' to find out," he said in a husky voice. "Damn' near every job we've pulled, there's been a gang of Feds on the scene. When we crossed out John Phelps, there was a Fed in the house where this Phelps guy was goin'. He didn't get a crack at any of the boys, but that was his fault and not yours. And you got the nerve to come back here to chisel in on the swag. Well, McAdam paid off to the Brain early this evening. We got our share and split it without countin' you in."

So the mob killed for money. They were hired butchers, directed by the Brain. X mentally reviewed the white-cross killings. A few of the victims had been wealthy persons whose fortunes had gone to one or two comparatively poor heirs. Those heirs had evidently split their inheritances with the Brain to pay for murder. But the majority of persons killed had been associated in some sort of business partnership. Usually the business was in a bad way, as in the case of the Corlears and McAdam firm. Many of these partnerships carried heavy life insurance of such nature that when one partner died, the other, or others, collected the insurance.

He remembered what Ingram had said, when the body of John Phelps had been found. Ingram had said that his insurance firm would suffer rather than the company in which Malthus and Phelps had been associated. Then that was why Malthus had been so upset. Malthus had made a deal with the Brain to remove Phelps in order that Malthus could collect the partnership insurance. Malthus was a murderer, and he had acted—

Some of the toughs in the room were taking off their coats. One of them leered at X. "Goin' to get roughed up a little, ain't ya? I'm goin' to like this a lot, smashin' the bones in your body. You always had the notion you were higher up than us account of you used to tote a gun for Wolf Hollis. You always—"

"Shut up!" Squid Murphy snapped.

A hush fell over those within the room. Somewhere, seemingly far away, some one was yelling in a raucous voice.

"Just a newsboy, Squid," Sally Vergane said.

"Shut up. That's what I want to hear." Murphy went to the little shuttered opening in the door that was nearest to the street. He opened the shutter, and the newsboy's voice quavered into the room:

"Ex-tree! Ex-tree! Body of Lewey Cassino found! Read all about it. Ex-tree!"

Squid Murphy slammed the shutter, pivoted, and flattened himself against the door. His face was black with hate. "So!" he said, huskily. "Boys, you know who we got right here in our family circle? No wonder we got G-men on our tail. This guy we thought was Lewey Cassino is Secret Agent X!"

CHAPTER VII

DOUBLE-FACED
DOUBLE-CROSS

X **CENTERED A** ring of guns that had killed often enough before and would certainly kill again. Murphy was behind his
men. His words lashed furiously:

"There's no foolin' this time, Mr. X. You're goin' to die on the
spot. To hell with the noise, boys. Burn him down just as if he was
Corlears or any of the others. We'll take our chances with the cops.
Let him have it!"

And then, the lights went out. Simultaneously, there was a with-
ering blast of gun-flame, its orange-red light illuminating a squirming figure on the floor in the center of the killers' circle.

"The Brain's here!" whispered Murphy, hoarsely.

"Want me to strike a light, boss?"

"Hell no! He'd shoot you down where you stand. Hold everything. Listen!"

The door opened, and the monotonous voice of the Brain
sounded within the smoke-choked room:

"Murphy, you're finished. This is the last leak. I told you to find
the squealer, and you've failed. Another of Aaron Malthus's partners was scheduled to die tonight, as you know. G-men were on
tap. They mowed down the rest of your boys like so much wheat.
True, four G-men were also killed, but there's no profit in killing
G-men. They got Lefty Laughlin, one of your best men. Either you
produce the squealer at once, or I turn on the light, Murphy. You
know what that means? Eh? Speak up, before I blast out your rem-
nant of a brain."

"Turn on the light, Brain," Murphy said. "Turn on the light, and
I'll show you the squealer. We got him right here. Lewey Cassino—"

"Nonsense!" the Brain interrupted. "Lewey Cassino couldn't get
close enough to a federal man to squeal. He's wanted for murder."

"No. Not Lewey Cassino. Cassino is dead. So is this guy."

"You're talking like an idiot," came the voice of the Brain.

And then, from another portion of the room, came the Brain's voice again in angry monotone: "Who said that? Who's using my voice? Don't move, anybody."

And again came that twin voice of the Brain from about the center of the room. "He's over here, you fools. He's Agent X. You may have thought you killed him, but you didn't. He's making a mob of fools out of you. *Don't let him slip.*"

Thus spoke Secret Agent X, in perfect imitation of the Brain's voice, as he moved cautiously through the dark toward the door. He had dropped to the floor on the instant that the real Brain had turned out the lights. Only one of his would-be murderer's bullets had touched him, and it had lodged in his perfect, bullet-proof vest.

In the basement room, all was confusion. The Brain was raging, snapping conflicting orders, for every order he gave was echoed by another order, given by Agent X. And X was moving steadily for the door, all the time ordering the men to remain exactly where they were.

"He'll get through the door!" shouted the Brain. "Stop him. I'm the Brain. He's the impostor."

"Don't mind him, boys!" shouted X. "I'm the Brain. Shoot at the next person who speaks, and shoot to kill!" He reached the door, opened it, slammed it without leaving the room. He flattened himself against the wall near the door, waiting, listening to the chorus of quick-drawn breath.

The Brain said: "Damn you! He's given us the slip. Get through the door. You can catch him yet!"

There was only a moment's hesitation before the whole gang rushed pell-mell through the door. When the last footstep had died away in the distance, Agent X drew a long breath.

"Brain," he said quietly. "I'm still here, waiting for you. Just you and I alone. Shall we finish it?"

Absolute silence. X took a hesitant step forward. He took out his small flashlight, held it as far from his body as possible, and flashed it. The light drew no gun fire. He fanned the beam around the room. The place was empty and as silent as the grave. Either the Brain had slipped out with his mob or had taken an exit made especially for his own use. Agent X sighed. With the Brain still at large, the white-cross killings might go on and on.

He left the building by the back way. There was one more scheme he might try to trap the Brain. It was exceedingly dangerous. It threatened the very foundation of his organization, for he would deliberately make himself a prospective victim for the Brain's murder machine.

As he hurried from Murphy's hideout, the plan formed completely. Charles McAdam had paid the Brain money for killing McAdam's partner, Corlears. Through partnership-plan life insurance, both the Brain and McAdam had benefited by the murder. Why couldn't McAdam form a second partnership, with the idea of gaining by the same nefarious scheme? Why couldn't Agent X, disguised as McAdam, form such a partnership? Who with? With himself, of course. Agent X would not only impersonate McAdam, but he would also act in the drama as McAdam's partner. And for his partner, what better alias could he choose than that of Elisha Pond.[40] Yes, that was the way—a fake firm formed by Elisha Pond and Charles McAdam, with Agent X the sole actor for both roles....

SALLY VERGANE had left Murphy's hideout as soon as she realized that the Brain was on his way. After all, she realized that she had unknowingly brought X into the hideout and feared that the Brain might vent his rage upon her.

Unknown to Sally, she and X had been followed, not by G-men, it is true, but by a golden-haired, persistent little shadow, Betty Dale of the *Herald*. Betty had made it a point to leave the Milan Café a few minutes before Sally Vergane had. She had waited just around the corner in her coupé, and had successfully followed Sally and the supposed Lewey Cassino to the hideout.

No sooner had Sally Vergane appeared at the back of the hideout, than Betty Dale was on her trail, and this time, as on one other occasion, Sally Vergane's trail led directly to the apartment house where Pamela Dean lived.

Sally went in the back way. A man stepped from a hiding place in the back entry and grunted a greeting to her. Sally told the man to come up. She wanted to talk with him.

Betty followed the woman and her bodyguard up the back steps. She watched them approach the door of Pamela Dean's apartment.

---

40   AUTHOR'S NOTE: *One of the Agent's most famous aliases is that of Elisha Pond, aged eccentric and philanthropist. It is in the name of Pond that a large sum of money has been deposited for X's use. Pond, known to dabble in all sorts of businesses, was the ideal character X was to adopt in this instance.*

She watched Sally Vergane produce a key and unlock the door, after which Sally and her pug-faced bodyguard entered the apartment.

Wide-eyed with astonishment, Betty tiptoed toward the apartment door. Either Sally and her companion were contemplating larceny, or the unthinkable was true—this underworld woman, ex-moll of a notorious gangster, was that woman of fortune, Pamela Dean, herself.

Betty listened at the door but could detect no sound. Her heart jumping madly in her throat, she tried the door. It was locked, the key remaining in the lock. She opened her purse and took out a pair of peculiar, needle-nosed pliers. This was an "oustini" such as hotel thieves use to turn keys from the wrong side of the lock. This instrument, a souvenir which Agent X had taken from a petty thief, early in his career, had been of use to the girl reporter before this.

She managed the instrument skillfully, and unlocked the door. In another instant, she found herself cautiously breathing the perfumed atmosphere of Pamela Dean's living room. There was the rumble of voices in the room just beyond.

Betty Dale tiptoed to the door of the bedroom and ventured a peek inside. The pug-faced watchman was there and also Sally Vergane. Or was it Pamela Dean? Actually, she was witnessing a metamorphosis. Sally Vergane had slipped a luxurious, dark-brown wig over her closely cropped blonde hair. Her dress lay on a chair beside the dressing table. Sally Vergane, wearing the most expensive underthings, was doing things to her plain face with creams and tinted powder.

No doubt about it. Sally Vergane was the glamorous Pamela Dean. Sally Vergane was speaking in an odd voice that was a mixture of her own voice and the cultured diction of Pamela Dean.

"I have played this game fairly to its limit," Sally was saying. "I think we have given them something to remember Wolf Hollis by. Our chief difficulty will be in finding some one on whom the Brain can place the blame."

"A fall guy," the pug-faced man said and began wandering aimlessly about the boudoir.

Fearful lest the man's wanderings bring him into the living room, Betty replaced her oustini in her handbag and hurried from the apartment. Sally Vergane was Pamela Dean. This was news that Agent X would value highly. She must phone him at once.

WHILE Betty Dale was excitedly reporting this news to Bates's office, Sally Vergane, perfectly fortified behind the glamorous veneer of Pamela Dean, was in her living room, talking to her watchdog.

"You've been faithful and square to Wolf and me, Twist," Sally said. "We've netted exactly one dozen G-men to date by arranging encounters for them with Murphy's gang at the scenes of the white-cross killings. I'll never rest until I send a whole squad of them to hell at once. Wolf would like that. He hated the Federals. But we're in a dangerous spot now."

The man called Twist nodded. "I'd better get back to my post. You think up something smart." He turned the key in the door, tried to open the door and failed. "Funny," he grunted. "I'm sure I locked that door when we came in."

Sally Vergane was on her feet. She stamped a fluffy, blue mule irritably. "Are you sure? Oh, how could you be so careless!"

"I locked that door, damned sure!" growled Twist. "Somebody's been here, that's all."

Sally Vergane's eye roamed about the room and alighted on a scrap of white cloth on the floor. She pounced on it, catlike, and held it aloft. "A woman's handkerchief! I've seen it somewhere. Wait!" Her breast heaved. The fury of hell gleamed in her eyes. "I know! She used it in the restaurant. She must have dropped it from her bag."

"Who?" asked Twist.

"That nosey little blonde reporter with her blue-eyed, baby stare," she said venomously. "She's been here. Then, *she knows.*"

Then out of the fury cloud on Sally Vergane's face came a slow, unlovely smile. "Twist, we've got it! The Brain is trying to find out who's been squealing and sending G-men to the scene of the white-cross murders. Perhaps he suspects me— But not for long. The girl, don't you see? Betty Dale can be framed so that the Brain will think that *she* has been peddling the information."

Twist nodded his misshapen head slowly. "I get it. She's the perfect fall guy."

CHAPTER VIII

KILLER'S MARK

AN UNEVENTFUL DAY passed in which X and his staff of operatives gathered much information regarding Charles McAdam, partner of the late Randolph Corlears.

McAdam was an unscrupulous attorney who had several times been on the verge of being removed from the bar. He was a member of a well-known business men's club in which X, as Elisha Pond, had no difficulty in gaining membership. Many other men known to the Agent were members of the same club. Among them were Thomas Ingram, Dr. Ormand, Major Hatfield and Nelson Birr.

How Nelson Birr, private secretary of Aaron Malthus, could afford to belong to a club was a mystery to Agent X. Birr's salary certainly must have been rather slender, for Aaron Malthus had been on the verge of bankruptcy for some time.

That evening, kindly old Elisha Pond checked coat and umbrella at the club and mingled freely with the other members. None would have guessed that this wrinkled, white-haired gentleman of the old school was the feared and notorious Agent X. His eccentricities in the matter of dress would have made Elisha Pond the butt of many a joke, were it not for the fact that his wealth and generosity purchased a vast amount of respect.

Mr. Pond paid particular attention to Charles McAdam, with a definite purpose in mind. When the news broke that a new business partnership of McAdam and Pond had been formed, none of the club members would be greatly surprised. So it was that McAdam seated his pink-porkiness at a table opposite Elisha Pond in the club dining room. For an hour or so, Mr. Pond's shaggy white head was seen close to McAdam's pink scalp. The two were engaged in earnest conversation.

"Wonder what old Pond is up to now?" asked Major Hatfield of Dr. Ormand.

The doctor smoked his pipe and shook his head doubtfully. "If it's a matter of business, Pond better keep his hand on his bank book. McAdam would skin his own brother."

Thomas Ingram, who overheard the conversation, stepped up to say: "Don't be too sure. McAdam met his match when he met Elisha Pond."

Earnest and confidential as their conversation seemed, Mr. Pond and McAdam discussed nothing more important than a theoretical law problem. X's first task, in forming the fake partnership of McAdam and Pond was to remove McAdam to some safe spot and keep him prisoner. Then, disguised at one time as McAdam and at another as Pond, he would manage an apparent business deal between the two.

But before he could successfully impersonate McAdam, it was necessary for him to make sure that he was familiar with McAdam's characteristic actions, and especially with McAdam's handwriting, so that he would be able to sign McAdam's name to a partnership agreement without exciting suspicion.

Not all of the Agent's attention was on McAdam, however. At a table, not far distant, one of the members dined quietly alone. That man was Nelson Birr. And X watched him closely, though covertly.

Nelson Birr concluded his meal at approximately the same time that X and McAdam finished theirs. He opened his wallet and carelessly tossed a bill down as a tip for the waiter. As he closed the wallet, a scrap of paper, hardly an inch square, slipped out and fluttered to the floor. Birr did not notice this, but Agent X did.

As he sauntered from the dining room, still chatting with McAdam, X picked up the paper and thrust it into his pocket.

Later, in the card room, X and McAdam were joined by Dr. Ormand and Thomas Ingram. Dr. Ormand suggested bridge. X declined. "Never play anything but solitaire," he told them. "Ah, there is a young man after my own heart!" He nodded across the room to where Nelson Birr was idly toying with cards at a lonely table.

"A new member," explained Dr. Ormand. "Doesn't seem to make friends or want to. Perhaps you can pull him out of his shell, Pond."

"Perhaps; I'll try," X said. But he walked away from, rather than toward, Nelson Birr's table. In a small reading room off the card room, X took out the slip of paper Birr had dropped and looked at it. It had obviously been torn from the lower right-hand corner of a much folded letter. On the paper were the words... "as my worthy successor."

Beneath this, where a signature should have been, was a small circle of ink centered by a cross. It was the sign of sudden death.

Nelson Birr—silent, friendless Nelson Birr—had dropped the paper bearing the fatal sign. Agent X recalled the man's peculiar actions that night at Malthus's house. He again saw Nelson Birr, mysterious, cagey, armed and ready to shoot. Nelson was not marked by the sign of sudden death; he carried it in his pocket. It was imperative that he question Birr at once. It would be no mere catechism, X resolved. Birr would be taken to the Agent's own crime laboratory and there submit his soul to the closest scrutiny that science and the keenest pair of eyes in the city could produce.

X opened his medical kit, which he always carried, and took out a small vial. Then he slipped it into his pocket. It contained chloral hydrate, familiar, quick-acting knockout drops which X employed. Dropped into a highball, the stuff could produce a coma not unlike a drunken sleep. Once Birr had taken the drug, it would be an easy matter for X to get him to his crime laboratory.

THE AGENT entered the card room and proceeded at once to the table where Nelson Birr sat. Birr looked up quizzically, his handsome, blond face flushing slightly. Agent X thrust out his hand. "I believe I have not had the pleasure."

Birr smiled slightly, introduced himself, and shook hands. "And you, of course, are Mr. Pond. I am a secret admirer of yours, sir. Your philanthropies are most commendable."

"Thank you so much." Agent X sat down, waved Birr into the chair opposite and sighed. "Stuffy place, isn't it?"

Birr raised his eyebrows. "I find it much to my liking."

X chuckled. "Odd, isn't it? I mean, we're all rather old codgers here, with the exception of Ormand. Being a doctor, he finds it to his advantage to cultivate the acquaintance of gentlemen who have one foot in the grave, no doubt.... Ever play double solitaire, Mr. Birr?"

Birr shook his head. "Quite a game, isn't it?"

"Oh, quite. Learn it by all means. Suppose you and I go into that small room over there where we can concentrate. I'll teach you in no time."

"Delighted." Birr stood up. X hooked his arm through the secretary's arm and steered him toward a small, private room.

X uttered Pond's crackling chuckle again. "We'll have a game to ourselves with something to drink on the side, eh, my boy?"

Birr smiled. "I'd like nothing better."

The small room where X had suggested that Birr learn the game, was actually an alcove near a small stage which the club sometimes used for entertainment purposes. There was no door to the place, but it offered sufficient privacy for X's purpose.

They consumed three, rather potent, highballs before X had managed to cover the simple rules of double solitaire. It was no difficult task for a man of X's skill in sleight-of-hand to doctor Birr's fourth highball with the drug. So it was that shortly after the game itself, Birr began to nod.

"Damned stuffy in here," he commented, playing the wrong card.

"So glad you agree with me," X said pleasantly. "And, if you'll pardon me, you can not play a queen on an eight spot, my boy."

Birr corrected his error. "Feel queer," he mumbled. He tried to stand up, but flapped limply across the table. X got up, stepped quickly to Birr's side.

"Hullo, what's happened to the youngster?" a thin voice behind X said.

The Agent turned, saw nervous Thomas Ingram looking into the alcove.

"Too many drinks, I'm afraid," X said.

Ingram turned his head slightly and called: "Dr. Ormand!"

"Oh, it's nothing to be alarmed about," X said hastily. "I noticed Birr was becoming a bit foggy. Couldn't keep his mind on the game."

Ormand came up. His eyes glistened brightly behind his rimless glasses as he pushed in front of Ingram. "What's the trouble, Birr?" he demanded. Birr, of course, did not answer. Ormand stooped over, sniffed, though how he could have smelled anything above the reek of his under-slung pipe was a mystery. Then he picked up Birr's glass and sniffed it. Then he sniffed at Birr's slightly parted lips.

Agent X inwardly cursed Ingram's nosiness while cleverly feigning anxiety. Dr. Ormand turned quickly to X. "Who was your waiter, Mr. Pond?"

"Number six, I believe," said X. "What's the trouble? Nothing serious, I hope?"

Ormand grunted. "Nothing except that the waiter has evidently tried to poison Birr. His glass contained chloral hydrate. I hardly think a lethal dose was given. However, we must not delay a moment. Ingram, have some one get strong coffee. Be quick about it, man!"

Major Hatfield and other club members came up. X knew that if he was to spirit Birr out of the club now, he would have to be a magician.

"Poison, you say?" Hatfield cried. "This is serious!"

"Not necessarily," Dr. Ormand contradicted as he coolly caressed his pipe. "Not if Ingram hurries with that coffee. I believe some one has merely given Birr a sleeping potion."

INGRAM came bustling up with Waiter Number Six in tow. The waiter was pale. His hand shook so that had not Ormand seized the coffee cup the waiter surely would have spilled the liquid. Ormand, with X assisting him, got a cup of the hot, black liquid into Birr.

"I think he'll be all right," Ormand said.

"But," Hatfield insisted, "this matter needs looking into. Though I am an investigator by profession, I should like to have the police here at once. Suppose you call the police, Ormand, while I arrange to have all exits guarded."

"Oh, really," said Ingram, "is such formality needed?"

Dr. Ormand's eyes rooted the waiter to the floor. "I believe so," he said, quietly. He turned on his heel, and with Hatfield at his side, left the room.

Ingram wrung his hands and danced worriedly around X. "I don't like the publicity this may mean, do you, Mr. Pond? What will our wives say?"

"I've no idea," declared X. "I haven't met mine yet."

Ingram groaned. "Lucky man! I propose that we get this thing over as soon as possible. Suppose we were all to submit to a search. Wouldn't that satisfy justice? I mean, the man with the poison bottle—it does come in bottles, doesn't it? I'm frightfully ignorant on the subject of murder. Ha, naturally, eh?"

"Naturally," X said, without enthusiasm.

"And inasmuch as this isn't really murder," Ingram sputtered on, "and poor Birr will suffer nothing more than a headache, why the devil can't we find the culprit ourselves and shut the matter up? A search would reveal the bottle."

"Ingram," said one of the club members, "you're making a colossal ass of yourself. Inspector Burks of the Homicide Department, seeing you act like a jumping jack, will be apt to clap the cuffs on you."

"Cuffs—homicide." Ingram held his head, and he was holding his head when the lights went out.

"What the hell?" some one cried.

Agent X leaped into the card room. "Probably a blown-out fuse," he said soothingly.

"It's the murderer!" cried Ingram. "I know it. He's going to escape!"

"Keep calm, you fool!" some one yelled at Ingram. "Look! There's a light now—that spot light in the balcony—the light we used at the last show."

The keen beam of light cut across the room, finding white, taut faces of the club members in the room.

"What the devil's happened to the lights?" demanded Dr. Ormand, who had just run up.

"Fuse gone, no doubt," X said.

"Or the murderer trying to escape!" cried Ingram. "Who's missing? Watch that waiter!"

"Nobody's missing," boomed Major Hatfield, as he joined the others. "I've guards posted at every exit. As soon as the police arrive, we'll search everybody."

A search was something that X dared not risk. He had all of his special devices with him, as well as the incriminating bottle of chloral hydrate. The Elisha Pond alias was too valuable to him, as it was his means of obtaining necessary funds, to have it discovered that Elisha Pond was Agent X. No, before he would allow that, he would declare himself Agent X and tell every one in the club that he was impersonating Elisha Pond.

A man clutched Agent X's arm. It was Dr. Ormand. "Damn it! We've very nearly forgot our patient. Birr should show some signs of improv—"

Ormand's sentence hung in mid-air. His keen eyes were staring in the direction of the alcove. No one had noted it before, but the spotlight, the only illumination in the room, was directed at the table where X and Birr had been seated.

Birr lay exactly as they had left him; there was nothing alarming about that. What was stranger than anything else was the spot of light itself. Its yellow circle was centered by Birr's form and also a shadow—a shadow that was a perfect cross.

The circle and the cross—the sign of sudden death....

Ormand and Agent X leaped toward the alcove at one and the

same time. They crowded shoulder to shoulder as they stooped over the man on the table.

"Not a mark," Ormand muttered. "Nothing but that damned shadow of a cross. Yet the man is dead, do you hear? Nelson Birr has been murdered!"

CHAPTER IX

"MEET MR. X."

MURDER. THE WORD was breathed around the room. Horrified eyes were anchored on that motionless body, on the cross and circle sign that seemed to have stamped out life.

Agent X was momentarily stunned by this revelation. He had picked a spot in the murder puzzle where Nelson Birr seemed to fit perfectly. Yet Birr was dead, and Agent X was at a loss as to how that death could be explained. It could not have come from the drug X had placed in Birr's drink, for the dose had been only enough to produce a coma. Plainly it was the work of the same person who directed the white-cross killings.

"Don't suppose Pond had anything to do with it?" Ingram was heard to whisper.

"Absurd!" snapped Ormand.

"But wasn't he drinking with Birr?" Ingram insisted.

"Pond, where the devil are you?" demanded Major Hatfield.

"Here," said X in Pond's mild voice. He stepped nearer the ray of light, and Hatfield came up to him.

"You've no objection to my searching you, have you, Pond?" the major asked. "It would stop some ugly insinuations."

X's muscles tensed as he answered: "I have every objection," he said acidly. "The mere suggestion of a search is the gravest insinuation I have to face, Major."

Hatfield's bronzed brow furrowed. He took a step nearer. "If it wasn't for your unimpeachable reputation, Pond, I'd say you were trying to conceal something."

Some one pressed against the Agent's right side. X turned to see Ingram darting back into the shadows. Ingram exclaimed: "He's got a gun! I felt a gun in Pond's pocket!"

Major Hatfield's teeth clenched. "I'm going to search you, Mr.

Pond!"

Hatfield put his hand out toward X. But he had scarcely touched the Agent before X's left fist shot out and up, straight to the point of Hatfield's chin. The major had traveled the world over and had seen much of war, but never in his life had he encountered such a blow as that. His long body struck the floor.

"Mr. Pond, Mr. Pond!" a clubman shouted excitedly.

But Mr. Pond was running toward the door of the room to stop suddenly as a spotlight pierced the gloom and centered upon him. More lights were gleaming through the doorway, and Inspector Burks could be heard bellowing: "Why the black-out here? What's the trouble?"

"Stop him!" shouted Ingram. "Stop Pond. He killed Nelson Birr. He's just killed Major Hatfield. He'll kill us all!"

"Pond killed some one?" Burks roared. "You're crazy. I—"

"Look at him!" yelled Ingram. "He—he's growing!"

Police flashlights focused on a figure in the center of the floor— a figure that had been Elisha Pond's. Age was dropping from the man's shoulders. As X straightened up, Elisha Pond seemed actually to grow. It was as if a magnificent character actor were showing them how his miracles were wrought. There was Elisha Pond's wrinkled face above a tall, sinewy, youthful body. And on Pond's lips was almost boyish laughter.

"You're quite right, Inspector Burks," came a voice that was not Pond's, yet came from Pond's lips. "Elisha Pond did not kill Nelson Birr. You will find that Elisha Pond is quietly sleeping somewhere in this club. Gentlemen, I want you to meet an old friend of Inspector Burks. Gentlemen, meet Mr. X!"

And with that, X's right hand raked across his face, instantly altering the plastic features that had identified him as Pond. At the same time, he tossed a mysterious cylinder to the floor directly in front of him. As police guns barked, a cloud of dense black smoke broke from the cylinder to form a screen which effectively masked X's movements.

"Watch the doors!" shouted Burks. "He'll not get away this time. Send somebody to fix the lights. Damn that smoke!"

To follow Agent X as he moved about the club in the darkness, would have required bloodhounds. Even when they found him, they did not know him; for he was on the floor of the washroom, apparently asleep. It was Inspector Burks, himself, who came very near to falling over him.

Burks turned his flashlight on the recumbent form of an old, white-haired man whose features were unmistakably those of Elisha Pond. There was an empty drinking glass close by which Burks's detective sense told him had contained chloral hydrate in solution.

THE INSPECTOR fell to shaking Pond by the shoulders, little suspecting that he actually had Agent X in his hands. As Hatfield and Dr. Ormand came into the room, the lights came on. Agent X's eyelids fluttered.

"Coming to," murmured Burks. "That devil drugged him."

"That devil" opened his eyes and muttered feebly: "Where am I?"

"You're okeh, Mr. Pond," Burks said kindly. "Mr. X handed you some knockout drops and has been impersonating you all evening. Disguised as you, he's murdered a man, that's what!"

"I—I remember now," X said. "I was having a little indigestion. A man came up to me here. I thought he was a fellow club member. He gave me something for my indigestion."

"What'd he look like?" demanded Burks. Then: "Oh, hell, don't answer that question. He never looks the same way twice." Then Burks did something that, knowingly, he never would have done: he helped Agent X to his feet.

Not only had X cleared all suspicion from the name of Elisha Pond, but he now had further opportunity of investigating the mysterious murder of Nelson Birr. The shadow of the cross-and-circle sign was readily explained. Some one, undoubtedly the murderer, had simply and quickly cut out a silhouette, representing the cross and circle, from a magazine cover. This had been placed over the spot light which had been turned on the body. Consequently the silhouette had been projected on the corpse.

This piece of paper, Burks deemed important evidence. But in his zeal to trace the owner of the magazine from which the cover had been torn, Burks overlooked a vastly more important clue—a dark-brown stain, hardly more than a quarter of an inch across, on the card table cover on which the body was lying. This stain X quietly removed by cutting off a bit of the cloth and putting it into his pocket.

Shortly after, X left the club to go to one of his hideouts. He emerged a little later, a young man with commonplace features, and drove one of his cars to the United States Court House. Using credentials which represented him as a member of the city police force, he eventually entered the office of Special Agent Weston. As soon as Weston had had a look at the credentials X carried, the Secret Agent tore them up before Weston's wondering eyes.

"They're quite false," said X with a smile. "I used them as a means of entering only. I am Secret Agent X."

"Secret Agent X!" Weston repeated slowly. He leaned eagerly across the desk. "Can you prove that?" he asked in a whisper.

AGENT X reached into his inner coat pocket and produced an envelope which contained a message from X's official sponsor in Washington.[41] Weston read the message over twice. Then he stood up slowly, almost timidly extended his hand to Agent X.

"Naturally," he said, "I've heard of you. Now that I meet the man, I realize fully that what I have heard in Washington, concerning the great work you are doing, is not an exaggeration. This message from K9 clears up much that I haven't been able to understand."

X nodded and took back his sponsor's note. "The nature of my work, my methods of procedure, make it imperative that my official capacity be kept secret."

"But, Mr. Agent X, yours is a most dangerous position. I don't know how many times I've read of your capture by the police. Once, I even read that you had been killed by Inspector Burks. Is there no way of giving yourself official protection?"

X smiled. "I take pretty good care of myself," he said quietly. "If my real capacity were known to the city police, it would eventually get into the papers. However, this is not a social call, Weston. No doubt I've caused your men a little trouble, but I am actually working with them in an effort to untangle the mystery behind these white-cross killings. Quite by accident, I came across this slip of paper." X showed Weston the corner of paper that had dropped from Birr's wallet, and explained the circumstances under which it had been found.

"You have confided in me, Agent X. I am most happy to be able to cooperate with you in this matter. Because we did not wish to arouse public apprehension, we have kept the matter quiet. Perhaps I should begin at the beginning and tell you that the late Wolf

---

41 *AUTHOR'S NOTE: The Agent's Washington sponsor prefers that his identity be shrouded and that he simply be referred to as K9. It is through the activity of K9 and certain public-spirited persons, that Agent X is supplied with funds for continuing his war against crime.*

Hollis was illiterate. He could not even write his own name. The cross and circle, which the Safety League uses to designate the spot where fatal motor accidents occur, happens to be the mark by which Wolf Hollis was known. Any written order which he issued was written at his dictation and signed by his mark—the cross and circle.

"Knowing this, there are but two possible conclusions to the mystery: either Wolf Hollis lives, a maniacal murderer, or gang vengeance is taking its toll for the death of Wolf Hollis. You can take your choice, Agent X."

"I'd choose neither," said X quietly. "There is a definite greed motive behind these killings. The mob is directed by a hired butcher; I am certain of this. The man called the Brain kills for a price—kills anyone. Only one of the murders has been motivated differently. Nelson Birr was obviously killed because of that slip of paper, which I'll keep for a while if you don't mind. Birr had solved the mystery of the identity of the Brain."

"Possibly," said Weston slowly. "Birr was a life-insurance claim detective, working for Major Hatfield."

That explained Birr's suspicious actions to Agent X, who prepared to take his leave. "Inside of thirty minutes, I'll try to have proof of the identity of the Brain. I strongly suspect who he is, even now. But the proof I might obtain will be of little use to me."

"Why?" asked Weston.

X smiled queerly. "I am sorry I can not explain the matter. But I must catch the Brain red-handed. Goodnight—and my heartiest thanks."

A possibility of the Brain's identity was in X's pocket—a little brown stain on a piece of cloth from a card table cover. Yet it was Elisha Pond who had obtained that, and Elisha Pond was not supposed to be even an amateur criminologist. As Elisha Pond, X must catch the Brain red-handed....

Morning papers screamed about the murder of Nelson Birr, dead from chloral hydrate poisoning. His murderer was admittedly Agent X. About the only truth in the entire article was that Nelson Birr was dead.

Agent X tossed the paper aside, went to the phone, and set in motion the machine that was to turn out a trap for the Brain—a trap in which Agent X was to be the bait.

Harvey Bates and some of his men attended to the kidnaping of Charles McAdam. When McAdam became a guarded prisoner in one of the Agent's hideouts, X became Charles McAdam. Shortly after, it was announced that a new business firm had been established—McAdam and Pond, Investments. An office was opened, and there both Pond and McAdam might be found; but, because Agent X was playing a dual role of both partners, Pond and McAdam were never seen together in the same room.

Furthermore, to insure that neither partner would greatly lose in the event of the death of one member of the firm, heavy partnership-plan life insurance was written up for the new firm by Thomas Ingram.

There was nothing to do but wait. Eventually, the Brain would take notice of the organization and approach "McAdam" on the delicate subject of removing Mr. Pond from this earth, collecting the insurance, to the mutual benefit of the supposed Mr. McAdam and the criminal gang.

It was a neat plan—if it worked....

CHAPTER X

NETS OF STEEL

THERE FOLLOWED A period of ominous quiet in the underworld. It was as if a storm gathered on the horizon, waiting for something before breaking. Evening of the second Tuesday in April, three opposing forces were set in motion: the Brain moved to carry on his mercenary murder; Sally Vergane, vengeance mad, conceived a means of wiping out most of the G-men in the city; Secret Agent X made ready for the culmination of his scheme to trap the Brain.

Though she did not realize it, Betty Dale was calmly walking into the center of this perilous snarl of conflicting forces. Agent X had welcomed her information regarding Sally Vergane's masquerade as Pamela Dean. Betty was determined to add measurably to that information in an effort to aid the man she loved. So it was that when Sally Vergane asked Betty Dale to meet her at an appointed spot for another talk, Betty eagerly accepted, having no reason to suppose that it was an invitation that held no promise save death.

So eager was she to meet Sally Vergane at the Milan Café that Betty Dale took no notice of the pug-faced drunk who staggered into her when she was within a block of the appointed place. She hurried on to find Sally waiting for her outside the dingy door of the restaurant.

Sally looked worried. She clamped her fingers on Betty's arm. "Say, Miss Dale, you don't mind if we get out of this neighborhood? There's a man that's been botherin' me inside this joint. You know how it is. Tough how hard it is for a girl, down on her luck, to keep on the level. I know a place where we can go that's better than the Milan."

Betty was agreeable. Had she noticed the face of the driver of the taxi Sally hailed, she might have recognized the driver as the same pug-faced fellow who had bumped into her on the street.

The taxi took them eastward, but by such a circuitous route that Betty had trouble keeping track of the direction. It was not until the taxi rolled into a garage that Betty realized that she had been nicely tricked.

Sally Vergane drove the muzzle of an automatic into Betty's side. "Now, you cheap little sob-sister, you're goin' to meet Squid Murphy. He'll give you somethin' to print in your paper!"

Betty measured the lank blonde beside her. Had not the pug-faced Twist turned out of the front of the cab and come to Sally's assistance, Betty would have put up some sort of resistance. But after one look at Twist, Betty realized the seriousness of the situation. Propped between two guns, she was hurried from the garage and through several dark rooms into Squid Murphy's new headquarters. Murphy and his men had left the one-time speakeasy as soon as they learned that Agent X had been visiting them in the disguise of Lewey Cassino.

Squid Murphy looked Betty coolly up and down, his hands in his pockets, his fingers squirming. Then he gave Sally Vergane a fishy stare and said: "What the hell? Don't bring dames around here—even good-lookin' ones. Ain't I got enough trouble just keepin' an eye on you?"

"Look the kid over, Squid," Sally said.

"Ain't that what I been doin'?"

"I mean give her a frisk. I got an idea you want this dame, dead or alive."

Squid's pale, twisting fingers darted into the pockets of Betty's coat. The girl reporter watched, astonished and afraid, as Murphy brought out a piece of paper, opened it, and held it to the light. Betty had not seen the paper before, but she realized that the collision she and the pug-faced man had had on the sidewalk had not been an accident.

Murphy's lips twisted into an ugly smile. "So you got the dope on this joint, did you? You was goin' to hand it over to the G-men, was you?"

"I haven't the slightest idea what you are talking about," declared Betty. "Furthermore, I advise you to let me go at once."

"She don't know what we was talkin' about!" Murphy scoffed. "She wants to go home! Well, baby, wait till the Brain gets a load of this!"

THAT same evening, Secret Agent X was in McAdam's Elmhurst home, sitting quietly and alone, as he had sat on several previous evenings. He had put in rather a hard day at the new office, acting first the part of Mr. Pond and then appearing as Mr. McAdam. Tonight, some sixth sense warned him that his patience would be rewarded.

At about nine o'clock, every light in the McAdam house went out. Either some one had cut the wires or opened the master switch. X felt certain that he was about to receive a visitation from the Brain himself.

Doors opened and closed quietly. Agent X never moved from his chair, gave no indication that his nerves were taut, that every sense was on the alert. Velvety footsteps approached the very chair in which X sat.

"Are you there, Brain?" asked X in the voice of McAdam.

"Yes," came the Brain's answering monotone. "What is it you want, McAdam?"

"How did you know I wanted you?" X stalled.

"Obviously, the formation of the Pond McAdam combine was for some blacker business than the swindling of investors, McAdam. Have you exhausted all of your portion of the funds realized from our last job?"

"The need of money is not pressing," replied X, for he had thoroughly investigated McAdam's finances. The insurance money gleaned from Corlears' murder had helped McAdam out of a scrape that had endangered McAdam's bank account and personal liberty as well. "I merely thought that inasmuch as the first job was so clean we ought to be able to repeat it. Pond seemed a likely victim, and I have seen to it that the firm is heavily insured."

"Then you would like to see Mr. Pond in the center of the white cross, eh?" the Brain asked.

X's hand strayed to his pocket. He was tempted to take his flashlight and turn it on the man's face, but he strangled his curiosity. After all, if his deductions were correct, he knew the man to whom he was speaking. And besides, it was evident that the Brain did not rely entirely upon the darkness to conceal his identity; from the muffled quality of his voice, X judged that he wore some sort of a mask. No, it was better to play the game until he caught the Brain in the midst of his hired killers.

"That's the idea exactly," X replied in answer to the Brain's question.

"And quite agreeable to me. But what shall be the terms?"

X had no idea what the Brain charged for his murderous service. It was better that he did not state any exact amount. "Suppose we make the fee the same as it was for the Corlears job."

"Thirty per cent of the insurance to go to you, then?"

X rubbed his hands greedily. "That's fine."

"Very well. I'll draw up a contract and deliver it tomorrow night." And the Brain stole through the darkness as quietly as he had entered.

But hardly had the door closed behind the Brain than Agent X was on his feet, following. The Brain had evidently possessed himself of a key to the McAdam house, for he locked the side door after going out. X watched through a window. The Agent's mind was like a super-sensitive photographic plate that instantly recorded every detail of the man's figure and stride.

A moment later, X left by the same route the Brain had taken. He hurried to the front of the house, looked down the street, and saw the Brain entering a parked car in which he had evidently driven to the McAdam house. X ran back to the McAdam garage, got in one of his own super-charged cars, and drove it to the edge of the drive. Just as the Brain got his car started and was leisurely wheeling it around the corner, X sprang into his car and followed.

The Brain's car headed down Northern Boulevard to Forty-second, crossed the bridge into Manhattan. From there on the trail kept close to the river to end abruptly in front of an apparently deserted loft building.

Agent X had driven with one hand all the way while his other hand had been occupied with artful changes in the plastic material that covered his face. When he left his car, about a block from the old building, his face was that of a younger and leaner man than McAdam. He had only to slip out of his padded coat, that had helped him simulate McAdam's fleshy body, and he seemed quite another person.

He approached the door through which the Brain had passed. It appeared of flimsy construction, yet the weight of the thing, as it yielded to one of the Agent's master keys, told him that it was backed by solid steel.

BEYOND the door was dark, silent emptiness. X entered cautiously and explored the room without benefit of light. He hesitated only a moment, opened a door leading into the next room, and stepped across the threshold.

Air swished. Instinctively, X jumped aside, but not far enough to escape the chill, weighty thing that landed across his shoulders. He twisted around, his arms flinging out to grapple with thin, flexible steel ropes woven into a net that tightened quickly about his body. Every fully developed muscle in his body strained against that metal mesh, but it was being drawn tighter and tighter.

He jammed his arms down to his sides, kept every muscle distended in order to obtain more play in the trap of steel rope. Still, the net tightened until he was practically helpless, standing upright in spite of the weight of the net.

There was derisive laughter in the darkness, followed by the monotonous voice of the Brain: "It was a fifty-fifty split, Agent X. It was agreed between McAdam and I that I was to get fifty per cent of the proceeds for the killing of Corlears. Had you objected to the seventy per cent I demanded for killing old Pond, I would not have been suspicious of you."

"So," said X softly, "you led me deliberately into a trap. I am afraid you've let yourself in for a lot of trouble, Brain."

"The most fruitless bit of bluffing you've ever attempted, Mr. X," the Brain chuckled.

There was a second of silence followed by the sound of men moving cautiously through the dark. Then lights came on. Agent X looked out through the steel mesh of his flexible prison. Six tough-looking men, three of them with drawn guns, stood in the room. There was no sign of the man X knew to be the Brain.

It would have added measurably to the Agent's worries had he known that Betty Dale was a prisoner in the same house.

AT ABOUT the same time that the Brain had led X into the trap made ready for him, Sally Vergane left the building where Squid Murphy's men held X and Betty prisoners. There was fever heat in Sally's brain, and the fires of hate burning in her eyes, as she got into the fake taxi where the faithful Twist waited for her.

At Sally's direction, Twist drove at a furious pace to the apartment where the glamorous "Pamela Dean" lived. There Twist was directed to wait. Once again, Sally accomplished her metamorphosis. This would be the last time, she declared. Sally Vergane was dead—Long live Pamela Dean!

She dressed with extreme care and left the apartment as the beautiful and seductive Pamela Dean. Then Twist drove her directly to the headquarters of the federal agents. Ten minutes later she came out, a gleam of insane happiness in her eyes.

"Wolf Hollis," she whispered, into the darkness. "Dear, dear Wolf! For every bullet in your body, a G-man dies tonight!"

She did not care how many of Squid Murphy's men were killed. They could fight it out—G-men and gunmen. The point was that she had directed the Feds against Murphy's whole crowd, against Murphy's all but impregnable hideout. Men would die on both sides, but she would count only the dead that wore the badge of the Department of Justice. Justice? This was justice!

She opened the door of the cab, started to get in. The toe of her pump slipped on something on the running board. She looked down, caught her breath. "Twist!" she said hoarsely to the man in the front seat. "Twist!"

Twist made no answer. He lay across the back of the front seat. Cushions of the cab were splashed with blood and white paint— white paint drawn in the form of a crude circle. And struck across the body was a white cross.

Sally Vergane stepped back, turned around. The back of her hand smothered a scream. Out of the shadows came the figure of a man. There was the threatening gleam of gun steel in his hand.

"Miss Dean," he whispered. "The guns are silenced. I can kill you as easily as I killed Twist, but I would rather not at this moment, Miss Dean. Or shall I just continue to call you Sally?"

"You!" Sally breathed. "You—"

"Yes," said the man slowly. "I have been following you, and I am delighted to learn of your treachery."

"You—your voice—" Sally gasped. "Like Wolf Hollis's. No—no, it can't be. He's dead."

"And I tell you that Wolf Hollis still lives!"

CHAPTER XI

BEHIND THE MASK

THE STEEL NET was drawn down tight and secured to X's ankles by means of ropes tied to the four corners of the net. The mesh looked so tight that it seemed it must bite through clothing and into his flesh. Actually, this was because every muscle in his body was distended to its fullest. A second of relaxation, and he would be able to move his hands and arms to a limited degree.

"So this is the famous Secret Agent X!" one of the gunmen sneered. He swaggered up to the net and shoved his gun into his belt. "And he's caught in a net just like any other sucker. Don't worry, fella, soon as I frisk you we'll get you out of there and into a nice coffin."

The gunman, his hands working through the opening in the net, emptied X's coat and trouser pockets of their useful miscellany. But as the gunman moved to search X's vest pockets, something happened. Agent X suddenly relaxed. The steel net hung a little loosely about him. His right hand darted to his lower right vest pocket, slipped in beneath the gunman's clumsy fingers, and pulled out something which dropped to the floor beneath the gunman's feet.

"What the hell!" the searcher gasped. He stepped back, yanked out his gun. But his heel came down directly on top of the fragile glass vial which X had dropped. This vial was filled with the Agent's anesthetizing gas, forced in under pressure.

The man who had searched Agent X was the first to go down under the powerful gas. As it spread about the room, men staggered crazily and flopped to the floor. Agent X alone remained standing, his locked lips smiling slightly. If he could hold his breath long enough, until he could work his way over to the door, he believed that a few minutes alone would enable him to free himself from the net.

Though he was hobbled by the rope that tied the net to his ankles, he could move his feet inches at a time. He shuffled slowly across the room. Sixty seconds, counted by the hammer strokes of his over-burdened heart were required before he could reach the door. His vest pockets, as yet unexplored by the searcher, contained, among other things, his master keys. If the door was locked, he would have little trouble.

He tried the knob. The door was locked. He got out his master keys, selected one which was most likely to fit the lock, and thrust it out between the strands of the net. The key went partway into the lock and stuck there. He pulled it out and tried another. It failed to enter the keyhole at all. Another and another key refused to open the lock.

He dropped to his knees in front of the door and tried to see through the keyhole. Something obstructed his vision. The key, of course—the key to the lock was inserted from the opposite side of the door. Again he tried the master key that he knew would open the door. He jammed at the key in the lock, but still it refused to move. Whoever had locked the door from the other side had turned the key so that it could not be pushed out.

That meant tool work. And his tools had been removed by the searcher. Desperately, he turned and shuffled back to the man who had searched him. He procured his case of tiny, tempered tools and started back toward the door.

It is impossible for a man to kill himself simply by holding his breath, yet Agent X came very near doing that very thing. His vision was blurred with red. He could hear nothing in the world but the pounding of his own pulse, rapping in the arteries at his temples. It was coming and coming fast—that moment when he should be forced to gasp in a great lungful of that sleep-producing atmosphere.

He shook his tools out on the floor. It was chiefly by means of his sense of touch that he found the needle-nosed pliers. Something snapped in the Agent's brain. His lips sprang apart. His aching lungs rebelled against the control of their master. He drank deeply of his own poison, coughed once, dropped flat on his face in front of the door.

IN another room at the rear of the building, Squid Murphy paced the floor. Five of his best men were in the room with him, two of them occupied in guarding Betty Dale who was seated in one of the two chairs in the room.

Squid Murphy felt edgy. He didn't know why. It just seemed to him that he had a seat on top of a volcano.

"It's the dame and the X-guy!" Murphy growled, flashing Betty Dale a glance. "I can handle the cops and the G-men, and not twiddle a finger, but these nosey dames and the X-guy—they make my head itch. Tell you, guys, if the Brain don't show up pretty quick, you knocks the dame and the X-guy. What's eatin' the boys anyway? I told 'em to bring X back here. Go see what's eatin' 'em, Pike."

A lean, sallow-faced youth, who looked hop-fed, complied eagerly with Murphy's order. Pike left Murphy's sanctum and went through door after door until he came to the front part of the building where X had been trapped.

He found the door locked, twisted the key, and pulled the door open. Six men, like six corpses, lay on the floor of the room. A seventh, confined in a steel net, lay at Pike's feet. It was like stumbling into a morgue.

Pike took a step backward, tripped and fell flat. Something was hooked around his ankle. It was the hand of the man in the net.

Pike tried to scramble to his feet. But the man in the net, despite the tangle of steel mesh surrounding him, rolled and squirmed, grappled with Pike. Pike tried to cry out, but fingers that had the same steely strength as the net itself, pinched on his throat and slowly, surely, choked him into unconsciousness.

When the first effects of the gas had reached X's lungs, he had fallen purposely so that his face was near the bottom edge of the door. Enough pure air from the outer room had reached him, in that position, so that his recovery had been much more rapid than that of the others in the room.

He had come to, just in time to hear Pike's footsteps outside the door and had simply played dead until Pike had the door unlocked. The anesthetizing vapor had dissipated sufficiently, so that the air was no longer dangerous. Agent X hastily gathered his tools, selected the sharpest, hardest blade among them, and began work on the steel wires of the net. Five minutes later, he was a free man. He quickly gathered up his weapons and equipment which had been taken from him, and quietly left the room.

SQUID MURPHY'S patience lasted about six minutes. Then he swore he'd find Pike and bring him back dead.

"He's had time enough," Murphy declared. "You guys watch that dame. I'm goin' after Pike."

Murphy left the room and went to the front of the building where he found Pike, still unconscious, an empty steel net, and the Agent's six guards still under the influence of the gas.

Murphy paled. He got cold all over as he realized fully just what kind of an opponent he had met in Agent X. He stumbled on unsteady feet from one exit to another of the building, checking up on the men who guarded the outer doors. No, no one had left the building. Murphy passed a trembling hand over his face.

"Cripes, the X-guy is loose, in here with us somewhere!" Then he snapped his fingers. "We got him. We'll put a slug in his brain, if he don't get us all first!"

Squid Murphy hurried back to where he had left Betty Dale. More members of the gang had drifted into the room and were lounging about, leering at Betty. Murphy slammed the door of the room and flattened himself against the panel. His fishy eyes skated from one face to another. A crafty smile smeared across his lips.

"Gotcha, Mr. X," he said. "Gotcha this time."

Murphy's men looked queerly at their leader. "Who in hell you talkin' to?" one of them asked.

"Mr. X," laughed Murphy. "He's in here, damn him. He *would* be here, tryin' to rescue the dame."

"Are you nuts, Squid?" one of the crooks jerked. "I ain't X. None of the boys is X."

Murphy's fingers danced on his chest. "Sure—crazy smart. You don't know who X is. He's never the same guy twice. I got a feelin' he's right here in this room."

Betty Dale's pulses quickened. She knew that Murphy's way of learning X's identity depended upon some terrible ordeal for her. If X was in the room, at the slightest threat against her, he would reveal himself. That meant death for Agent X. If he wasn't in the room, she could look forward only to agonizing pain.

She drew a long breath and fixed Squid Murphy with a blue-eyed stare. "Don't be absurd," she said scornfully. "I know Agent X. If he were in this room right now, you'd know it the worst way."

Squid Murphy's lips twisted. "So you know him, do you, baby? That's fine and dandy, that is." He walked across the room, opened a steel box, and rummaged among tools. Finally, he picked up one that suited his purpose and turned to Betty.

Betty's fingers clenched until it seemed that her fingernails would penetrate the palms of her hands. There was an electric soldering iron in Murphy's fist.

Absolutely ignorant of the fact that Betty Dale was in the same building with him, Agent X was concentrating every effort to out-witting the Brain. He had no idea how much time had elapsed since the Brain had trapped him in the building. Perhaps by now the elusive killer was miles away. But there was only one way to make certain—search the building.

Three doors opened on the hall in which he found himself. He decided to try the one to the right of the door he had just closed behind him. He found it locked, all the more reason why the room beyond would bear close investigating. Again his master keys were brought into play. He opened the door softly and found the room beyond dark.

X listened and detected the faint sound of some one breathing. He stepped into the room. The Brain always moved in darkness. Perhaps the other occupant of the room was the man he was hunt-ing. X drew his gas pistol and moved quietly in the direction of the breathing sound.

"Brain," he said quietly, "I've come."

LOW LAUGHTER sounded within the room. X's body tensed. He waited. Nothing more came out of the blackness. X unclipped his penlight from his pocket. Had the Brain given him the slip again? He ventured a beam of light that stabbed across the room. Instantly he ducked and chopped off his light. Nothing happened. Yet his light had centered upon a man who sat in a chair and wore a black hood and mask over his head.

X took another step toward where he had seen the man. "Brain," he whispered again, "don't move. I'll shoot at the slightest sound."

Again came soft laughter. X scowled at the darkness. He turned his flashlight on again and stepped boldly up to the man in the chair. The muzzle of the gas gun pointed at the man's masked face. Queer, glittering eyes watched him from slits in the mask.

"You disappoint me, Brain," X said. "After all, I expected a little more resistance at the finish."

The man moved stiffly in his chair, but said nothing and simply stared in fascination at X's gun. In the masked man's right hand was a rusty nail. He was scratching on the arm of the chair with it—making queer designs that consisted chiefly of a cross surrounded by a circle.

X drew a quick startled breath. Was it possible?... His left hand shot out and tore the mask from the man's face. For a long moment, X was silent. The face of the man in the chair was a distorted mask of lifeless looking flesh. The mouth was set in an open-lipped snarl. His head was twisted on his shoulders at an odd angle. As he stared at Agent X, he laughed that soft, idiotic laughter.

Agent X nodded. He understood now why the man in the chair continually scratched the sign of the cross and the circle. The cross and circle was his signature—all, perhaps, that his crazed brain remembered of the life he had lived before. For the man in the chair was Wolf Hollis, the feared and hunted, reduced to a crippled imbecile.

Somehow Wolf Hollis had escaped the G-men. The burned body that had been found among the ashes of the house that had been his last stand, must have belonged to one of Wolf's henchmen. Perhaps one of the federal men's bullets had lodged in Wolf's brain, resulting in his paralysis and feeble-mindedness.

Wolf Hollis was not the Brain. He hadn't brains enough to plot the killing of an ant. But somehow, some way, the Brain planned to use Wolf Hollis. The Brain had marked every murder with the cross-and-circle signature of the illiterate Hollis. Clearly, he intended that when the showdown came, Wolf Hollis should bear the blame for all the crimes.

But if Hollis were to be the fall guy for the Brain, Hollis would have to be found dead; for no one would ever believe that this imbecile was the man behind the white-cross murders. That meant that in all probability, the Brain would return to kill Hollis....

FRAME FOR A DEAD MAN

A **QUICK RAP** on the front door of Murphy's loft-building hideout brought two guards to their feet. With guns drawn, they approached the door. One of them peeked through a hidden slot.

"That was the Brain's signal," the guard said to his companion. "It's him, all right, and he's got a dame with him."

The guard unlocked the door and admitted the Brain and Sally Vergane, still in the guise of Pamela Dean.

The Brain and Sally crossed to the room beyond. The Brain turned on a light. His face was covered from forehead to chin by a black silk mask. He carried a silenced pistol in each hand.

The girl looked pleadingly at the masked man. "Wolf," she began in a choked voice.

"Please refrain from calling me Wolf Hollis," said the Brain. "The similarity between my voice and his is due chiefly to your imagination."

"Then—then—"

"Keep still, Sally. I told you that Wolf Hollis is alive. I'm taking you to him. He's been with me a long time. I've been running this for him. He's slightly—shall we say, he has retired?" He nudged the woman into a dark hall, unlocked another door, and thrust her into another room.

"Wh-where's Wolf," Sally whispered. "That's all I want. I gotta know if I'm all right with Wolf."

The Brain pocketed one of his guns and took out a flashlight. The searching beam bored the gloom and centered upon the figure in the chair, the crooked body of Wolf Hollis.

Sally Vergane stared, wild-eyed, at the man in the chair, at his hideously distorted face and madman's eyes. "Wolf!" she screamed.

*Wolf Hollis's moll had Betty Dale covered
when a pug-faced fellow bore down on them.*

"Wolf, what's the matter? It's Sally." A sob choked her off. She ran across the room to fall on her knees before the man in the chair. She seized his hands. "Wolf, say something. Wolf!"

The man in the chair stared dully down at her and laughed his soft, mellow-witted laughter.

Somewhere in that room was a shuffling sound. The Brain's flashlight darted toward the corner, picked out the upright form of a man whose commonplace features were unmistakable. The Brain had seen that face once that evening under circumstances he was not likely to forget. It was the man he feared, his mind telegraphed. It was the man he had trapped. How that man had escaped from that trap, the Brain didn't know. He knew only that that man must die, for he was Secret Agent X.

Even before the man he feared could take a step toward him, the Brain fired. His shot was surprisingly accurate for such hasty aiming. Without a groan, the man pitched forward to the floor.

A triumphant oath spilled from the Brain's lips. He crossed quickly to the man on the floor and dropped beside him. His shot had penetrated the center of his victim's forehead. He was stone dead.

The Brain heaved a long sigh. "Dead," he whispered. "Secret

Agent X is dead. I can sleep again! The whole underworld can rest. I've killed Agent X."

Somewhere, outside the building, came the rattle of machine gun fire. The Brain's moment of relaxation was gone. His body stiffened. G-men were outside the building, acting on the tip Sally Vergane had given them. G-men—what in hell did he care for G-men? Hadn't he just killed Agent X, greatest of them all? Wasn't everything set for a safe walkout, leaving Murphy and crazy Wolf Hollis holding the bag? Wolf Hollis—the man ought to be dead when the G-men found him; or better still, the G-men ought to kill Wolf.

The Brain sprang across the room to where Sally was sobbing beside the laughing man in the chair. The Brain clubbed one of his guns and brought it down on Sally's head. The girl slumped to the floor. The Brain chuckled, leaned over, and took one of the madman's hands in his.

"Wolf," he said, "you hang on to this, understand? Just like I give it to you, you keep holding it."

He pressed one of his pistols into the man's hand. When the G-men came in and saw Wolf Hollis with a gun in his hand, they'd shoot to kill.

The Brain hurried across the room. "Now, for the getaway," he mused. "Down into the basement, through that manhole, and into the sewer. As simple as that. Only, coming out of a sewer with a mask on—" He shook his head. "Not so good. And a man in my position can't be seen popping out of manholes at any time. I have to do better than that. Now, if I came out with some one—" He chuckled and glanced at the dead man on the floor.

"Agent X," he said to the corpse, "the idea is almost worthy of you!"

BETTY DALE had been endowed with more than her share of courage. Though there was a terrified trembling going on inside of her, her face was a rigid, fearless mask as she watched the electric soldering iron begin to glow in Squid Murphy's hand.

Murphy planted a knee on the chair where Betty sat, then bent over her. "You got one more chance. If Mr. X is in this room, you'd better point him out. If you don't, I'll force him into the open. He ain't the kind to sit around and hear a dame's eyes sizzle."

"How many more times must I tell you that he is not in this room?" Betty cried.

Squid Murphy sneered. "Ain't that tough! Well, baby, here it comes!"

Murphy moved the soldering iron slowly toward Betty's face. Its pyramid tip pointed directly at her right eye. She felt the terrific heat of the glowing metal, shrank back as far as possible into the depths of the chair. There was a scream in her throat, locked there, choking her until she could hardly breathe.

Sweat stood out on Murphy's brow. "I'm goin' to jab, Agent X," he said hoarsely. "You've got a chance to save this skirt. It'll be damage no doc can repair, after I've jabbed. You hear me?"

The soldering iron quivered. Murphy snatched a breath. The iron leaped forward....

Lights went out. In the sudden darkness, the tip of the soldering iron glowed like a red eye and slowly faded. Murphy swung around. *"The Brain!"* he hushed.

Somewhere near at hand came the rattle of machine gun fire again.

"The Feds!" one of Murphy's men gasped. "They're shootin' in the front door."

"The Feds," said a low, monotonous voice, *"and* the Brain!"

A flashlight held in a black-gloved hand beamed through blackness and spotted Murphy and the terrified Betty Dale. Murphy dropped the soldering iron.

"Get to your posts," the Brain ordered. "We'll have to shoot it out."

"We'll give 'em hell!" one of the men yelled as he drew his automatic and started for the door. "Let's go, you guys!"

Murphy's men scrambled from the room to scatter through the building. Squid Murphy, in the light of the Brain's torch, pulled the chair, in which Betty sat, out from the wall to reveal a hole about fifteen inches square.

"Murphy," said the Brain, "what are you doing? Get out there and fight with your men."

Murphy uttered a strained laugh. "Like hell! I'm gettin' my share of the dough and gettin' out."

"Those Feds will shoot you down," the Brain warned.

"Nix. I got a hundred grand in this bag. I gotta live to spend it!" Murphy yanked a leather satchel from the opening, swung around, and started across the room. The Brain stood in his way, a black and ominous shadow. Murphy paled. "What you goin' to do, Brain?"

The silenced gun in the Brain's hand plopped. An expression of blank amazement crossed Murphy's face. His knees melted under him.

Betty stared down at Murphy's twitching form, screamed, and sprang to her feet.

The Brain came at her, snatched up the bag containing Murphy's money, and hooked his arm around the girl's waist. "Keep still," he warned. "I'm saving you, Betty Dale!"

Betty struggled in his powerful grasp. "Let me go!" she panted. "I don't want to be saved by—by you, a murderer!"

The Brain dragged her through the room and to a door that opened on the basement steps.

"You're the Brain," Betty gasped. "You're not trying to save me. This is some sort of a trick."

The Brain said nothing. They had gained the basement. The gun battle between the G-men and Murphy's mob roared thunderously above their heads. In the basement floor was an opening which had been closed by a manhole cover. The Brain picked Betty up, carried her to the opening, and dropped her through.

She fell a distance of about eight feet to the damp floor of the sewer below. She got up, turned around, and started to run. The Brain's light slashed ahead. In another moment he had caught up with her.

"Try to escape, and I'll kill you," he said quietly. "Now walk straight ahead."

Betty clenched her fists, tried an angry blow at the Brain's head.

He ducked, laughing. "Try to see behind the mask, Betty? Well, when you see my face, it will be a short walk out of this life. When we get to the end of our underground journey, it may be necessary for me to take off my mask and tell the police how I rescued you. They will accept my word above those mad-sounding utterances of yours. Soon after, because you know the truth, I will have to kill you."

"You're mad," she said scornfully. "Do you think you can escape Agent X? He'll go through anything to get you, Mr. Brain!"

The Brain chuckled. "He'll have to go through the fires of hell. I killed him with a shot directly between the eyes."

"You—you're lying!" Betty stammered.

"Oh, you think—" The Brain stopped. From somewhere behind them came a strange, shuffling sound. The Brain dropped the bag of money. His left arm, holding his flashlight, looped through Betty's arm. In his right hand, he held his silenced pistol.

THE BRAIN'S light quivered on the twisted, hideous face of Wolf Hollis. The man dragged his crippled body along the passage. The silenced pistol the Brain had pressed into his hand, pointed stiffly at the Brain himself.

"Hollis!" the Brain said hoarsely. "What the hell are you doing?"

"Following you, Brain," came the reply from grimly twisted lips.

The Brain muttered an oath. "He sounds almost rational. Yet he couldn't regain his sanity with that federal bullet pressing into his brain."

The twisted man shuffled forward until he was within ten feet of the Brain and Betty. "Rational, did you say? Never more so!" He laughed softly. "How beautifully you'll fit into the electric chair, Brain. A portion of the loot is now at your side. I find you abducting an innocent girl. I have seen you commit murder. Furthermore, I have undisputable evidence that you killed Nelson Birr because Birr had uncovered your secret, by finding a portion of the note which Wolf Hollis had dictated and signed, appointing you his successor.

"The Birr murder was one of the cleverest unpremeditated crimes I have ever encountered," went on the twisted man. "You found Nelson Birr under the influence of a non-lethal dose of chloral hydrate. You administered the approved antidote for chloral hydrate—strong coffee. But in that coffee, you placed nicotine. Even a non-lethal dose of chloral hydrate, when fortified by nicotine, becomes deadly. The nicotine was readily obtained in the form of tobacco residue from the catch-basin of your pipe. Placed in the coffee, it was unnoticed. Your only error was spilling a drop of the tobacco juice on the card table cover.

"Examination of that stain told me what it was. Who but you would have had the necessary scientific knowledge to pull such a murder trick? Who but you, a world-famous authority on potential murderers, would have been able to pick out men like McAdam and Aaron Malthus—men who had motives for murder, lacked the nerve to commit them, and would be willing to pay you for doing the job.

"My evidence can be further substantiated: the handwriting on the scrap of paper which dropped from Birr's wallet, was identical to that on the note placed around the butt of the automatic you handed me, proving that the illiterate Wolf Hollis dictated the message Birr found to you. And why should you have helped me by passing me that gun when the police held me in Malthus's house? Simply to alibi yourself and preclude any suspicion I might form about you."

"Then—then," the Brain stammered, "you're not Wolf Hollis?"

"An absurd question! It was all a matter of mistaken identities. By means of makeup, I simply switched identities with Wolf Hollis. It was Wolf Hollis you killed, not Agent X. I am Agent X. The Wolf Hollis who allowed you to press this gun I have into his hand, was Agent X."

The Brain laughed. He turned his pistol quickly and pressed it against Betty Dale. "This young woman tells me that Agent X would do much for her. And if Agent X comes a step nearer, he will be able to consider himself her murderer!"

Agent X flung the empty gun straight at the Brain's head. The Brain ducked, released Betty Dale, and flung himself at Agent X. Fists thudded on flesh. The Brain was a windmill gone mad. He had power that terror-stimulus had doubled, but he lacked the cool, fighting nerves of Agent X.

X took blow after blow, but always ducked under killing haymakers. The Brain's breath was coming in desperate sobs. He was quickly wearing himself down, yet he felt that X's telling blows were hammering him with more power than before.

"Damn you!" he shouted, as one of his punches cleared the point of X's chin.

X laughed, coldly, disconcertingly. "Save your breath, doctor. You need it!" Then he closed in for a quick finish. A blow to the belt doubled the Brain over. A hook to the jaw straightened him out again—out on the floor.

Agent X sprang to Betty Dale and seized her in his arms. "Dear, I hadn't the slightest idea you were here! I'd have torn the place apart—"

"Let's not talk," Betty whispered. She raised her lips to his.

WHITE light speared through the darkness. Agent X swung around, his body shielding Betty against this new, unforeseen danger.

"Put up your hands, Wolf Hollis!" cried a familiar voice. Special Agent Weston matured from the gloom. Behind him were half a dozen G-men. Agent X raised his hands above his head. "So you've cleaned out another rats' nest, Weston? Allow me to congratulate you!"

Weston came closer. "No funny cracks, Hollis. This time you won't get away."

"I'm not trying," laughed X. "I wish you'd search me. Inside a secret pocket of my coat, you'll find that note signed by a person known as K9. It will identify me."

Weston's jaw dropped. "You—you're—"

"Look for yourself, Weston!" Eagerly, Weston sought out the note when he had read on a previous occasion. He turned to his men. "Boys, this man is all right!"

A G-man grunted: "Looks enough like Wolf Hollis to be his brother."

Weston laughed. "He's everybody's brother—twin brother!" He shook X by the hand. "We've rounded up the whole crew, the Dean woman and all. The Dean woman must have been giving us the run-around before, but this last tip was genuine enough. But who's this?" Weston dropped beside the unconscious masked man on the floor. He jerked off the mask. "Dr. Stuart Ormand! What does this mean?"

X smiled grimly. "It means the chair for Dr. Ormand and another triumph for the F.B.I. Helpless, because of a bullet pressing on his brain, Wolf Hollis was merely a tool, a fall guy for Dr. Ormand, the Brain, cleverest criminal brain I have ever met. His true identity was not even suspected by his own henchmen. His profits from his mercenary murders must have reached something well over a million. All of his killings were trade-marked by Wolf Hollis's cross-and-circle signature, so that Hollis would get the blame. He got on all right until he had to pull that cover-up murder of Nelson Birr, because Birr had the dope on him.

"I'll be glad to hand over the proof that will find Dr. Ormand guilty in any court. But right now—" he turned to Betty Dale and smiled gently. "Well, Weston, you interrupted some rather important business of mine—mine and this young woman's."

www.ingramcontent.com/pod-product-compliance
Lightning Source LLC
Chambersburg PA
CBHW061036030726
47504CB00002B/398